Always My Love

by

Lee F. Patrick

The Coalition of Shifters

Always My Love

Javari Press
Calgary, Alberta, Canada.
http://www.javaripress.ca/

ISBN: (Ebook) 9781895487-27-5
(Print) 9781895487-28-2

First Ebook Edition December, 2020.

Cataloguing Information is available through
Library and Archives Canada.

Set in Gentium Book Basic and produced solely with ethically
sourced and recycled electrons from Canada.
Print version sourced through the United States

Previous Publications

Novels:
Coalition of Shifters: **Lonely Together** 2019
Mind Games: **The Alanyo Heir** 2018
Assassins Justice: **Alter Egos** 2017

Shorter Fiction/Poetry
Into the Darkness *Mythaxis #24, December 2020*
Who Profits? *The Trench Coat Chronicles, Celestial Echoes Press November, 2020*
Ultimate Evil *Sirius Science Fiction (on line) June 2020*
Assassins Justice: **Recruit** *Javari Press June 2020*
The Giants Dance *Polar Borealis #13, January 2020*
Reborn *The Twofer Compendium, Gemini WordSmiths, December 2019*
The First Fatality *Polar Borealis #11, September 2019*
The Runaway Apprentice *Enigma Front: The Stories We Hide, August 2019*
Coalition of Shifters: Ethan and Monster *Javari Press, July 2019*
The Carina Project *Javari Press, March 2019*
Assassins Justice: Man's Best Friend *Javari Press, February 2019*
The Promised Land *Manawaker Audio, 2018*
It Was a Dark and Stormy Night *Polar Borealis #5, Jan/Feb 2018*
Dark Reflections *Wild, Wicked and Sparkling (Starklight Press, October, 2017)*
Shadows in the Mist (poem) *Polar Borealis #4, August 2017 (Prix Aurora Award finalist)*
The Fire Mage *Enigma Front: Burnt (Analemma Press) 2016*

Acknowledgements

Thank you to those who helped with various aspects of this and earlier stories about Ethan and his journey. Javari Press of Calgary, Alberta, my wonderful Gary with his help with formats, consultations on cover design, and delicious suppers. (And cups of tea when I hit a snag in the storyline.) Also to various friends and fellow writers who helped out with bits of plot issues or just let me natter somewhat incoherently at them.

Please consider providing a review of this work on Amazon, Kobo or Goodreads. Or tell your friends. You can also request that my books, or any other small press authors, be carried by your local library. It is difficult for a small press author to reach further than their own circle of friends and acquaintances without the help of their readers.

I thank you in advance for any efforts on my behalf!

There have been upsets in the world since the first cases of Covid-19 were reported in early 2020. Too many have suffered with this illness and will continue to do so or have died.

In Ethan's Earth, this tragedy has not and will not happen. It lurches along the same way it did in 2019. The big problems are the same.

I salute and applaud all of those who have gone to work in grocery stores, hospitals, care facilities and generally have to be around people to do their jobs. Stay safe! (And wear masks when you are in crowds!)

I also salute those who have stayed home to continue working and to all those who have figured out the technologies that let us meet in cyberspace until it is safe to do so in person.

If you like my Facebook page, you'll hear any of my writing news before it becomes public. Come over and let's chat!

Lee F. Patrick
Calgary, Alberta December 2020

Prologue

My name is Ethan Carson. This bit is my life so far, just so that you're up to speed on what's already happened before the start of this part of my life story. A lot of my past isn't pretty, or things I'm happy about. Sometimes I wasn't sure I wanted to continue living. But I did anyway and now don't really want to die, as you'll discover.

However. My life has, on occasion, sucked beyond all measure. There have been a few bright spots over the years, but on the whole, if I developed total amnesia, I'd be way ahead of the game and be a lot happier. At least until the hunters came after me again.

I have a cougar living in my head, sort of. No real idea how, but I'd inherited the ability or whatever, from my father, and back further. No one was really clear on that part of the story, at least the bits I've been told.

Even the Coalition of Shifters, a mercenary group who mostly seemed to be the good or at least okay guys, don't have a real clue about their own history. But they actively seek out shifters living in the world to 'join' them. Or else. They 'recruited' me with three trank darts while I was trying to slip out of the Seattle area before they caught up with me. I woke, pissed off, in a small cell. Then they took me to one of their secret, mostly underground bases to have my dad convince me they were the good guys. I was still uncertain of that assertion when I left under cover of night about six or seven months later. Still wasn't, now over a year after my escape.

I'd thought that I'd been orphaned at the age of eight. Men in suits surrounded our house and then it blew up. I was in a Prohibition era smuggling tunnel when that happened, waiting for my family to join me so we could escape and stay free, though I had no idea why *anyone* would want to hurt or hunt us. I mourned my parents and baby brother. The foster system didn't work well for me. Then, at the age fourteen, my left hand became a cougar's paw. Fully. Tan fur and claws that were, and are, needle sharp.

The beast inside me woke up and decided it had to protect me. From anything. Anyone. Bad dreams, you name it. If I was afraid or angry, Monster, as I called him, was ready to rip apart what or whoever upset me. I was extremely thankful there wasn't another kid in my room at the foster home and that I was partly insulated from bullies at school by my association with Carlo, the younger brother of Esteban Morado, one of the neighbourhood drug dealers. I also earned money delivering drugs and whatnot for his businesses to have enough to eat. Because of my arsehole foster father. Monster did not like him, as you might guess.

Gordie, who ran the foster home as a way to earn extra money, planned on telling my social worker I'd run away. In reality, he was going to sell me into a brothel in the very near future as he had done to other foster kids. I left for the streets instead. Monster helped protect me from most of the dangers I, we, faced out on the streets. I came into a significant payday at seventeen and headed for the forests despite still being underage. The first night we were completely out of sight and hearing of any person, Monster wanted to go hunting for fresh meat. It scented a deer nearby. We became a cougar, which totally freaked me out, though I wasn't positive what I'd turned into until I heard it chirp, which is a really weird sound. I'd listened to various critter vocalizations and recognized it. I'd only had my hands visibly shift before.

Monster's ability to see in the dark and smelling gun oil and other scents had kept me safer in the city, now he provided warmth and meat.

Full shift. I could watch what the cougar did, but Monster was in complete control. I could make suggestions, but when it was really focused on a stalk, I was just a passenger. Like it was when we were in human form. Sharing which form we were in made it happier and easier to deal with. Besides, during the winter, having fur was a very good idea.

Life for the next few years was okay, but we were lonely together. Spotted hunters a few times and moved out of the area as fast as I could. While in Banff Park in western Canada, I met an older cougar shifter. Marshall, or Marsh. He normalized me, as the shrinks would say. There were others like us out there. And the hunters, but he had a few more suggestions on how to stay away from them. Staying *out* of cities was at the top of the list, but I'd already figured that part out.

My own luck in evading the hunters ran out in the Seattle area five years or so later, as I said. Eventually, I was tranked and woke up in a tiny cell. Then I found out that my parents and little brother Sam *weren't* dead. They'd been living in the relative luxury in one of the Coalition's secret bases ever since the explosion. While I endured the foster system, mourning their deaths, they'd been safe and secure. As might be imagined, I did not take that news well. I was beyond pissed. And still, I was glad to have them back in my life. A blip of happiness that soon faded.

Other shit happened. Some things that just pissed us off. Having to finish high school was the least objectionable, although doing book reports was among the trials I endured. Having everyone believing rumours that I had killed a number of (unnamed) hunters belonging to the Coalition didn't help, either. The suckage escalated on an exponential scale. (See, I used a math expression to prove I learned something in those classes. Yay, me.)

Eventually I sneaked out of the compound or maybe they let me go. Picked vegetables at a farm in the southeast for a couple months, then headed further south to spend the winter in a giant swamp. Seemed like a good idea as a place to hide. Mostly we did okay once we figured out the best way to kill a large constrictor. Lots of small bones, but there wasn't much else to eat since the feral, invasive constrictors eat up most of the smaller mammals, birds, and everything else. A public service, of sorts. With the number of eggs each snake could lay per year, it seemed a never ending and probably losing battle for the long run.

We also made decent money selling snake skins and skulls so I didn't have to risk casinos or big cities to get supplies. As an added bonus, we didn't encounter any hunters from either side down there. On the other hand, Monster became very tired of snake as the main course for every meal about the same time the summer's muggy heat began to ramp up and the mosquitoes started biting, so we headed north to find a new range. I didn't take his grumpiness seriously at first. He then ripped up the tarps that kept our little camp dryish. From the look of the clouds, it would be raining sometime that afternoon. I can take that sort of hint, so packed up everything else we had and headed for dry land.

Here's what happened to us next.

Ethan Carson/Borgan

Somewhere underground, USA

Chapter 1

I didn't really regret leaving the swamp. Monster was also happy, even if his fur time had gone down to rarely as we travelled the highways, getting rides mostly from people in cars, not the truckers as we'd done for so many years. We were dry, there weren't as many mosquitoes eager to chew on us, the vehicles had air conditioning, and snake was definitely NOT on the menu. For good, as far as he was concerned.

Atlanta, Georgia is a nice city. Parts of it anyway. I had no reason to wander into any upscale neighbourhoods or the downtown core, since my current cover, and reality, was that of a homeless person. My last real home had been with my parents. The years I spent in foster care did not count as having a home in my reckoning. I wasn't sure if I should count my time in the Coalition's underground lair, but the suckage there made me lean toward it not counting. Or maybe half time.

The less reputable parts of the city were where I found a decent squat while I looked for casinos to raise more money for my travels. I cached the bulk of my camping gear high in an abandoned warehouse so it was invisible from the main floor. Even in full daylight, I couldn't spot the big pack with my eyes. Monster, of course, saw it easily. Pattern recognition.

With my small duffel (containing most of my money in case someone did find the big pack) in hand, I found an abandoned city bus map and located a local library to do some research on where we might head next.

The guard at the library's main entrance gave me a glare but since I was as neat and tidy as possible, thanks to a travel plaza's shower facilities earlier that day, she couldn't refuse to let me in.

The start of the Appalachian mountains wasn't that far north of us, and I checked on locations of various parks, making notes in my new map book. I'd stopped in a used book store. It was a few years out of date, but major roads don't move very far so it would do for now.

A young man drew my attention from research. He had the same sort of beast as Karl, the mission leader I'd dealt with at the Coalition's underground lair. So far, the only people I'd encountered with this critter were of African descent. So lion, leopard, or maybe cheetah. Monster wasn't quite sure since we hadn't seen any of them shift, but it was a big cat.

The young man didn't look happy, but that was *not* our fault. Three other guys were hovering nearby. Watching him.

They weren't hunters who might also be after me, since the only ones I'd seen wore suits. All the time. No matter if they were in a slum or a forest. It had the advantage of making them easy to spot, so I didn't care.

The guys acted like ones I'd known before I'd left Toronto. Gang members. Probably also drug dealers. Monster obliged and sniffed, but they weren't carrying guns, at least not at the moment.

After a brief interchange of quiet comments with the kid, the gang left. The shifter tried to focus on whatever he'd been trying to read but didn't look like he was having much luck.

Monster thought of him as a kitten. Too young to be out on his own. In reality, I guessed he might be fifteen or maybe sixteen.

He soon gave up studying and packed up his books. I finished off the few notes I needed to make for now and followed him out. A block later, he stopped and looked back at me. I smiled without teeth and joined him.

"Why you following me, dude?" Then he blinked, confused.

"Because I'm like you. Different critter, though. Can we talk?" Being in a city meant I had to change my usual routine in meeting another shifter. I didn't want *any* fur showing where there were cameras to see it. Monster purred at his beast. A growl, but that seemed to be from his stomach, not his beast. There was a burger joint slightly down the block. "Come on. I'm buying." The kid hesitated, then nodded.

The tray was pretty full when we left the counter. Burgers, fries, onion rings and tall drinks. He chose a seat in a corner, not popular with the other customers.

"What are you?" he asked. "And what the *hell* am I?"

"My name's Ethan. I can shift into an animal form. You can too, or you will once you get older. I have a cougar. Not sure what you are exactly, but it's a big cat, but not another cougar. There's wolves as well." I took my food off the tray and pushed the rest toward him. Hunger won, at least for the moment and he started to unwrap one of the pair of double burgers with everything.

"Shifters have been around for a lot of years. I'm guessing your dad passed, some time back?" A nod as his mouth was full. "Didn't tell you what he was. Same problem I had. Didn't know what was going on when my hand changed. I was fourteen." Another nod.

"How's home, or are you in foster? That's where I ended up. Supremely sucked." He swallowed.

"Home sucks too. Mama married again. We have his three kids living with us now. Oldest is ten. Youngest's three. Mama's having another."

"So, bedrooms are cramped, you're the designated babysitter, you have no real privacy and the drug dealers want you either as a runner or a dealer. Maybe both. Right?" At least Ron, another kid I'd helped, hadn't had the second set of problems. His three young nieces thought of him as their big brother who could be jumped on early in the morning and existed only to play with them, be their sitter or help with their homework. Early morning play was *not* a good idea for a young shifter with a beast primed to rip apart any attacker before the human could stop them. A sliding lock on the inside of his door had pissed off his sister and protected the girls.

He paused to stare at me, the burger halfway to his mouth. A nod.

"It does sound like a supreme suckage. Your dad have any relatives you know about?"

"No. He never said nothing about them. Three years since he died. Wrong place to be. Two gangs fighting over turf and he was in the middle when they started shooting. Cops tried to tie him into the gangs, but that didn't work. They were pissed that they couldn't steal all our money and the house. Spoils of illegal activities, they said. It still cost a lot for the lawyer to help us keep everything. I think that's mostly why Mama got married again. We were pretty broke with just what she made at the grocery. I work there too, ever since I could."

"Still?"

"Just summers and school breaks now. Mama insisted that I concentrate on school the rest of the time. Wants me to get the diploma. But..."

"How's the step-Dad?"

"Okay. We get along. Knew him before my dad died. His wife had cancer. Diagnosed just after she had the last baby. Died because they couldn't afford more treatments. Sold their house and everything. Didn't make a difference. But those guys in the library? They've been after me for a couple months now. Talking about how I'd make a lot of money to help my mama, and they gonna protect me, shit like that."

"Get you involved and throw you to the cops to rot in jail if they need a patsy. Did some deliveries for a dealer when I was a kid."

"You still in the life?" A wary glance.

"Not any more. Came into serious coin when I was seventeen. Headed for the hills. Been wandering ever since. Have you ever seen guys in suits, just hanging around your place, or maybe at school?"

"Seen them a couple times now. They don't come close, but that's why those guys think I'm working with narcs. Idiots don't believe narcs never wear suits unless they're going to court to testify agin' guys like them.'"

"True that." I debated for a moment on what else to tell him. "I got caught by the suits once but got away. Their style of doing things was very not mine. But. Could be a place you'd do okay and be safe. Still have to finish high school, but there aren't any gang bangers or cops around to give you grief. I can give you a free contact number."

"But you left..." He stared at me. Daring me to tell him the truth.

I sighed again. "I did. Shit happened that was maybe because of a spy from another group. Maybe. My shit. Not yours. Gimmie your pad." Slowly, he pulled one from a side pocket on his pack. I wrote the number down. "Don't lose it. Or you can just go over to the next suit who shows up and ask them to take you in. Lots of them don't have beasts like we do. Yours should be able to tell who does and doesn't."

"It knew you were different once you got close," the kid said.

We didn't talk about much else related to our situations, just finished the meal. As we were leaving the burger joint he turned.

"Korry. Thanks, man."

"No problem, Korry. Ask your mom again about any relatives your dad had. Male ones will have the same kind of critter you do."

"I will. What can I do for you, Ethan?"

"Not much, Korry. But. You know where a casino is? I want to hit one for travelling money and that's the easiest way. Beast keeps me from having tells at poker. Once you get to eighteen, can be a good way to raise money to be anywhere else."

"Dude, gambling's seriously illegal here. No casinos, not even betting on out of state horse races." Korry said. "You don't wanna go to the other games without back up. Especially if you win."

"Well, I guess I need the bus station then. Heading out to Mexico. I'll stop off in another state where it is legal. Louisiana, maybe." I'd heard of the riverboat casinos in a diner on my way south to the swamp.

Our short cut through an alley was perhaps a bad idea. The three dudes came around the side of a garage. Obviously they'd watched us leave the restaurant but managed to stay far enough away so Monster hadn't sniffed them.

"Korry, dis guy your narc? Thought you was for real, but you just leading we on."

"That's us," I said. "What are your teachers doing all day? Snorting the coke you sold them?" The dudes stared at me. Confused. I grinned.

"Leading us on," I said. "Not we. Seriously. However bad your grammar is, I'm not interested in talking to any of you. Vanish. I'm not police of any form so I don't honestly care what sort of shape you're in when Korry and I leave here."

They stood there, still confused since I wasn't playing by their usual script of bluster and intimidation. The two on either side of the middle dude looked at each other. Middle dude glared at me. Only one to fight. I hoped he'd be smart and give up on his first bounce off the pavement, but I didn't think he would. He'd have to prove he was in charge once he went down the first time. Top dog never lost a fight or the littler dogs ripped their throats out. Two broken legs *might* keep him down.

"He's not a narc," Korry said. "And you idiots been coming after me this whole time, remember? If I was working with a narc, I'd have joined you first time you asked, maybe the second. You'd be in prison already." The back two looked confused. They must be sniffing their own product.

"Hold onto my bag for me," I said to Korry as I slipped the duffel off my shoulder. "This won't take long."

"What won't take long?" Korry asked as he took the duffel. Confused.

"The fight I'm about to win."

Leader dude laughed. He was taller and wider than me. Monster growled. Korry heard *that* noise and stepped away from me. Quickly.

The dude pulled out a switchblade but the other two moved back. Good. They might have enough brains to survive to true adulthood.

I smiled again. With teeth. Then I leapt forward and hit the dude in the stomach with my left hand. He'd been watching my right. He folded over and fell to the ground.

The two dudes stared at their leader in shock. Wait. Damn. The idiot wasn't breathing. Not wanting a murder warrant out on me, I turned him onto his back from a foetal position and started CPR. The whoop of air going in a few compressions later meant he'd be okay and I stood up.

"Take him away and don't bother Korry again. None of you will survive the next time." The two dudes stared, then I picked up the switchblade and retracted it. "My fee for your educational experience." I put it in my pocket. "Shoo."

Their leader was waking, so they pulled him upright to stand between them and headed past us. I turned to watch them go and saw that Korry was staring at me as well. I went over to him and took back my duffel.

"How?" One word but a big question.

"Partly the beast, but I learned a long time back that the best defence against a dude like him is a sudden and full-on attack. Like... If a guy says you have to the count of ten to do whatever, they're generally going to wait for the entire count before they do anything to you. So *you* attack on six or seven. Three if they're counting down. Works really well. Ask your beast to help you with its strength. Or if you want to run faster, it can help with that. One way to get away from idiots like those."

Korry left us at the bus station and headed home. I went back to where I'd stashed my big pack now that I knew where the station was. Maybe I'd see him again, maybe not. I just hoped the idiot thugs wouldn't ever bother him again.

About a week later I was in another city. It was the same one I'd been in to 'retrieve' a thumb drive full of critical information that might have been a total set up, as I never saw the item. My first mission for the Coalition. A half day by car south of the compound, by my guess and a hard look at my big map book of North America. A complete set-up to make me think the Coalition wanted me to be one of them. Or at least keep me and Monster under their control, especially since I was the only shifter who could do a full shift. Was I the only one in the world? I didn't know.

I wondered what questions they'd asked me under the drugs but I accepted that I'd never know now. It was about a year now that I'd managed to remain free. I had to count each day I stayed that way as a bonus. I guessed they might not think I'd come back to this part of the country. That I'd stay well away from the one compound that I knew a location for. We'd see.

The truth of my past might have shocked the leaders. My body count was low compared to others in the life I'd been forced to live on the streets, but I had killed several times to save myself over the years. Deliberately. Let others die from Monster's claws or told the gangs I'd worked for which new set of idiots were trying to steal their product or their money. I didn't feel all that bad about doing it. The Law of the Jungle is the same on the streets. Life near the top of the food chain was far better than scrounging at the bottom. The gangs paid better but there were other hazards to life and limb. Prison or death.

I briefly debated going to a particular downtown park and seeing if the woman who'd smelled good to Monster had permanently routed her asshole sort-of-boyfriend. She'd smelled good to Monster and that meant he wouldn't object to me dating her.

A breath later I abandoned that terminally stupid idea since she had no idea that a few men could shift into partial or (for me) full animal forms and the rest of the world was not on the 'need to know about me' list. I couldn't afford that kind of mistake if I wanted to stay out of anyone's cells. I found the bus depot again and bought a ticket at the last minute. Then I headed north east away from the open farmland. I'd get off in a medium-sized town and find a ride at a truck stop to break my trail. Just in case I'd shown up on anyone's camera system and the Coalition or the government teams managed to identify me and get a team onto my trail quickly enough to actually follow us.

A month later I had a nice little cave set up in a national park. Originally it had been a bear den but that had been many years back and there had been no recent sightings of bears or any scent of them. I'd dug out rocks and dried up bear poop for a solid week before we moved in. The mountains here were low compared to other places we'd lived but we'd scented no recent cougars. Natural ones, that is. They don't like to share a range and I didn't want to kill one unless it was trying to move into my space. In fact, there didn't seem to be any of the larger predators anywhere around the area. Good and bad. Good that Monster wouldn't have to fight anything above our weight class and bad that we would be seen in fur by an occasional hiker if the wind was in the wrong direction.

I guessed that the local hunters must really thin the deer herds back during the fall. Either way, there were plenty of other smaller animals for us, unlike in the swamp, where there was little other than snake for the few larger predators (like us) to live on.

These hills also had flocks of wild turkeys. Yum. Monster highly approved of this range, so I'd settled in as best we could without going back to Washington (the state) to retrieve my old gear. I didn't want to risk being that visible. I might head back that way in a year or three. If the hunters showed up here, I'd head back there, grab that gear and move south into Oregon. Northern California was another possibility.

There were a bunch of campgrounds adjacent to the park which meant hikers during the weekends and holidays. Occasionally there were a *lot* of people in every campground. And on those days I went hiking with my small backpack. Just a chance to be among people and not worry about who saw me. Occasionally I was invited to join a campfire after the hike. They wanted to know things about me but I had worked out a cover story and told them my campsite was nearby but not the one we were in. Everyone seemed to believe my story, or at least didn't challenge it out loud until after I'd left.

No one I scented there had a beast. That didn't surprise me. I knew that we were pretty rare out in the world after fifty or more years of both shifter organizations tracking down any lone shifters.

There was also at least one other sanctuary, probably out west, that the shifter family I met on that first mission was headed for. I thought about trying to find it occasionally, but it was better I stay away from any group. The Coalition really wanted me back under their control and I didn't want to put any other group at risk of their recruiting methods.

I also hoped that Korry wasn't having much more trouble from the drug dealer I'd nearly killed.

The people who hunted us might have thousands of shifters in their compounds. The one I knew had five hundred permanent residents, more or less. About a third or so were shifters from babies to their eighties. All of them male, of course. The older adults tended to be semi-retired, like Dad. Over the age of twenty to about sixty or so, they were mostly part of the teams that went out into the world and did stuff to support the compounds, help hunt down other shifters, raid naughty drug dealers or cartel members and I'm not sure what else. That life was behind me. Maybe. I hadn't encountered many young shifters out in the world. Ron, the first one we'd met, was currently at a Coalition school after running away. Perhaps. He called his family every couple of weeks according to the last letter he'd written me. He'd be safer staying put.

I had no idea of what had happened to the other adult shifters I'd met out in the world after our initial meeting. The Coalition and the government teams were very practised at finding the lone kids. I doubted many of us stayed free long enough to become old shifters. Not any more. Too many cameras.

Korry might have given the Coalition a call if his life continued to suck. That would give them a general idea I was still alive, but since we'd left Atlanta the next day, I figured we were relatively safe from being tracked from there. I'd also told him that I was heading for Mexico. He seemed honestly sorry I was leaving so soon, but hanging around Atlanta meant suits with trank guns would soon be swarming around the neighbourhood and after both of us. There are too many cameras to stay hidden for long in any large city.

On the plus side to my current location, the many local campgrounds also meant lots of discarded stuff in the Dumpsters that I could use to make my lair more comfortable. The bins were bear-proof from habit, but not people proof. I just had to be careful not to let the lid lock down while I was inside. That would have been a problem. I generally folded my duffel or pack over the locking mechanism. I found useable stuff about every third trip, like the tarp I was currently folding.

One corner was badly frayed from flapping loose during a windstorm last weekend but most of it was still intact. As a bonus, it was a dark green so I could use it as an outer door for my cave. Crucial come winter winds. Then again, I might stay in fur for most of it. That prospect didn't bother me as much now as the first time I was setting up camp in the wilds of southern Ontario at seventeen. Monster and I were getting along better than before.

My left upper arm and shoulder ached at times but didn't really slow us down much in the hunt. After so many years with few large natural predators, the local wildlife was primed to run at people smell, not cat.

That was slowly changing near my main cave, but we'd still have the advantage for quite a while longer. I could always find another cave or build a hut as a hunting base on the other side of the national park from my main cave to give the prey around it time to recover their numbers.

It was midweek, when there were only a few campers around. Monster heard a vehicle coming and I slipped into the forest and back up to my cave. It was mid fall and time to prepare for winter. I used the cash from my various mostly legal ventures like hunting boas and selling the skins along with my pay from the veggie farm to get more at a Native casino not too far away. As usual, I'd keep enough for a stake for the next time so I didn't need to spend much time in the local towns. In, get a pack full of groceries, and get out. That made it harder for anyone on either side to spot me. I also had plenty of places out here to put a body or four where they wouldn't be found quickly.

Monster thought of eating them, but I wasn't sure if I could become a cannibal. Or was it cannibalism if the beast was eating them? Philosophy. Who knew I had it in me? A new way to spend my evenings, at the very least. I'd scouted the local deer trails, found several nearby ponds with cattails and locations for other wild edibles. At least once a week, I'd dragged a section of dead fall closer to the cave entrance to build up my wood supply. Still, I had time to relax, read, and let Monster play.

I'd bought a used soccer ball with a pump at a Goodwill on our way here. Monster like batting it about and was very careful not to use his claws on it. I was glad he could have fun. Playing with other shifters might be better, but I still didn't want to go back to the Coalition. I wondered if the government people were any better. Probably not. I still wasn't certain which group had blown up our house, despite what I'd been told about that night. I wouldn't trust any report I was given. Both groups would have excellent forgery departments and Monster might not be able to tell if a prepared shifter lied to us.

When I moved from here, I still might try to find the shifter family I'd met. I still didn't know what sort of critter they were. Korry was the same type but hadn't known anything about his father's ability or any sense of which type he had. Monster still couldn't quite figure it out. The family I'd helped had only needed an extra three or four hundred dollars to get where they were going after the hunters showed up near their house. Again, the Coalition or the government group? I guessed food costs, gas prices and mileage. Came up with a big swath of territory. Still, planning was a way to spend time when the weather sucked.

I also had a thought on escaping the heavy-duty shackles the Coalition used. They were thicker than the normal kind and made of titanium, not steel. I was stuck in the cave during a heavy rain thanks to the remnants of a hurricane and we didn't want to get soaked in either form.

I had my big pot full of turkey stew ready to reheat so we didn't have to go hunting for another day or three. The run off from up the hill was filling my tripled tarp water reservoir so I wouldn't have to make any trips down hill with the ten litre water cube for a while. That was just tedium but at times necessary since there wasn't a stream in the cave area.

My idea was that if I could slow down the shift from human to cougar (or the reverse) while moving my hand, the other form might end up on the outside of the shackle, not the inside. I tried to picture what I wanted to happen for Monster, but he didn't seem to fully understand what I was trying to do. It was way easier to communicate with Monster than when I'd first left civilization at seventeen, so he was more like a big pet cat now, except that he hunted to feed both of us. Just thinking about petting him or rubbing his ears made him happy and I'd hear a purr in response, usually just in my head, but occasionally he used my vocal cords if he was very happy about what he'd done.

Idiot beast. I talked to him quite often, mostly to hear a voice. Any voice. Even my own.

My last attempt nearly resulted in me having my left index finger stuck in a thin branch. I stopped trying after that. The beast almost understood, but he just didn't have the smarts to make the technique work. I shrugged. That might change in a few years. Monster was getting smarter each year. I still wasn't sure how or why. Was it a normal progression or were we different than most shifters since we shared the body and worked together to survive? I was sure that we were a better team than any of the other shifters and their beasts.

I just had to make sure neither side got their hands on me again. If the hunters came around here, I'd stalk them for a change. Monster liked that idea and purred. It almost felt like he licked my face. Weird. But living with him now was like having a big cat where you didn't have to change the litter box every day or two.

His current attitude was unlike the past where he only wanted to kill anyone who annoyed him or frightened me. Why had that changed? And how had he become smarter over the years? Unlike most of the shifters' beasts that I'd met at the compound. I wasn't sure any of them could do... well, anything that the human half didn't specifically order them to other than shift hands to paws if they sensed danger to their human half.

Why was Monster so advanced? What about the few other shifters that I'd met out in the world? Next one I encountered, I'd have a list of pointed questions for them. See if their beasts were as limited as the tame ones I'd met so far.

More damned philosophy. It made more sense than the dratted book reports I'd had to do before I left the Coalition. Them, and the other high school courses I was told that I had to work at so I could go out on missions, I did not miss at all.

Chapter 2

Winter up in the hills didn't suck too badly. Four or five dumps of snow less than shin deep. I, really Monster and me, killed a good sized buck deer before the first snowstorm and dried and froze the meat. There were lots of cattail roots in the boggy areas to supplement the venison and I'd snuck into the farming areas with my largest pack several times after their main harvest was over to pick up any abandoned squash and potatoes. I had more than enough to eat without depleting my canned or dried goods which would force me to go shopping sooner than I wanted, unlike the swamp. There weren't many campers once the snow started and being a park, there wasn't any hunting allowed.

Staying in beast form was okay and it was warmer. After a little while, Monster hadn't minded much if I used his eyes to see what was going on. I took to wearing my hunting knife on a collar whenever we went out in fur. It sort of looked like a tagging thing, so that was another layer of protection. For example, if Monster found a deer with a broken leg, it was easier to partly butcher it in place than it was to lug the whole carcass back to the cave. Getting rid of the bits that neither of us would eat meant the smaller predators rejoiced in the free meal at that site and didn't come up to the cave to try mooching a meal from us.

Life was pretty good. I was lonely, but that was a fact of my life now. There wasn't anything I could do about it. Staying in a town meant the Coalition would be after me within a few days. Or the government people. I had to stay off the grid and be as invisible as possible.

Monster liked to watch the families down in the campgrounds, if we were in fur or not. Especially the kids. I tried to understand his reasons. About all I was able to determine was that he found them interesting. They needed protecting. From what, Monster didn't seem to know, or couldn't tell me something that was so complex an idea. But they had to be kept safe. I wondered if he had finally understood that I hadn't been safe when I was a child in the foster system. Hard to tell, but keeping kids safe instead of wanting to eat them was a good thing in general.

Another soccer ball was left behind at one of the campsites in the late fall. It had rolled down into a gully and the family likely thought that it was already packed up, so didn't bother look for it. Once the leaves dropped, it was visible. I brought it back to the cave. Monster liked playing with the two of them in the open area in front of our main cave. I knew he wanted to play with other people but that couldn't happen now. Sometimes on those long summer and fall weekends, we could play pickup soccer games in the campgrounds which satisfied us both.

I also thought about the family I'd helped occasionally. I hoped they'd found safety from their contact and hadn't called the Coalition for *help*.

Late spring again. I'd been here about a year now. Two years since I'd escaped the Coalition. I found a package in the woods above one of the campgrounds on my usual route. A heavy duty dark green garbage bag, with a hand-written tag. *Ethan*, it read.

"Shit." I looked around. No one. Back down at the bag and calmed a little. "It's been here a while. Dust all over."

The beast sniffed. Two scents he knew, once I opened the bag. Mom. And Sam. A faint purr at the recognition. "Are they sure that I'm here or is the first step in a trap? Been three weeks since I was near here. If they left it here, the scent would be gone from the outside after the rain last week. Should I take it?"

I sighed. Would I have approached them if I had scented them in the campground? I wasn't sure letting them or anyone know that I was here was a good idea. Bigger question was how had they found me? Should I pack up and leave? Find another range north or south of here?

There was more than enough time to move and set up before winter came. Maybe go north until August, then head south for veggie picking. The spring and summer heat in Florida was nasty, but for the few months of real winter, it would be okay. I'd stay in the swamps and live off pythons. There were a few birds down there to provide a change of pace. But we never hunted big alligators. Their armour was too thick for Monster's claws and teeth. Though, the smaller ones were tasty and I could possibly sell those skulls, along with snake skulls and skins to make enough money to buy more supplies than I usually needed. As a swampie, the local shopkeepers were used to seeing me and there hadn't been any reports of a cougar in the area, which was a bonus since it would alert the hunters that we were there.

If I took the package, they might be sure that they knew where I was. I left it there for two more weeks. Checked all the nearby campgrounds each weekend, late at night, once everyone was asleep so no one could see me in fur. There were no familiar scents and no sign of anyone with a beast, or a suit. I finally took the package apart right where it was, in case there was a tracker inside it.

There was a note inside. No obvious tracker but the Coalition had tech that was really small so I couldn't be sure unless I soaked the contents in water for a month. And that might not be enough to wreck the tech that I'd seen and begun to use.

Ethan, the note started.

We're so sorry. We had to be away. A critical event was happening at one of our smaller bases. I did leave you a note. Karl said that he'd told you. By the time we were able to return, you'd left. We're sorry that you didn't feel right staying here with us. Yes, you were allowed to leave, Ethan. We do want to keep track of you and hope that you'll decide to come back to us. But only when you're ready. It was after midwinter when we finally discovered where you were. It looks like a good place. Dad's a little jealous of your new range. We've tried to go camping a few times a year but it is hard to manage the time away. It might be easier now that Sam's grown up enough that we don't have to worry about him shifting if he's startled by a loud noise. We might go alone or with another couple or two.

Our leaders managed to trace all the rumours back to Justin eventually. No one ever suspected that he might be a government spy. He did go missing for a short time four years back, trying to track one of their agents, he said. It seems that they quickly turned him instead. Dad and I don't know all the details, but it's likely that he sent the government hunters word about Marshall. Tim was notified about him showing up and being identified, as were all the other team leaders. He, of course, told his team as Bill told you. He also learned that you were going and where the campground was.

How Justin's lies affected you is now well known. We had a procession of people apologizing when his perfidy was revealed. That was three weeks after you left. Dad just snarled at them. So did Sam, when he returned from his training. He really misses you and wished that he'd gone to the gym and played with you and your beast, in whatever form you were in.

We've wondered where you were ever since you left. It eased my heart when you were found. We'd hoped that the government group hadn't found you first.

There's three hundred dollars in the bag and a portable solar panel, a high capacity battery and a string of LED lights. There's also a cell phone and charger that works with the battery. Text messages are shorter and safer than calls. Check it every few weeks. Please? We'll try to warn you if the other side shows any interest in that area. There are three numbers in the memory. One is to us directly, the other two to local contacts north and south of the park.

By the way, Sam managed a full partial change last week. He did pay attention to your advice but this was the first time it all came together properly. He's quite proud of his tail. Since that was the first time it manifested, he fell over several times because he was trying to grab it to get a better look at it. I finally held it for him, though I was laughing so hard I could barely see. Dad had the camera, and was laughing even harder than I was. I'm surprised he managed to keep it mostly pointed in the right direction.

We have video for blackmail later.

Love

Mom and Dad

That answered a couple of questions, but not if I should leave or what might happen if I went back to the compound. I doubted that everyone would be glad to see me if I just showed up again. Different chickenshit would probably continue. I checked all the packaging and there were no extras that I could see. The phone was an older model. It was shut down at the moment and I left it that way and took out the battery just to be sure. I knew the techs could put things in just about anything to do almost anything and I didn't have the ability to tell what might be different from a normal phone even if I could figure out how to take it apart. Putting it back together and having it actually *work* was another issue.

I took the entire thing, including the outer bag, up to the cave and stashed it all as far back as I could. All the dirt and rocks around the cave should keep any transmitter I missed from revealing my location. If I did call anyone or check for messages, I'd put the battery back in far from my cave and other places where I stayed. I'd also make sure there was only one cell tower nearby so they couldn't pinpoint my location.

The lights were neat, but since it was late spring, I didn't use them much. By the time the sun went down I was more than ready to get to sleep. I dithered just about every day about calling them or just leaving the phone buried in the cave forever. Or moving out of the area entirely. Take my essential camp gear and find a new range to hide in. The beast didn't have a solid preference. There was good hunting here and no other large predators. It was our place. I rubbed my aching left shoulder and the beast purred.

I wondered again if anyone else's beast ever acted like mine. Maybe not recently, but long ago. Marsh's beast hadn't been able to shift much, but he'd been over a hundred and twenty when they died. A young or a tired beast couldn't shift more than paws, I guessed. So that didn't really answer the next question I had. What *was* our maximum life span? Living in a compound with access to medical aid and not a lot of stress might give a shifter another twenty or thirty years of good health.

It did mean that the beast helped the human half stay healthier longer. How old were the oldest shifters? Dad was over sixty but looked nearer his mid forties. Did each shift reset our ageing clock or did the beast just repair whatever internal damage occurred during the non-shifting times? Would it be different for those who never really shifted?

Marsh had been on the move for most of his life, with a few short stints when he was younger trying to have a real life with a wife and a job. With regular meals and such, how long could a shifter with a motivated beast live? A lot longer than most people, I guessed. More philosophy to fill my time. I did not regret leaving the school books behind, but maybe I'd get a notebook from a store to jot down my thoughts.

"Shit. Can't do that. If someone found it, that would blow the secret. Unless I wrote it in a kind of code." Also a bad idea since I'd have to remember the code. I'd just have to keep the ideas in my head. Maybe discuss them with Mom and Dad: if and when I did go back. Still not likely.

I finally checked the phone about two weeks later. I was nowhere near my main cave, but high enough to get a signal from a nearby tower. Just in case. The single text message was from the local number. Dated nearly two months ago. If I responded they'd know I was around here, or at least that I'd found the damn phone and the gear. The local contact had probably come out to check if the package was still in place every few weeks. Did it really matter if they knew I had taken it? After all, a visitor from the campground might have taken it. With Mom's note, that blew the secret of our existence. There hadn't been a sudden spate of campers, with or without suits, so maybe they assumed I'd taken it.

Reply to let us know you have the package. Updates will follow biweekly.

After a little fumbling on the tiny keypad, I managed to type a reply. *Got it.* I pressed send then I shut the dratted thing down and headed back into the cave to put it away. On the way back, there was a stupid turkey that just looked at me instead of running or flying away. It came back to the cave with me. Monster was pleased at the easy meal. Yum.

Chapter 3

It liked the new den. Not full of dampness and tiny buzzy biting things, but warmth and much good hunting. No more big slithers. They were tasty but the tiny bones were hard to eat around. Ethan finally decided to come back to proper forests after it made sure he understood that it wanted to leave the damp place right away. They belonged up high, not in the damp place with wet fur that never dried properly.

The small ones It watched were kittens, it knew. Kittens had to be protected from predators. There were bad males who liked to hurt kittens. It would make sure that Ethan helped protect any kittens that were in danger. The ones it saw here had good males and females who protected them.

Might they have a kitten or two of their own? First, it knew, they had to find a female who smelled good. There had been two. But Ethan wouldn't go to find those females again. There was danger if they went to the one from the park. And the dark female already had a mate and a new kitten to come. It sighed. The old one had such a wonderful female. It was good that the old one and the protector had remembered the good female when they ended.

Perhaps Ethan would bring out the ball again soon. Maybe they could find another like it and they could both play. Maybe soon they could find a female who would play other games with them. Then they would have their own kitten. Its beast would be raised to be strong and it would protect that kitten from danger and they would all play together.

Would they go back to the big cave? Maybe a good female was there now. It liked living in the range, but Ethan needed others like him to be happy all the time.

Chapter 4

We were in beast form about two weeks later, looking for small game. A grouse, turkey or marmot would have been ideal, but really, anything would do at the moment. Even a squirrel or three. The deer were still lower in the hills than I wanted to haul a carcass up to the cave, but if I didn't find anything small soon, I'd have to lug a deer back with me. Without any kill, I'd have to open stew cans or packages of the dried stuff or head to a pond and haul out more cattails. Then I'd need to go to the stores to replenish the stash. What caught my attention, however, was an unfamiliar series of noises. It was hard to make out, so it took me ten minutes or so to determine what it was. It finally clicked: a crying child. Monster figured out which way we had to go before I did. Of course.

She, I thought, although it's hard to tell at that age, was sitting in the middle of a winding deer trail, crying for her mommy. She had a death grip on a brownish stuffed toy and wore a t-shirt, pants, and sneakers. We circled her first. No other recent scents. She had come up one of the many winding deer trails and obviously had no idea that she could just follow it or any other trail back down hill to the campground she'd come from, or a nearby one. Either would get her back with her family. Too young to have any sense. I never considered not helping her. No parent would suffer the loss of a child if we could help it.

There was, however, no sound of a hysterical mother or father calling. At least not yet. Why not was another question. Would anyone abandon a child in the wilderness? Not likely, I hoped, but it was possible. It was much more likely was that she'd followed a butterfly or a bird as it flitted along, then was surprised to realize that she wasn't in the camp any more. Thus the tears.

I suggested we sit down. To my surprise, Monster did so, but kept watching her. I considered options. Monster thought of her as a kitten. He liked watching the kids playing. Even when we were in a city park on our way up here, any time he saw kids playing, he wanted to watch for a while, even if he had to watch from my eyes. I didn't mind. Seeing kids growing up happy and with their families made us both feel better.

We strained our hearing. No one was calling yet. Still. Damn. I didn't have my clothing pack with me, so I couldn't shift back to human, be a hiker and simply carry her back down to her family. It would take at least three hours or so for us to reach the cave, grab some clothes and the pack and come back here. She might still move a considerable distance in that amount of time, and there were other, smaller predators in the area that would just see her as an easy meal. I wore my knife collar as usual and that would have to stay here. I shifted one arm and detached the collar, then hid it under an old fallen tree for retrieval later.

This could be an idiotic thing to do, but at least I could save the child in a form that wouldn't raise questions. There were occasional sightings of cougars in and around the park. I guessed that most if not all of them had to be us, given the timeline. I'd checked in the back issues of the largest town's paper in the library when I'd gone down for a major supply run in the late fall. If I was lucky, no one would believe that a wild cougar had walked a child out of the woods. If the full shift was so rare that I really was the only one able to do it, that gave me more protection that the government hunters would discount any stories. Though, Justin would have told them about me and what we could do. But would they trust him enough to act on that information? Since the Coalition already knew we were here, it wasn't like I'd be giving away our location.

Monster, I thought. *We can help her walk back to the campground. So she'll be safe. Okay?* I pictured us in fur walking downhill with her. Then happy parents hugging the child. A pause, then I sensed assent. Monster withdrew and I was in charge. Mostly, I thought. I stood us up and didn't have trouble balancing or walking once I stopped trying so hard. Four points of contact made it relatively easy to walk in a mostly straight line. I wouldn't want to try running or fighting in cougar form, but Monster could take over for those needs. Good enough.

I circled her again and came up the trail so she could see me. Her eyes went round and she clutched the toy closer. It was a tan colour. Not obviously a bear but beyond that I didn't care. We sat, then lay down. And kept purring. She stared at us, not realising the danger if Monster was a natural cougar.

"Is you a good kittys?" she asked.

I purred louder but didn't move. She used the toy's front leg to wipe her tears away, stood and slowly came toward us.

"I gots a little lion," she said and held the toy out so we could see it.

It's an African lion, I told the beast. It was close enough to what we looked like for a small child.

"Has you gots big tooths, Mister Lion?" I wasn't going to quibble about being called a lion instead of a cougar. She was too young to know the difference.

I showed our fangs, a little, so not to scare her. Monster still watched from the background of our mind. He purred at me and her. Odd. It did make this easier to do. There was nothing around to harm her physically except us, so maybe he figured that I knew more about human kittens than he did. Which was sort of right. At least I'd been one. And had Sam for that short time. If we were attacked, Monster would either get us out of here or deal with the threat.

"Wows!" Then tears threatened again. "I'se losted. Do you knows where my mommy and daddy are?"

I stood and bunted her, then turned and took two steps down the trail. Stopped and looked back at her, purring all the time. I added a chirp, which always sounds weird. She didn't move. I circled around her and bunted her from behind then walked past her. She followed us now, still clutching her toy.

She insisted on holding our tail after a little while, which the beast put up with. I decided to take a shortcut to the nearest campground so we could pass a small spring in case she was thirsty. I drank at the pool first, then she did. The sky was getting darker. We couldn't make it all the way down the hill before full dark. She could have been walking for maybe four or five hours. Or she might have panicked in the mid-afternoon and run until she was out of breath, which would increase the time needed to get from where we found her to the nearest of the campgrounds. Even if that wasn't where she'd come from, she'd be safe.

Why weren't there sounds of people calling for her? That aspect of the whole thing bothered me a little. No, it bothered me a hell of a lot. But again, they might still be closer to her starting point, not realising how far she could run or exactly when she'd left their site. Had a human predator approached and frightened her? I couldn't shift back to human to ask her anything as that would really confuse her and her parents would have her in a mental hospital right after she told that story for the first time. Being saved by a cougar was marginally better, but not ideal.

Well, Monster and I could have kept moving all night, but she would keep falling in the dark and was probably pretty tired and hungry by now. I found a mossy spot and lay down. She ended up by our stomach, so she stayed warm enough to get a good sleep. The beast liked having a kitten nearby, for reasons that eluded me.

I'd flashed a few memories of me as a child so Monster would get the idea. The first time I was allowed to hold Sam. My decision to be the best big brother ever. He purred in agreement. I still didn't understand why

Monster felt this way. And how he had changed over the years.

Male cougars don't help raise the cubs they father and might attack any young cougar, especially a male, who came into its range. Maybe the beast did share my childhood memories of snuggling with Mom *and* Dad to watch TV or if I had a nightmare. Hard to tell, but Monster had sensed a tiny beast within the pregnant lady. She wasn't showing any tummy bulge so she wasn't far along. How fast did the beast develop? Puberty must play a role but it made no sense to me. I only know my first shift was at fourteen. Monster just wanted to kill whatever threatened or frightened me for years afterwards. Its claws were lethal. Still were, but it wasn't as eager now. Almost like he waited for instructions.

Dawn was just a hint of light in the sky when I woke the child up. She didn't want to pee while we watched. Very odd. We were on our way fairly quickly, possibly due to her being hungry but there was nothing for her to eat. The berries were still hard. I kept hearing rumbling noises from her stomach. I took a people trail that held her faint scent when we crossed it but we couldn't move fast with her short legs. Riding me wasn't an option given the uneven terrain and her continued death grip on her toy. Cougar shoulders and backs are kind of bony, which would make it hard for her to hold on with only one hand. Might even be im possible with two.

After twenty minutes or so, I heard several voices from down the trail. Male. All calling for Cindy. I looked back at her. She recognized the name. Good. Search and Rescue, I guessed, or at least helpful people from the campground. I was surprised they hadn't been out last night, but maybe they'd only just arrived or had gone up other, more likely trails first. There were a *lot* of hiking and animal trails around here. Without a scent dog to get them started on a direction, a lot of searchers were needed to cover all the possibilities.

Whatever. I could hand Cindy over to them and not go any further downhill. They'd be up here in a few minutes. I twitched our tail out of her hand and bunted her to the ground. A small growl to imply that she should stay put and wait. The voices were clearer now and Monster detected multiple scents on the up-slope breeze. The group was on the trail below us. Monster leaped us off the trail and headed for cover up higher on the hillside. I wanted to ensure that little Cindy would have a happy reunion with her parents. Otherwise, there would be an accident. Fatal.

Then I'd have to leave since everyone in the adjoining counties with a gun would be after the killer cougar. I realized that I really didn't want to move at the moment. I liked our current range. So did Monster. So I hoped these people were sensible and official.

The first person who caught sight of Cindy was male, with a sort of uniform on, as I expected from the voices. He stopped and put up his hand. "In sight. Everyone halt. I don't want to frighten her into running away from us. Be tough to get her to stop."

He came forward slowly. "Hi, there, sweetie. Are you Cindy?" No response that we could hear but he smiled and moved closer. She must still be sitting. Monster was also curious about the interaction and came forward to watch with me. Possibly to take over if anything went wrong.

"My name's James. Your mommy and daddy were really worried that you left the campground yesterday and asked me and my friends to come help look for you." He was out of sight now but not out of hearing range. Or our claws if he did anything we didn't like.

"The big lion helped me yesterday, Mister James," I heard her small voice now. "Then he told me to wait here when we heard you calling."

"That's great, honey." His voice said he didn't believe in any big lions helping little lost girls in any forest outside of a kid's book. Good. "Can I carry you? We'll get back to the campground faster that way. And I have a snack bar if you're hungry."

"Yes, please. I'se hungry, but the big lion didn't have any snacks. He took me to a place to drink and we had a nap on the ground when it got darks. His fur was really soft and warm." The sound of ripping paper and soon I saw them again. James was holding Cindy was in his arms and the rest of his team waited further down the trail.

"Called it in," said another man. Lots of relief in his voice. He must have a little girl at home. "Other teams are heading back to base. Parents are informed and coming to our starting point from the search HQ."

Cindy turned to look up-slope. "Thank you, Mister Lion." And then she waved. I saw confusion on most of the faces. Excellent. No one would put any stock into anything she said about friendly lions of any kind in the woods. In a few years, she wouldn't believe it either.

I waited until they were all out of sight and hearing before I suggested that Monster head up the hill so we could retrieve the knife collar. We'd spend the next day or three in the cave, just in case people started searching for a nearby lion or cougar. That also meant dried or canned food unless we tripped over a critter or two on the way there.

We didn't even spot a squirrel. Sigh.

There are always downsides to being a hero, but I did feel good about helping her. No telling what might have happened to Cindy if we'd gone in a different direction from the cave to hunt yesterday. I firmly pushed the thought of finding her body in the woods away. I didn't need any more nightmare material.

Hordes of people infested the trails the next few weeks, even on the weekdays, all with cameras in hand, as I'd guessed might happen. I just sighed and stayed human, in case anyone found my cave. There weren't many cougar tracks near the cave since there was considerable bare rock but out further, they were pretty likely. I hadn't been that careful about not leaving sign above the paths the hikers generally took.

A guy squatting in the forest was believable if a ranger found me. I'd have to leave if one did, but that didn't really bother me. There were other, smaller caves not too far away if I wanted to stay in the area. And after a few months, I could move back in here, since it was the largest of the caves I'd found. The others were good for waiting out a rainstorm, or for a couple of days to hunt in a different area.

I stared at my dwindling supplies. Time to take advantage of the increased people traffic to do a supply run, since with so many campers, I wouldn't be easily recognized by the staff. The clerks would be concentrating on restocking shelves and running the till, not in memorizing faces or making small talk with the customers to pass the time, asking questions like where were you from and what did you do for a living.

"No hope for it, Monster. We need to brave the grocery store." At least I still had a decent amount of money so I wouldn't have to bother hitting the casino first. I washed up, trimmed my beard way back so I didn't look too much like a homeless guy and braided my hair so I could hide the length under my coat. Then I grabbed my smaller pack and a decent carrysack that I'd found in a trash bin. We headed to the main roads via a game trail that intersected with a marked trail leading back to one of the larger campgrounds' parking lot.

Maybe two thirds of the sites were still occupied and a bunch of people were packing up. Must be a Sunday, not that I really bothered keeping track of what day it was. Maybe the excitement of the rescue was easing off with other news attracting everyone's attention.

"Howdy," I said to a couple with a big truck and a trailer. They were likely to have room in the back seat. "You heading out? Name's Ethan."

"I'm Joy and that's my husband Kris." Joy smiled at me. Kris was a big guy, taller and heavier than me. "Did you see the lion?"

"No lions, but there were a lot of cougar tracks higher on the slopes. But I'm nearly out of food, so I wanted to bum a lift to one of the stores." Two little girls came from the toilets, holding hands. "You have any luck seeing anything?"

"Weren't really looking," Kris said. "Our daughters, Mia and Ella Jean. We'd already booked the camper and the spot so we just came out. Didn't expect the whole furor that happened."

I smiled at them, and Monster purred. Both were older than Cindy, probably just school aged for Mia and a few years older for her sister.

"Daddy was real upset when the little girl went missing," Ella-Jean said. "We had to promise we wouldn't go outside the campground without an adult."

"A good thing," I said. "Cindy was really lucky, however she was found. There's a lot of wilderness out there."

"We'll be about twenty minutes," Kris said. "Tuck your pack in the back of the truck for now."

It didn't take much longer to leave the campground with me helping Kris tote the heavier things. The family let me off at the intersection where the store was and headed for the highway. I'd entertained the girls on the way there by describing various critters they hadn't seen on the tourist trails, like the turkeys. The girls weren't sure I'd been telling the truth. I was tempted by a selection of the swampie stories I'd heard at the diner but restrained myself to just the truth. Joy promised they'd look up the local wildlife on the computer when they reached home.

The grocery store was a fifteen minute walk away. It wasn't massively crowded at the moment, so I was able to walk in and grab what I needed rather than waiting in line just to get in the door. The fifteen or so folks in the store were discussing the lion. Still.

"Just like that cartoon, with the boy who thinks his toy tiger is real," said a middle-aged woman two people in front of me to the cashier.

"There have been cougar sightings in the park for over a year, Ma'am," the cashier said. From the tone of her voice, she'd said that a lot of the past few weeks. "There really is one out there. People have seen it. With cell phones so handy, they took pictures." One of them, blown up to 8x10 or so, showed us stalking a wild turkey. From the slightly grainy image, the photographer must have been well out of Monster's sniffing range. An advantage of the full shift was that people were mostly cool with a cougar in the park, but they wouldn't have been so relaxed if anyone spotted us in a partial shift.

"But would a wild animal do anything like that?" the woman asked.

"Not that anyone can figure. Maybe it was like the castaway and the soccer ball on that movie." Several people seemed to agree with nodding heads. I had no idea what film they were talking about so kept my mouth shut and nodded when someone looked at me.

"Where could a cougar have come from?" asked someone behind me. "I didn't think there were any in this part of the country."

"Our best guess so far is that it was a pet and got too big or the owner got scared of it. Then they just dumped it out here. It must have been old enough when it was taken that it already knew how to hunt. But it stays well away from the farms and the campgrounds. We don't bother it and it doesn't bother us." A murmur of agreement.

It was now my turn at the till. Rice, flour, dried beans, salt, their biggest bag of chocolate chip cookies and a block of lard would fit into my packs. And a big bottle of apple juice that I might have to hand-carry. "You've been up there?" The man behind me asked. "See anything?"

"Spotted a bunch of tracks up high in the hils," I said. "Caught sight of it last week up near the lake. Beautiful animal."

"Would it... kill a child?"

"Don't know," I said. "I do know cougars don't like dogs. But I doubt any wild animal would have walked her down the hill. At least all the fuss has been good for the economy here, having all these extra visitors."

I paid. The cashier gave me a quick smile for distracting the guy behind me, at least for a little while.

The gas station also had a lot of business at the pumps. The downside was that most of these people were leaving the area, not heading back up the hill to the campgrounds.

"Sucks to have to carry all the food up by ourselves," I muttered. Then I noticed there was a short line over at the big propane tank. "That might be a better place to ask. People stay here for long, they'll need to refill their tanks for cooking." I wandered over and put on a 'gosh, did you know there's a cougar out in the woods' face. Got a ride in three minutes.

Two days after I settled back in the cave, a cold downpour arrived from the north west and all the dirt trails turned to mud soup. The cougar/lion seekers all went home to dry out their gear and clothing. And we shifted, with relief, then headed into the forest to hunt for fresh meat. Two grouse were slower than the rest of the flock.

A week or so later I checked the phone from the top of the same hill I'd used before. The only message was from a week ago. *Cindy. Was that you?* I sent back *Yes* and shut it down. No use denying it as we were the only possibility.

I thought again about leaving. But I didn't. There might have been a couple of normal hunters out here to check on what might be going on, but they hadn't bothered me. So I would continue to mostly ignore them.

The moment Monster caught the medicinal scent of their dart guns, we'd start hunting them. Either side. It wouldn't matter what side they said they were on. If they weren't on *my* side, I didn't want anything to do with them. And the only person who might have qualified to be on my side was Marsh. Since he was dead, I couldn't, wouldn't trust anyone. Not right away.

Chapter 5

Summer was wonderful in the hills. Small and young idiot animals became my lunches and suppers. More campers provided odd comforts for the cave. I found a succession of novels in the bear-proof trash units during my prowls at the campgrounds and took them up the hill. I had read a fair number of books once I left school and my horrible foster father Gordie. I kept them hidden because tough, ass-kicking gang members didn't do such sissy things and I didn't want get into a fight over a book.

I'd seen the list of books I had to read for the dammed school work in the compound. Those were annoying. Just because they were old didn't mean they held any real value. The ones I found out here weren't old idiot classics but more modern novels.

The one that had werewolves and other types of shifters as major characters just made me laugh. I checked the *other books* listing in the front and was impressed at how long the list was. Then I wondered how I'd missed the genre, but mostly the books I found were ones that other people didn't want any more. These might be keepers. At least while I stayed here. There was no way to carry them with me if I left here suddenly. Weight and volume are the important consideration in moving quickly and my survival gear and food trumped any reading material. I hoped that reading them out of sequence wouldn't get me confused by leaps in the overall story line, if there was a coherent one.

I wondered how close the nearest used book store was. I could use the others I found to buy different ones and recycle them back through the store once I'd finished them. Next time I was near a larger town I'd go around late at night and look to see what other sort of stores they might have. The local librarians would ask for ID and an address to borrow books. I didn't have either for this state, even though I still had the ID Tim gave me on the first mission which said I was from out west. Sitting in the library to read wasn't an option. I don't read nearly that fast and staying in any camera's range for that long wasn't an option I wanted to

risk our freedom on. The government group maybe didn't know I was
here and I really didn't want to deal with any hunters or leave because
one of them spotted us.

I was lounging on an old cushion in the sun reading just outside the cave
on a gorgeous late autumn day when I heard voices far down-slope. One
was sharp in tone, adult male and annoyed. The other, softer voice was
hard to make out. What the man said wasn't really clear, but just his
pissed off tone made me wonder what was going on. It was mid week,
which meant fewer campers and the whole rescue lion excitement had
thankfully died off with the falling leaves.

We'd let maybe a dozen or so seekers get near enough for good picture of us in fur once the rush of visitors dropped off. Those sites weren't
anywhere near our caves. A few idiots tried to approach us but we didn't
let any of them get close enough to try making friends. A sharp yowl and
we headed away from them. Two or three times we rushed right past
them so they were knocked over. Or they had thrown themselves out of
our path and claws. From the various comments I'd overheard over the
summer at various campgrounds and the grocery, the abandoned pet
story had gained a lot of traction. It also explained how we'd suddenly
appeared here with no nearby sightings to lead a cougar here from a
wildlife park or from way out west. I'd have to remember that rationale
if we stayed in the east. I could even report seeing myself and start the
story just to be sure it got into people's heads.

Was the noise below us from a pair of hikers having an argument
about which way to go? Another lost child? Not likely. Maybe the government hunters believed Cindy's story when no one else did and decided to stake out a child to try to attract me once all the tourist excitement had died down. A stronger possibility. That meant I couldn't be
seen in full shift near whatever was going on.

I reminded myself that a homeless guy hiding out in the park was
doable. I'd seen plenty of them in the wild areas near cities. And had
stayed in those camps myself from time to time while I won money,
bought supplies and stayed closer to escape avenues. My stuff here certainly qualified if anyone actually found us.

I put my book and cushion inside the cave and fetched my smaller
pack and wallet ready for a hopefully short trek. All my extra cash went
into the secret compartment at the bottom of the pack, just in case I
needed to leave here quickly. Then I sighed and tucked the dammed
phone in an outer pocket of my jacket with the battery in, but didn't turn
it on. I might have to leave the area for a while or forever, depending on
what was going on. *Crap.* Then again, winter was coming and it would be

harder to move around and not leave tracks in the snow, which I'd have to do to hunt.

The lion seekers might come back once there was a solid snow cover and it would be hard, if not impossible, to hide from them unless I stayed in fur all the time. They'd be confused to find a person alone up here, well inside the cougar's range and a major competitor for the same types of food. Not to mention any sudden changes in those tracks from cougar paws to bare human feet or the reverse.

Another option was to head out of here, stay human in the biggest city I could reach quickly and hit casinos whenever I needed more cash. Stay in a cheap motel on the edge of a town, dye my hair again. Find a new range to live next spring or just come back here. Throw the damned phone into a river and hide better. Not stay in one place very long so they'd have a harder time finding me. Maybe we would head into the deserts of the south west or in northern Mexico. That had been one of my possibilities when I'd come here. Might be a better option now. Cougar actually lived out there, I knew from my early research. Might confuse any watchers that there was now an extra one. Winter would also be easier down there with no snow and not as much rain as the Seattle area had on a regular basis. Nevada also had a lot of legal casinos which meant I wouldn't have to go to a larger city to find one.

Another option was to head back to Florida or Georgia for the winter. But we'd need to get a boat first thing. I doubted the canoe we'd used was still where we left it. Monster and I lived on the damned snakes for months. No hint that we were making much of a dent in the population, which meant the population was extremely resilient. A strong hint of crankiness from Monster at that thought. Okay. Snakes were off the menu. At least not a steady diet of the big ones. That left heading out west or further north. Or going back to the Coalition.

We walked along a deer trail that mostly paralleled the hiking trail but lay higher on the hill. Plenty of cover so I wasn't visible. A young boy stood on the real hiking trail, slowly looking around him, but I didn't see the source of the adult voice. Monster was interested in the child below us once we were within sniffing range. Still seemed weird that he wanted a kitten. His desire must be my desire for family bleeding through from the human part of me. Maybe. Or not.

I missed Sam. Both as he was now, and as I remembered him as a toddler. Was he out on one of the teams now, finishing off his training? Hunting other shifters out in the world the way I'd been hunted? Or were the teams trying my tactic of just talking to the shifters they found? Asking them if safety and security (and full plates of food they didn't have to hunt) was better than scrounging through dumpsters or slowly starving.

The boy we spotted was older than Cindy. Maybe six or a little older. There was another, recent male scent on the trail that made Monster growl. The boy had been left here deliberately. That spoke to bad guys of one sort or another trying to find me. Or a shifter like me. I took the phone out of my pack and glared at it. Then I put it away. I needed more information before I pushed a panic button. Or I could just leave the boy here. The beast didn't want to do that.

Still, we circled the boy and he didn't notice us. No one else was nearby right now. The person who'd left him here hadn't left the trail near here and there was no sign or scent of anyone else. There were a lot of deer trails, so he could be below us to keep an eye on the boy. We settled near him but still out of sight and I started to think. How would I track the boy if I were the one who had left him here? A transponder? In his clothing, or maybe swallowed. I thought those would take a couple of days to work through the gut.

The beast kept our nose sniffing. The boy smelled familiar to Monster. Suddenly I realized why: He had a beast. A cougar like mine, but so tiny. Did the hunters think that I'd rush to a child who carried a beast? The boys who carried them at the compound smelled different to Monster from normal kids, even as toddlers. I wasn't sure most shifters could tell the difference when the boy was so far from puberty.

I hadn't bothered to tell anyone in the compound that Monster could even detect the beasts in toddlers, babies and long before they're born. Keeping Monster's full ability hidden was a good idea. Or they'd be hunting me in earnest and trying to ensure I had kids, even if they had to drug me. They might already have sperm samples from the various times I'd been unconscious. I might already be a father. No way to tell, unless I went back and managed to force Dad or Karl to tell me. I really hoped any kid of ours had a decent home, even if we never saw them.

Damn. I have to keep our head in this game, *not worry about shitty things that I can't ever hope to control.*

I moved further up-slope to ensure I could get a signal and took the phone out. Leaving a shifter in the hands of the government, or whoever these guys were, didn't set well with me. Plus, I could use a comfortable place to stay for the winter. I'd see how they behaved this time and decide if I wanted to stay when the excitement was over. I hadn't really forgiven the Coalition for the drugged questioning. Either time.

On cold, damp days my left shoulder still ached. Maybe they would finally fix it if I went back. The gunshot was the shooter's fault, likely also Justin's, but I was sure the medics could have done a bit more at the time than put a small bandage on either side of my shoulder. There hadn't even been any stitches. I'd looked in the mirror before I left and saw the wider scar on my back. Living in the compound meant that I could stay human and wouldn't need to use that arm for anything other than carrying a meal tray until it properly healed.

From what Mom's letter said, it seemed that the leaders had grown a brain about their idiot procedures. If they sent me out on another assignment, I might slip away once it was over if I decided to leave. Along with all of the team's cash if the attitude hadn't really changed. I could and would head out again. With prejudice this time.

No new messages were on the phone. I sent mine. *Boy about six years left in woods near me. A trap. Might have transponder. One of us. Ideas?*

I settled in to watch the area below me and the boy. A little flutter of leaves lower down, but only one or two trees at a time. Someone moving? The wind shifted to up-slope as it usually did mid-afternoon, which also brought the scents of several other people out there, spread along a major trail along the lower slope. How could they see or hear the boy?

About a half hour later I heard a response buzz on the phone. Wonder how long it had taken them to realized I'd sent a message and for them to contact a compound and find out what they were supposed to do about it. If anything. If they wouldn't help I'd have to leave here with the boy. Dead men would attract attention of the wrong kind, especially if Monster was involved.

Likely a trap. Can have a van at the intersection of 590 and the Willett trail head at nine pm for pickup. Taking him with you a good thing if you can do it safely. Haven't spotted any known hunters in past week. No idea who these are. Will check registrations at the campgrounds near you once you and the boy are safe. Try not to leave any blood trail or overt evidence of your beast's involvement if deaths are necessary.

Okay, see you then, I sent. Shut the phone down and stuffed it into my pack. I was glad they were onside with getting us and the boy out of here. Maybe I'd come back for my cave stuff in the spring. Or not. It was just stuff. I had all my money and ID in the pack, along with my last three energy bars, two bottles of water and two cans of chicken stew to tide me, well, now us over until the pickup tonight. And the opener, plus my latest books if we had to wait for pickup. I stood and headed down the other side of the hill so the hunters wouldn't see me.

The boy stared as I came along the hiking trail. I picked up an old branch as a walking stick on my way downhill and put a smile on my face. It had been well over two hours since I'd heard them talking so they might think I was just a hiker if they realized I'd stopped to speak to the boy. They had to be close enough to hear or see him, so they could catch the shifter. However, there was a lot of bush between the two trails. If I didn't speak loudly, they might not figure out that I was here.

"Hey, kid," I said, stopping as soon as he stood up. "What're you doing up here? Are you lost?"

He didn't know what to say but he was panicking by the fear smell. He'd been told to wait here until the lion/cougar showed up, no doubt. He wasn't expecting anyone in human form. The idiots who'd left him should have known about the possibility. Who were they? A new group after lone shifters? That led to other questions I had no time to consider.

"Hi?" A quaver in his voice. Not normal lost child behaviour. There had been plenty of discussion about Cindy in the grocery store and the campgrounds. Parents telling their kids what to do if they were lost. Mostly to stay IN the campground unless they were with an adult.

Other Search and Rescue people held little classes just about every weekend in most of the campgrounds. Monster approved of teaching the kittens about being lost. Cindy had at least stayed put once she got tired, but she'd come a long way before that point. The team that found her would have taken at least another day to reach where we'd encountered her, if they guessed right on which of the myriad deer trails above the hiking trails she'd used. Or if they'd gotten a scent dog onto her trail.

"Kid. It's okay. What's your name? I'm not going to hurt you. I want to help you. My name's Ethan."

"I can't goes nowhere." Tears threatened. "I has to stay here."

"Why not? Don't you want to go back home? The woods aren't that safe for a kid your age. There's lots of wild animals up here."

"He said had to stay."

"Your dad? Is he mad at you? Is he punishing you?"

"No. He bringed me here and say to wait."

"For what, or who?" I was playing clueless, just in case the hunters could hear us. With the wind blowing up-slope, they might not.

He collapsed in tears but didn't make much noise. I knelt so I wouldn't loom over him. Kneeling also made it less likely we'd be spotted.

"Hey now, kid. It's okay. Did he hurt you? We can go to the cops. They'll help." Well, with any normal kid, they would. Rural cops seemed to have more ties to the people they lived among than the ones in the cities I'd seen. Would actually help rather than just ignore a problem. But it didn't matter in right now. With a beast, he couldn't stay out in the world by himself. That left keeping him with me or both of us going to a compound. I wasn't exactly thrilled with either option but couldn't abandon him to these men.

"They puts me in a zoo!" I moved closer and finally was able to touch him. He was thin, wearing just a t-shirt and shorts. Shaking. Cold to the touch and I heard his stomach rumble. Starved as well? The beast growled. Kittens needed caring for. That man was not doing a good job. A sense that Monster was trying to contact the boy's beast. Hard, since he wasn't anywhere near puberty. At least, he didn't look old enough to me. I opened my pack and pulled out my sweatshirt. It covered most of his body so that would help him stay warmer, although his legs were still exposed.

"A zoo? Why?"

"I can't tell nothin' 'bout that," he wailed quietly. That finished any amusement I felt. Poor kid. But he might still be a plant. On the other hand, I needed him to trust me. Right now, so we could get out of range of the hunters before one of them caught sight of me or heard us talking. Well, it had worked for the other shifters I'd met out in the world.

"Maybe I can show you a secret," I said, still speaking quietly. "I was afraid of being put into a zoo when I was younger. Before I learned to control it." His head came up and he stared at me. I wriggled my fingers to get him to look at my free hand, then Monster changed it into a partial paw long enough for him to get a good look. He stared at my hand even after it was back to normal.

"You like me?" The last word was almost a squeak and his eyes were round with shock. He probably hadn't ever seen anyone shift for real. Maybe pictures. Probably lectures.

"Yes. I can take you to a safe place. What's your name?" The damn compound was the only real option for him. Keeping a child with me up in the hills would be difficult. Staying in a city was even worse. The local Child Welfare would not ruin his life more than it already had been. Not many other options for him other than the compound.

"Victor. I'se bait, he say. To gets you. You gotta run now!"

"How many men came with you, Victor?"

"Five in the big car." He wiped snot and tears onto the sweatshirt.

"Good enough. Let's go on a different trail so they won't see us. I know people who can get you to a safe place. What about your parents? Do they live with you?"

"No. Some kids like me. And lots of *them*." So there were others who needed rescuing. Kids *and* probably adults. A problem for later. The tears started again. I pulled out a granola bar and picked him up. "Eat up. There's water in my pack once you finish that off."

"Does you change a lot?" Victor asked about an hour later. He'd finished the bar, had a drink and then a brief nap while I carried him. The sweatshirt had warmed him up. The deer trail we were currently walking along wasn't on the hiking maps so I doubted that the hunters would have it under surveillance.

Only five men nearby that Victor *knew* about. Five well-trained guys was a reasonable size for a normal team trying to take down an inexperienced shifter. More would leave a lot of traces that could send a shifter into hiding or out of the area completely. They'd also need a second vehicle to carry all their camping gear or they might have a very big van or a motor home. Either would be noticeable in a campground given that they were mostly closing down for the winter. Notice wasn't a good idea given their agenda.

Two or three small groups could cover more campgrounds. But they only had one boy out here. That Victor knew of, I reminded myself. Other teams could be on either side of them. Just in case the current group spotted me. They might be wandering up in the hills looking for the cougar with trank guns. I had to work out other possibilities. Tactics and strategies weren't really my strong suit.

"The beast helps me to looking for food so I know where a grouse or turkey might be hiding. I can change more than just my hands if I need to," I said. Despite his fear of the hunters, he still might be a plant. Revealing the full change could be dangerous. A small stream was up ahead and I put him down with relief to refilled my water bottles.

"Are you okay to walk a little?" He nodded. He took my hand. He wasn't that heavy but my arms were beyond tired. My left shoulder had a dull ache all the way down my back and into my upper arm. I'd have to carry Victor on my other side the next time. We made it a good way down the trail when Monster smelled a man down below us. I knelt immediately and pulled Victor down beside me. "There's a bad man down there," I said quietly. "Did the men give you anything like a big pill to swallow this morning? Or it might have been even a couple of days ago, before you arrived here."

He shook his head.

"Don't worry about it then. Stay put. I'll go see who is down below us. And don't make any noise. Okay? I will be back for you." If he tried to attract attention or warn the hunters, I'd know he was a plant and I'd just leave him here. Get myself to the rendezvous and never come back. Five to one wasn't good odds during the day. At night, I'd have a better chance against them, especially if they kept looking for the boy once it got dark. I might have help from whoever was coming to pick me up.

Victor nodded, pulling his legs up under the sweatshirt to keep them warm. Why hadn't they given him more clothing? To make him glad when they took him back to camp each night? So he wouldn't think about running away?

I kept my pack on just in case and let Monster direct me to the watcher. He wore a damn *suit* of all things. No attempt at camouflage or even trying to look like a hiker. At least he'd lost the tie. Maybe they figured no one would be around during the week this late in the fall. What an idiot. He had a dart gun by the medicinal smell along with usual gun oil of a pistol. Neither weapon was visible and he used binoculars to scan the upper slopes. He wouldn't see us if we kept low. I didn't want to attack him right now as that would reveal our line of travel.

A double click and he put down the binoculars. Took a radio from his belt without taking his eyes from continual scanning up-slope.

"Anything yet?" A gruff voice.

"One here," the man said. "Got nothing so far. Just a frickin' squirrel or some sort of rodent." Three others also admitted negative results. Victor was right. Five of them. Still only one of me, so the odds weren't much different. They didn't use names, which seemed odd. Then again, that also meant no one nearby had names to associate with them. I'd bet their ID was totally bogus and so was the vehicle registration.

"The kid'll still be there," the gruff voice said. "He's too scared to cross us. At least he's not crying like yesterday. That was seriously getting on my nerves. Wanted to slap him into having some sense."

"Still a stupid risk to use him," the one near me said. "We don't have many of them his age or older." That was good news I could relay to the Coalition. And maybe they'd be able to trace these guys and free all the shifters and kids they held. Monster thought that was a very good idea.

Another issue was where had they taken Victor from? Did he have parents that were grieving, or dead, even if they didn't know they had a son? Or were they trying to breed shifters and why? How was another issue. I know that under those circumstances, I'd kill myself as soon as possible and take as many of them with me as I could manage before I had any kids. Whoever I'd contacted must have already alerted the local compound. Maybe they could get a team out here quickly so I'd have help dealing with the suits.

"Keep your eyes peeled," the gruff one said. "It might not be nearby. Could have a big range with plenty of game if he's not showing much in the local towns to buy food. We'll pick the kid up near sunset and move south again if it doesn't show in two days. Out."

I headed back uphill and found Victor where I'd left him. They hadn't referred to any other team with them so odds were decent that they were here alone. That would make it easier to deal with them once it was dark or I had reinforcements.

"Let's go. Quietly. There's someone down there."

"Did you kills him?" Victor whispered.

"No. Well, not yet. I need to get you out of here to somewhere safe first. I don't want the others to guess which way we went. I want to be able to sneak up on them later. It'll be easier that way."

Victor managed another good stretch of walking, then he started to slow. Little or no exercise from living in a cell, I guessed. I picked him up on my right side, gave him another bar to nibble on and kept moving.

We made the intersection around eight, according to the phone. I hadn't bothered with watches since I left the cities. My 'day' was sunrise to sunset during most of the year. An hour to wait but that was better than being late for the pick up. I pulled out the can opener and the spork. Victor, soon full of cold stew, slept with my sweatshirt and jacket around him. Monster obliged with enough fur on our body under my clothes to keep us warm without those layers. I left Victor dozing and circled around the area several times, just to be sure the hunters hadn't figured out our plan and we'd been tracked here by something inside Victor's guts. If they'd given him anything like that.

One of the men should have gone close enough to where they'd left Victor for an occasional sighting. Just to be sure he stayed put. Or put a camera up a nearby tree rigged to send pictures to their phones. Or some variation on those methods. Once they realized he was gone, they'd have to figure out which way he went and if I'd found him or he'd just run away. Our road was actually not on the same feeder paths as the local campground so they might not know it existed. Lots of maybes. But...

A dark van pulled off the road around nine and the driver got out and headed for the tree line. He was sort of visible from the road as he pissed.

"Ethan?" A soft call that wouldn't carry far. I didn't recognize the voice as one of the hunters. So I could, maybe, trust that he was on my side. Our side. At least for the moment.

"Over here. So's the boy. Sleeping. Five men set him up as bait for me. Don't think there's any electronics on him but I can't be sure."

"Great. We'll check him later but the van is shielded. You want to come with us?"

"For now. Five to one isn't great odds, even with the beast. My cave is fairly secure and I doubt they'll find it. I don't really need anything from there right away. It's safer not to risk fetching it right now. It's just stuff that can easily be replaced if I want to head back out into the wilds."

"You should stay in the back with the boy for now. That way no one sees another person up front with me. I'll park nose out as I usually do near the house and we're set back fifty yards from a side road. No one will spot you or the boy going into the house though the back door."

He opened the rear door for me. Four or five packing blankets for us to sit or lie on were the only things visible. No one hiding. I could see out the front, so getting gassed went down as a possibility. A dart gun was still an option, but Monster didn't smell any darts.

I listened and Monster let me know that there were no car sounds, or any other people around. I tossed my pack inside first, then picked Victor up and carried him to the van. Victor woke when the engine started but seeing me reassured him.

"I'm Neil, by the way," the driver said, turning slightly in his seat to look at us. "About a half hour til we get to our safe house. The boy okay?"

"A little scared. I think he's probably getting hungry again." I put humour into the last sentence.

"Pleases," Victor said in a small voice. "They dint give me any food in the morning. Ethan gave me two bars and stew while we waited for you. And water."

"We have fresh pizza at the house," Neil said. "You both like the meat lovers kind? We had two large ones delivered a little while ago. We often do that so it won't show up as unusual."

"What is pissa?" Victor asked. "Is it food?"

"Really tasty," I said. "Like a big piece of bread with a tomato stew on top. Meat and melted cheese on top. Kinda." My stomach growled at the thought. I enjoyed pizza but it was not easy for me to order in to a campground without a tent and car to account for my presence. The cell phone was a necessity for that, along with a credit card. The smell up at the cave might be noticed. The stews I usually made were always a worry, especially during a busy weekend. I'd eaten at plenty of pizza places when I was in civilization and could just use cash. Deep dish with lots of meat toppings. But not anchovies. They were just wrong and Monster agreed with me.

The safe house was a long ranch-style on a big lot that backed onto woods. A wood fire burned to take the chill off the evening by the trail of smoke from the chimney.

Carol was about shoulder high on me with reddish curls and freckles. Neil looked mostly Native. Victor had nearly fallen asleep again so I carried him in. Neil brought my pack with him.

Victor roused enough to eat two small pieces of pizza, drink a glass of milk and brush his teeth before falling asleep again. There might have been a sleeping pill in his milk to encourage the nap but he'd had way more exercise today than he was used to. He was locked into the same type of small room I'd seen before but he didn't object. There was only one of them. I left my pack in a real bedroom. It also had a window that would open and there was no real fence at the edge of the property if I chose to leave in the middle of the night. We then had a video conference with Karl and three other folks I didn't know.

None of the other men were introduced, but all four were all pissed at the thought of a breeding program that wasn't theirs. That didn't really surprise me. Once Victor's guys were no longer a problem, I might just head back to the hills before anyone decided that my participation in the Coalition's desire for stronger shifters was suddenly a priority.

"They said they didn't have many boys Victor's age?" Karl asked.

"They did. Victor told me there are a bunch of boys and a lot of *them*, by which I think he meant men like the ones out in the woods. There must be a group of women to have the kids but he doesn't remember his mother as such. We didn't talk much, since sound carries on the wind and I wanted to get us both out of the area before we really started to chat. Five to one isn't good odds, even for me, needing to protect the boy. But the men were scattered along one of the main trails, as if they expected me to immediately head down toward the campground that's below that area once I met up with the boy. I think they also expected me to be in fur. Not sure how they planned to take me, but my beast smelled that they all had dart guns."

That might be a way to take them down tomorrow. A dart in each, maybe at the campground as they came out of the tents. Then, whatever.

The men started talking to each other about what I should have done and what I could or should do now. I wasn't encouraged to participate, as Karl glared at me the moment I started to say something, so I took advantage of the lull to get another piece of pizza. At this rate, there wouldn't be any left for breakfast.

Chapter 6

I'd told Karl everything I'd learned from Victor and what I guessed about the five guys. The bit about them not having a lot of us was good news to everyone. Who these guys were was not comforting. None of the government types had ever tried anything like this before to catch lone shifters. And they might know the fully shifted cougar was me, thanks to Justin. I wondered if there had been any sightings of him since I'd left.

"So what do we do with these guys?" I asked, once they finished dissecting what I'd done or should have done. "Leave them here to wander around and try to find Victor in the hills or take them out as soon as possible? Stick them in the cell here or take them to a compound until they give up their bosses and the location of their facility?"

"Their people probably know what campground they used," Karl said. "Killing them increases their interest in the area. I know you wanted to save the little girl, Ethan, but it was terribly reckless. A lot of people visited the area once word spread. The story spread very quickly on social media and we couldn't contain any of the feeds. We expected to see some of the known government people on the cameras, but there weren't any. They might have sent a new recruit or two but we can't be sure. At least the story of the cougar as an abandoned exotic pet explained where it came from for the official record. It's happened on occasion in various parks, but the animal is usually killed within a few months because it has no idea how to hunt and goes after livestock and people instead of deer and such. If you leave with the boy, they may think that someone shot the cougar for a trophy but didn't want anyone to know they'd done it."

I shrugged. "An odd thing happened with my beast when I found Cindy that day. Natural cougars, especially males, are not interested in kittens or cubs of any kind. My beast is. Have any other men seen the same behaviour or am I an outlier on this as well?" That Monster had the same idea years ago was a detail they didn't need to know right now.

"We'll ask around. But based on your father, he's a dad, not just a sperm donor. Same with me. I'd guess it's a human trait influencing the beast." The others nodded. I still didn't know what Karl's beast was. All that I'd met so far were dark skinned. Full Negro or part, by their looks. Had their beast come from Africa and that was why the program had chosen them? I knew about lions, but there were lots of other predators there. I didn't need to worry about just now. I might ask Karl directly if I did return to the compound with Victor.

"Back to the hunters," I said. "What do you want me, or us, to do now? Kill or capture? I need some help either way. Five on one with no blood is tough by myself."

Neil and his partner Carol shrugged. "We're here mostly as a way station," she said. "Young shifters, as well as runaways from the nearby area have hidden in the park over the years. We've brought them in fairly quickly. We also keep track of natural cougars or the few wolves or wolf-dog packs who pass through. We're not trained in assault tactics."

"The hunters were scattered today?" one of the others asked.

"Quite far apart, but with radios and probably regular check ins. I didn't think to check the phone for the time I heard them call in. I wouldn't be able to take all of them out if they're that scattered and warned that I'm after them. How long til you could send a team up here to give me a hand? Or just two guys, at least. We can work from either side once they're spread out. Or we can take dart guns into their campground at night. Get them all that way. Pack them up and... whatever."

"That's still a problem. It's going to be two or three days before I can get you any solid help," Karl said. "Minimum. That station is the only one close enough to your location. All of our seasoned teams in the surrounding area are on assignments we can't pull them from quickly. We don't want to risk kids waiting for their first assignment if these guys are professionals. To fly anyone in would attract the wrong kind of attention. The hunters could call in or leave before any real help gets there."

Carol giggled into the silence. "What if the hunters are sick or asleep tomorrow morning?" Neil and I looked at her. "Instead of using the dart guns, which leave marks, if it's better they die very suddenly. A little addition mixed in with their morning coffee. I can guarantee they won't be moving fast if they each have a cup or two. That should even the odds for Ethan and Neil to contain them. Take extra pills dissolved in whiskey to be sure they won't wake up once they're asleep."

"A good idea," Karl said. "The bodies shouldn't be left at the campground, either. They would be found too quickly. Are there any tracks that off-roaders or dirt bikers use for the hunters to drive down? They'd be city idiots who got stuck and died of hypothermia or something reasonable for the official record. The enemy might guess that they were killed since Victor isn't with them but that's okay. We don't want the local or state police doing a lot of investigating into their cause of death and getting in our way."

"It's not really cold enough for hypothermia at the moment. But I have just the thing," I smiled. It wasn't a nice smile and showed a bit of tooth. "It'll give nearly the same result. Heard of an incident at a small town grocery store a few years back. Happened way out west in the fall. Guys went up the wrong road in a Jeep with intent to joyride where motor vehicles aren't allowed. They tried crossing a creek and got stuck midstream. Decided to walk out the next morning. The tailpipe went under water during the night as the creek rose from a storm far enough away they didn't realize what was happening. They were cold, so they shut the windows tight to keep the heat in and turned on the engine. Carbon monoxide poisoning killed them. There was also considerable alcohol involved from what I was told." Several men chuckled as they pictured the scene. Karl grinned with teeth.

"They weren't found for at least a week since no one knew where they'd gone after they left home. They hadn't left a message behind on where they planned to go or what they were going to do. They might not have had a plan when they left, but still didn't bother to phone home before they lost their cell signal. Coverage in the area was spotty, I heard. Lots of hills." Karl nodded in agreement.

"That also hides exactly when these guys will have died. Their bosses might still suspect it was me, but they won't have any solid information and with no more cougar sightings, they'll assume I've bugged out with the boy. Or Victor could have just run away and they were chasing him when the accident happens. That also helps keep Neil and Carol off their radar. No outside help or involvement." Murmurs of agreement.

"Shouldn't we keep them here so they can be questioned first?" I asked. "We could park their van behind the house so it's not visible from the road or we can take them to another site for questioning once they're unconscious. Dump their van in another campground or a chop shop once we have them all tucked away."

"Higher says they should die quickly in case the others have their own reinforcements nearby. These men might not have mentioned them and not told the boy either," One of the others said.

"You could hang around the area for a couple of weeks before coming in, just to establish that the cougar is still around and they're not." Another the dark complected shifter. "Keeps them all guessing and you'd have help by then. Collect another set or two. We'd certainly keep a few of them to get all the information we'd need to take them down."

Karl snickered again. "If there's no one awake in the campground, you could just spike their coffee supply with the sedative tonight. Then you pack them up and take them into the hills. You won't have to chase them all over the area and carry them back. Faster and much less of a chance of Murphy visiting and screwing up the plan."

"That we can help with," Neil said with a smile. "We have a four-by that can get us in and out of just about anywhere in these hills. It also has a tow cable if we need to drag the van further into the stream so the tailpipe is well under. I know a good place that other people have been stuck in over the years. Mostly they're idiots who don't have a clue about being off bare, dry pavement but think they do. No one's died from monoxide poisoning, but it's certainly a possibility. I can help that become the accepted version since I work part-time with the rangers."

I sighed, seeing that comfy bed I'd bounced on recede into the future. Damn. "We need to spike the coffee supply tonight. I don't know what they'll do tomorrow. They have to know that Victor's long gone by now. They might have called for reinforcements or already sent in a report that he's vanished. No way to tell."

"A late night," Carol said with the hint of a sigh. "On the other hand, they might spend a day or two looking for Victor before they call in to cover their asses. Find Victor before they have to admit that they screwed up. If they don't have many shifters, then Victor's loss will hurt their agenda, whatever that is. I'll stay here for now and make sure Victor doesn't panic if he wakes up."

"I doubt he can shift anything at his age," I said. "He's far too young. But protect yourself if you go in."

"I will. I'll get the bottle of sleeping pills and crush them up while you two get the gear ready." I wondered why this station might have a large bottle of those pills but maybe that was a common item on their inventory, no matter how small a base it was. Monster was slightly grumpy about the idea of taking any sort of pill. But making sure the hunters died and the boy was safe balanced that out. Especially since we weren't the ones taking the pills.

A short time later we were in the dark red four-by heading back to the camping area. It would take about a half hour to reach the most logical campground, Neil told me. Most of the men would be asleep by now. Hunting anyone, even a child, in the dark was mostly futile.

"Karl suggested that I tell you that we're the reason the Coalition knows you're here," Neil said just after we left the house. "We called in to update them when you first contacted us about Victor. That's also why the guys for the video conference were ready so fast. They knew the approximate time I'd get back to the house with you and Victor."

"How'd you first spot me?" I asked. I didn't really expect him to tell me the truth but had to ask. Like scratching an itch when you know it won't do any real good, but you do it anyway.

"There hasn't been a cougar or any shifter in the area for several years. Our station was going to be shut down and we'd move to another location that's seen more recent activity. Then one, you, showed up. Word had gone around to all the compounds and safe houses about you being able to do the full shift. And that you were in the wind. Carol and I weren't sure if you were here, but there were no other cougar reports in the surrounding area to account for a natural cougar's travel to get here. We sent that report up the chain and got back a message that said it might be you. Used some trail cameras and that proved there was a cougar, but not who it might be." He glanced over at me so I shrugged.

"Local people were nervous when the first sightings came in, but all of them were well away from the campgrounds. No missing livestock or dog attack reports from the hikers. Folks started to relax. There were a lot of folks out in the trails after you walked Cindy back, but no one found any tracks. That confused the entire storyline, but there were lots of other pictures before and after that incident to prove there *was* a real cougar in the forest. The abandoned pet story gained a lot of favour."

"That was my plan. I should have gone up near the lake as fast as we could right after the searchers found her and made sure a hiker spotted us in fur, just to make everyone decide that it *couldn't* be us since a natural cougar wouldn't travel that fast. I only go near the campgrounds during the weekdays. And not generally in fur where I would leave sign. Not many people are around then. I know to stay away from the local farms and dogs. The beast really doesn't like them, just like real cougars. We've never attacked a dog, but we haven't encountered many. If I'm on a trail with the chance of meeting people, I'm in human form, so it just growls at them in my head. I don't try to make friends with the dogs either. Tell the owner I'm allergic and that satisfies them."

"Good excuse to use. Anyway, I put small cameras up in the trees near the waste bins at three of the nearest campgrounds to the bulk of the sightings. Caught you at two of them over the next few weeks. Facial recognition did the rest."

"When did you get that?"

"Late fall when we finally had a good picture. Once you were identified, we were told to ignore you. Then a package came up with one of our regular supply drops. I was surprised that you took it. I checked on it every week or two, whenever my job took me past there. Might have pulled it, or put it in another location, probably higher up if you hadn't taken it when you did. We didn't want anyone else to find it."

"Shit happened before I left the compound," I said. Monster growled inside me. I didn't want to explain the details. Again. "I dithered for a couple of weeks on opening the package, and more in using the cell phone. Only reason I called about Victor is that it would be hard to take out five men by myself and not leave traces of blood. If anyone decided the deaths were caused by the cougar, I'd have to leave here. One plan was to grab the boy and using their car to bug out once the men were dead. Take their money and credit cards and dump the car at a chop shop so no one ever knew what happened to them. But still, taking care of Victor by myself would be hard. I'd have to be closer to supplies. Stay in or near a town, but that would mean I'd be identified pretty fast from all the cameras around these days."

"That makes sense," Neil said. There was a slight stink of fear coming off him. If he was mostly untrained in fighting, I wouldn't have any problems in taking him out if he was in our way. The beast approved.

We stopped well away from the campground so no one would associate our engine noise with his vehicle. If they noticed it at all. It was just midnight. We'd talked about more general things after his confession. Carol was a wolf shifter's daughter but Neil wasn't in any of the bloodlines. His great-grandparents had been guards who helped the others escape or were also pissed at whatever they'd been told to do. Whatever that actually was. There were a lot of people on the teams. Shifters and normals, working together.

Why had Justin turned on the Coalition? Money was an obvious reason, but he could already get just about anything he wanted in the Coalition. Maybe he'd been 'recruited' like we'd been and found a relative in the other group. I should ask Karl what else they'd discovered about his activities. I could understand why the leaders would want to keep most of the details quiet, but Mom suggested that everyone in the damned compound was now on my side. I seriously doubted that. We'd see. I'd leave Victor there and head out again if the chickenshit hazing and nasty rumours started up again.

I really hoped that our return wouldn't start another round of all the single women trying to 'attract' me. But I had a nasty suspicion they'd be trying to drape themselves all over me to 'atone' for doubting me. That was so not going to work for Monster. I wasn't sure what his criteria were. Smell was the word I used, but it was so much more than that. I just wished I understood what qualities or traits that he was looking for. Maybe he didn't know either. He just knew what he didn't like.

Damn. More philosophy. At least I had something to think about while I waited for the men to wake up tomorrow morning.

So we could kill them.

Chapter 7

I stripped down, put various things, including my clothes and boots, into my emptied pack, put it on, loosened all the straps, and shifted.

"Good thing you can keep the pack with you," Neil said. It was a weird fit, but we'd brought supplies in using the pack fairly often and Monster was used to it. Eliminating the hunters was also a pleasing thought to him. I was starting to wonder again just how smart Monster was becoming. I might try my handcuff escape trick again if he could finally understand what I was trying to do. Another project to work on.

I wouldn't come back here right away, but I could clear out the cave once we'd dealt with these hunters. The gear might be helpful to another shifter Neil and Carol had to help. We were near enough to the compound I knew that I could pop back here in a week or two and make sure a couple of hikers saw the cougar to further confuse the thugs' bosses. If they let me out again so soon, that is. They might send someone along as a minder who would call in if I vanished on him.

I'd found a new book two days back and hadn't started it yet. I might finish the current one on the way back to the compound. If they didn't drug me for the entire trip. I didn't think they would any more. But I could be wrong. If I was, well, I'd gotten out once. I could do it again, but they wouldn't see it coming when I left. The easiest way was up into the ceiling by way of the bedroom closet so they wouldn't see me on any of the corridor cameras. I'd have an entire night to exit the building. Or I'd hide out in the Shipping area and go out with another team. Either on or under one of the big supply trucks.

All but one of the hunters were now asleep in a big six man tent, and that one was nodding by the fire. They hadn't put their food and such into their van, which was a bonus, since the interior light would come on the moment a door opened and there would be noise of the door sliding which might wake up a sleeper. I slipped back into human form but kept the beast's night vision so I could see everything. Pulled my boots on to protect my feet from rocks but otherwise didn't bother with the rest of my clothes. It was a little chilly but bearable for the short time I'd need to be in the open. I hoped. Monster obliged with a light coating of fur but no other shift. Then he purred as I thought about rubbing his ears in thanks. The hunter by the fire yawned, checked his watch, and stood up to head for the outhouse. I smiled at the wonderful opportunity this made and started to move. His shuffle through the bits of gravel hid the small noises of our own travel.

I began rooting through their gear as the outhouse door banged closed. Found the large can of coffee at the top of the second box I found and opened it. Mixed the powder into the upper layer. It didn't look the right colour to me, but putting darts into the men would mean puncture marks. They were small, but the local coroner might wonder if the marks were relevant once the bodies were found. That could be a few days from now or next spring. No way to tell, so we had to be careful.

I finished up and hid behind a line of bushes before the man came out of the outhouse. He slumped by the fire, tossed another log on, then checked his watch. Another big yawn that I echoed. It had been a long day. I smiled, then headed back to where Neil waited, still in human form, but pulled on a sweatshirt and pants once I was far enough down the road that no one would hear me. The wind was getting brisker than I liked but with the short fur under my clothes, I was fairly comfy.

"It's in with the coffee," I said softly. "I'll stay and watch them in case they get a call or decide to bug out early. You should get back home and only come up when I phone. That way everyone sees both of your vehicles in the yard all night. Might not make any difference in the long run, but I'd rather take precautions. There's just one man on watch, so I still don't know if there are any others from their group in the area. They could be in campgrounds scattered around here to try to spot me so these guys could reposition Victor each day. They're likely still in suits so they'll be easy to identify once you can check all your cameras."

"Good idea. Do you need anything? Maybe a sleeping bag? I always have basic camping gear in the back."

"No. I'll shift back and settle in above the campground to keep them in sight. It's still a warm night for the beast. It can add extra fur during a shift in the winter so we stay nice and warm."

"See you tomorrow, then."

He left quietly. I undressed again, put all my clothes into the pack after a quick drink, shifted and headed back to the campground. There was a place we'd used before to observe this campground but I didn't go anywhere near it tonight. There were astringent smells. Disinfectant. A trap lay underneath. A net, I thought. A regular cougar might have been fooled since there was no trace of human smells. The hunters must have found the spot earlier today. We'd probably shed enough hairs to be noticeable over the past months while lying there. Good thing the lion-hunters hadn't noticed it. Then again, they'd missed almost *all* of Monster's footprints. I'd found quite a few of them once I started looking. But none of those folk were real trackers. I wondered if any had bothered to come, given the various fanciful stories I'd heard at the grocery and campgrounds after Cindy's rescue.

I moved further up the hill and settled in. Monster was being very cooperative. I thought about stroking his ears and he started to purr. Very quietly, so the noise wouldn't give away our position. We were sort of wrapped around each other. Less lonely. I napped a little but Monster stayed alert. He wanted to be sure that these men suffered for frightening the kitten. Its kitten? I might have a new little brother to look after. That would be okay. Victor needed a family if we couldn't figure out where his real parents were right away. I wondered if Mom would be interested in adding another son to the collection. I'd have to send a message to her and Dad once we returned to the safe house. Or I could go higher up the hill and text them myself. Maybe once I finished packing up the gear in the cave, I'd send a quick message. Then again, Karl might have already told them what I was up to. Being proactive to keep Dad happier. And Mom.

Coffee was a prime consideration for the hunters the next morning. They started the first pot before true dawn. The man making it didn't hesitate at the colour of the grounds. Good enough. Monster's colour vision was different than the human version so maybe that's why it seemed different last night. Each hunter had at least two cups, I guessed, then split up and headed off in various directions with food bars and water bottles in their pockets. One went to the net trap first, then moved up the hill past it. Oh well. We waited until he was well past us and followed.

A half hour later he slumped to the ground. A faint snore. Monster wanted to piss on him but I managed to stop him. I shifted back, pissed near him to satisfy Monster and dressed. This hunter hadn't gone that far, which was good. He was heavier than I was but with the beast's help, carrying him was fine. If they all managed to get this far from the campground it could take hours to fetch them all back. Maybe an extra sleeping pill or three should have been in the mix.

I reached their camp and dumped the hunter into the back of the van. Then I took out the cell phone and called Neil to help me pick up the rest up. If he could get close to where I found them with his vehicle, I wouldn't have to carry them all back here. Lots faster to dispose of them at any rate. Random people interested in camping might show up and that would be a bad idea.

"Victor's doing okay this morning," he said. "Carol gave him a pillow and a blanket last night. He expected a locked room without any comforts at all. I don't think they kept him in anything else, actually. But he does like pancakes, sausage and juice. She hasn't gotten a lot of information yet, but her opinion is that he was out in the world with these guys for only a couple of weeks. They seemed to move from one area to another on a schedule, searching for shifters. There weren't any other groups that he saw but one of them called in every second day. Maybe they were after you, but the mission leaders think it was more of a general fishing expedition. Too bad we can't question really them before putting them down. There aren't many people out on the trails this time of year so hiding the van behind the house is easy."

"Or we just keep one of them. Bring him to your place and send an interrogator with talkie drugs. One night and we'd have a lot of information, then we could add him to the others." No one listening to me again. Was it because I was still considered a 'new guy' or did they think having a good bond with Monster meant my ideas weren't worth anything? *Damn chickenshit again. Would it ever stop?*

Karl said that all of them were to die last night. One missing would mean more searchers out in the hills once their bosses learned of their deaths. Personally, I wondered if we shouldn't just keep all of them and leave their van in a crowded area with the keys in the ignition. More chances to get real information on where they were from. However, their bosses would guess they'd been caught and that might motivate them to do something nasty and fatal to their prisoners. So maybe this was a better ploy. Maybe. But one extra night of no contact might not make much of a difference to their bosses.

"Good enough. Maybe we'll learn more once he's used to us. I guess that he hasn't had any schooling." My stomach rumbled at the thought of that nice hot breakfast. I'd had a breakfast bar and two sausage sticks with water. *Yippee.*

"Carol agrees with that. Basic reading so he can follow directions or write reports. Not much else. He's still pretty young, she thinks. She's looking for some picture books in the basement. Leftovers from when we moved in. If he can read those, it'll give his new teachers a baseline."

"I think he was also kept on short rations. He might be older than he looks but I doubt he knows when his birthday is. The teachers should start him with grade one or even earlier, no matter where his reading level is now." I wouldn't mention the idea of book reports until we were back in a compound, safe from these guys. Didn't want the kid to bolt after all the trouble we were going to. Then again, it would be years before that special hell would start.

"Carol will pass that on. She was going to see what sort of books she can find in the nearest little library if she can't find anything at the house to read to him. Start testing how much he knows. I'll see you in a half hour or so."

I'd returned three of the closer goons back to their site but hadn't started to break down their camp yet. Neil walked in, just in case.

"Two more still to find," I said with a sigh. "I might have to shift back to track them down. Hope they're near..." The radio I'd taken from the first one down crackled. I'd tucked it into my jacket pocket so I could overhear any conversations. So far, they'd been quiet.

"Guys," said a strained voice. "Are you okay? That stew last night must have been off."

I smiled with teeth at Neil, pushed the talk button and groaned. "Yeah. Feel crappy. Heading back. You?"

"Us too. Just near the out..." We faded behind the van and watched as the final two men, holding each other up, come into sight. That was a relief. We didn't have to waste time chasing them down. We smiled at each other and Neil handed me a pair of cleaning gloves so we wouldn't leave fingerprints on any of their gear.

They made it to the camp and fell over. Not into the fire pit but it was close. I piled the last two in the van with the others while Neil broke down the tent and such. We just stuffed the gear into the van for now, not bothering to be neat or organised. We had to get out of sight before any new campers or the person who took the registration info from the little box by the outhouses came by to check on the site. I drove the van and let Neil out when we reached the four-by. He took the lead since I wasn't sure where he figured was the best place to arrange the scene.

I knew all the trails higher up the hills but hadn't bothered to memorize the smaller roads near the campgrounds. Didn't want to risk being seen much by hikers in fur near the campgrounds, especially after rescuing Cindy. Then again, acting more like a natural cougar helped convince the locals that Cindy had imagined the lion who brought her back toward the campgrounds. Too late now. If I did stay with the Coalition, maybe I could come back here, maybe with the family, for an occasional holiday. Staying in the campground would be odd, but we could have several runs in fur at night. Maybe find a turkey for supper. Monster approved. The domestic ones were far blander than the wild ones.

Neil stopped a short distance from a stream I recognized. There were lots of small rocks underfoot so we didn't have to worry about footprints.

"We need to properly pack all the gear up before you drive it into the water, so we don't splash around down by the stream-way. It isn't likely that any tourists will be out so far during the week, but you never know who might want to come and be one with nature. Had a search for a wo-man like that last spring. Family found their car north of here. Didn't leave any notes or text anyone where they were. Sort of like your idiots out west. If no one else thinks of it once they're found, I'll remind the boss of our incident. It's similar enough to get the point across."

"Good to think of possibilities." We pulled the gear out, strewing it about to separate the gear by type to make it easier to pack it up neatly, then pulled out the people and leaned them against the side of the van.

Neil pulled a big bottle of sleeping pill laced whiskey and an elec-tronic thing out of a carrysack from the four by. Then a pair of doctor-gloves. I raised an eyebrow when he used the thing to take the men's fin-gerprints along with pictures of their faces and whatever ID they were carrying. Then he took out several long cotton swabs in holders from an insulated bag.

"Another way we can find out who they are, if they're in the system," Neil said. "And people from one of the bigger compounds will run their pictures against all the hunters we've ever encountered. As well as all the camera footage where we've seen other shifters. We have access to a number of classified government DNA databases as well as the 'learn your ancestry' ones, so that might get us a hit, or at least give us a clue if they're closely related to anyone already in there. Any hint who these guys are is a good one. Be hard to find out who they are otherwise."

"The IDs are probably fake, so that's a lot of searching," I said as I put another set of gloves on, just in case the police thought to check for other peoples' fingerprints. I started to pack the gear not quite neatly, as if they'd been in a hurry to leave the campground and didn't really care if it wasn't neat and tidy, just inside and mostly compact so the driver could see out the back window. There were only five sleeping bags. What had Victor used? I spotted a blanket that Monster knew had Victor's scent, so I put it on the four by's hood. We could always throw it away if Victor didn't want it. Leaving it in the van might confuse whoever found it. Monster was happy the suits were going to be dead soon and purred.

Neil finished doling out the first bottle of whiskey and produced a second. "First one had more sleeping pills. Getting drunk is a typical be-haviour once they get stuck," he said. I nodded. "If this bottle is tested, it just has the whiskey. I'll rinse the first one out a couple of times to be sure no trace of the pills is left behind, then pour in some whiskey to coat the inside of the bottle."

He'd gone to each man and poured about a shot each into them once he finished with their ID. Kept at it until the second bottle was about half gone and they weren't really capable of swallowing. Several competing snores were nice to hear. Not having to fight them was also a plus. I could have taken down two of them together, not all five at once. There would be a lot of claw marks if we'd had to fight them that way.

Next, we heaved the men into their seats except the leader. He'd go in once the van was in the stream way since I needed to drive the damn van and I wanted the seat belt in place. Knocking myself out or getting thumped in the head was not part of the plan for the next few hours. We had too much to do once we left here. I also didn't want to be even partially disabled once we were back in the Coalition's clutches. I wasn't sure if a quick shift or two would heal a concussion within a day.

I went over to the stream and spotted the ideal place to run the van in. There were big stepping stones for hikers but it was actually deeper just downstream from that point. The real vehicle crossing was about five metres upstream and the access was partly hidden by overgrown shrubbery to discourage idiots from trying to drive any further.

City people in a hurry wouldn't stop to look for the safest place to cross. They'd just assume they could drive straight across since the way was all rocky and the stepping stones were right there. The parks people should put a couple of big rocks to block vehicle access to the stepping stones. They probably make some changes after finding the 'accident'. A gate to protect the real access from idiots would also be a good idea. If Neil didn't mention that idea, I'd tell him so he could bring it up later.

I backed up down the trail, built up a decent speed and made it about halfway through the stream-way without triggering the crash systems. I wound the window down and looked back at Neil. I saw two thumbs up which meant the tailpipe was already under water. Excellent: we wouldn't have to mess around towing it further in and the men would be dead sooner, without a chance to wake up. I left the engine running, turned the heater on full and rolled up the window. Then I went around the outside of the van and released all the seat belts as I went, as would happen once they were stuck.

The leader was limp and that made it hard to get him into the driver's seat without getting him all wet but I managed. I went slightly downstream before leaving the water so I wouldn't leave more drips. The half-full whiskey bottle was now on the console and I tossed the empty on top of the gear in the back. Neil had wrapped each hand around both bottles in different places. And multiple times. I was very impressed at his attention to detail. I'd taken mental notes while I loaded the gear. Monster still wanted to piss on them. He settled for me pissing on a tire, which would be clean enough by the time they were found. A half hour later

Neil headed back to Carol and Victor. I headed up to the cave to get all my gear out or buried. The fact that the 'cougar' vanished about the same time as their men died would make their bosses search elsewhere for Victor. Keeping them from realising who I was would be important. I'd mention the idea of me coming back here to establish my alibi, as it were, but I doubted the leaders or Karl would agree to let me come back on my own.

The sun was nearing noon when I reached the cave. I hadn't realized I'd accumulated so much stuff when it was all sorted. Good thing I had the bigger pack for major moves. I left the tarps and such in there. A lost person might need them and any critter who used the cave after our scent faded wouldn't care about them other than as something to lie on. The few vegetables and dried meat in my larder I tossed into the tree line for whatever critter might need an easy snack.

The next afternoon I called for pickup and Carol would come to fetch me. I checked the 'accident' site on my way out and all five men were dead. Their faces were all bright pink. Good.

"All good?" Carol asked as I came out of the woods. "Neil was on shift today. Couldn't easily get out of it. Victor's having a nap downstairs. I did lock him in when I came to get you, but he didn't seem to mind."

"He's used to a room like that. I'm just glad I have more strength than a normal. I had a lot of shit up there," I said. "It's just inside the tree line." My big pack, the smaller one, the carrysack and a tied-together tarp had the rest of my gear. She blinked in surprise.

"Didn't want to leave much evidence in case their buddies came looking for them or me," I said. "You and Neil might want to put a bunch of really small cameras in all the campgrounds. I'm sure they'll come looking for these guys at some point."

Carol nodded. "We'll also catch license plates at all the campground entrances and at the registration kiosks. Guys in suits will be easy to flag. More chances for facial recognition to link these men to others we can track down and question one of them for details."

A few minutes later all the gear was in the van and I sat in the back so I'd stay out of sight.

"How's Victor doing?"

"Good. He sleeps a lot, then eats everything I give him. Did you see your message? Karl forwarded it to us in case you were staying dark."

"From who?" *Karl or...*

"Your parents. They like the idea of another son. Or a grandson. However you want to settle who Victor's primary caregivers are."

"I didn't bother to check the message thing," I admitted. "Not used to having tech around any more. But I'm glad they're happy about the idea.

Staying with them would be best, I think."

"Especially if you keep going out on long missions," Carol said. "Gives him continuity."

"Plus he'll have two big brothers to help take care of him."

I moved all my bundles into the upstairs room, then went down stairs to see Victor. Monster was happy we'd rescued him. So was I.

"Hey Victor," I said when the little cell door opened. "You want to come upstairs and help me sort my gear? I'm not sure what I want to take back with me or what to leave here." I planned to leave the food, but keep the cooking gear and so on.

He stood up, not sure what to do. He only understood being in a small room. Alone. A steep learning curve was ahead, but we'd help him.

"Victor. Did anyone at that place ever hug you?" I kept my voice gentle. By the confused look on his face, I knew the answer was no.

"Hugs are a way of showing that you like another person." I held out a hand. "Can I show you?"

That nervous head bob meant yes, I hoped. I went down on my knees to even out our height difference and opened my arms. "Put your arms around my neck. Okay?" He approached me and did so. "Now you're hugging me. I'm going to hug you around your chest. If you want me to stop, just stop hugging me. Okay?" Head bobs. I gently wrapped our arms around him and Monster was purring so loud he hijacked my vocal cords. Victor started to imitate him, then started crying. He didn't let go so I didn't either. We made it up to the main level about a half hour later. There must have been a camera down there because Carol was ready to feed us and give Victor another hug.

In the interest of making Victor feel safer, he slept in the same room as me. He started out on a cot but crawled in with me during the night. Monster must have known he was with us, but I only woke up just after dawn because Victor's arms were around our neck and he was crying.

Two days later we headed back to the compound in a passenger van that Karl sent for us. A day and a half at highway speeds with no stops except for gas and bathroom breaks, they said. Two drivers, neither of whom introduced themselves. They did help shift what remained of my gear.

Victor was a little nervous around them, but we took the second set of seats so we could ignore them. They kept the radio on and didn't talk to us. Carol had found a few simple story books and one that showed numbers and counting so Victor could be amused, though he liked to watch the scenery and even the towns. The bad guys hadn't let him sit up high enough to look out the windows in the van, so the world was still pretty new to him. We also had a pool lounger on the floor in case Victor wanted to sleep. Mostly at night but short naps after every meal.

The next morning after we finished our breakfast take out, Victor got a half sleeping pill. They didn't bother handing one to me, which sort of surprised me. We weren't actually that far from the compound, but I'd known that already. I knew where it was so they didn't have to bother any longer. It was a relief that they might be trusting me now, even if I had escaped from them. We'd see what they did next. The beast seemed happy at going back there, maybe because of Victor. Monster *was* more aware than before. But I wouldn't mention that or we might be back in another tiny room with a locked door, being studied. With no option but to die by our own claws.

We turned off the highway about twenty minutes past the rest stop where I'd found that first ride from when I left here. The minor road didn't seem to have a name or number, just a break in the painted lines and a No Exit sign. The median between the two sets of roadway was mostly level, so a car or small truck could go to and from the exit without people being suspicious. The dirt road had deep ruts and puddles from a recent rain. We went slowly, but still bounced around for about ten minutes, then the surface became nice flat pavement.

"It's another ten minutes along here, then we turn off into a grassy track," the driver said. He still hadn't introduced himself.

"Wondered how people drove in and out for various missions," I said. "Big trucks with supplies or people in them use to the main gate, which is nicely paved?"

"Yup. There's cameras along here, so if there's a tourist or maybe a spy for the others, they get detoured toward a broken down bridge with just enough room to turn an average car around. Most folk just have a picnic if they manage to get that far, then leave. We have cameras to keep an eye on them. See the fork just there?" I glanced past him and saw a line of small evergreens, similar to the others scattered through these woods.

"Those bushes are really good fakes," he said. "Like the ones used for movie close-ups. A gate mechanism can cover the real fork. Most folk never bother to come past the potholes near the highway. Maybe one or two a year. The gate is tested about once a month. In case."

"Good to know." *Hard to get out or to sneak in. About what I'd figured.*

About twenty minutes later, we were in a tunnel. The big rigs couldn't get through here, so there had to be two access points in Shipping. There were probably cameras along here too. With the possibility of solid barriers to block access, and they might be airtight. Not a way to escape. The rigs were possible to get out on. Or I'd just go over the fence again unless they'd rebuilt the square corners into curves. But I doubted they had.

Chapter 8

It sniffed. Ethan was looking at a thing on his lap as he often did. He'd thought about rubbing its ears and liked the purr that resulted.

The scent coming from the woods below them was different but familiar at the same time. There was a kitten. With a tiny one like it was.

Ethan understood at once. Good. They would have a kitten without bothering about a female. Finding one that smelled good was very hard.

There were others. Hunters who did not take proper care of the kitten. Ethan sent for aid. That was good. All the hunters would die. So they could not hurt other kittens.

Ethan prepared well for keeping the kitten safe. Staying away from hunters was good. Unless all of them could die quickly. The tiny beast within the kitten was so small. Like the other kittens it sensed in the big cave. It paused. Would they go there with the kitten? The male and female would make Ethan not sad. The older kitten might be there. It would try to talk to the small protectors inside both kittens. So that the older kitten would have a strong protector. It would talk to the small kitten's protector too. That would help it grow faster so it would protect the kitten from other bad things. It was sure.

Maybe there would be a good female in the big cave now. Having this kitten to play with was good. But it still wanted a kitten of its own.

Chapter 9

Mom and Dad were waiting for me when we arrived just after noon. "Ethan!" said Mom. I'd barely gotten out of the van when she ran towards me. She started crying the moment she saw me. Dad nearly broke my ribs when he finally had his chance to hug me. Mom hadn't wanted to let go. Monster purred in my head. Very smug.

"This is Victor," I said once they'd calmed down and I could breathe. He slept on the pool lounger on the floor between the seats. Looked cute and pathetic at the same time. Way skinnier than a kid his age should be. "He'll sleep for another hour or so, I think. Can we take him up to wherever I'm living until he does? I don't want him to wake up here for the first time on a gurney in Shipping. Or alone. That was a serious bummer. I think he'd panic that the hunters grabbed him back."

"Of course, dear," Mom said. "Do you want him to live with you as well? We only set up a one bedroom for you, but we can certainly find a two bedroom if that's what you want."

"I don't know," I said. "But I'm the only person he knows here, so he won't panic as much when he wakes if I'm with him for now. Don't know what might be best for the long term."

"We'll sort it out," said Dad. "Sam will be along shortly. He said he had something to take care of."

A guard that I vaguely recognized came toward us with a gurney. The guard who'd tranked me the first time I'd woken up here. I smiled. With teeth. He didn't look happy. I didn't care. Neither did Monster.

Dad took the gurney from him and I transferred Victor, then put my smaller pack underneath. "I'm keeping that one with me for now. I don't care what your normal procedure is. If it vanishes from my rooms, I will tear the place apart until I get it back. Understand? The rest of it is my camping gear. Don't throw it out. I may want it for a holiday later." The guard nodded. Fear stink spread from him. Dad noticed and added a frown in his direction.

We left before he actually fainted. Monster noticed his shaking hands.

Victor lay on my couch when he woke up about two hours later. I was re-reading my history text from the beginning of the chapter. Yes, I still had to finish the dammed high school GED, according to Mom. I was in a different apartment but my clothing and such, including *all* the dratted books, had been boxed up after I left.

They'd been hopeful that I would return voluntarily. Well, they'd been partly right. Without Victor to worry about, I wouldn't have come in. Just killed the hunters, whoever they worked for, and moved on, using their van to get far from the cave. I'd have all their cash and credit cards to buy food and other supplies for my next range.

I'd dump the damned cell phone and find a new range to make our own. At least until the Coalition caught up with us again. At least I knew how they'd identified me this time. I'd have to pay more attention to places where a camera could be hidden. It must have been really small or I would have noticed it and either avoided it or dropped it out of wherever they'd attached it from behind.

"Hey Victor," I said. "Glad you're awake. Headache?"

"No." He looked around, confused. "Where is we now?"

"My apartment. You're safe now." Well, as safe as any shifter could be. More or less. "Are you hungry?"

Quick nods and a hopeful expression. I smiled at him. No teeth.

"The bathroom's just there. After that, we'll go to the cafeteria. There's always food available to nibble on." His eyes were round.

While he was behind the closed door, I phoned Mom.

"I'll be along in a few minutes, dear," she said. "Sam's just finishing taking his clothes away. So Victor will have his room instead of camping out with you. Sam insisted on it."

"Thanks. I think Victor needs a mom and dad, not just a dad who will probably be out of here a lot if Karl has his way."

"Of course he does."

She hung up and I felt that old pain return. I'd needed a mother and father but hadn't had either for so long. I wasn't sure I was over needing them. Maybe that was one reason why Monster was on side for us to come back here. He purred as I thought about rubbing his ears.

Victor came out. He'd even washed his face and hands.

"There's a bunch of kids near your age here," I said as we walked down the corridor. Victor held my left hand in a death grip. "Did you ever meet any other adult shifters where you were?"

"No. Stayed in little room most of the time. Saw the mean men and others same as them. Know other kids but I'se not sure how many was there." Then in a small voice. "Is the mean mens dead?"

"They are very dead. They won't ever hurt anyone again."

"Good." A hint of anger. "I stay with you now?"

"Well, with my family. My mom, dad and brother live here. I'll be going out on missions, to help find other shifters in trouble and rescue people. We want to find who else the mean men knew and find all the other kids and shifters from where you were. I was on a holiday of sorts when you met me."

The simplest explanation of black ops and why I was living in the mountains that I could come up with quickly. He didn't need to know any other details about my history right now. Maybe when he was older and actually curious.

His grip tightened. "Alone here?"

"Never." We reached the cafeteria door and I pushed it open. A couple of people were having coffee while they looked at reports, but it was otherwise empty. Noises and smells from the kitchen said supper prep was well under way. I led Victor over to the single cold buffet table. "There's always snacks here."

Victor's eyes were round at the sight of so much food. Definitely starved for most of his life. I picked up a tray and poured two glasses of milk. "Do you want me to choose some things you might like?" He nodded. I'd ask later what sort of things he'd ever eaten or Mom could. Stew and bars had been familiar, but what else had they fed him? I put sausage sticks, cheese, an apple each and a short stack of oatmeal chocolate chip cookies on a plate and added a knife to cut up the apples.

We sat on the outer set of tables and I gave half the food to Victor, then cut up our apples and removed the core bits. Easier for him to eat.

He ate slowly, savouring the different tastes, the same way he'd eaten the pizza and everything else at Neil and Carol's, and the takeout on our trip back here. We were about half done when I caught Mom's scent as she came in. She fetched coffee for herself and more cookies to share and came over, letting Victor watch her approach. She sat down on the other side of the table from us.

"Hello, Victor. My name is Lucy. I'm Ethan's mom." Her smile made me feel warm and safe and she wasn't even focused on me. "Did he tell you that you'll stay with me and his dad?"

"Hi?" A quick nod.

"It's a much different place here than where you were before," Mom continued. "You'll have your own bedroom and go to classes to learn a lot of wonderful things. There are many other children about your age to play with. There are boys like you and they'll be able to change shape when they get older. Other boys won't ever change. You'll start to meet them tomorrow morning, or maybe during supper tonight. Okay?"

Another quick nod. "Have another cookie."

When we left the cafeteria, Victor held both our hands. We passed several shifters in the corridor and they all smiled at Victor. I knew he was calming because my hand wasn't being squeezed in a death grip any more. Monster was happy that the boy was less stressed and kept purring at his beast.

Mom had been to the stores section of the base while we were on route, it seemed. There were clothes that would fit Victor in the dresser and closet. Carol must have sent along his measurements the night I brought him there. With a sleeping pill in the milk that first night, he'd be out while she measured him and I was headed back to the campground. I thought he'd gone to sleep too easily but he'd had a lot more exercise that day than his body was used to. And a very full stomach.

"All for me?" he managed to ask.

"Yes, dear," Mom said.

"Not have so much extra at bad place. Just one set. When washing." He stared at the dozen shirts in all different colours hanging up in the closet. Then he started to cry. I let Mom handle that hug.

Sam was in the living room when I came out. "Is he okay, Ethan?"

I took a deep breath. "He will be. Never had more than two sets of clothes. No friendly adults there and not a lot of time with the other kids. Looks like you get to be a big brother now. I don't know if he might be older than six or so, but the doctors will have to figure that out."

"Assholes. Hope we find them soon. Lots of guys will volunteer." We both grinned.

"Thanks for giving up your room to him. He needs a family."

Sam shrugged. "I'd been thinking about moving out anyway. None of my friends still live with their parents. I'm sharing a four bedroom with my friends who are also joining the teams. It'll a bit strange to get used to, but we'll do okay. At least we don't have to learn how to cook."

"Either way, I appreciate it. I'll probably be going on missions since I did come back, so Victor needs the stability. No idea what team Karl has in mind for me now. I did okay with Bill and his guys."

"Bill's new team is down in Mexico at the moment. Oh, Karl had an idea after you left. He told me yesterday, when we knew you were coming back with the boy. You, because you can shift all the way, get to help play with the younger kids. So they really aren't afraid of the change. Me and a few others have been showing them our shifted hands but the teachers don't want to scare them with a full partial. The older teens are better with that version, especially if we can still talk."

"Makes sense. Do they want the kids to watch me shift?"

"That's the plan from what Karl said. The kids watched my hands change. Thought it was fun after a while. Theory is that it will be easier for them to do a full shift if they aren't scared of what we look like."

"What about your tail?" I smiled. Sam grinned.

"That's harder to get to come on its own," he admitted with a grin. "I have to concentrate for my beast to remember to bring it in."

"Mom said she has video of you the first time it showed up." Sam laughed, which is when Mom and Victor came out of the bedroom.

"Hey, Victor!" said Sam. "I'm Sam, Ethan's brother. We're brothers now too!"

Victor smiled. Monster purred so loud I was surprised no one else could hear it. Proud of our... Kitten? Whatever. I was glad that he was happy at being back here. I was still waiting for the cost of our return to be brought up. Missions to find other shifters or stomp on drug dealers were a certainty, but what else might Karl and the leaders have in mind?

Dad came over to my apartment the next day. Mom had taken Victor to school and was staying with him so he could get used to the idea. He'd need a lot of help to get up to grade one, I thought. We hadn't talked about what sort of learning they'd given him and the other kids but he could barely sound out words and though he knew the names of numbers, addition was not a skill he'd been taught. A dedicated teacher would be needed to get him up to the first grade level.

"What's up, Dad?" I asked when he came in. I'd been reading the dratted history text while sprawled on the couch. "Victor okay?"

"He's fine. This is your debrief," he said, pulling a small recorder out of his pocket. "Karl and well, quite a few others want to know what you've been doing since you left here."

"And you drew the short straw?" I put the book down and sat up. Dad sat in the chair to the side of the couch.

"Sort of. I volunteered when the subject came up. Your reactions to being drugged finally got through to various people. Now that you're back, no one wants to give you a good excuse to leave."

"Wow. The leaders must've grown a brain while I was gone. Maybe. So, turn that thing on and let's get the interrogation over with."

I started the recitation after I was outside the wall and heading away. I guessed they had hidden cameras to track me while I was inside. Dad didn't object.

"Found the highway thanks to the beast and headed to the rest area just south of here. A couple of rigs were parked there overnight and I found a ride heading further south the next morning. Swapped to another rig and ended up in Georgia. I spent the next five months or so picking veggies and trapping rabbits. I wasn't sure what day it was when

I left here, so figured it would be easiest to stay in warmer climes when winter came. I wasn't sure how long I'd have to set up supplies and fire-wood if I went north."

Dad stared at me. "Picking vegetables? And why trap the rabbits?"

"Meat for the ongoing stews. There was a communal kitchen that people who knew how to cook rotated through instead of being out pick-ing. Less effort for everyone else and we could pick longer. We went out in fur most nights. The beast liked midnight snacks and there were a lot of rabbits in the area. The pay was pretty decent if you don't blow it on booze or drugs, which only a few of the younger men did. Most of the people were families. Hispanic and probably illegals, but they were good people. Staying there also kept me off any cameras as long as I didn't leave the farm, which I didn't have to do. I had a stash spot for my pay that kept it safe. It was a good place to hide out before going anywhere else. Once the harvests were over, I headed for the nearest swamp. Southern Georgia, just north of the Florida border. Mostly decent place to spend the winter and stay out of sight."

"A swamp? What did you live on? Alligators?"

"Not the big ones. Too tough for us to kill, even with a machete. Snakes were our main meat source. There's a lot of really big ones in there. I made enough money to buy food by selling the skins and heads to a guy who sold tourist stuff so I didn't have to spend much of the money I earned from the farm. That was useful once I reached my range in the park and needed to buy more supplies and gear."

"Were the snakes poisonous?" Dad still seemed unhappy about my diet. I might ask him about that later, not while I was obviously being re-corded. The leaders would probably be recording and observing wherever I was for the next few months, in case there was another incid-ent of people not liking me.

"No. Constrictors. Couple of different species but mostly Burmese py-thons. Three metres and up were the ones we went after. Smaller ones don't have enough meat to bother with them. Years back and still, people dump their pet snakes into a swamp when they grow too big for a little fish tank and those snakes have little snakes by the hundreds. There isn't much else to eat there, because the snakes eat up a lot of the small mam-mals, frogs and the birds. Sometimes each other. So we were doing a public service. When spring came, just before I left, we stomped on whatever nests we found, or had boiled snake eggs for meals. They weren't bad if you got to them just after they were laid.

"Then the mosquitoes started hatching and the heat along with the humidity made my beast cranky. I woke up one morning and it had shredded my tarp into small bits. It wanted out of there and ensured I knew it. So I packed up, sold the rest of the skins and so on that I had to the tourist stand and headed for a motel to transform from swampie to hitchhiker. Getting new clothes was high on the list. Everything I had was pretty worn out by that time."

Dad snorted. "I can imagine. Then you met with a young shifter in Atlanta? Korry did call in, by the way. He's at our school now. Home was too tense for him to stay there. The gang leader you nearly killed hadn't done anything overt, but he'd spotted several of the members around his house. The step-dad was also on his case about the gang-bangers circling around. His mom wasn't totally on side with him leaving, but came around. She was told that Korry's grandfather had been in the Union army and we'd finally traced his descendants for our scholarship program. He sends her letters and calls once a month. She's happy."

"Figured the banger were going to be a problem, but Korry had to realize it. It can be hard to jump into the unknown based on one encounter. I guess he already told the contact what I did for him."

"He did. We were relieved that you'd shown up anywhere and were okay. Mom was very worried. She didn't want you to leave. Um. We guessed you were *not* going to Mexico as you told him." I shrugged.

"The rumours and all that shit got to me, Dad. Marsh dying, and you guys weren't here. Not even a letter. Did they really not tell you what happened at the time?" I really wanted to know.

"We heard nothing until we returned here. Expected to see you with Marshall. I had words with Karl, the leaders here and a few others. The fact that they'd driven you away." He shook his head. "I do understand why you left, Ethan. But I'm glad you came back, even if it was just for Victor. I more than half expected you to leave your range after you found the package Mom left for you. We had several discussions on if we should have sent it in the first place."

"Thought about leaving after I found it. Guessed there might be extra tech in the phone, so I never kept the battery in it unless I used it. And that wasn't anywhere near my main cave. Just in case a team tried to find me before I wanted to come back."

"Then you found Cindy on one of the trails."

"Yeah. We'd gone out to hunt that afternoon. Turkey or grouse, but I didn't want anything really big like a deer since the meat would go bad before I could eat it all and drying it means keeping a fire going which means hauling wood, which was a pain since there wasn't many small dead trees around. We were cougar with just a knife on a belt I used as a collar. No clothing to get bloodstained, since it was a warm day. There she was, in the middle of a deer trail, clutching her toy lion and crying. It would have taken us a couple of hours to get back to the cave, grab my clothes and return to her. There *are* other predators in that forest, Dad. She wouldn't have had a chance if one of them found her. So I hid my knife collar and we brought her downhill. Once we heard the searchers, I left her there and went uphill to observe. Just in case the people calling her name had a different agenda than just getting her home."

"The news coverage was quite entertaining," Dad said with a smile. "Everyone had a different explanation for a while. Then the imaginary friend that her toy represented took over. You should have a look at those comics if you don't know them. You'd like them, I think. There's a few in the library as I've spotted a couple in the cafeteria. Not the whole set, but I don't think there's a coherent story line."

"Maybe. I realized later that I should have gone to a popular hiking trail or lookout really fast and been spotted in fur so it was more obvious she wasn't with *us*. I heard some of the rumours when I went to get groceries a few days later. There were so many people around the next few weeks that no one suspected that I didn't actually have a campsite no matter when I met them. I did let some tourists get close to us in fur, then ran away to show that we weren't approachable. It seems that people thought that the cougar was an abandoned pet which was okay. Anyway, the guys who brought Victor there must have guessed I was the reason. Any word on who they were?"

"Nothing so far. I agree that questioning at least one of them might have been prudent before they died. The government group is an outside possibility, but we've never heard of them doing breeding like that, sort of factory style, before. The ones we have in custody are being questioned again, if they'd ever heard of that kind of operation. It could take a lot of time to find a connection if we aren't lucky."

"Neil and Carol were helpful, but having someone else who was trained to track and fight would have been better. The last two guys actually came back to camp on their own before they passed out. That saved us a lot of time in getting them and their gear out of there."

"And from there you came back."

"Yeah. Anything else?"

"The men with Victor. Any sense you have on their level of training?"

"Good radio skills. Five guys made sense for hunting against just one inexperienced shifter. They should have done a lot of things differently since I wasn't new to shifting, though. Made sure they had eyes on Victor the whole time they left him on the trail, or at least checked in with him or had a bug on him so they could hear if he encountered anyone. I worried about a transmitter in his clothes or his guts. If they spotted a random hiker talking to Victor, they should have been prepared to at least trank him, me. Just in case I was the shifter. For some reason they seemed to expect us to show up in fur, not human form. Maybe because that's how I encountered Cindy. It would have been way easier to rescue her in human form than in fur. No big deal."

"Take her to the edge of a campground and tell her to go to a family? Otherwise you'd have been hailed as a hero. Lots of media coverage with your picture. People would have wondered who you are. We already knew your location, but the government hunters might have shown up. "

"Yuck. These guys, I was up at my cave, heard one of them talking to Victor and went down to investigate, so I had my wallet, phone and my small pack with clothes and food in case I had to bug out."

"It sounds like they might have training, but not much experience dealing with shifters. Any attempt to hide their scent on the boy?"

"No, they either didn't think of it or maybe didn't care. They had no idea how to hunt a shifter. But all were solid. Muscled. How well they might have fought... no idea. My first plan was to get Victor out and maybe ambush them one at at time as they searched for him the next day. But I couldn't guarantee that they wouldn't be damaged in the process. The beast was pretty pissed about how thin Victor is. He was cold when I met him. Shivering. Good thing I'd packed along a sweatshirt. It went down to his knees, so he was able to warm up."

"Then Carol suggested the sleeping pills to even the odds."

"Much better and faster. It was a bonus the campground was deserted. I think they might have chosen that one because there was no one else around. Five big men and a little boy would be noticed. They were wearing suits, so that's a tip off for any of their friends who show up looking for them. Any idea on others in the nearby campgrounds?"

"Not that I've heard. I think you're right that they were alone. I'll pass everything on to Karl. He should have the other campground info from Neil in a day or so, since the park tracks visitor numbers. We'll also check cameras for that vehicle in any other campgrounds or parks. The plates should show up on traffic cameras or other locations. Their van's plate number hadn't been issued yet, but had the right stickers, and two years of them so no one would bother checking the registration unless they needed to. The men had to come from a fixed base, after all."

"Do you need anything else?" I asked.

"Did you get any practice in on your Spanish while you were away?"

"I did. Most of the pickers were Hispanic. They understood me okay but I sometimes had to ask them to repeat a word or sentence because they didn't speak clearly or used slang I didn't know. I also learned several new ways to swear, but Joseph won't be interested in that."

"The swearing could help if you're in South America and trying to deal with the locals."

We both grinned. Book learning versus reality.

The next day was an outside day. Victor held my hand as we went out the doors into the sunshine. Monster purred.

"Mister Ethan! You came back!" Peter trotted over from his parents' blanket, then stopped to look at Victor. "You're the new kid, right?"

A nervous head bob from Victor. "This is Peter. Peter, Victor. He's never been outside much. I rescued him just before I came back."

"Wow. We're going to practice soccer. Do you want to come, Victor?"

"Never play," Victor said very quietly. "Just be in room."

"I'll show you how to kick the ball. It's okay." Peter smiled and got a small one from Victor. I followed along to watch, after I dropped my shoes on our blanket. Monster promptly shifted our feet to the partial. He wanted to play with the balls too.

Peter and two smaller boys that Victor knew from his classroom started to dribble balls up and down the grass. "It's hard at first," Peter said. "But you'll get stronger all the time. We practice in the gym, but it's better out here."

By the end of the afternoon, Victor had a good idea of how to get the ball to move forward. Peter had a new little pal. We all had supper together. An inner table but no one tried to sneak up on me. Monster purred at seeing the boys together.

Chapter 10

Damn near every time I left the apartment by myself, people, both shifter and normal, approached me to try to apologize about believing the lies Justin had spread. Mom had warned me right after Victor went to bed that first night. I hadn't quite believed her. Then I realized she'd been downplaying the need the denizens had to expiate their sins, as Mama Consuela might say. Victor wasn't in the cafeteria when I reached my limit of the drama queens. He didn't need to hear what I said.

"All of you listen up," I said loudly. "Yes, you all believed Justin's lies. Now you feel bad about it. Get over it. Next person to try apologizing to me is going to be gagged with their own shirt. Do you all understand?"

A murmur of agreement. "Tell anyone who isn't here. And by the way, ladies, don't bother trying to attract my attention. I am not interested in finding a partner right now. My beast doesn't like any women we've met here either, so don't bother trying. It just annoys my beast." I sat down at my usual place at an outside table and relaxed. The buzz of conversation was muted, but what snippets Monster helped me hear indicated that they wouldn't risk the gagging. Good. One problem solved.

Karl showed up at my apartment a few days later. I was back at the idiot school books. The geography and history was generally interesting but the Spanish I remembered from my youth was of the city slang variety with lots of swearing. Not the type of language that they wanted me to use and I'd mostly done okay with the non-slang version Joesph had insisted that I use. I'd learned more street Spanish while crop picking but it wasn't really proper either. If we were in jungles, I doubted that getting verb tenses right would matter that much.

I glared at the damned CD player. What the locals' slang and idioms were would be more important. Maybe the local teams would have a better clue. And if the mission leaders would let me go into areas without a lot of people, it would be easier to stay off everyone's radar.

"The docs want to try an experiment, Ethan," Karl said. "There's been considerable debate over the years on where the energy comes from for the change. One camp says there's no energy cost and the other..."

"Says there has to be," I finished his sentence, leaning back in my chair. "Of course. I'm pretty sure there is an effect. If I activate a lot of the beast's senses or rapidly change bits of me back and forth in a short time, I'm way hungrier for the time since my last meal. The shifters who do the full partial must have noticed it as well."

"They did. The science geeks have tried various tests with them, but they aren't satisfied with the numbers. They say it could be because the internal organs doesn't really change much for the partial. Skin and fur mostly change. Bones and muscle have more variation, they said. What we want to do is pretty simple according to the docs," Karl said. "We put you into a large box, which is sitting on a spare industrial sized scale they've hijacked from Shipping. They take an initial weight, then you shift. Weigh you again. Maybe cycle through a couple of times to see accumulated difference. Or if it takes more energy the more shifts you do."

"So no food or water," I said. "They should put a container in there that I can piss in. Big wide mouth Thermos would be easiest."

"Any other problems?" An eyebrow went up.

I took a deep breath. "The beast is *not* going to like being in a box or cage. Trust issues again, Karl. Still. I came back here because of Victor. No one else, not even my family. I couldn't keep him safe out in the world by myself. I'll work for you doing missions and experiments like this. But. You, the leaders here and whoever else runs things need to know coming back really wasn't a choice I made for *me*. And if I get wandering feet I'll head out. Again. I hope your security isn't as pitiful as it seemed the last time. I know what the small access tunnel is like, so I wouldn't try that route. If you or anyone else tries questioning me with drugs and torturing me to shift out of beast form, I'll kill them. Tell the leaders I mean it. If they want to sacrifice an idiot so they know I will do it, that's fine. Just keep Tim and Nate away from me. Unless you want them to be the example. Or if you catch up with Justin, we'll be *very* happy to motivate him into talking about what he's been up to and why."

He nodded, almost dismissing my last comments. "We'd shut down and moved several of our sensors and such that night. But you guessed that. Still, you made it out of the building faster than expected. And climbing the wall was impressive. Claws on your feet, too?" I nodded. There might be claw marks in the concrete that told them how we'd left.

"For money to live on, it would have been hard for you and Victor without a way to earn enough money other than by gambling. Single guy and a small kid would have raised red flags, especially with no real documentation. The DNA testing of those hunters is in process. We haven't found the names from their ID in any database we can access. And that's most of them. The camera footage search is ongoing. We've gotten a shit-load of it over the years. What can we do to make the experiment work?" Karl always swapped topics like that. Figured that people would keep up, didn't care much if they couldn't. I found it annoying. So did Monster.

"If it's a big enough platform, like the size of a regular shipping pallet, I can get the beast to just sit on your scale. If it's upset about being in a cage, it won't settle down and the science people will have a hard time getting a good reading with it moving all the time. I can't imagine there's a big difference per shift."

"We'll just try the scale then." Karl looked at me, then up at the ceiling, thinking. "Without the box. See how that goes. The docs also want to do a full workup on your metabolism and the beast's. They're always trying to figure our how to adapt their equipment and sensors to what the various men can shift to. A problem is that the beast is in charge when you fully shift. It wouldn't appreciate having patches of fur removed so the docs could glue down the sensor pads. If they put them on you first, they might not be in the right place after you shift. Not much of a problem with a full partial."

"I agree." I'd told them about Monster being in charge myself. And Karl had seen how hard it had been for me to change back to human when the beast was riled. They didn't know how much more the beast and I could do together now. I stood up and walked a little to calm Monster and thought about ear rubs. He was confused by the rapid subject changes of our discussion.

"That part is going to be tough, Karl. Best I can think of right now is that I do your metabolism tests without calling on the beast and again while it helps me but we don't do any real shift. I know that I can run faster and can lift more with its help and nothing is obviously shifted. Might just be muscles but I never noticed much of a size change. Maybe do the full partial for a third run. I didn't usually do that since it's pretty noticeable if normals are around, but I did shift to it if I needed to move quickly without losing clothing or my pack. I just take off my shoes and socks. That's also how I climbed the wall. That form runs a lot faster than any human can. If I'm going that fast, I use the tail to help keep my balance, especially on uneven terrain. Works really well."

"They've run metabolic tests like that on everyone. They shifted as much as they could on the second try. I'm not sure if they tried your variation. Maybe we should add it to the list, depending on what your tests show."

"First, the weight thing," I said. "When do they want it to happen?"

"A day or so. They'll have to calibrate the scale system without the box." Which meant they'd already built the thing. A hint of a growl from inside me. The first instalment of the price for keeping Victor safe.

I grinned instead of bitching. For now, at least. "I guess that they just needed a standard scale before, because everyone else was able to stand on two feet with a small platform using a regular scale. Four feet need a lot more room. Our paws are pretty big for our size. Helps stay on top of snowdrifts during the winter, not fall through the crust."

Karl nodded, but was sort of tuned out of what I'd just said. Obviously he didn't really care as long as I agreed to go along with the plan.

"So, what kind of beast do you have?" Monster still couldn't tell but I really wanted to know what I might have to deal with if I left here again. "I'm pretty sure it's some kind of cat. The beast can tell the difference between the cougars and the wolves, but there are only two dozen or so like you here and it's confused. Korry's the same sort of beast." That sort of got his attention back on what I was saying.

"I'm a lion. African, not one of the other big cats from there like leopards or cheetahs." Monster gave a brief purr, now that he knew what that beast was.

"Wow. Is that why you're so dominant?" Karl was well over two metres tall and had to weigh well over a hundred twenty kilo or so. That meant his beast would be huge. Much bigger than we were. Heck, even Sam was taller and weighed more than I did now. Courtesy of my foster father's greed and his desire to keep me skinny and short for the brothel he planned for my future. Monster growled at the memory. I wondered if Monster was smart enough to make us taller the next time we came back from a full shift. Might add a centimetre or two each time. If he could figure out how to make it happen or I could explain what I wanted.

Karl looked confused. "Dominant? What do you mean?" I blinked, returning to the conversation. I was surprised that he'd responded.

"Yeah. Why are you confused? Can't your beast tell if other beasts are more or less dominant to yours?"

"Because I don't have a clue what you're talking about, Ethan. Who do you think are the leaders here? It's not me. I run the missions and their personnel, not the whole compound. You met our three leaders at the hearings before you left."

"It's not about being in charge of a department, sort of." I sat down. *Shit.* How much more advanced was my beast than the others here? A lot, I guessed. "I just know from the beast. Like Tim was an alpha wolf. Dominant. But he wasn't high on the human side even though he was a team leader. You're in charge of missions, and you're *the* dominant beast here. At least, the most dominant that I've met and that includes the three leaders. My beast senses that dominance. That's one reason I could control it when the boys came into the gym when we first met. It liked playing with you, knew you outranked it so it was primed to obey. Sort of."

"What about your father? Is he truly dominant to you or does he get respect because he *is* your father?" *Damn, he really wants to know about this concept. No idea why.*

That took a bit of pretending to think and communing with Monster, mostly to keep him calm and not give away all of our secrets. Karl sat down to wait. "Mostly because he's my father," I finally said. "His beast is less dominant than mine, but there isn't a huge difference. Sam isn't as dominant as Dad is, but he can get away with more because I and the beast see him as a cub. Actually, a kitten. Same with Victor. Kids get a... free pass on behaviour from the beast, most of the time, anyway. It let Cindy hold its tail, which I was kind of surprised at. I was more in charge that time even though we were in fur. Because I'd been a kid so I knew more about them. That's the best way I can describe it for now."

"This is quite interesting, Ethan. What about the other shifters that you've met? How does your beast view them?"

"Most of them are... lesser. Not as dominant as it is. That was one reason the beast was so cranky when we met. It liked our play fighting and was pissed that it was interrupted. Sam was the only one in the group who would have survived if it truly took over. If they all showed submissive behaviours that might have saved them. I can't be sure, though. Its first reaction to danger is to kill whatever is in our way. It might never change." But it had changed over the years. Slowly. We still needed to keep our secrets.

"Because Sam's still a kid to you, your beast sees him that way as well. Is that changing now that you're getting used to him as nearly adult?"

More pretending to think, mostly calming Monster by rubbing his ears. "I'm not sure, Karl. However old Sam is, he's still my little brother. Before the house blew up, I wanted to be the best big brother ever for Sam. No one was going to pick on him. I had grief at school and wished I had big brother to look out for me like my friend Carlo had. No one messed with him once they knew about Esteban. He ran drugs and protection in the neighbourhood as well as the local bodega. I had some slack from the bullies because I was friends with Carlo, but it wasn't a direct connection so I still had grief when Carlo wasn't around."

"I'd like to tell our shrinks about your idea, Ethan. It seems to be leakage from the human to the beast. We know about the beast influencing the human, as that generally results in incidents we need to clean up and hide. But the other way... I don't think we ever considered the difference in our beasts' instincts from their natural forms. You're right. Cougar males in the wild don't care about their kits. Would kill an interloping male in their range, even if it was their own kitten, from what we know."

"Wolves and lions do family things. Protect the cubs is a top priority for them. There's mostly wolves here, aren't there?" I already knew that, but wanted to keep Karl talking. Encouraging his hope that we were going to stay and be good. For now, or until spring came around or Victor didn't need to cling to me so much.

"I agree. So maybe the cougar line shifters didn't think twice about caring for their kids in the early years. Had sex with a woman and moved on. Didn't care or possibly know if she had a child if they had a short term fling. That was natural for their beasts. Low fertility rates would also make them and the other sorts assume that they were completely infertile so they didn't have to worry about using any kind of protection. Not that there was much available other than the rhythm method until the 1960s or so." Karl stared at me, his fingers drumming on his thighs.

"Cougar are still the most common kids we find out in the world. At times the link is two generations back. Like Marshall." A growl from Monster at the memory of the blood staining the old shifter's chest.

"Shit-disturbing again," I said with a grin. "My speciality. Well, back to the books. I'm not allowed to complain in public. I have to set a good example for Victor, his teacher said. Even about the dammed book reports." Karl smiled and left. I went to the bathroom to cover my thinking from the cameras I knew were active. We were so much more than these quiescent beasts.

Monster purred in my head, smug and proud. That would give us more advantages if, and when, we wanted to leave here again. At least no one had messed with my pack. I tried to stay with Victor, Sam, Mom and Dad for meals as much as possible. That discouraged the stinky females. At least none of them had tried wearing an entire bottle of perfume again. A glare kept most of them away. Several had still tried to chat me up as we were in line at the buffet tables but none of them were acceptable to Monster, so I ignored them. They were sensible about the cold shoulder and didn't try to apologize after my announcement, but they were still circling near us, hoping for whatever rewards might come with having our kittens.

Chapter 11

Three days later the scale was ready. Four science types (one normal male, three females), three guards with dart guns who did have beasts in case Monster decided on what might be a very good/very bad course of action. The guards stayed near the walls in the gym so they'd have a clear view of everything that went on and Monster couldn't quickly reach them. I just hoped they had made it impossible for their camera systems to ever be hacked again.

"I passed a guard on the door," I said to Karl. "Good idea." Keeping the number of bystanders low was a good idea. Monster had never been this close to a lot of people. I planned to do lots of ear rubbing while he was out. Maybe we could get a ball or three from the storage closet for him to play with in between shifts.

"I thought if your beast thinks I'm dominant to it, I can help you if it gets cranky after a while."

"Good plan." I turned to the science woman who seemed to be in charge. She was older, maybe in her mid-fifties. Medium blond hair mostly hid the grey. Brenda, according to a name tag. "What's the actual procedure you want to use? Karl was pretty clear on the plan when we first talked, but I know things always change when crunch time comes."

"We're starting with a fairly simple protocol, Ethan," she said. "We weigh you, then you shift and we take another reading. Wait a half hour, then you shift back. Another set of weights. And so on. A report on how you feel each time. Any discomfort or odd feelings. If you say you are fine, I expect that you could easily complete a five mile run without call-ing on your beast. Depending on what these results show, we might change the protocols to help refine our data for another set of tests. Do you understand?"

"Yes. Having to stop halfway through an infiltration would not be a good idea. Screwed up timing would be the least of it. What can I do for the half hour? Just sit around? That might be harder for the beast. It gets bored and might not understand what you're trying to do. One reason I didn't want to try using your box system."

"That makes sense. The beast can wander around the gym. That's why we're in here rather than in the small lab we'd planned to use at first. A little play with Karl could keep it from being bored, or it could have a nap. I can have your school books brought in if you want for when you're human. Ideally, we should have the same amount of exercise for each iteration to account for any discrepancies in your weight. We currently plan to do four sets of changes. I *do* want to know how you feel after each one. We don't know what the effect of rapid, full changes is. We did trials with those able to do the full partial, but our results weren't reproducible. They were almost random. We aren't sure why, so we have more tests scheduled for them once we test this method with you."

"How about a couple of sheets of paper with things like Good, Bad and It Totally Sucks? Maybe add YES and NO pages so I can answer simple questions. That way I can still try to communicate while the beast is out. We were better at sharing control in the hills since I wasn't as nervous about staying in fur for long stretches last winter. And maybe get out a soccer ball or two if it gets bored. It likes to play with them." I let a hint of a blush out. "I've done that out in the world when I was sure no one else was around. Didn't want *that* to show up in a video anywhere."

"Good idea. We're treading a lot of new ground, Ethan. Thank you."

I nodded. I still didn't trust these people, not completely. But they were the best alternative I had right now. At least until next spring. My parents would take care of Victor, even if I vanished again. It might be harder to stay hidden than I thought. If there were people comparing camera footage from anything that took pictures and stored them, I could show up on any grocery store or casino footage. If I left I should head down to Mexico or up into the wilds of Canada. Nastier winters in the north, but lots of land to roam in and small towns without a lot of cameras to shop in. I could become a snowbird. Summer in Canada and winter in Mexico. The beast perked up at the thought of birds. I didn't have time to explain the difference right now so I thought about stroking him. Silly thing purred.

One of the other women wearing a lab coat, younger than the rest of the science types by a big margin, came over from a computer. No name tag. "We're ready to start when ever you're ready, Ethan."

"Okay," I said after a deep breath. She was different than the other women. Then it clicked. She smelled good to Monster. That could be a little complication for the test. Or a huge one. I blushed, very involuntarily, and everyone looked at me. I tried not to stare at her. "Um." I swallowed. "Um. Just so you know, miss. My beast has decided that it likes you. This is really, really rare. I doubt it will do anything to harm you, but it might come over to sniff you. Just treat it like a big pussycat and it should be okay. Rub its ears, maybe." I'd be able to control him. I hoped.

"Another outlier behaviour?" Karl asked.

"Yeah. Maybe. I'll tell you about it when I'm human next cycle." I went behind the equipment and stripped. *Shit.* I'd have to reveal more of the beast's abilities. But choosing a mate type behaviour wouldn't give them much of an advantage. There had been only two other women I'd ever met who'd gotten the same reaction from him. I still wasn't sure if the lady with the shifter family was interesting to Monster because of her smell or the fact that she was pregnant and there was a very tiny beast in her son. The lady at the bogus pickup site was a definite yes. However, Monster wasn't really interested in any other pregnant ladies that we'd seen here or out in the world. He could sense the foetus but the mothers weren't acceptable by whatever criteria he insisted on.

Wait, I might actually have the chance to start a relationship. That'll stop the other women from bothering me. I hope.

The science guy came behind the barrier and gave me a big towel to wrap around my waist. "Thanks."

I stepped up onto a steel plate a little over a metre square. The controls didn't look like a simple industrial scale. Another lie. It was supported on all corners and sank slightly as my full weight came onto it.

"If I sit down, it might be more stable for your measurements," I said. "And the beast should fit okay lying down."

"Good idea," the yummy one said. A smile. The beast really did like her. I wondered what her name was. I sat and it didn't take much time until Brenda nodded.

I suggested a shift, but kept the beast lying down. A deep breath and the woman smelled even better. Monster started to purr.

"You can get up now," Brenda said. "Walk around. Get your ears scratched if that helps keep your beast calm." The others present mostly restrained their laughter but we heard several snickers from the guards.

We stood up and leaped off the platform. Cold, hard metal wasn't comfortable to lie on. The woman came toward us and held out a hand.

"Hello," she said. "I'm Melissa. I should have introduced myself before you changed. How do you feel?"

She had four pieces of paper that she put down but we sniffed her hand first. A quick lick. She tasted good too. Then we put a paw on the Good sign. They hadn't bothered with an 'It totally sucks' sign. Not a surprise. Monster was being really focused on sharing his body with me right now. It wanted this female to be ours. Mine. Whatever.

"Excellent." She smiled at us and we were happy. The purr's volume went up. "Maybe we can walk around the gym a couple of times?" Her eyes flicked over to Brenda and she nodded in agreement.

Walking outside would have been better but Monster and I were both happy to be near her. Then she sat down on a mat and we curled up beside her. The feel of her fingers rubbing just behind our ears made the rest of the time pass quickly.

"Time for the change back," she said. The beast wasn't happy about that and stopped purring. "We can talk then, Ethan. Even though, I probably won't be rubbing *your* ears."

She stood, so we did too. We jumped up onto the platform and lay more or less on the towel.

"We're getting another reading of your weight, Ethan," Brenda said. "Okay, you can change back."

Melissa turned her head slightly and I shifted. Pulled the towel over my lap to hide a definite erection. "It's safe to look now," I said. I'd never had this kind of physical response to a real woman, even the two that Monster had approved of. *Shit, I might be able to have a real relationship.* The thought freaked me out but Monster purred in my head to reassure me that all was well from his end. Finally.

She turned back and smiled. "Your beast's fur is extremely soft, Ethan. I'm sorry if I was carried away. I've worked with natural cougars, lions and wolves in my training. They were retired movie animals, habituated to people. They'd learned to really liked physical attention during their careers. The main reason they had such careers in the first place. However, there have been many attacks and accidents over the years in the industry, even with hand-raised animals."

"I'm not at all sorry about the ear rubs. Neither was the beast. It really likes you, which is beyond rare, like I said."

"And we have our reading," said the science guy.

"How are you feeling?" Brenda asked.

"Great," I said. "We may have to redo your test without Melissa around, just in case. The beast is happy with her around. I doubt that it would do anything to drive her away."

"We'll try any variations another time," the other woman said. "For now, we'll just keep on as we planned. I'm very happy that your beast is calm about all this. If we need to do a repeat, it won't be upset if Melissa is here with you. We'd make sure she was available when we do schedule the next time. You two, or just Ethan, should walk three times around the gym, then sit down on the mat to replicate the first cycle." I managed to wrap the towel around myself and secure it. Mostly. If we did this again, I wanted a bath sheet or a big bathrobe for this part.

"Think of it as a kilt," Karl said with a grin.

The three of us ended up walking. I was sure everything that happened in here was being recorded so I only minded a little. The beast was happy Melissa was still with us. He was more present than usual. I was slightly surprised no one else could hear the purring that echoed through us. I did not mention it, not now.

"Explain the attraction thing, if you can," Melissa said, beating Karl to the question. "I'd never heard of anyone mentioning anything like that."

I tried, mostly without blushing. "The beast, from what I've sensed just now and over the past maybe five or six years, is seeking a mate. Whenever I'm in a place with lots of people, it's paying attention to all the women we encounter. Walking on a street, in a grocery store, that sort of thing. By the way, the female is for me, not another cougar for itself. It's ignored all the female cougars we've encountered in the mountains. Haven't been many of those, but it just walks away from their territory. I was glad of that. I wasn't sure if it mated with the cougar female if the kittens would be normal cougars, or human babies." Both of them nodded, though Melissa's eye were wide.

"Since you're the first full shifter we know of, that is a legitimate concern," said Karl, his eyes wider than usual. "I'll pass the idea on to the science types, but I'd hope there wouldn't be any offspring at all."

"The beast also likes kids," I said. "Treats the idea of them as kittens who need protecting. Doesn't matter whose kid it is. That's one reason I could save Cindy. And then Victor. It's seen a lot of kids here, like young Peter. It wanted me to help him when he was being bullied by his brother. But it's picky about who might be suitable as a mate for me. Very picky. So far, there have only been two women we've met that it's approved of. One was out on a mission, with no way to move forward with anything like a date. The second one is you. Two out of possibly thousands of women over the years. You smell good to it, Melissa. Very good." *Glad I kept from blurting out that there were really three good candidates, not just two. Did Monster really care that she was from another line?*

"So none of the women living here smelled right to your beast?" she asked. "Is that why you didn't try to start any relationships when you used to live here or when you were younger?"

"No and yes. As a teen, I was living on the streets and girlfriends were not in my world view. Being alone was safer since there were spontaneous shifts to worry about, like most teens. Whenever the beast heard a loud noise, for instance. The only two times I... paid for companionship, the beast really didn't like them and I almost lost control. So I never tried that again. Nobody should die just because I tried to have sex with them. This was about..." I had to stop and count back. "Seven years back, maybe eight. The first woman I ever met who did smell right was the one in the downtown park on the first mission I did."

Bogus as it was, it had given the beast ideas. That was after the pregnant lady it liked, so maybe that contact had jump started its interest.

"But with her, and me, you don't feel any..."

"Discomfort, rage, I'm not sure what word to use. But I'm pretty sure..." I shut up and blushed, not wanting to presume how Melissa felt.

"That if you were in bed with Melissa, it would be a wonderful experience?" Karl asked. He was grinning, the bastard. I was sure the news was going to spread quickly to the other leaders.

A surefire way to keep me here and happy about it. Might not be a downside to finding someone to be with. A girlfriend.

"That would be a yes," Melissa said. She was grinning too.

"Time to sit down," Brenda said from her console. We went to the mat and did so. I had to adjust the towel so I wasn't flashing anyone.

"How do woman deal with short skirts?" I asked. "Never mind. I don't think I want to know." All the women laughed *at* me. Not *with* me.

"How do women in relationships differ from ones who are single, Ethan? Or do they?" The third woman, who wasn't wearing a lab coat, approached us carrying a chair. She smoothed her knee length skirt down and kept her knees together so no one, meaning me, could look up her skirt, since her knees were about head high for me sitting on the mat. "I'm Alicia, by the way. I don't think we've actually met before, Ethan. I have seen you in the cafeteria on occasion."

I had to ponder again. Decide how much to reveal. "You look kind of familiar but we never spoke. Good to meet you. Anyway, the beast ignores them as potential mates once it, we know about the relationship or if it doesn't like their scent. The scent was the most common negative by far. I can check ring fingers but the beast smells a man's scent on her. I think." I shrugged. "Or something. I never tried to quantify any of these reactions before." I'd done so occasionally, but hadn't really concentrated on it. Didn't have the need out in the wild. No women of any kind around us unless you counted the ones in the campgrounds.

"In the next few days, try to recall anything about other encounters," she said. "How did your beast know that Melissa was available?"

"It didn't, really. But there was other male scent on her. At first, it was her smell that attracted it." I paused, trying to decide the best way to explain a reaction I didn't understand either. "I'm using the term smell, but actual scent isn't the only thing that it notices. I just wanted a simple word to use rather than just waving my hands around in the air because it's too complex to explain in one or two words." Melissa smiled.

"The beast likes her more than the one we met in the park on my first mission. It wanted to challenge the asshole who'd been bothering her that day. That would have been a really bad idea and it took a lot of effort to convince it not to rip the guy up in public." *Then we'd been drugged and tortured into shifting back to human.* A hint of a growl from Monster at the memory. Then it sniffed Melissa and purred happily.

"I'm glad you didn't," Karl said. "That would have been impossible to cover up if it shifted any part of you in that crowd. Too many cell phones." He turned to Melissa. "*Are* you in a permanent relationship?"

"No." She blushed this time. "I graduated university from a vet program last spring. I concentrated on zoo predators, which was as close as we can get to the shifter types. Then I spent three months with the film animals for real world examples. Most recently, I worked in one of the other compounds with another vet to get the practical side of working with shifters. There are med staff here for people but no trained people on the animal side. There's been a need for several years and I'll be travelling to other nearby compounds and safe houses that have shifters, especially if they're older. We need more information on the ageing process to determine when shifters should actually be retiring, not just using their chronological age to decide what they should be doing."

"Did you date on the outside?" Alicia asked. Another blush which made Monster purr more. He really liked her.

"Yes, but never seriously. My mom suggested dating while I was at university so I wouldn't stand out. My father lives in the southwest with my mom. He's cougar. So is my brother. Actually, both my grandfathers are cougar. They're mostly retired now but help out by training young shifters in tracking and such. Both of them can do full partial shifts even now. That was considered very unusual when they were young."

"We encourage the lines to stay relatively pure," Alicia said at my puzzled look. "This is the first time we've encountered the scent attractor, or whatever it really is, that I've heard of."

So why did Monster like the lion lady so much if it mattered? Maybe it didn't. Mom isn't from any line and I don't think Dad's mom was either.

"Better ask all the other shifters else if they've noticed it," Karl said. "Or just ask what made them decide on the woman they're with. The term used might vary depending on how much of a change the man can do with their beasts or how good their bond is."

"Nearly time to shift back," said the male scientist.

"Well, you can rub our ears again," I said to Melissa. She smiled.

The next two sets of shifts went okay. While human, Melissa and I talked about our pasts, small talk to get to know each other. I didn't mention the shit I'd gone through before I'd left for the forests, but did talk about Mama Consuela and how I became sort of Catholic. Melissa didn't seem totally adverse to at least becoming a friend. We had time to move slowly. Monster just walked or sat by her and kept purring while she rubbed his ears or neck. Karl went outside the gym with a cell phone in his hand. He didn't mention who he'd called or why, but he was smug when he returned.

Then while the beast was out, we tapped the Bad sign.

"Definitely the last one then," Melissa said. "Changing back immediately might make you feel worse. Do you feel up to walking right now?"

The beast answered by not getting up. I tried to concentrate on the symptoms. Mild nausea. A bit of cramping in my gut. I'd pissed the last time I was human and that was being factored into my weight.

A short nap later the beast felt better. We tapped the Good sign. Melissa came over and we did our three laps of the gym, then had a little time on the mat before it was time to shift back to human again.

The nausea was worse but I managed not to spew. Mostly because I hadn't eaten lately. "Shit on a stick," I muttered. I rolled onto my side, faced the wall and didn't plan to move until it subsided.

"Looks like we're done then," Karl said from behind me. "Can you talk yet, Ethan?" A hint of amusement in his voice, the arsehole.

I held up one finger of my left hand. The middle one. Snickers from the various guards. They'd probably all holstered their dart guns by now.

"Just rest, Ethan," Melissa said. "We'll get our reading, then we have a bottle of water for you."

Another nap. That seemed to help. The science types were staring at screens when I woke. The guards were sitting on the bleachers, no weapons to be seen as I expected. Bored. There was a fluffy blanket on top of me, since I was mostly lying on the towel.

"Are you feeling better, Ethan?" Karl hovered over me.

"Kind of. Is there any sports drink around? Not water. That was a 'Totally Sucked' reaction, Karl. Not sure if we could walk even a kilometre. Even now."

Melissa brought over a bottle. I lifted it and realized there was a blob of cotton on the inside of my left arm with tape holding it down. "We took a blood sample, Ethan. We should have done one each time you changed. If your beast doesn't object, we'd do that the next time or just do them when you swap back to human."

I kept sipping the drink. Nectar of the gods instead of terrible, which meant I really needed it.

"It will take us a day or three to analyze our data," Brenda said. "We may want to do another complete run, just to compare to this one."

"I see how I feel tomorrow," I said. "I'm heading to the cafeteria once I finish the bottle." I waved the sport drink, now half full. Another muscle cramp in my left shoulder. I rolled it a little but it still ached.

"We'd do the same time interval, but maybe without exercise."

"I'm not sure the walking made much of a difference, Brenda. But I know one thing today did prove." They all looked at me. "Too many full changes in a short time and I'm useless in any kind of operation."

Karl nodded. "Exercise or fighting might make it worse over a short period, Ethan. That could use up more of your available energy. We might want to try a shorter time frame with more exercise next time. Just two sets each of you and your beast."

I groaned. "Why did I come back here again? Oh yeah, my life's ambition was to become a lab cougar." Everyone but Karl laughed. He knew everything I'd said in the interrogations. I wondered if this *was* a good idea. To let them, and everyone else in the compounds, know what my limits were. On the other paw, my limits might be far beyond the average shifters I'd be working with. I had to keep the leaders satisfied that I was going to stay. Let them think Victor and my family were the reason. The beast now seemed—smug. At finding a potential mate, I thought. Melissa and I needed to talk. But first, food. Then a shower and my clothes instead of the dratted towel. Maybe the other way around as the nausea threatened to return.

Chapter 12

I didn't actually eat much after going back to my place and curling up in bed for another nap. I just hadn't felt hungry after I had a cursory shower and dressed at the gym. I forced myself to eat a sausage stick that I had in the small fridge and almost hurled. The bad part of sleeping was the dreams that kept waking me up. They were more like replays of all the times I'd fled from hunters but in these dreams they caught me.

Somehow Sam was always a toddler, no matter how old I was, and the goons threatened him unless I did whatever they wanted. I didn't shift in those dreams, which kind of surprised me. It was almost like the beast wasn't in my head anymore. Totally weird.

The third time I woke thrashing in the covers I gave up and took another shower since I was sticky with sweat. I'd change the sheets later. The beast was back and also grumpy but I couldn't isolate a reason. Maybe because my dreams had bothered its nap. Then I worked on the idiot history course until I heard a knock at my door.

"It's open!" I called as I turned to face it. It was Melissa. The beast roused a little, but it seemed to feel as crappy as I did.

"Are you ready for... Gods, Ethan, you look terrible. What's happened?"

"Didn't sleep well last night," I said. "Nightmares, so I got up and started working on the dratted history course I have to finish."

"How much did you eat before going to bed?"

"A bit. I wasn't that hungry after the nausea went away." I shrugged. "So I didn't bother going to the mess hall."

"You need to eat." She grabbed my arm and pulled me toward the door then stopped as she realized I was barefoot. "You used a lot of calories yesterday. Where are your shoes?" I sat down on a kitchen chair once she let go of me. She tried to pull me up and that did not work.

"Shoes are in the bedroom. I'm still not that hungry, Melissa." She dropped my arm and headed behind me, coming back with a pair of slippers Mom had brought over and I'd never worn. Bare feet or real shoes were my usual choices. I'd worn the dressier shoes as little as possible, since the noise annoyed Monster. It's harder to stalk prey if they could hear you coming. The runners were a good choice for daily use since they didn't make much noise in the corridors.

"These will do for now. Get up. Now."

I honestly didn't care enough to fight her right now. She towed me to the cafeteria and sat me down at an outer table. Before I knew it, there was a tray in front of me. Apple juice, pancakes with too much syrup, bacon, sausage and a trio of eggs over easy. Most likely Mom had told her what we usually ate.

"Eat. Now." She sat and stared at me until I lifted the fork and had a half a sausage. They'd also been doused with syrup. Monster roused a little. He liked that Melissa was here with us.

By the fourth forkful I realized we were starving. Melissa smiled as we started to pay more attention to the plate and less to her. She went and fetched a much less full plate for herself. By the time I finished, my nagging headache had vanished and I felt more human. Well, as good as it ever was. Monster also seemed happier, but I wasn't sure if that was because of the meal or that Melissa was with us. I hoped that we could start seeing each other. Friends to begin. Hopefully more. Monster would be cranky if she refused us. We might have to go to another compound, or she would. If there was a serious need for a vet here, they'd have to move me. Away from my family and Victor.

"Brenda calculated that you lost about sixty grams each shift," Melissa said once I had finished everything on the plate. A very serious face. "The loss did increase in the last two shifts, which didn't surprise me. I'm guessing that most of the loss came from your liver and any fat reserves you have-or had. That's where spare energy from food is stored, by the way. The blood sample we took showed that your metabolism goes into high gear to do the change, then it seems to settle down and goes back to normal while you're in the other form. There's no ongoing calorie increase for being in the other form, at least that's what we think at the moment. We might need you to stay in fur for a couple of days to be sure. We'd have to weigh everything you ate or drank. Plus everything you... eliminated. I doubt your beast would be happy at a fast of two to three days."

"Out in the wild, cougars eat just a few times a week. Depends on what they can catch, or what they've cached. Water would be more often. I think that the full changes so close together just made it worse." She nodded. "We can probably stay cougar for a longer time, but I think it would be better if we weren't here with all the people around. Seeing a cougar wandering the halls might freak them out and it'll be bored if I just stay in the apartment. And the sports drink? It tasted great instead of terrible. I know that's always a bad sign."

"Your electrolytes were also depleted, Ethan. Doing that many full shifts in a short time is a..."

"Very bad idea." I shrugged. "That's the only time I've ever done so much shifting in such a short time. Generally I stay in the form for a couple of hours, at least. Or I just shift enough to do what's needed."

"Like the other shifters do. Just their claws, for instance."

"Sometimes that's all you need. It might be okay if I drank or ate between shifts to replenish those reserves. That might be an easier test to run. Lots of exercise to use up my reserves and at least a sports drink with sugar to provide a jolt of quick energy after each shift to fuel the next round."

"Sugar or other high-carb or high protein foods with a sports drink might be best. Brenda wants to schedule more tests to determine what the optimal mix is. We'll also find out how well the other shifters react to the same sort of tests we're planning. The teams need to know about the problem, but they may have already taken precautions without knowing the details of why they needed to do so."

Oh joy, more testing. On the other hand, out during a mission in the field or just in the world, I need to know how to stay on top of anything. Everything.

"I know from one mission that the people who set up our gear gave us maybe three times the amount of food we really needed. Don't know if they expected us to carry it up a mountain, but we might have finished it off if we had three or four hungry teens with us instead of just the one we were looking for." *I should write to Ron. See how he was coping. And Korry. Let both of them know I came back. See if they can become friends.*

Karl joined us on the last bits of conversation with a coffee for him and a large glass of orange juice for me.

"On an infiltration, you could go through a perimeter in beast form to evade the sentries, then shift just a paw to a hand to open a door or type an access code onto a keypad, then shift it back and continue on. You could carry a sports drink in a harness along with some assorted high calorie snacks if you have to do several complete shifts in a short time. That would work no matter what form you're in."

"Could do. When we went hunting in the mountains, I usually shifted to cougar at my cave so I didn't have to worry about my clothes getting bloody, then went downhill away from the campgrounds to hunt. Washing clothes by hand was a real pain. I carried a knife on a short belt that I used as a collar. Kind of looked like a radio tracker, at least from a distance. Once I made the kill, well, it depended on how big the animal was.

Birds or small mammals, the beast would just carry them back to my cave and I'd change back there. Deer, I'd change at the site, roughly butcher the carcass and either cache a haunch up a tree or carry it all back to the cave. Most of the deer in the last range weren't that big, so if I left behind the stuff I wouldn't eat like the intestines, head and lower legs, I could carry the rest in human form with help from the beast. Leaving those bits behind also meant the scavengers didn't try to follow me back to the cave. Time of year also mattered. I did figure out how to wear my small backpack in full shift for warm clothes after a winter hunt. I scavenged garbage bags out of the Dumpsters." Melissa smiled at me.

"Did you ever go after cattle or sheep?" Karl asked. "We didn't hear any word of missing farm stock around that park. One reason the station guessed there was a shifter in the area instead of a natural cougar. Then we had a decent picture from near a waste bin, which identified you."

Mostly what Neil had told me, so probably the truth. Or they'd decided beforehand what to tell me. Might be the truth, or not. It didn't matter now.

"I didn't want the ranchers out hunting me since they wouldn't respect the park boundaries if they were cranky. Besides, full grown cows are too big for one predator my size to tackle and if the herd scents a threat, they gather together so that nothing can get to any of the calves. Sheep, well. I hate the taste of wool so they was never on my list unless I was really hungry or found one already recently dead from a car or truck. Every so often I grabbed a big road kill, but only if I was travelling, it was a recent death and I didn't want to waste time or money on a diner. I'd find a spot away from the road and shift to let the beast eat.

"I tried to stay away from all the major roads in my ranges. Deer, mountain sheep and goats aren't that bad eating. You have to be very careful of the antlers and horns in cougar form. They didn't spook as quickly if I was human, since they weren't hunted much in most of the parks I stayed in. I made a rough spear to slow them down, then I could change and finish them off. Thought about a bow and arrows but never tried them. They're bulky to carry if I was swapping ranges." And my shoulder couldn't take the strain after the torture.

"And there weren't many poultry operations near your latest cave. Maybe the odd coop in a yard."

I shrugged. "I left those chickens alone unless one escaped on its own. Marmots aren't bad eating. Small enough to carry and two or three days worth of meals for a decent sized one. There were a lot of them near my cave, just before your guys caught me in Seattle. Not many around where I found Cindy and Victor, but they like bigger mountains than the Appalachians. We also love ducks, grouse and geese. Wild turkeys are excellent for a couple of meals. There were lots in the last range. Fall and spring are the best times for the water birds if there's any lakes or ponds as stopover points nearby."

"Once you finish eating, you should have a short walk around the building. Then a nap," Melissa said. "Then have as much lunch as you can eat. No shifting at all unless there's an emergency."

"That sounds like a plan," Karl said with a smile. "Maybe for the next test, just have Ethan do a full partial shift. See if the same issues come up and if there's a difference in how much energy it takes. We have a couple of dozen or so team members in residence who can do a full partial for comparison as they cycle back from assignments."

"I'll talk to Brenda and the science team. I'm not sure the scale they used the first time was as sensitive as this one, which might have been why the earlier results were uneven. Doing the test with whoever is here first also ensures Ethan has time to fully recover." She turned to me and looked delightfully stern.

"I want you to come to the med centre with me after lunch so I can check your shoulder. Your cougar's gait was off a bit. I'll do an X-ray of your left shoulder and one of the beast's in a few days, once you can shift safely. I'll need to compare those with any done earlier of your shoulders, and I have sample X-rays of what normal joints look like for each form. Maybe I should also get a set with you in a partial shift. Just to be sure of what might be wrong. I think we should also get complete sets from all the shifters here. I'm not sure any other compound has that sort of detailed X-rays either, so I'll pass that on through my medical contacts. We need to know what the uninjured joints and bones look like for everyone, not just the shifters. At least everything is digital now. If a shifter is away from their compound, the file can just be sent to a closer one anywhere in the world if they're injured."

Karl glanced at me but didn't say anything about what Tim's team had done to me. Then the damage from the bullet that killed Marsh which really hadn't been treated properly. The combination hadn't really healed back to pre-injury status. Well, I had sort of intended to get my shoulder checked out if I came back. Now I had a doctor on my side, along with the general feeling of guilt at how everyone had treated me.

I finished the juice, managing to hide a belch behind the glass. "A trip to the head and I'll go walkies."

I wasn't surprised to see Melissa waiting outside the washroom door. Monster purred in my head. It would take a serious betrayal to force him to start planning to leave here. Well, I was thinking that way myself. Being alone in the mountains was hard work and winter meant I'd be more alone than usual. Having anyone be in my life was a novelty. A normal relationship, even if was technically a threesome, had a lot of appeal.

And Monster, at least, seemed to want a kitten or kittens of its own. Well, mine. Or ours. Maybe that interest would help my sluggish libido. I might have to let the doctors know about that issue. Maybe later. Right now there was a woman nearby that both of us were attracted to. She was the most important thing in our minds.

"Thanks for waiting," I said. "Anywhere in particular we should walk? Something you might like to see down here?" We started toward the gym. We could walk in a big circle and not get lost if we weren't paying attention to where we went. "There isn't really much to see, though."

"Not really. I was surprised that no one goes outside here."

"It kinda sucks. The beast would prefer to live somewhere we could go outside whenever we wanted to. The outside days are maybe twice a week when it's nice out. No idea how they set the schedule. Might be random, or it depends on the weather forecast. No one wants to go out in a thunderstorm, after all."

"Did you meet many other shifters out in the world?"

"A few. Not sure where they went after we met. Why?"

"Mostly I've been wondering how they deal with injuries," she said. "Broken bones, being gored by a deer or slapped by a bear. I doubt any of them would go to a doctor or a hospital."

"Bears were the main reason I left Banff some years back. Lots of hungry bears fall and spring and we'd be outclassed in any conflict." I snorted a laugh and got an 'Explain Yourself' Look. "I washed dishes in town for some money to buy supplies and went to Mass one Sunday. Chatted with the priest after. He was confused that I didn't have any romantic encounters to confess. Then he assumed I was gay and got flustered. I just told him I didn't care either way and he calmed down. But really the beast didn't want me anywhere near a woman it didn't approve of. We hadn't met anyone at that point."

"A lonely life."

"We were lonely together. Sometimes I was really mad at Dad. Thought that he was the reason we'd been targeted back then. In reality, it could have been me. If a shifter got close enough to detect my beast."

"Someone sensing your Dad was more likely," she said. "At eight, many shifters can't detect the beast. Not like yours can. It took the best care of you that it could. You really never had a girlfriend before?" A smile that warmed our heart. Monster purred in my head.

"No. When I was on the streets, the beast might shift and betray what we were. And it didn't like any of the women I knew. So we stayed out of their way. I heard stories from other guys and saw some nasty break-ups." I paused. "Did you know that most guys are scared shitless whenever a girl comes near them? Very dangerous creatures, girls. And then women. Well, women are even worse. Especially when they under-stand how to use their feminine wiles on poor males like me, who have no idea how to carry on a conversation that isn't about work or some-thing equally inane." *Why had I said that? It was the truth, but...*

She giggled. "You're doing fine, Ethan. I didn't date much when I was growing up since the boys I knew were more like extended family, given how few kids were in that compound. That one is among the smallest. At university I knew I couldn't get serious about anyone. So my feminine wiles aren't very well developed. What I know about you I like. You risked your life to rescue Victor and Cindy. You fought for Korry. You and your beast are protectors, and that means that you are a good man. That's a fine place to start. However you got there."

I blushed. "Thanks. I never had any good male role models in foster care. Three different families, who all saw fostering as a way to make money. Then there were a lot of criminals and gang-bangers who were not that good at relationships. I had sort of a grandfather who liked to tell stories about when he was young. Mama Conseula's father. I worked for her son, doing various sorts of deliveries. Mostly illegal ones, though my friend Carlo and I also did food deliveries from the bodega to older folks, especially during the winter. Toronto's winters could be very nasty. Well below freezing and lots of wet snow. The one time we wintered in southern Georgia was nice that way."

"Tell me about your good times and the bad ones. We'll swap stories until lunchtime." A smile that made us so happy Monster took over our voice for the purr.

I was surprised to see Sam and his buddies in the gym a week later. Melissa was with me. So were Dad and Victor. There were signs on the doors. 'Warning! Full shift implemented. Do not enter!' A dozen or so soccer balls were near the middle of the room.

"Full shifts?" Victor asked. He turned to me. "You is really a cougar?"

"Yes. We can be the partial, or fully shifted. Most shifters just do a partial. Are you scared of the cougar form?" A tiny head bob. Maybe he'd seen some 'after the kill' pictures of a natural cougar hunting.

"It's okay. Stay beside Dad and Melissa when I change. Then you can decided if you want to stay and play with us."

Victor grabbed Melissa's hand. I smiled without teeth and went over to the side. Stripped quickly, facing the wall.

Okay Monster. We finally have friends to play with. The little kitten's not sure about playing with us, though. A breath and we shifted.

Monster didn't object as I watched out our eyes. He started to purr. Ignoring Victor for the moment, he headed for the balls. Sam and his buddies backed away, but Monster pounced on a ball and batted it toward them. Sam caught on first and went to his full partial, including his tail, and kicked the ball back toward us. Monster sent it to one of the others. Soon all the balls were in motion.

After maybe ten minutes, Monster turned toward Victor. Walked over and sat just outside of arm range.

"Do you want to pet him?" Melissa asked gently. "His fur is really soft near his ears." Victor glanced up at her, then another tiny head bob. He took the first step toward us but Dad came too.

Melissa's hand was soon on our head. Monster started purring. Victor took a few moments longer, then he touched our head. Monster angled our head so that he could rub our ears. It does feel good.

The older boys stayed off to one side so Monster wouldn't feel surrounded and panic. That was another reason Melissa was invited.

"Is so soft," Victor said. Monster sensed that he was relaxing.

"Let's all play," Dad said. "You and Ethan versus the rest of us. Okay?" We chirped in agreement. We stood and bunted Victor and turned to return to the balls.

When we shifted back, my left shoulder ached. "A bit too much exercise today," I said to Melissa as I dressed. "But it was lots of fun."

"Can I does that soon?" Victor asked. "Or just partways like Sam?"

"We won't know until you're older," Dad said. "Next time Ethan shifts, do you want to come play again?"

Lots of nods and a big smile. "Maybe Peter comes too? Or just cougars can come play here?"

"Doesn't matter to us," I said. "Peter saw my hand turn to a paw. You can ask him if you want at supper. He might be scared like you were at first, but we can let him get used to the idea." A bigger smile resulted.

"I think we'll start to get others coming out," Sam said. "I just wish we could go outside and play there. I kept slipping because I didn't want to mess up the floor in here and had to keep my claws from coming out to gouge the wood."

"How good are you guys at seeing in the dark? That's one way to be outside and not have to worry about people spying on us." Sam grinned. "We could practice that in here if we can shut most of the lights off."

Bill and his wife came over to my usual table just after noon with a stroller between them. Melissa was in the medical area with a patient and I'd come in alone for a change.

"Congrats on the little one," I said. Monster purred in my head. Maybe at the baby's beast.

"Yeah. He mostly sleeps, still," Bill said. "Last night, unfortunately, wasn't one of those. Now, of course, he's out like a light."

"I'll try keeping him awake this afternoon," his wife said. Danielle, I remembered. "Might not do any good, but I don't want to turn our schedules completely around."

"He'd swap back the moment we arranged it," Bill said. They sighed.

"Your first kid?" I asked. Bill nodded. He was four or five years older than me, so that surprised me a little.

"Took a while to find the right woman," Bill replied. "Kind of like you, though my wolf didn't seem to care like yours seemed to. I did."

"You're back doing missions," I said. "After almost a year at home. Maybe the baby misses you." They both stared at me. I shrugged.

"Hey, I have no idea on how or what babies think. Maybe even less of an idea. My beast really likes the idea of kittens. Babies. Since you were around a lot his first year, maybe that means something. You were just away for a week or two, weren't you?"

Danielle looked at Bill, then down at the baby. "I'll have to track his sleep schedule and see if there's a difference when Bill is around," she said. "I know other moms who are having problems with their infants now that the dads are back on duty. All are shifters, though the effect might not be as pronounced in non-shifter families."

"We had to track down a drug dealer," Bill said. "Took longer than we figured. You would have been helpful. Maybe you can come out with on the next assignment. If we can talk Karl into letting you join us, that is."

"I am so ready to get out of here," I replied with a smile. "Even the thought of tracking a drug dealer through a stink-ridden slum doesn't seem like a bad idea."

Danielle rolled her eyes at us and the baby decided to wake up and demand a diaper change. It will Bill's turn, it seemed. My eyes didn't quite water. Maybe the reality of infants might dampen Monster's desire for a kitten of our own. Or he'd just withdraw until the gas warfare was over. That wasn't a problem natural cougar dads had to deal with. But any boy child of mine would have a fierce protector by his side, encouraging his own beast to be far more than the dull ones that most shifters in the compound seemed to have. And the girls, well, no one would mess with them either.

Chapter 13

Ethan wanted to go to the big cavern. It could come out and play. It purred. Fur time was good. Maybe there would be a ball. Or two.

There was a strange big flat thing in the exercise place. Other things that reminded it of the time its leg was hurt. Hunters with dart guns where it could not reach them easiy. The dominant and others without beasts. It growled. There would be no play here. Ethan stroked it and it calmed. For now.

Then a young female came near them. It sniffed and started to purr. A female that smelled so good! The others ones it had found were other places. Not here. Could this one become Ethan's mate? Then they could have a kitten! It would help that protector grow strong.

Ethan sat on the flat thing and asked it to shift. So it could meet the female properly? They walked around the exercise place and then the female sat down and let it sit next to her. Then the female rubbed its ears and neck. It purred and no one tried to make it go away. Ethan was quiet but liked the female too. Good. There would be a kitten. Like the lion female and the others it scented here. The small kitten from the forest was good to be with, but it wanted its own kitten. It would teach the tiny beast many things while it grew. That kitten would not be lesser.

Ethan wanted to shift back. It didn't want to. But maybe they could play with the female later. It sat on the big thing and it brought the other shape back. The female walked with Ethan and the big lion, then sat with them. There were words but it didn't try to understand. Was it a new sort of game? It liked playing with the ball much better.

The other sat on the big thing and it could come play again. And have ear rubbings from the female. It purred.

It was unhappy. Even the female couldn't help it feel better with ear rubbings. Ethan was unhappy too. It slept. When it woke, it felt better. But too soon the female wanted it to return to the big thing. When Ethan took over, it went away. Back to its place. Warm and dark there. It would feel better soon. Ethan was safer in the big caves than in the forest. It could stay here and rest. When Ethan was better, it would return.

Some light times later the female wanted to it to lie on a small hard thing. Ethan rubbed its ears. This was to find out why the foreleg and shoulder hurt sometimes, it understood. That was a good thing. It had tried to make it better but the leg kept hurting when they hunted. It did not understand why but that leg was hurt by the bad ones.

It wrapped itself around Ethan's mind when the female asked them to be close. They saw pictures that it did not fully understand but they were different than the form they had now. Ethan asked it to make sure the foreleg and shoulder looked like the picture from now on. So they could run and chase balls easier. There would be no pain.

It purred and made Ethan's shoulder different. Now it knew how to make itself better the next time it was in fur. The female took good care of Ethan. There would be a kitten.

Playing in fur was more fun now. The older kitten with others were in the big cavern. There were many balls to play with. The mate was there, with the small kitten from the forest. Ethan let it shift, telling it the small kitten was frightened of it.

It played with the older kittens first. To show the small kitten that it was safe. Soon they all played together.

It purred at all the kittens' beasts. To help them wake and grow strong so they could protect their others when they left this safe place.

Ethan and the mate slept together, but did not try to make a kitten. Maybe. It was not sure how kittens started, just that they were very small at first. It sniffed. A hint of a special scent. Of the female that the old one remembered when he ended. A sense that its ears were rubbed, then the scent was gone. Was that female also happy that Ethan now had a mate? It was happy and purred.

Chapter 14

I woke slowly. My nose was full of a wonderful scent. Melissa had spent the night with me again. I opened my eyes to see her watching me. Smiling. Wearing nothing but the sheet, which showed off her curves.

"Good morning, love," she said. "Sleep well?" I purred in response. It echoed in the bedroom, startling me. Melissa didn't seem as confused as I was and her smile grew.

Wait. What? I lifted a hand. But it wasn't a hand. It was a paw. I chirped. Well to be honest, we chirped. The beast had become bolder about shifting on his own in the past three months. Melissa had shown Monster how to properly fix our left shoulder. I couldn't follow the jargon but a major tendon or two were damaged in both forms and weren't repaired during the shifts we'd done. At least it didn't hurt any more.

She's not going to mate with us in this form and she can't change shape. I pictured myself in human form and Melissa twined together. The beast sighed. It was getting easier to communicate with more words and fewer pictures. As I watched, the paw became my human hand.

I sat up and checked the rest of our body. "Sorry, Lissa. I'm not sure why that happened. Or when."

"I was warm all night, at any rate. Truly, you don't know why?"

"Um. The beast really likes you." I blushed. "It's happy you're around. So am I. Like I said when we first met, it's been hunting for a mate for me for a couple of years. I'd mostly given up on trying to find anyone, especially while I was out in the world. It didn't like any of the women we met here and I wasn't sure I wanted to stay with the Coalition anyway."

She sat up, letting the blanket pool in her lap and smiling. I blushed again, distracted. The beast purred inside me. "Then you found me," she said. "Or the other way around. You know, I think it might be a good idea to give him a name."

"What? Who? The beast?" And she'd called Monster *him*? I'd always tried not to use that name out loud or use anything other than it as a pronoun to match what everyone else here seemed to use.

"Yes. From what I've seen over the past few months, he has a personality and habits that are distinct from yours. He's very different from the other shifters' beasts I've treated. A lot of what he does also doesn't reflect what's normal for wild cougars. It's a topic the shrinks have been debating the past few weeks. Mainly from my observations of you and how he reacts to various stimuli. Alicia is on side with the idea." She paused. "I know you and the other shifters use it to refer to their beast. But I don't think *it* applies to yours at the moment. If that was ever an accurate description, given what you two can do together."

"Why not?" *How much had we given away of Monster's abilities?*

"He's not... I don't have an easy term to use for what I understand of your bond with him. Also, using *him* and a name might help the minimal and partial shifters to do more. Help strengthen their bonds with their beasts. Superheros always have different names than the one they use in the outer world. I think that it might make it easier for the teams to be able to refer to their beasts as the source of a feeling or sense of danger if there are non-shifters we don't trust in the area. The information could have been sent on a private channel the outsiders don't have access to to help explain to them if they question it."

"Makes sense. And the shrinks are onside with using normal people names for the same reason? Not Fido, Wolfie or ones like that?"

This had to be the strangest early morning conversation I'd ever had. Strike that. It was the strangest. Time of day didn't matter with the current topic. Having Melissa intimately in my life also meant it was harder to keep the beast's abilities as hidden as I wanted. But if we were going to stay here for the foreseeable future, it wasn't as much of an issue any more.

"That would keep anyone from listening in and guessing what's really going on. The teams have had problems for years, I learned. The shrinks are kicking themselves because they should have thought of it ages ago."

"Well, it could work." She smiled at us. "Especially since it might help shifters connect more with their beasts. That might let them do more of a change or just be able to use more of their beasts' abilities." Certain physical manifestations were happening to me under the sheet. "Do we have to get up right now and spread the word?"

"Not really. Did you have a plan for how we should spend this morning?" She asked. Another smile that melted my heart.

"I had an idea that I think you'll like." She bent over and kissed me. The beast, Monster, purred louder and retreated slightly.

Mom looked at the book in front of me later that week. "Is there an announcement you and Melissa need to make, Ethan?" An eyebrow went up. I'd just finished a solo lunch in the cafeteria and managed not to spew the juice still in my mouth.

"It's not what you hope, Mom. No, Lissa isn't pregnant. Yet. She suggested I pick a name for my beast. Apparently the shrinks want all the shifters to do the same thing. I thought that I'd read the names in my head and see if I can tell if my beast likes one more than the others."

"Hmm. But the other is a possibility?"

"I have no idea. Still early days, I think." We'd been sleeping together for two months now. We hadn't quite moved in together but my libido was slowing rising. I still hadn't told the docs about it. Then again, I still hadn't really seen any medical person longer than it took them to hand me sleeping pills for my next mission. Other than when Lissa helped figure out what was wrong with our shoulders.

Alicia came over to the outer tables and joined Melissa and me at lunch a few days later. "I wanted to talk about how we can help other shifters develop, Ethan. How did you start working with Dave?"

"Smelling for things like gun oil or cigarette smoke when I was moving packages for various drug dealers. Started doing that when I was eleven or so to get money to eat. My first hand shift was at fourteen. I left the foster home and started living on my own soon after that. Dave could tell if an enemy was lying in wait for me, so I didn't have many encounter with idiots trying to rob me or whatever. That cut down on the chance of his claws shredding whoever was trying to ambush me. Why?"

"What about identifying certain people? If they are a shifter or not? Perhaps starting with the members of your team. There was an incident a few weeks ago down in Venezuela. A shifter in full partial was on an infiltration. One of his team, a normal human, was also working his way in. They surprised each other as the trails they were following intersected without warning and the man was injured. They had to air evac him to the nearest compound for immediate surgery. He'll recover, but it will take several months for him to return to his team."

"They're sure it was the beast taking over from the shifter?" Melissa asked. Alicia nodded.

"Not that surprising," I said. "It must have happened before. Dave's been wound pretty tight on stalks out in the woods when we were living out there as well as parts of the missions. If one of our guys came in from the side, he might lash out. Surprise isn't good for the beasts. He gets... tunnel vision, sort of. Highly focused on the prey in front of him to the exclusion of everything else. Necessary for a predator looking for a meal, less good for a shifter in the middle of an operation, where there are multiple enemies who can come from any direction at any time."

She nodded. "Ideally, I'd like to have the adult shifters help develop it as a game, then we can start showing it to the older teens and work our way down in age. We don't know when the beasts begin to develop."

"Dave can detect beasts when the boys are young," I said. "Playing with the littler kids, he knows their beasts are still sleeping. Not the exact term I want to use, but the beasts aren't really aware of what's going on around them at that point."

"And the teens? Once they're starting to shift?" Melissa asked.

"Less asleep." I shrugged at their expressions of confusion. "I know, that's not really helpful. Sorry. It took years for Dave to get to where he is now. Fourteen, more or less. Shifters aren't going to see any fast improvements. The guys are going to get bored. So are the beasts. One problem is living in underground places like this. There's no real stimulation for them, especially for the teens. An afternoon or two each week outside, or the occasional camping trip is about it. There's no real danger or need for the beasts to protect them, unless they're older, working on a team and in actual danger. With those constraints, it might be too late to help the older shifters develop a tight bond with their beasts." I paused.

"They might get better, but I don't think they'll ever manage to get as good as Dave is now. The younger ones have a much better chance but they'll need to get out more, not wait until they're preparing for the teams. I wonder how much difference there is between those who stay in compounds like this one or more open ones. Or the school place, since I guess there's a lot more outdoor training there."

Both Ron and Korry were there. Their last letters were all about their shifts. And grousing about the English classes. I have to start doing more missions so I can get the rest of Joseph's ongoing idiot book reports off my to-do list.

Alicia nodded. "You worked with Dave from the beginning of your shifts. And out in the world with much more danger than we, living here, can imagine." I nodded. "I had an idea on my way over. What about following a specific scent? We can blindfold the person and use the gym. Use a scent that lasts for a little while, say only a few hours."

"You could put cameras up in the rafters," Melissa suggested. "Track the person laying the scent, then see how close the trackers are."

"Or the beasts could start following the earlier shifters instead of the actual scent." I added, shaking my head. "Wait. That's a problem in tracking anything. Kind of like following a critter in the snow. Real animals don't try to set up a fake trail, but people on the run do. You might ignore everything but the disturbed snow or even walk in those tracks, which messes them up. If other people had followed along that same trail before you started, you'd never see anything else, since you're all following the footprints of the first person. You don't realize the target backtracked from a point like a stream, went up a tree via a hanging branch, then came down ten metres off to the side and is long gone now. The first tracker reached a spot where they lost the original trail and just kept going, hoping to pick the trail up again but the fourth one can't tell who went where because of all the other scents and no clear tracks."

"I see that would be a problem if you're the third or fourth in the sequence." Melissa said. "Which makes it harder to arrange any scent training in a pristine environment."

"Same as why police always want to limit the number of people in an area if they're using any scent dogs to find a missing person. Just telling the difference between a shifter and a normal human might be easier to start with," I said. "There wouldn't be any bias on the previous person's score. Blindfold a shifter and run a group of ten or twenty team members or so past them. Keep track of the results, so the people can see if they're improving. If you want a bigger sample with fewer people standing around staying quiet, have them mix up the order on the second round. Or have the first couple go in between the rest. As long as you have a camera on, it'll be easy to double check the scores."

"We could start with men only," Melissa suggested. "Once a shifter can get all of those right, add identifying the type of beast, then if the subject is a woman, and finally guessing actual identity."

Both women looked at me. "What are you doing during this afternoon, Ethan?" Alicia asked me with a smile.

"I think that I can probably make a very educated guess at this point. I was going to work on the history course, but that can wait, I assume."

"You're a very clever man for a man still in high school at your age." Melissa's dimples came out. Alicia tried to keep from smiling wider. But failed. I sighed. *Damned courses. I wish I was done with the damn book reports.*

After lunch the next day Karl grabbed all the teams and guys on paternity leave currently in residence: thirty-three men, three teams including Bill's, and we went to a large room I'd never seen before. It was near Shipping, I thought. One office chair sat by itself. A small table holding a camera system behind and slightly to one side of the chair were the only furnishings at the moment.

"You've all heard we had an incident," he said, once we'd all made it into the room and milling around, mostly according to which team they were in. "So now we're adding new types of training for the shifters to help develop your bonds with the beasts. First thing we're trying is this: Can you tell who is a shifter and who isn't. Once you get those right, we'll add variations. We're working on other techniques for later."

Alicia stood up. "The first run is to show you how much a beast can do. Ethan will use Dave to show you how accurate he is."

"Is this why you dragged a bunch of older shifters into a conference room yesterday?" I didn't see who spoke or recognize the voice from near the back.

"Yes. That was to test the concept. Today, you get to see the results for yourselves." She held up a thick blindfold. "Once Ethan can't see you, I want you to form a line. Not by teams, but as randomly as possible. We're recording this test to show to other compounds. We want all our shifters to improve their bond with their beasts. We're hoping that a bet-ter connection will cut down on friendly claw incidents if the beasts de-velop more of an awareness of who their team members are."

I took the chair and Melissa handed me the blindfold. *Hey Dave, more games to play*, I thought. Dave purred. Smug at how good he was.

Lots of feet shuffling noises. "They're ready, Ethan. Guys, listen up. Once you're done, go toward the end of the line, but don't follow the same order when you do. Okay? First one to the mark on the floor."

Footsteps. Shuffling noises as the rest of the line moved forward.

Beast. A picture of a wolf. "Wolf."

Another. Just a person silhouette. "Human."

And on. And on.

"That's the last one," Alicia said eventually. Dave was bored early on but I kept thinking about rubbing his ears so he kept with the program. I pulled off the blindfold and blinked in the bright lights.

"Some of you came through twice," I said. We hadn't bothered with identity for this round. I figured we only knew about half the men by name, which would skew our results. Mostly because we hadn't worked together and no team guys wore name tags around here.

"Fifty correct. Out of fifty." Karl was smiling. With teeth. Dave was more smug now, watching from behind my eyes. "There's sixteen shifters here now. Who's next?"

"In the interest of time today, we'll do twenty each for the rest of you," Alicia said. "And we'll schedule practice sessions at least two or three times a week. You can also practice by yourselves whenever you can get a group together. We might also be able to use the teens as prac-tice subjects but only if their beasts are well developed. They're also go-ing to be doing this training once we iron out any kinks, so it gives them an idea why and how."

"For this run, just try for shifter or not," Melissa said. "If you know the type, say so. Bonus points."

Dave caught a few grumbles from the shifters. Being challenged to do more with their beasts wasn't what they thought they should be doing with their downtime. *Tough.*

Chapter 15

It was confused. Their mate wanted it to be called him. Like the other. Like Ethan. And a name. It had a name, it knew. Monster. The other was looking at things again. Not having fun. Maybe they could play with the balls later. With the older kittens. And their kitten. The female might like to play too. It liked when they played in fur.

Ethan put down the thing and picked up another. *Monster,* he said quietly. *Melissa thinks you need a different name. I used what I did because that's how I saw you back then. When you first changed part of me. You weren't very awake then. Now you can do so much more. That's why the new name.*

It didn't remember many things from when it was that small. Just that it had to protect the other. Protect Ethan. It would also protect the mate so they would have a kitten and Ethan would not be sad and alone.

These are people names, Monster. I want you to choose one. Okay? The other started saying words that it didn't know.

It settled and listened. A few words sounded nicer than the others. But it wasn't sure how to let the other, Ethan, know.

Ethan stopped talking. *We'll try again later.*

More time with the mate. The female was good. They would have a kitten. Hopefully soon. Ethan read words slowly. For its new name. It chirped on one that it liked best. Dave. Ethan read others that sounded similar, but it only chirped again when he said Dave.

It was in fur more. The others all called it Dave then. Sometimes they played with balls in the big cavern. The mate and the kitten from the woods played too. Being here was good now. Ethan was not sad.

Another new game. Who had a protector and what kind. It showed Ethan the types. The lesser ones showed how asleep they were. Even the big lion was not as good as they were. Ethan rubbed its ears. So did the mate. Dave purred.

Chapter 16

Karl intercepted me as Melissa and I were leaving the cafeteria two weeks later. "Got a special mission for you," he said. "Briefing in one hour, in my office. Be there." Then he walked away.

Melissa looked confused. I shrugged. "He doesn't like to waste time. It can't be a crisis, or he wouldn't be going to eat. I'll find out what's up in an hour. He won't say anything even if I followed him back into there and talked to him while he eats. It's really annoying at times."

"Well, you can work on your history in the meantime. Joseph won't be peeved at you if you need to head out. Again."

"I will be *so* happy to have the damned GED over with," I said with feeling. But each mission meant one fewer book reports I had to complete, which made the trips bearable. I had to ask Joseph how many were still on the list, and maybe check with other teachers to be sure he was telling me the truth.

An hour later I was outside Karl's office. No shifters or normals to be seen or sniffed. Of any team. Which was strange. Dave didn't sense anyone other than Karl in the office. I'd been mostly working with Bill's new team since I returned, since there wasn't another based here that needed an extra shifter. I knew I wouldn't find out anything out here, so I knocked, and went in when Karl made a noise that might have been 'Come in'.

"Am I heading out on my own? Why?" I asked as I sat down in the visitor chair without waiting for permission because Karl hadn't bothered to look up. Another annoying habit of his.

"Not a chance on solo missions, Ethan. And it's not anywhere near here. Africa. Western jungles. The only reason you're going is because we want and possibly need a full shift, but with as much control as possible. The only Lion near there who can do a full shift isn't as reliable in having his beast do what's needed as you are. No one had told us about him before we admitted you could do the full shift. Also on the down side, he's from a different group of shifters than the one we need to work with and there are issues between the two groups. We're neutral in that conflict. The group we're going to visit thought we were joking until they saw the footage of you shifting when I was testing you. We can't afford any civilian casualties even though we'll be deep in the bush when it goes down."

"And the mission is?"

"It's a rescue. Between ten and fifteen young women were kidnapped. The first report was pretty vague on numbers since it was sent out right after the raid. Some girls managed to get into the forest and didn't come out until they heard their mothers calling for them. The girls were kidnapped from relatives of one of our allies out there. The ones responsible have vanished into the jungle and it's going to be difficult to track them down. They haven't contacted anyone about a ransom yet or even to boast about their raid, so we aren't even sure who is responsible."

"You want me on a long flight, alone? Where lots of shit can spook Dave into shifting something? We've never been in a plane, but I've heard things. Sudden drops and changes in pressure. Hell, even just taking off could confuse him. And what about the crowding and the noise? Being squished between people he doesn't know for hours without respite isn't a good idea. No idea how long the flight might be from here to wherever." I shook my head as gruesome possibilities flashed through my thoughts. None of them had happy endings. "The Coalition has some big jets, don't we? You could also keep us asleep for the whole trip."

"It's very time critical mission, Ethan. We don't have time for a cargo ship to get from here to there. Our own planes and pilots who could do the distance are committed to other operations." He stared at us for several minutes. "Definitely not economy. Business class. Bigger seats, fewer people. And I'm going with you. That part was already set. I can speak a few of the local languages. Worked there as a liaison for ten years back when I was younger. A half sleeping pill should keep Dave calm. Maybe we can take one of our smaller planes to the airport instead of driving, just to give him a bit of experience. That might work, or we just rent a small plane with one of our pilots at the wheel in case of a shift."

"Could work." A deep breath.

"You've *never* flown before?" He seemed honestly confused, and he shouldn't be. He'd been the one asking questions when we were drugged.

"Didn't want to risk it," I said. "Plus the obvious danger of Dave getting upset and visibly shifting, there's a ton of cameras in all airport terminals and I figured that would give anyone looking for a shifter plenty of time to get a team in place by the time I landed. No chance of slipping away on route like I could with a bus, a train, or just plain hitchhiking. I usually had a big backpack full of camping gear, so I'd have to hang around the luggage thing before I could leave. Sitting duck. Well, cougar. Staying on the ground had a lot of appeal. You already know that I usually hitchhiked or took a bus to go long distances. Did you forget to ask about any flying experiences while I was drugged?"

"Okay." He ignored my last comment, as I guessed that he would. "We'll leave late tomorrow. That way you can sleep part of the longer trip if we can get the right seats booked and no one will be suspicious. We'll put you on the window side. That way I'm between Dave and the other passengers. The dominance thing might be useful if he gets upset."

"And you'll need to bring a dart gun in case I can't control him. Do they come in plastic?"

"I'll have ID as an air marshal as cover for any weapons I need to carry on the plane. I'll have a briefing package together in the morning. Go tell Melissa. I have work to do."

Melissa stared at me when I got back to my, now our, apartment. "Karl wants to take you and Dave to Africa? Why? Aren't there other shifters there already who can do the job?"

"It seems there's a dozen or so young ladies who are part of an ally's extended family who were kidnapped a few days ago by some very bad people. The locals need, or think they need, a full shifter in order to rescue them. Apparently there's a lion who can do a full shift near there, but their groups don't get along. I have no idea what their actual rescue plan is. I'll know more tomorrow."

"Do you want to go there?"

I took a deep breath and let it out slowly. "I'm honestly not sure, Melissa. Dave's reaction to flying is my major issue but there are others. It seems that none of my concerns truly matter to Karl. I knew I would have to do missions for him when I came back here with Victor. The weight test where we met? That was a part of it. Along with finishing the damned high school courses. The new missions with Bill's and George's teams when they need an extra hand. There's always a price for things. It might not be money, but more like favours. The Coalition has done things for me since I came in so I kinda need to do what Karl asks me to do, even if I don't really want to."

"That's not how we work, Ethan. Everyone's looked after, no matter what happens to them."

"The entire world works this way, Melissa. The Coalition paid for your schooling, right? What would the elders think if you decided to set up as a film animal vet in Hollywood or somewhere else and leave the compounds behind? You don't shift, so there wouldn't be any problem with the government folks finding you, though that's not certain. You're an information source on locations of compounds and safe houses if they know you're related to a shifter."

She stared at me.

"If you did leave, the leaders might decide you needed to repay the entire cost of your education since they'd footed the bill. In full. Could you do that? Out of your savings?"

She almost spoke to deny that possibility, then looked thoughtful. "What about the other missions you went on before you left? Why did you do them?"

"Paying back room and board, mostly. Trying to change at least one team's mind about how to approach shifters out in the wild. I wanted try preventing other young shifters from the mental trauma of the stalking and tranking that I went through. Don't know how far that idea's spread since I've been gone, but I think it's getting better."

"Do you think Karl or the leaders here or anywhere else want you out in the world alone, Ethan? They let you go once, hoping you'd come back. And you did."

"For Victor. I debated just killing the men with him and taking Victor with me, but that would have been difficult, if not impossible. I'd have to find a very isolated range but one with enough game and other kinds of food to keep us both fed. More danger if I was caught while getting supplies. Leaving him alone in a camp out in the wild wouldn't have been a good idea. I couldn't risk taking him with me into a city. For one, kids aren't allow in casinos, so he'd have to stay in a motel room which costs money. I occasionally used them to have access to hot water and privacy, but more often I found a squat in an abandoned building or an encampment with a bunch of homeless people. Those are very bad place to leave a young child alone. So there was no good option but to come in."

Maybe I could have joined the migrants picking fruit and veggies, but there still would have been questions about how we were related. But it could have worked. Plenty of other kids for Victor to play with and I could have taught him basic reading and math. Along with the other kids.

"And now, you've gone on several short trips with different teams."

"Room and board, again. Giving Dave some outside fur time. Dave doesn't want to leave you behind, Melissa. Considering how many women we've met over the years, you're the only one where I have a decent chance at a life with anyone. I've been so lonely ever since I was eight. You're always my love." I couldn't say anything more. Monster purred inside my head and Melissa held me, us, tight.

Victor was almost harder to tell. I'd warned Mom first and went to their apartment. "Hey, Victor, wanted to let you know that I'm heading out on a mission late tomorrow." I kept my voice calm.

"With Mr. Bill or Mr. George?"

"With Mr. Karl this time. We're going to help a group of shifters in Africa. I'm not sure how long we'll be gone this time. Like Pete's dad. Sometimes he's away for a week or two helping good people get away from bad ones."

Victor grabbed us around the neck and started to cry. I just hugged him back until he let go.

"Lots of bad thems?" He asked finally. A very quiet voice.

"Yes. Very bad men. They kidnapped some friends of the shifters there, and we're going to get them back home to their families. I will be back, Victor. I'll bring you a present, okay?"

About twenty minutes later he was calm enough for me to leave. Mom gave us glasses of milk and cookies once he stopped nearly strangling me. Since I faced the kitchen area, I saw her put a sleeping pill into Victor's. Separation anxiety, she'd explained to me the first time I'd headed out after arriving with him. I had a lot of reasons to come back to the Coalition now.

Dave did *not* like the noise in the smaller plane, or the sensations as we took off. Even with a half sleeping pill, it was hard to keep control. I just kept picturing us rescuing a group young girls being menaced by evil thugs with guns and rubbing his ears. I also kept my hands on my lower thighs so any claws would go into them rather than the upholstery of the rented plane. I felt a few pricks, but they weren't deep. I wore dark pants to help hide any blood. Plus bandages and an extra outfit in my carry-on.

The plane finally levelled off, reducing the noise and pressure. Karl looked over at me. "Okay? Is Dave calming down?"

A deep breath. "Yeah. The moment we get seated in the other plane, I want a full pill. This is not a great idea, you know."

"Our first plan was to be another set of thugs. Have you as our prisoner, going for a big ransom. They'd want part of that, we guessed."

"That implies a second plan," I said. "And changed recently?" There hadn't been *any* plan in the info he'd given me before we left the compound. Just general comments on the local jungle: very thick and tall, with variously sized paths for foot and vehicle traffic and lots of critters that might want to snack on us. Or that Dave might want to snack on, which made him happy. Ostriches weren't local, which was a relief. We'd seen a nature program on them and getting kicked could kill us no matter which shape we were in.

"Yeah. Locals weren't in favour of that one. They know more about the general type of the most likely thugs involved. Anyone with you might be recognized as being not-thugs, which blew that plan. So we're going to be escorting you on a leopard hunt and look for them with that as a cover for going down marginal roads and such. They'd assume you had a lot of money and want to do a ransom."

"Sounds better to me. So we'll all have weapons and such. What name am I using?"

"Borgan will work. We have all the docs ready. Including passports, credit cards and so on. The thugs won't ask questions about your current home, just how much money can be raised to buy your freedom once they grab you. With any luck, they'll all be dead after we recover the girls, so won't ever be able to share that name around."

"And once we get caught, we cut through the ropes late at night and remove the obstacles to our health and happiness." I smiled.

"Good way to put it. I'll have to remember that one."

We were met by a uniformed security dude as we landed in the early twilight at a big airport, possibly on the coast. No beast within him, which made sense. "I'll escort you to the check in. I also have your Marshall's ID and a weapon, sir." Dude didn't look at me, just Karl. Dave was a bit distracted by the jet fuel smells. A hint of the ocean? I was just happy he'd calmed down after a little while. And the landing hadn't been nearly as bad as the takeoff.

Thanks to that dude, and another one who pulled our rolling luggage once we reached the terminal, we took back ways, away from the crowds and those pesky cameras. The government guys might be interested in us. I wondered if they had anyone working here or if they just hijacked the camera feeds like the Coalition probably did.

The jet was huge in comparison to the plane we'd taken to wherever airport this was. We had a brief view of it through the wall of windows at the departure lounge.

"You need anything?" First Dude asked, without really looking at me. I might ask Karl why later. Plausible deniability that he'd met me?

"Trip to the washroom would be good. That way I can zone out on the sleeping pill once I get on board and not worry about making a mess."

"Good idea," said Karl.

The other dude went with me. Waited at the washroom entrance, which was nice. There was a bulge in his armpit, but he wore a security uniform, so no one bothered us.

Dave, I thought at him. *It's a bigger plane. Like a really big bus. It might bounce a bit like the ferry on the waves. We'll sleep a lot. Nothing on the plane will hurt us.* I pictured the ferry we'd taken from Vancouver Island years ago. The waves had been pretty high that day. Smaller boats, mostly moored, bounced a lot. He purred at the memory. I just hoped he'd stay calm when the reality hit.

Boarding had just started when we returned. I joined Karl in the line and First Dude handed me a passport with the ticket inserted.

Dave sniffed at the stewardesses but thankfully didn't do anything else. Our seats up in the front were a lot larger than the ones in the other plane. Fair bit of leg room, which I didn't really need. Karl handed me a half sleeping pill.

"I've got the other half ready. See how he reacts first." I shrugged and took it. Rubbed Dave's ears so he started to purr.

Take off was worse than the small plane: more pressure and lots more noise. Dave growled the entire time, but with the noise level, no one could notice that he was using my vocal cords. Except for Karl. Maybe.

Thankfully the noise and pressure dropped early on. According to the ticket, we had a direct flight to wherever we were heading. Karl said that we would be met by the shifters with transport so we'd head out to the bush directly after we landed and retrieved our gear.

The in-flight food was okay. I took a blanket and pillow when they handed them out and took a full pill. I encouraged Dave to snuggle near my mind, which was about the best way to keep him calm that I knew of.

By the time we started descending for landing, Dave was fairly calm about the whole thing. Even some minor turbulence as we started to des-cend didn't truly bother him. On the other hand, I held onto the armrests whenever that happened. Tightly.

"I'm amazed," Karl said. "Didn't take as long as I thought it would." I'd been reading a magazine from the back of the seat in front of us be-fore the bouncing started. I hadn't bothered with the little TV.

I took a deep breath before I tried to answer him. "I tried to get across the idea that the plane a boat that flies like a bird. We've seen a bunch of nature shows with storms. We've also been on a ferry in choppy seas, which gave him a real life reference. Sort of. Seeing the boats going up and down in the waves must have stuck with him."

"Good." Karl wore his little smile. I started to worry. "How do you think he'd do with parachuting?"

"You aren't kidding." Dave roused a little at my sharp inhalation but a few ear rubs and he calmed. "We take lots of time. Showing him a camera feed from a jumper for a couple of iterations to start with."

"That is part of our normal training course, you know."

I sighed. "You just get us into a perfectly good plane, now you want us to jump out of one while it's still in the air. Probably in the dark."

"Only way to reach a number of missions," Karl said. "South America has been on my ass wanting you to go help them out. They were really pissed when you vanished on us."

"You had the control then, Karl. You still do. All I wanted was to be treated okay. You should have just asked for information."

He looked over. "Would we have gotten it?"

"Probably. Explaining *why* you needed to know about various things would have helped get the answers you wanted. Like Dad did with the debrief when I got back with Victor. I gave you everything you wanted that time, didn't I?" *And more.*

He didn't reply. I turned back to the magazine since the plane wasn't bouncing any more. The seat belt light went on and we looked out at the ocean and clouds below us. Dave purred a little.

Chapter 17

We were escorted by a security dude to a specific customs agent, who didn't examine our bags, just stamped our passports. Two big guys, each at least a head taller than me and bulked up, met us just outside the terminal. Both wore long tan pants and plain grey T-shirts. Karl recognized one of them, so that was okay. Getting picked up by the enemy would make the trip more of a bummer. Dave was a bit withdrawn, which kind of surprised me. Ear rubs helped. Both dudes had lions, which I expected. I doubted there were any other types here. The dudes weren't as dominant as Dave, which helped him more.

They can't shift as much as we can, I told him, picturing them in not even a full partial with mange, with us in total fur. *That's why we're here. To show them how great we are. And rescue the girls.*

"This is your prized cat?" one asked with a sneer. "He is small. I could break him wit one hand." The locals I'd heard while we waited for our luggage had interesting accents. Almost a sing-song way of speaking no matter what language they used.

"I can get back on the damned plane and leave," I said. "Or we can go find the girls. I will fight any of your guys to show how bad-ass we can be if you need proof. Expect a lot of blood. None of it will be mine."

"Ethan," Karl said. "This isn't a dominance thing."

"Yes, it is. You're the dominant here, Karl. I'm next. Then those guys. I am *not* putting up with any chickenshit. Not any more. If I have to, I'll just leave. Dave can get us through anyone who tries to get in our way."

The dudes looked confused, then looked around for another person. "Dominance?" said the second. "What do you mean by that word? And who is Dave? Did he come with you? Where is he?"

"Ethan has a very strong connection with his beast. Calls him Dave. Stronger than anyone I know. I warned Rìnmáyọ̀ about the local attitude toward other types of shifters before we left. Told him to send his best guys to meet up with us. I'm seriously doubting his ability right now."

"Slow down, Karl," said another voice. A cargo van had pulled up near us, but Dave had been focused on the two dudes. Growls, not purrs.

"Rìnmáyò. What gives? You wanted us here. Now this?"

"We have little contact with any other forms, Karl," he said. "As you know from your time here. And so we tend to see them as..."

"Lesser," I said. "Big mistake with me, dudes. Size doesn't matter so much with the beasts. Attitude does. And Dave's got it. He doesn't like any of you. I can hear him growling in my head. I'm going to have to show you all what we can do before we get much further. I can go back home right now. Or your people stop all the chickenshit hazing."

Rìnmáyò looked at Karl, who shrugged. "We will see what you can do once we reach our base. Shall we leave?"

"Fine for now," I said. One of the dudes opened the side door and I saw benches against the far wall. I picked up my pack one handed from the trolley and tossed it inside. Karl rolled his eyes but said nothing.

The trip took about two hours. We went from modern city to suburb to rural to jungle with occasional villages. Dave kept sniffing the air once we were away from the airport since we only had a limited view out the windscreen. Cooking used different herbs so those smells were different. Karl and Rìnmáyò had a conversation that I ignored. The two dudes were up front so I didn't have to play nice with anyone right now. I didn't say anything, just read my book. I had to go back to near the beginning since reading while taking sleeping pills doesn't help in remembering what the heck was going on. Eventually, we stopped. Lots of people were outside.

Rìnmáyò opened our door first. The dude in the passenger seat got out and he blocked that doorway once Rìnmáyò was out. Karl put a hand across my chest. "Let him warn the crowd," he said. I shrugged. I heard Rìnmáyò talking in one of the dialects. Maybe so he could say things I wouldn't understand. Maybe only a few of their people spoke English, which would make sense out here. No need unless they wanted to read textbooks or novels in English.

The time was late afternoon, by the angle of the sun. When we were allowed to get out, the crowd stared at me, so I stared back.

Mostly men were at the front, women to the sides and kids running everywhere, mostly with just shorts until they were near puberty. Dave sensed the beasts. Most of the men had them, unlike the compounds that were mostly normals. I wondered what their history was. A lot different from the bits I'd been told so far. I wondered again what Marsh had actually known about our origin.

A really old dude was at the front of the group. Short hair, all white against very dark complected skin, wrinkles you could get lost in. Taller than me by a full head. And dominant. Even more than Karl. He was the true leader of these people. He had a cloth wrapped around his torso that went down to near his knees, not the shirts and pants or shorts the others did. No idea what it meant. Maybe that he was in charge here. On the other hand, shifting with that on meant there was nothing to possibly constrict the beast's movements.

He spoke in what seemed to be the same language as Rìnmáyọ̀ had used, then a middle aged dude standing beside him translated for me. And maybe for Karl, but I doubted that he didn't speak a major language here. Maybe he was a little out of practice after so many years away.

"Welcome, brothers," he said. "Our leader is Adésọ́lá. We have met few who can sense their brothers as you can. Come and be welcome. Any help you can give us in finding the lost ones, we appreciate your efforts."

Dave sniffed and approved of both men. "Thank you, brothers," I said. "To find those lost is a good reason to travel. To meet others in fur, that is another." I sort of bowed my head at the old dude as he heard the translation. He smiled, with teeth. So did I. So, apparently, did Dave. Awed noises went through the crowd. The fangs thankfully receded as I closed my mouth.

"Come with me," said Rìnmáyọ̀. "We have set aside a house for our guests. There is a banquet tonight, then we leave tomorrow early in the afternoon in the most likely direction to find the kidnappers and their victims."

"Okay." I went to pick up my pack but a trio of teen boys grabbed it first. They seemed surprised at the weight. I had a set of armour in there, plus a few other toys. The bag would not, the first airfield escort said, go through a normal customs check. Going or coming. They hadn't. So far.

Most of the buildings were one level with a dark reddish finish. Some sort of thatch covered most roofs, with shiny panels on them.

"Thanks," I told the boys when they dropped the pack in one of the bedrooms. This house had four bedrooms, a basic gas kitchen, bathroom, dining room and living room. It wouldn't be out of place in any suburb I'd ever seen. I guessed that few people had stayed here. No personal effects at all, but woven decorations were on all the walls. Karl and Rìnmáyọ̀ were in the living room when I joined them. "New house?"

"A few years old now," Rìnmáyọ̀ said. "We have occasional visitors who insist on the amenities but most of our people don't care about them, except for lighting. We have solar arrays on all our buildings and an interesting and ever growing collection of truck batteries to store the results. Since we are near the equator, day and night are nearly equal all year round. Having lights allows us to do much more and learn many things." That explained the shiny panels I'd seen. It made sense and would be a lot cheaper and less noisy and stinky than running generators all the time.

"Good enough. What did you tell the crowd when we arrived?"

"That you might be shorter than most of our men, but any insults would be met with claw and fang. Anyone stupid enough to annoy you would be left to suffer without medical aid."

"That should cut down on the idiots." Dave was smug.

Despite Rìnmáyọ̀'s little speech, I wasn't very surprised that before the banquet, Karl and I were 'invited' to a gathering of the shifters. Mostly big guys, all but a few of them taller and heavier than me. I doubted the short ones had finished growing since they had the slightly unfinished look of teens almost through their main growth spurt.

"One challenge and they'll drop the chickenshit?" I asked Karl quietly. A sigh replied. "Okay. At least I *hope* they drop the idiocy with just one. Otherwise this might be a very short trip. I am not putting up with it any more. I can head west and find the coast if I have to." North would end up at the Sahara Desert, which would not be easy to cross. Jungle we could deal with. Unending sand, maybe not.

A long welcoming speech from Adésọ́lá that Karl translated with a few words. Basically, this is the dude who's going to help us find the girls. He's a bad ass and he's going to prove it right now. If he can.

A big guy to Adésọ́lá's left stood once the speech was over. The local champion, I guessed. Dave went on alert. There was suddenly no one standing in the middle of the gathering and that included Karl. I took my boots and socks off, then stood and dropped everything else. I didn't want anything to constrict or limit Dave's actions. I didn't really want to kill this dude. Not unless we had to. He might be a nice guy, after all. The rest might also get cranky which would mean we'd be leaving here with no money and no clothing. Harder to get back to Melissa.

Dude did a full partial shift. No tail, so he either wasn't that good or he didn't want to give us something easy to bite. A breath and we were in fur. Totally. Karl's muttered comment about showing off was hidden among everyone else's gasp. Dave stepped forward and yowled. *Challenge accepted, dude. Get ready for the pain to begin.*

The dude held his hands far apart to try grabbing us against the side of the crowd. Dave knew what to do from the fight training we'd been through. He leaped and scored against the dude's right arm with his left paw as we leapt past him. The outside this time, so we wouldn't hit an artery by accident. That arm went down. Dave whirled in place to face the dude again. Next would be a hamstring on the opposite side. Then the throat.

We just need to show how good we are. We don't have to kill. Not him. Not now. We just need to impress these shifters so they know what we can do.

I was right next to Dave's mind but he was getting to the hyper-focused state where I couldn't influence him. Muscles tensed all through our body. *Shit...*

Dave yowled again. The old dude stood and two guys came out with bandages to our bleeding opponent. A lot of ear rubbing and telling him we'd won calmed Dave. A chirp, which always sounds weird coming from a big cat. Then I stood up, my left hand bloody.

"Are we done here?"

The crowd cheered and surrounded us, but they were smiling. We'd made the right impression. Eventually I had a few minutes to wash my hands and get my clothes back on just before we went to eat.

The banquet was good. Wild meat, not cow. A nearby platter had quail sized birds, which made Dave happy. A large beaker of something was placed in front of me. I took two sips and moved it away. Highly alcoholic, which wasn't something I wanted to finish. A shot would be okay, but the beaker was the size of an iced tea glass. Or larger.

Adéṣọ́lá noticed my restraint. "I never drink much," I said. "That could leave Dave in charge. And I'm not sure what he might try to do if anyone else who is too drunk to know better annoys him." A pause for the translation. Then a smile. I went back to the food.

There were also acrobatics by the younger men and boys. About a third were partially shifted. Still no tails. Maybe I'd ask once we were back here with the girls.

There was a noise out in the living room that shouldn't be there. Dave woke me with a growl. Soft footsteps. The bed frame didn't squeak when I stood up and moved to the side of the door. When it opened, we were hidden behind it. A faint stink of fear, and more of excitement. More damn chickenshit. I was pissed. So was Dave, so I had to rein in my own anger. Blood spray might mess up the room and annoy our hosts.

The invader had a knife in his right hand. Good thing we were on that side. As he moved away from the door we were on him. One hand held his knife hand and my other arm went around his throat in a choke hold. A gurgle and he was out within a minute. Good.

A deep breath, letting him slide to the floor, in case he had a friend behind him. Dave didn't sniff anyone else lying in wait out in the main room, so I found a web belt holding up the kid's shorts and tied his hands together with it. I generally wore briefs to bed while on a mission, so I just picked the invader up and took him out to the front porch. Karl must have heard me swear as I bounced against a wall as the body shifted on my left shoulder, as he came out a few moments behind me. He'd stopped to pull on his pants. Not the thing to do when there might be an actual emergency.

"What's going on, Ethan?" he asked. "Who's he?"

"Attempted murder or maybe just assault, but he lost," I replied. Dave growled. I dumped the invader onto the ground at the bottom of the stairs. Still out but he'd wake pretty soon. Dave relayed that the kid was still breathing. Two dudes were nearby and Karl put the porch light on so we could all see what was going on without shifting our eyes.

A kid. Maybe sixteen. Maybe younger. I looked at the knife in my hand. Steel blade, good grip. An expensive weapon out here, I guessed.

"What has happened?" asked one dude as they approached, hands nowhere near their weapons. Good. And they knew English.

"You know him?" I asked. The dudes turned him over slightly and nodded. One checked for a pulse and shrugged.

"Babáfẹ́mi. His father you scratched before feast. He is boy in our eye. If he were to mark you, even a small scratch, he would gain status. Become man. Perhaps thought to go on mission with visitors."

"And now?"

"Remains boy. His father will not be pleased with his attempt." A few other dudes were looking our way. Night sentries, I guessed. "You should send for Rìnmáyọ̀," Karl said.

Pretty soon the kid, Babáfẹ́mi, was awake but he wasn't moving. I was sitting on the lower step with my feet on his back. Rìnmáyọ̀ and Adésọ́lá arrived together. A few more men followed, mostly because they were awake and curious. Not his father. Possibly so he wouldn't slap the kid silly for a totally dumb stunt that could have gotten him killed.

Rìnmáyọ̀ sighed. "He is alive?"

"For the moment. Came into the house, and my room, holding this knife. Took it from him, choked him out and tied him. What do you want to do with him?" I held up the knife as evidence.

Explanation to the old dude. More talk back and forth. Dave wanted to shift our feet so the kid would feel the claws pricking his ass. Rìnmáyọ̀ turned back to us before he did it on his own.

"He is yours. Do with him as you please. That is the price of failure."

I looked over at Karl and raised an eyebrow. "Anything?" A nod.

I thought at Dave. *An older kitten. His father's defeat. Wanting to show he was adult. What to do with him?* Dave provided a visual. I had to clamp my jaw shut to keep from laughing. Dave purred.

"Okay. Dave's got a punishment in mind. After that, he's your problem. We don't need anything else from him." I set the knife down, then dropped my briefs next to it. A deep breath and Dave was there. We saw a shudder go through the boy as we came into sight. Maybe he'd use his brain the next time. Crossing the stupid line might get him killed if he didn't start to use his head for something useful.

Then Dave pissed on him. I hadn't realized we had to go that bad but maybe Dave had arranged for it during the shift. Then he picked up the knife and briefs in his mouth, without my prompting, and headed back to our room. He put the knife and briefs on the bedside table and jumped up on the bed. Purring the whole time. I debated going back outside once he shifted us back, since I could hear people talking. I decided getting back to sleep was a better idea. The next few days were going to be busy ones and my sleep cycle was serious out of whack with all the time zones we'd crossed. We'd be off into the forest later today so getting synched to when dawn arrived was more important than nattering. Besides, I'd find out anything important once we woke up. Karl came in just minutes later, closing his door without disturbing us.

Next morning, after a decent breakfast, Karl showed me around the village, since he'd been here before. There was a school with mostly female teachers, which made sense with all the shifters here. All the classes once the kids were over puberty were segregated between the boys and girls. Under that, they were all mixed together. General studies at first, then specializing? It made sense.

I didn't see the champion or his son but didn't really expect to. All the adult men seemed to size me up but no one else said or did anything that might be a challenge. *Happy day, no more chickenshit.* Dave roused a little at the thought of birds, but settled quickly thanks to a few ear rubs.

Lunch was in the house with the three guys who would be my 'guides', along with Karl. All spoke excellent English in that sing-song accent, which was easier to understand the more I heard it, which would help us coordinate.

Oluyẹmí was their team leader. "We have a good jeep with a hidden GPS system. We will also carry a unit openly, so our enemies will be satisfied that no one can find us. We also carry a satellite phone, which we can use to arrange the ransom if they do not have one. My other three men will be shadowing us and can arrange for others to come depending on how many enemies there are once we are in their camp."

"Is there a listening device in the jeep as well?" Karl asked.

"One of the radio settings activates it." Táíwò said. "We have basic supplies for a week and can call for resupply if needed with the sat phone. There are smaller animals in the area that we can hunt for meat and can go to nearby villages where we can purchase other supplies and possibly learn if anyone has seen the kidnappers." A pause. I wondered if he knew any of the missing girls. Maybe a relative if the men found wives outside of this village unlike what the Coalition preferred to do. That this village was full of shifters seemed to be an open secret around here.

"We would prefer that you not actually shoot a leopard, Ethan. They are becoming rare in this area as more land is cleared for crops."

"Fine by me. I can miss it if we actually find one, or just shoot a few rounds into a big tree and pretend I spotted one but missed. Any shots should alert the bad guys that we're in the neighbourhood." They all nodded. "Not having to chase them around will make our trip go quicker. Better for the girls' recovery if we get them out sooner than later." There was also less chance that they'd bond to their captors and join in the fight against us.

Mid-afternoon was hot out in the open but comfortable under the trees. The jeep was had a very good muffler system, so we didn't scare off all the critters in the immediate area. As day shaded into dusk, we set up a camp near a tiny creek. I had the best tent to myself as the white idiot, everyone else shared the other. A tarp covered the kitchen area in case of rain or, more likely, to stay out of the hot sun.

"I can do a quick sweep of the area once it's dark," I said. "Dave likes the fur time and he doesn't get much while we're in the compound. His paw prints might be mistaken for a leopard, so if the thugs spot them, our excuse for being here makes more sense."

"Almost a down-side to his ability to aid you on a mission," Oluyẹmí said. "How do you cope with his need for exercise?"

"I use the gym when we aren't out in the wild. Warning signs on the doors just in case. Sometimes we go outside when it's dark with other shifters to practice infiltration and teach their beasts about shifting their partner's eyes so we don't need lights. Half the folks are freaked out by the idea of us being in fur though I'm not sure why. Dave also likes to bat around soccer balls. My younger brothers love coming to play with him, along with some other kids. Shifters and normals. My girlfriend Melissa comes out when she isn't busy. So do my team members and their families. A few others, when they're available.

"Dave's very good with the kids. Thinks he needs to protect them, which is more or less what I've told him about why we're out here. Rescuing stolen girl kittens from very bad men who aren't treating them well." The men nodded in agreement. "He's not really smart, but I can get ideas and instructions to him. Mostly he follows them, except when he scents something tasty."

There wasn't much wildlife around when we checked late at night. There were also no thugs in the area. Dave climbed several of the trees, just to have fun. I didn't try to stop him. And the marks might be mistaken for a leopard's, in case the thugs were moving around here too.

Opinion was divided on what they were doing: settled in place to let any hunt go past them, or moving every few days. I agreed with the staying in place group. We'd see who was right. Hopefully in a few days. I didn't want to be away from Melissa very long.

I also had to find Victor a present. Maybe I'd ask one of the guys what a seven or so year old boy would have here as a toy. Or a tool, like maybe a bow and arrows? That would also make a dandy weapon on a strike team. Silent and death from a distance. No risk of being injured in hand to hand fighting. With Dave's help, I'm sure we could pull a very powerful bow. They could be used to take out sentries that were high up without bothering to climb up to reach them. Or to shoot a line up high to climb to an access point in a stronghold.

I'd have to mention the idea to Karl on our way back. Depending on how we travelled back to the compound, maybe we could check out a sporting goods store to see what might be available commercially. First I'd have to convince him it was a good idea.

Once we were back in the village, I'd ask if they used bows for hunting, or if they just did a partial shift and ran down whatever was going to be on the menu that night.

Chapter 18

The first bird boat was small and noisy. Ethan kept rubbing its ears. After a while, Dave started to relax. They would find the lost female kittens. So that others could have a female that smelled good to have more kittens with. The bad ones who hurt the kittens would all end. They would not go to the wonderful females like the old one had.

The big bird boat was much noisier. Ethan wanted to sleep and it was dark out the clear thing in the wall. This must be a long trip. It tried to remember some of Ethan's travels when it was small. The big stinky things sometimes travelled for long distances during the dark times. It settled around Ethan's mind to make sure no one bothered them. There were odd scents on two females near them but Ethan did not react to them. That was good. They had a good mate now.

The new place when the other bird boat stopped was full of strange smells. The first two males thought they were weak. Dave growled. They would soon learn. With blood if they did not submit.

They went to a large place. With many protectors. Most males had them, which was different from the big cave. Ethan asked it to show how much better they were than these others. The lion did not have a tail like it did. Still, the challenge was simple. First to bleed lost the contest. They had played games like this before, though in the big cave, it did not use claws to truly wound. Here, the lions needed to learn how powerful it was. So they could rescue the girl kittens taken by bad men.

Night came. The bed was good but Dave kept alert. A noise outside the den was not proper. It woke Ethan. The older kitten held a knife but had not shifted so it did not know where they hid. Soon the kitten slept.

They took the kitten outside. Ethan spoke to guards. Others came to watch but would not interfere with punishment for the kitten. It had sought to prove adulthood, Ethan told it.

It pissed on the kitten. The lions and Ethan all approved. Then they returned to the nice den to sleep.

Chapter 19

Three days later, Karl spotted a set of recent vehicle tracks in the mud as we crossed another track. We ignored them and kept going, I grumbled loudly about the lack of the leopards that I'd been promised and Dave scented at least two thugs in the nearby brush.

We'd just packed up our gear after breakfast the next morning when we were surrounded by at least a dozen thugs. I just hoped these were the right thugs. Otherwise, Dave would have a fun time in fur tonight.

I had no idea what they were saying, but having a dozen automatic weapons pointed at us meant we were on the wrong side of the power equation. Oluyẹmí was knocked down for yelling at them.

"Get the hells out of here," I yelled to add to the confusion. "I've come here for a leopard and I hadn't gotten it yet. Damn thing moved on me yesterday and I want it in my sights again before I have to leave!"

At least one of them understood English, since he stared at me when I yelled, then muttered a translation so the thugs near him guffawed.

"You not go anywhere now, American pig," the thug said. "You pay us much, or maybe your life is all you steal away from our country."

Then we were tied up and had to walk a couple of klicks to their camp. I played the stupid, obnoxious white hunter until they gagged me. Dave wasn't that concerned, since I kept showing him pictures of happy rescued girls and all these thugs lying in their own blood. Thankfully none of them heard Dave purr. On the other hand, they might think that I was growling at them. I could tell the difference but they wouldn't. The jeep puttered sedately along behind us with its hidden GPS telling the other lions where to come and find their camp.

Thankfully, these were the right thugs. At least, there were several young women who looked recently beaten and cringing making a meal. Our food, including a small antelope Dave had brought down yesterday went into their supplies. Good thing we'd already eaten breakfast. The thugs looked like they needed resupply of their own. Or some decent hunters who didn't need an automatic weapon to take down dinner.

"Bingo," Oluyẹmí said as he identified someone from the list of possible thugs. The thugs couldn't hear anything, but using our beasts' sensitive hearing, we could communicate easily.

We were pushed into a small hut that was made of thin saplings pushed into the ground. Other saplings made a framework for the roof, which was overlapping large leaves, already starting to wilt in the heat.

The door was the same construction, but a short chain and an old keyed padlock held it shut. Empty at the moment and it looked to have been recently built. Just for us? Certainly re-roofed within a day or two. That also meant it couldn't be solid enough to slow us down much.

We huddled in the middle so we could talk. The thugs could see us through the half-arsed walls but we could also see them. "I have seen at least two of these men in the databases," Oluyẹmí said softly. "This group is feared in our country and others. We should have had more men closer, so they could be with us on the night. I do not think the rest can reach us in time. For any clean up, perhaps, but we are very outnumbered now."

"These thugs won't be feared for long," I said. "None of them are wearing real body armour and they'll find the hooch in our supplies before too long. Go with claws, as long as you can manage once we bust out. Not tonight, they'll still be on alert. Tomorrow or the next day should do." I flexed my fingers. If Dave could do a long claw, we'd be free quickly and then all the thugs would be very, very dead.

"I turned on the transmitter in the jeep the moment I saw movement from the tree line," Akinlabí said. "The transmitted conversations will also alert our people to bring a lot of extra help."

The worst part of the next two days was pretending to be an arsehole hunter who was now trying to buy his life from the thugs. There were a couple of gut punches, but no real damage. I guessed they didn't want to risk killing me before they actually had the money. On the other hand I did get a good idea of where the girls were kept at night and the spots they had for sentries.

They tossed me back into the hut after another sat phone call. Using our phone, which was a truly stupid idea, but I didn't see one in the boss's hut, so maybe they didn't have one or it needed recharging. "Money will be at the bank tomorrow noon," I said. "All of us will be released once that's confirmed."

The others looked relieved, at least until a pair of the girls came in with our meal. Starchy blobs, with assorted bits of other vegetables. A couple of half-ripe fruit that we'd split. No meat. Dave grumbled inside me. *Better food later.* And lots of ear fondling.

"We heard them talk, sir," one girl said quietly. "Once they have the money, all of you will die." She glanced at me. "They want to break you, sir. Not let you die until you grovel at their feet."

I tried to look suitably afraid. "God will help us. All of us." From her expression, she didn't trust me to be anything other than a rich idiot who didn't accept reality. At least, not right now. She'd probably change her mind once we finished with the thugs. This part of the country would be a lot safer for everyone once they were in the ground. Or food for various predators. The cycle of life. I didn't smile but Dave was pleased with the future I pictured.

The 'food' had the consistency and taste of library paste as usual. At least it had calories. As the light faded, we started to prepare.

The idiot thugs hadn't taken our clothing, boots or belts. They'd focused on our camp gear, rifles, and food supplies. And the highly alcoholic hooch. Dave made a nicely sharp claw and the rope around our wrists parted pretty quickly. Then I worked the small saw chain out of my belt and helped untie the others.

"Are you up for this?" Karl asked. I nodded, but he didn't look happy. No time to discuss why he was that way. We had a long plane ride to get home and he wouldn't be able to wander off and not answer me.

"You want the leader alive, Oluyẹmí?" I asked. "As a trophy of sorts, he could be useful. Would that help your tribe's reputation in the murky waters of thuggery?"

"If possible, otherwise we will make do with his head," Oluyẹmí said. His guys smiled, briefly. "Our men will bring cameras and such, so we will leave the bodies in place to show how they died. And Ethan, you will not be in any of the pictures. We have no wish to put you in danger from their allies, assuming any of them would care. Our people will also not be shown, but the photos will be circulated. Leaked through one of our contacts in Lagos to the newspapers and such. A potent warning not to bother us or our allies and friends."

Other thugs might decide to go after easier targets, but the lions might also expand the area they controlled or maybe just supervised. Protect more innocents as a welcome outcome, which was a pretty good idea. Possibly have more income to keep improving their standard of living and buy more batteries and solar panels.

"I don't really want to be a target either. I'm happier staying out of the pictures. There were other people hunting me before the Coalition found me. I don't want to advertise where I might be found, even if we're back in the States by the time they figure out I was here."

"Good idea," said Karl.

"Cut halfway through the middle poles on the back side of the hut," I said. "Top and bottom if we can. That should give us a nice door and I don't want to drop the roof on us right now. It could slow us down and wake the bad guys sooner than we're ready for them. Easier to deal with sleeping people than ones with their fingers on the triggers. Not sporting, but never give a thug an even break is our motto." Their teeth were very visible for a moment as they smiled. White against their dark skin and the jungle behind us. They all had longer canines than usual. So did we.

Táíwò lay so he was near the back wall and soon I could hear the sawing. Nice and quiet. We snored to cover the noise occasionally.

And it was slow, since he couldn't make much noise. That didn't matter much. Dave heard some crying from the largest hut, but none of the girls stopped breathing. The rest of us tried to sleep once the exit was ready. For now. Tomorrow would be a very busy day.

It was nearing dawn when we were ready, but we heard grumbling from the direction of the boss's hut. We were awake, making final preparations for our exit out the back of our hut. A glance around and we all lay down so we looked like we were still asleep. Karl slipped another rope back around my wrists, in case they dragged me out. Dave could cut me free if that happened. I also prepared to lose my boots, having already taken my socks off. I didn't want anything to slow Dave down.

I couldn't understand what the leader ranted about but Karl and Oluyẹmí were worried. "Their men in Lagos didn't check in on schedule. Our people must have taken them," Oluyẹmí said softly. "They should have waited for our signal later this morning before doing so. Perhaps they were planning a double cross: take the money for their own and our people acted to prevent their departure. Thus they could not call here."

The head thug, followed by his two main thugs, stopped outside the hut. The thug on the right unlocked the door. The two came in and picked me up by the arms. I toed off my boots as they dragged me outside and dropped me in front of the leader.

He slapped me across the face. Pretending to fall was hard. Dave growled in my head. Pissed. I managed to get my feet back underneath me and saw three thugs, with several of the girls in tow, coming out of the shadows. The light kept getting better as the sun continued to rise. A glorious day. *Shit was hitting the fan big time. Might as well attack with words to slow down whatever physical shit the thugs had in mind.*

"What's going on?" I shouted. "You've got your money. Let us go!"

"There is no money," he said and slapped me again, though not as hard so I didn't fall. "My men have not reported to me of their success in getting the dollars. What did you do, American pig?"

"What the hells could I do from here?" I sneered. "You wrote the script of what I should say. That's what I said. You heard me make the calls. I think your men took the money once it arrived and ran away. Why should they come back to this stinking jungle when they have a half million dollars to play with? I certainly wouldn't bother coming back to this dump of a camp with a cretin like you in charge."

The two thugs stared at each other, then at their leader. The thugs scattered behind them looked confused, then grew angry as a thug translated what we'd said. No one wanted to think they'd lost the money they'd already spent in their minds.

"Nearly ready," I heard Karl say. Rather, I heard it with Dave's help.

"That's not my fault," I said loudly. "You picked the wrong men to send to pick up a half million dollars. They'll live like kings now. All the women they want, all willing to do whatever they want, not the skinny girls you kidnapped and force yourselves upon."

"Now." Oluyẹmí breathed.

I was ready to leap up and Dave broke the rope, changing us to the full partial in a moment. The two thugs were in our way, but not for long. One claw on each hand was longer, more like a knife. The thugs clutched their throats as blood poured down their chests. Carotid flow goes a long way but we were mostly past them when it started.

"Keep the girls safe, Ethan," Karl shouted. We bounded toward them. None of the thugs had their weapons pointed toward us. Thankfully, at least three of the girls grabbed the guns nearest them and fell to the ground to keep the thugs from using the automatic weapons. Good. I heard roaring behind us as the lions shifted to their partials to attack. I caught sight of one out of the corner of my eye. Karl, since he was on that side of the hut. A thug raised his weapon but Karl was on him before it rose above knee level. More blood spurted.

The two thugs in front of me kept trying to get their guns back instead of running away or drawing another weapon. Between one step and another we were cougar. Thugs kept falling under our paws, now soaked in blood. Dave was careful where we landed, so none of the girls would be hurt. None of them were looking up that I could see.

"I'll kill these two!" the leader shouted. He had two other girls by the hair, holding them in front of him as a shield. Dave snarled and stalked toward them. One of the girls sobbed but the other watched us. I hoped she could get them both out of the way when Dave attacked.

Dave was hyper-focused on the leader. I was just a passenger now. He stopped about two metres from the girls, letting his rump fall a little. Not in preparation for sitting, but for a leap. A twitch of the tail and the girls fell, one dragging the crying one down. Dave was halfway to them as the girls began to move.

The leader was still alive. For the moment. I thought at first that Dave had missed his stroke. Or maybe he'd hit exactly where he intended to. Brachial artery, I guessed. Fixable with a hospital nearby or he'd lose the lower arm because of the tourniquet that could stop the flow and save his life. Karl, changed back to human, came up to one side of me. Blood dripped from his hands and my own.

"Oops," I said. The thug's eyes were still wide open and he'd seen me change back from cougar to the full partial to human since we'd sat on his chest while shifting. There was fear in his eyes. And he'd pissed himself. Dave was pleased. Very pleased. Táíwò helped the girls get out of the way. The crying one had stopped for now. Two other girls held her.

"You messed with the wrong people," Karl said as he knelt beside us. "None of your men survived. The pair you sent to retrieve the money are dead as well. There never was any money. We set up a trap. You fell for it. You'll be dead in a few minutes and we'll smile as we butcher your corpse for the leopards."

"I know things," the leader said. His eyes were wide as he went further into shock. "I can help you. Please."

"You never responded to a plea from anyone in your life, so I don't think you deserve any pity," I said. "Go to the hell you deserve."

One claw into his neck and the carotid went. A little spray but not much since a lot of his blood was already underneath him. Plus, I really wanted a bath before much longer. The heat in the hut had reminded Dave of the Georgia swamps. Not in a good way.

I found the nearby stream and cleaned up slightly downstream of the camp so we'd still have clean water. My clothes were possibly done for, but I tried to get what blood I could out. Táíwò brought my bag with clean clothes. I soaked them upstream of the pool before putting them on. I felt much better for being cleanish. And the damp clothing would keep us cooler. For a couple of hours at least.

Oluyẹmí gathered the girls by the main hut and Karl told me he was reassuring them that the thugs were all dead and a truck was coming to take them home. Several sounded sad at the idea. What would their life be after their trauma? Ostracized because they had the bad luck to be kidnapped? I hoped the team had a bottle of 'several weeks after' pills.

"Another few days and we'll be back on a plane," Karl said. "Would Dave will be okay with flying from now on?"

"Probably. I'll let you know once we're back home. The smaller planes might be easier on him than the big jets. All the other shifters should help reassure him." I sighed as I figured out the subtext of his question. "I'm guessing that we are not going directly home, are we?"

"No. There's a couple of quick jobs in South America that need a cougar to get close to the targets' sentry posts. A lot of our cougar shifters are down there rather than in Europe or elsewhere as there are no native wolves in those areas. The jobs are surveillance before we send in the troops. Won't take long. Once we're there, you can call Melissa and let her know where you are. And find her a nice present or two once we take out the drug lords."

"One of the cartels? I thought they were too big even for us to deal with?" Too many locations which means we'd need all the teams to hit them at the same time. Bill sort of explained why we didn't go after them when I was first with his team.

"These are baby members. Another mission is a nasty group of 'freedom fighters'. They want to stomp on the system, not improve it. We'll thin out their numbers. That's a job from the State Department, not the DEA guys."

"Are we propping up a terrible regime from people who really want to change the status quo?" These jobs had been arranged before we'd even left the compound, I guessed. Confirmed when we landed here and the big plane's interior wasn't shredded by Monster's claws or maybe after the small plane landed safely. At least I knew about the other operations before we were in the air to go home. Time to let Dave know what would happen.

Karl sighed. "A little of both, actually. The local officials are very corrupt, and several of their leaders will have accidents that will look like the freedom fighters took them out just before we eliminate them. A sad coincidence. The ones we're mainly after don't have any real plan for change. They just want to be the ones who are getting all the pay-off money. Knocking both sides down gives everyone else a little breathing room and a chance to make things better. The local shifters will establish a small compound there to monitor who takes control. They might even set up one of their normal people as the new boss. At least that way they can put any bribe money to use in making the locals' life better and keep other thugs from trying to take over the region. They'll also encourage farmers to grow different cash crops instead of drugs. Food and meat animals. Maybe coffee if it does well in that area."

"What about the cartel? Why take them out now?"

"A smaller gang split off from a more major cartel but they're terrorizing a valley full of people. Again, we may set up a small group there for long term security. If one group took them over, no doubt other thugs might try if it doesn't look like they have much protection."

That made me feel more optimistic about deaths I'd gladly help with.

The girls started making breakfast and slowly began to step on, not around the corpses, taking the long way around the cooking area to do so once they saw that none of us objected. One girl picked up a knife next to a corpse after she'd stepped on his crotch and only walked away when that part of his body was in much worse condition than it had been. Specific parts were detached. The other girls watched our reactions, which were to basically let them do whatever they wanted. More knives were taken from the various corpses and they were soon very busy and not with the food cooking on the various stoves or at the firepit.

"These wounds will also hide whatever signs we left from our claws and teeth," Oluyẹmí said. He'd just come back to the fire after helping a girl find another knife on one of the corpses. She'd broken her first one on the thug's eye sockets.

The rest of us kept the meal from burning while the girls were busy expressing their feelings. And cleaning up after. At least we had enough water by the kitchen area for the few hours it would take to be sure the pool's water was clear again. Once they returned, Oluyẹmí spoke to them and we retreated from the kitchen. The meal was ready to eat and he insisted the girls go first, and to eat however much they wanted. The thugs probably kept them on short rations so they wouldn't have the energy to try running away. They'd probably threatened to hurt the girls remaining if one tried to escape.

The girls also tried to wait on us once they'd eaten. Well, me, mostly. Dave wasn't sure what they wanted but none of them smelled good to him, so they were off the short list. And I was pretty committed to Melissa now. She'd always be my love.

The trucks with the rest of the teams arrived just after lunch. The general attitude was mostly pissed that they'd missed the fun early this morning. The camp was now a stinking, fly-attracting mess due to the blood and bodies. And the other parts scattered about. The new tents were set up on the other side of the creek. Upwind of the mess. Two older women stayed with the rescued girls. Dave heard a lot of crying.

What with establishing the identities of the thugs and generally tidying up; stripping and dragging the remains of the thugs into the tree line for the local small predators and finding anything saleable they owned, we didn't leave the site until early the next afternoon. The trip back was a lot faster since we didn't have to pretend to hunt innocent leopards and we had enough supplies that we didn't need to hunt for the pot either. I thought I spotted a leopard up one tree near the road, but couldn't be sure since we were going pretty fast. Dave couldn't scent it as the wind was the wrong direction.

Two days later, we pulled into the shifters' village. The girls were still with us, which I found odd. I'd thought that the plan was that we'd take them home right away. For whatever kind of life they could make now. It seemed there was another option on the table, which made a lot of sense when I thought about it while we were in the air to South America.

Adésọ́lá had two other old dudes I didn't recognize at his side when the trucks entered the village's open centre. There were a lot more male humans here than last time. The girls' people, I guessed. Come to witness their daughters' safe return? But what would happen to the girls back in their home village? Neither Karl or Rìnmáyọ̀ had mentioned anything on that aspect of the mission despite my asking.

"Please remain inside until I signal." Rìnmáyọ̀ left our jeep, which had the canvas roof up so Karl and I were sort of hidden in the rear seats. The girls were helped out of the lead truck and formed a small gaggle to the left of the old dude, *not* near the leaders of their village. Lots of talking I couldn't follow, so I elbowed Karl for a translation. He was closer to the action. I wasn't actually surprised that no one went over to the girls. Shunning for shit not their fault. Dave growled a little in my head.

"What's up now?" I said quietly but with a bite to my tone.

"Cole's Notes on the operation." He leaned back and stretched. "And lots of boasting. We'll go out in a minute. The other older men are human, from their allies, but they all knows about shifting."

"The girls are from their people?" I just wanted to be sure.

"Yes." Rìnmáyọ̀ waved and Karl stood up. "Show time."

"Literally or figuratively?"

Karl snorted and I followed him out of the back of the jeep. The old dude went into another spate of talking. The crowd was quiet. Completely. There were far more people here than I'd seen from inside the jeep. Dave sniffed. Most of the newcomers were human, not shifter. The rest of the villagers, or maybe just the girls' extended families.

"And now?" I asked.

"Time to shift, Ethan," Rìnmáyọ̀ said as he approached us. "These visitors need to see what we've been trying to accomplish. I would like to speak with you on how it happened for you, but today is a time for celebration. So, please?"

"Okay." No towels in sight so I took my shirt off first, then my boots and Karl held the shirt up while my pants came down. Then Dave stood there. *Very* smug. A few gasps of surprise from the humans. He wandered over to the girls and purred at them. No one fainted, which was a very good sign. Adésọ́lá started speaking again. One girl reached forward and Dave leaned into the caress. She was the one who hadn't flinched at our approach to the thugs' boss.

Does she smell good? Like Melissa? I thought. Pictured Melissa. No real answer. Soon all the girls were touching Dave. This was so weird. I caught a look at Karl. He looked baffled too. Dave then walked over to the old dude and the allied dudes. Sat down. Old dude smiled and nod-ded. We shifted back, then Rìnmáyọ̀ came over and handed me my pants.

"These girls will stay with our people," Rìnmáyọ̀ told me after the old dudes spoke. "They would be shunned among their own for what happened to them. But if they live here and become wives to our young men, at times their parents and families will come to visit them. And their children will be ours." The older women with the trucks, doubling as medics, had handed out pills the moment they set foot in the camp, I'd seen. All the girls had taken them. I wasn't sure how long it would take for the results, but it might also take a long time for them to even con-sider the idea of being with a man again. For a few, that might be never. Even for them, staying here was a far better option than going home.

"That sounds like a good idea," I said. "I wondered if your men found wives here or in the nearby villages."Another head bow at the old dude, who smiled back. Then it faded slightly. He said spoke to Rìnmáyọ̀.

"You were never initiated?" He asked me.

"I first changed a hand to a paw at fourteen," I said. "I wasn't living with other shifters at the time. I thought my parents and young brother were dead. The man who was supposed to look after me only wanted the money he was given for pretending to care for me. I feared him. And I feared what he would do if he discovered what I was. So I ran away. Lived on the streets of a very large city. Alone." I could see Karl's scowl, which vanished when he realized I'd seen it. More translation followed.

Adésọ́lá then had a question.

"And now that you live with the Coalition?"

"I didn't volunteer to join them at first. I was kidnapped. They'd been hunting me for many years. They still hunt any lone shifters that are out in the world. " Rìnmáyọ̀ spoke softly into Adésọ́lá's ear.

Karl's scowl was back, full force. The old dude spoke to him. No one translated for me this time.

"Later, we will discuss this more," Rìnmáyọ̀ said. "We do not speak of our problems in front of our guests."

"Sure. Anytime you want."

The party was extensive with all the visitors. They'd all brought food. Each girl had three or four suitors, which totally shocked them. Their families smiled, especially the mothers. A constant: mothers caring what happened to their daughters. The suitors were all young men, possibly just old enough to marry, I guessed. Completely unlike the thugs, which also might help the girls recover from their ordeal.

"We do not have enough women from among our people," Rìnmáyọ̀ said. We were seated together, with Olúyẹmí on my other side. Táíwò and

Akinlabí were outer bookends. Karl was with the old dudes. I saw them talking but couldn't understand a word. If he was pissed at what I'd said, I might not be going to South America or out of the compound at all once he had me back there. Still, I would leave if he tried to imprison me.

"We tend to have more sons than daughters. That is one reason we keep tribes of those who cannot shift such as these as allies. Together, we do not have problems with restricted bloodlines. Every year our young men go out to their villages to meet their young women if none of those here are right for them. It is considered an honour to come here to wed. A few of our young women who are not chosen within our village find a husband in those tribes, so we are doubly related. All are satisfied with this arrangement."

"I can see the problem. My father was also born out in the world from a woman that may not have known she carried a shifter son. And he married outside the bloodlines as well. I have no idea if that's why I can do a full shift and most shifters can't."

Oluyẹmí shook his head. "Do you truly believe that, Ethan?"

"I have no idea what the truth is," I said. "What I do know is that I have a much better bond with my beast than most shifters do. If I had to bet on a reason, that would be it."

That reassured them. "We will talk after about how you gained that depth of bond. Perhaps tomorrow."

"Short answer is that I had to use the beast's senses to stay alive in that big city I mentioned. Taught it how to recognize the smell of gun oil, among other things. It could warn me if there was someone around with a big gun." Dave obliged with a sniff. "At least eight, maybe ten guys here are armed. Not exactly sure which ones, but Dave can figure that out if we are near them."

"Formidable," Rìnmáyọ̀ said. "So on an infiltration, you can easily find the sentries even though they are quiet and attentive."

"Even if they don't smoke on watch and bathe occasionally. They can't hide from us."

We talked shop for the duration of the meal. Again, I turned down the local hooch after a token couple of sips. Most of the other shifters didn't drink much either.

Karl didn't say anything as we were escorted back to the house in the full dark. I slept soundly and well thanks to the very comfortable mattress. I'd used leaves, moss and the occasional cushion from a Dumpster for my beds in the various caves and improvised huts I'd lived in for years. Real mattresses were much nicer. No one bothered us tonight, thankfully. It had been a long week and a bit.

Chapter 20

Karl wasn't around when we left the bedroom the next morning. Rìn-máyọ̀ was in the living room waiting for me. There was a nice assortment of food on the coffee table, probably leftovers from the feast.

Two others came in a few minutes later. "They are leaders among our people, who seek to understand how to help our brothers-in-fur manifest more easily."

Akínlànà and Káyọ̀dé thankfully spoke fairly good English so no one needed a translation, which meant that our conversation would mostly be in real time, which was a relief.

I filled a plate and Dave came forward behind my eyes so he could watch. I figured I was going to get nibbles, mostly when they discussed what I told them. The abundance at the feast last night meant I wasn't that hungry so it wasn't really a problem.

"As I said last night, I think that working with the beast inside you has to start when you're young. Use their strength to help you do things, like lifting weights, trying to scent gun oil, or detect people who smoke. Talk to them even though they can't answer in words. Anything that engages them will help them develop."

"And for years while you were young, you were alone in the world," Akínlànà said. "No one else to speak with. As you said."

"Yes. The Coalition took my parents from our house, but I was in an old smuggling tunnel underground. I was told later that there were men from another group that sought to kill us. Neither group knew where I was, I think. Or the Coalition's people didn't listen to what my parents told them. Then the house blew up. I was found by regular police a day later and given to others to raise. A foster family. No one came to take me from there. The Coalition knew exactly where I was for eight years. When I learned that, I was very angry with the Coalition, and with my parents. That anger still comes out on occasion. Less now, but still."

"The man who sought only to profit from your care." Káyọdé nodded in understanding. "When did Dave start to awaken?"

"My first actual shift was when I was fourteen. My left hand swapped to a paw when I was angry at the foster family. Full shift, not a partial. I wasn't really aware of my beast as a separate part of me much before that. Though, I was remembering that time not long ago. I don't do that often. Bad things happened to me and Dave can't tell if there is an immediate threat to us when I remember those times so he tends to go on alert, looking for the danger. Primed to attack. They're hard wired to protect us from anything, even being surprised by accident." More nods.

"I had, well, feelings of danger before that first shift. There were bullies where I went to school. I think I was around eleven or so when the sense of danger started. I was near a corner in a hallway and I just felt— anger, I think. It freaked me out so I moved to the other side of the corridor and it went away. Those corridors were quite wide, about three metres. When I passed the corner, I spotted one of the worst bullies in the school standing there, leaning against the wall. He might not have been waiting for me specifically, but I would have lost my lunch money at a minimum if he'd been able to grab my arm, since he was older, taller and stronger than I was."

They discussed what I said in their language. Maybe so I wouldn't feel that they didn't really believe what I'd said. I took advantage of the break to eat a couple of tasty fruit slices. Dave wanted more meat to catch up from the meatless captivity, so I had a hunk of venison or the local equivalent next.

"Were there any other manifestations of your beast at that early age?" Káyọdé asked.

"Running was easier. Another way to bypass the bullies was to be faster than they were. Bullies are loath to have much exercise so if you were faster than they were, they stopped trying to catch you, unless they'd set up an ambush. I noticed in my gym class that running was getting easier. So was lifting weights. I used to make deliveries after school to raise money for food, since the man I lived with wanted to keep me alive, but not let me grow much. To stay weak so I couldn't fight back. That's another thing you and your youngsters can do. Ask the beasts to help your people run faster. Use their eyes outside at night rather than flashlights or lanterns. Their sense of smell when you go on a hunt. If you can do that there's no need for low-light gear for sneaking up on bad guys. Make games of these things to train your young men starting as soon as possible. And the older shifters, but it may be harder for their beasts to develop more if they are older. Maybe. I'm honestly not sure how much is possible. Um. I did have a question for you guys. Why don't any of you have tails in the partial shift?"

"What?" Akínlànà asked. "Tails? Why should we bother with them?"

"Tails are awesome. They're really useful if you're running on uneven terrain or to keep dodging around obstacles in a firefight. They help you balance better with just two legs. Your champion didn't have one when we sparred. I didn't see any when we fought the thugs or the young men who did the acrobatics before we left. That's why I'm asking."

"We." Káyọ̀dé managed the one word then stopped. They looked at each other. "We never thought they would be useful. Maybe. It is not what we are taught when we begin to shift."

"It can be difficult to get the beasts to add a tail. My younger brother says that he has to remind his beast to have a tail with the partial. Other times, they aren't really needed, so there's no problem. In the partial, sometimes our tail is down one pant leg. Other times I pull down my pants a bit so it can get out. Especially if I have to run. I can show you."

"We shall think on that issue. Ask our beasts to provide a tail to experiment with running. Perhaps while we play soccer, so there are many sudden changes of direction," Akínlànà said. "What else can Dave do? Now, not back when you were young?"

"Identify if a person is a shifter and what kind. We've started working on that with others in our compound and a video was sent around to others. Don't know if you got one. It's pretty simple: Line up a mixed group of shifters and normals. Blindfold the shifter and have his beast tell him which each subject is. We can do a round to show the other shifters, if you like. You can get more complex later. What sort of shifter, eventually who the person is."

"Tell?" All three stared at me in amazement and possibly envy. "Your beast *speaks* to you?"

Oops. "Not tell in words. He can't *tell* me things but he can *show* pictures in my head or do things like growl if there's a problem. A chirp if everything's okay. For the game, he shows me a stylized picture of what sort of beast a person has, or a human silhouette. Dave's gotten better over the years at understanding what I'm saying or thinking. I can use two or three word sentences and he gets the idea. Um, mostly. I used to need to slowly picture a series of actions to get more complex ideas across. That's also a lot easier now. Though, when the thugs were marching us back to their camp, I had to keep picturing girls being menaced by thugs and that we'd get to kill them all to keep him from starting that party early. He was very pissed at how the thugs treated the girls. He treats any child as a kitten. I'm not sure how exactly he thought of the girls. Maybe as potential mates for your people or maybe just as kittens. Either way, they needed to be protected and taken away from the thugs."

"So Dave is more like a well trained hunting cat than a true partner," Rìnmáyọ̀ said. "We know of these from our traditional tales but to keep such animals in these times requires extensive paperwork and permits. Each one with an official with his hand out for a bribe. And when our beasts are young, they are much like any young animal, it seems. The more one works with them, the more they understand and learn."

"Yes. I think our beasts' development really doesn't start until much later than our own does. Early on, they seem to be sleeping, to Dave. Unaware. Ten or so is about when the kids start to get limited contact. Mind you, when we're in fur, Dave is in control. Most of the time. The full partial, I'm still in charge. During the fight with the thugs, we were both very present, no matter what shape we were in. Having two minds to keep watch on your surroundings makes it easier to stay safe. Dave can be hyper-focused on a hunt and that makes it a lot harder to keep him from going in a direction that I don't want him to. That can also be a problem on a mission since he wouldn't see other enemies if they weren't in front of us. We're working on that."

More discussion. I thought about rubbing Dave's ears, which helped keep him happy. I really wasn't sure how much he was following.

"The games, Karl sent word about them," Rìnmáyọ̀ said. "We dismissed them. We thought that since they lived in such different places, that we were far beyond them. We need to examine those games more closely."

I swallowed a piece of venison. "Hide and Seek is a good one for your village. There's lots of dense brush beyond the buildings and fields. You could also do it in the village once your people get better at it since there are a lot more shifter scents here. That really helps develop the beast's tracking ability. Which scents are new, which are older. Did the quarry hide their scent by walking in a stream or did they really climb up that tree." All three nodded.

"Another of our people wishes to talk to you," Rìnmáyọ̀ said. "Then after we eat again, we would like to see your identity game."

"Sure thing. Where does the other person live?"

"Not far. On the other side of the village, near the forest. He is our... conduit to the gods."

"A shaman? Priest?"

"Yes."

"I just need a quick trip to the can and we can go, if there aren't any other questions for right now."

"We will wait for you outside." All three rose and left. Well, that answered that question. The shaman might have been another reason why we were here. Other than needing a white guy to run the scenario, they could have done the entire operation in house. Did the shaman just want to talk to us about the initiation or did they really want to know about the full shift? That another local group had managed it meant their street cred, so to speak, was lower. They needed to show that their people were as powerful as any other group. Basic gang posturing but with no real intent to start a conflict that could only be satisfied with blood and death. Maybe.

Oluyẹmí and another shifter had joined the group when I came down the stairs of the house. "Is there any special ways to show respect to the priest? I was sort of raised Catholic."

"Not really," the new shifter said. Fairly dominant beast. A strange scent on him. An incense? Dave wasn't sure but it just meant he'd be able to tell when this man came near us later.

People watched us walk down the street. I didn't see Karl but Adésọ́lá sat outside his house, talking to one of the leaders from the girls' village. He smiled at us so I smiled back.

Oluyẹmí and the new guy were in front, then Akinlabí and Káyọ̀dé on either side of me and Rìnmáyọ̀ behind.

"Weird sort of escort, guys," I said once it was clear the pattern was deliberate as we went around a corner. People stepped out of our way or waited until we passed by to cross the path. Dave was on alert.

"Custom for a boy to be seen by the priest," Akinlabí said.

"Twenty-nine. Not a boy," I said mildly.

"Uninitiated," Káyọ̀dé said. "And Karl said you were still studying. So, still a boy in our way of life."

"High school, not elementary. Which I didn't want to bother with. Still don't. But I have to keep plugging away to be able to come out on missions. Book reports suck big time." A hint of a snort from Rìnmáyọ̀.

We turned another corner onto a narrower street. Still just foot traffic, plus one or two older, gear-less bicycles parked at each intersection. They made sense. The village was a big place if you had to get across it in a hurry. We stopped at a small building, about five metres wide, on the edge of the village, nearest the trees. This one had white and back paw prints double the size of my hand scattered over the outer walls. The door was set low, about the right height for Dave to just walk through.

"Go inside. He speaks English as well as we do."

"Okay." I went to the doorway and crouched down.

The interior was dim, and I didn't see any windows. Dave obliged when I blinked so we could see. There was a curtained-off area that might lead to a bedroom, but this seemed to be the living/dining room.

"Welcome, Ethan." The voice was from a man not that much older than I was, with a beast that was almost as dominant as the old dude's. "Sit. Please. I am called Gígalolúwa." He pointed to a mat in front of him.

"Hello." I moved to the mat and sat down.

"We wish to offer you a chance to initiate here, according to our ways, since it is clear your heart is not with those you travel with. That they never offered we find as a mark against them."

I sighed. "A lot of their methods are just-- well, I'm not very impressed with how they operate. And yes, I would have turned them down if they'd mentioned an initiation. Because I did not trust them when I first arrived there. Um. I'm not sure they actually *do* anything other than maybe have a celebration to mark a boy's first shift."

I'd seen birthday parties in the cafeteria. Other parties sometimes but there hadn't been any candles on the cake. I guessed they were for shifting, since those were all for boys on the edge of puberty. Never for a girl.

"Is your attitude toward them changing?"

"Slowly, Gígalolúwa. I'd left the compound and my family, well over two years ago now. Couldn't see a future with them. A spy had been spreading rumours, poisoning everyone against me. To be honest, the only reason I came back was that I'd found five very bad guys with a young cougar shifter. Victor is around seven, and they were using him as bait to lure out an adult shifter, possibly to force him to breed more shifters. But they didn't know much about how a shifter works and what we can do with the beast's help. I did get aid to deal with them, but those men died. On my own and out in the world, I couldn't properly care for the child, so I went back to the Coalition with him. He lives with my parents now. For Dave and me, things have been better since then."

"But you still hold a core of suspicion within you."

"Yeah. I do. It might never go away. But I've met a woman who Dave doesn't object to. She's only the third we've encountered so far. Neither of the others were available, for different reasons."

An eyebrow went up. "As far as I can tell, it's a side effect of having a more aware partner. If the woman doesn't meet Dave's criteria, and I have no idea exactly what traits he's looking for or how he considers a woman acceptable. If she doesn't, he won't let us be together. Might kill the woman during a climax if I tried to have sex with them anyway."

"Are there any others finding this... issue? We have not, as far as I know. None of the other lion tribes we know have mentioned it either."

"Not that anyone's told me. It might not be as blatant as what Dave does. They might just have a bad feeling about one woman and it's love at first sight with another."

"Hold out your hand." Gígalolúwa's left hand extended and I did the same. He changed to a partial, so Dave did too. I had a sense that the other beast was well developed and they were communicating. I had no clue what they were talking about. Somehow. Dave started purring.

"So, our beasts agree. The initiation might also help your bond to increase," he said. "Come back here at moonrise, if you wish to embrace the ceremony. Fortunately, it is full tonight."

"I will be here. Making it easier for Dave and I to work together is a good thing. Anything special I need to do?"

"You should have a light meal in the mid-afternoon," he said with a grin. White teeth flashed against his dark skin. "We do not want either of you distracted by the growling of an empty stomach."

Only Rìnmáyò was outside the hut when I left. A couple of blinks later our eyes were back to human. He didn't say anything or ask any questions, but escorted me back to the house. He did try taking a different path but I didn't turn with him. "We can follow our own scent back along a route," I said. "That might be another good exercise to help the beasts develop for all your men, not just the younger ones. Have a guide walk them somewhere while they're blindfolded, maybe turning them around a lot so they aren't sure which way any turn is, then let them follow their own scent back to the starting point, maybe still without looking. Bonus points if they follow the exact route with all the digressions. You could even do it in the village so there's no bent down grass to give them a hint if they can see." He smiled at the idea.

I made a mental note to tell Alicia about this variation. Since a shifter would be following their own scent, there weren't the problems that we'd discussed before about the first tracker to go contaminating the trail for all the shifters after them. We could use the gym, or go outside so we could spread the trail out more. A camera high on the outer wall would help with the scoring. Maybe we could do it at night and give the men practice in using their beasts' night vision as well as the scent tracking practice. If we used blindfolds day or night wouldn't really matter.

"Hey, Karl," I said as he came in. A new assortment of food was on the dining table and I'd already made a plateful of selections, along with a mug of water and was just sitting down. "How'd things go this morning?"

"Good. They've sent word to the other local shifter groups that these thugs aren't a problem any more. We might have missed a few that were out on other assignments, and they'll all keep their eyes peeled for anyone trying to start up harassing isolated villages again." Karl continued with other details on the thugs. Obviously he didn't want to tell me how he'd explained the Coalition's recruiting methods.

"What about you? Do anything?" I didn't want to mention the shaman until I'd had a chance to think about what he'd said.

"Talked to Rìnmáyọ̀ and a few others about what sort of things Dave helps me with. Told them about the identity game, and they want to see it after lunch. I figure doing other things like following a person through town or out into the bush. Or following your own scent back to a starting point. Get the adults on side with it, then the younger men can start to develop more. You want to help run the games?"

He nodded and started to load a plate of his own.

Karl did the explanation of the identity game since I guessed a bunch of the men didn't speak English. Finally he turned to me. "Ready to go?"

"Always." Oluyẹmí came over with a folded over scarf and tied it around my head. *Time to show them again how great we are,* I thought at Dave, who came forward to identify the shifters. His purr echoed quietly.

"First one up," Karl said.

"Lion." With only one type here, that was also an easy guess. The line progressed. Murmurs from bystanders that I couldn't understand.

I paused. Dave was confused about the next one. We were about twenty bodies in. "There's something very different about this person. Dave's confused." A picture formed. Lion, but not the usual image he used. "What the hells?" I took the blindfold off. What stood in front of us was physically a big male lion with a gorgeous mane. Sleek and well fed. An older animal with serious scars from fighting to keep his pride over the years. But there was something very different. I'd sensed normal wolves and cougars before. This was *not* a normal lion.

Adésọ́lá came to stand next to me. "He is our, I do not know the word. Representative of our other form," Rìnmáyọ̀ translated.

"Totem," Karl said.

"That's not just a lion," I said. "He's different. Way different."

The priest, Gígalolúwa, came up to the lion's side. "Yes. He is very different from a normal lion. Now. He had lost the final battle against a younger male for control of his pride. We found him soon after and healed him. Now he aids our young men in the transition from youth to man. We will see you and your cougar at moonrise if you wish to learn more of your beast." They turned and walked away. Karl came to my side a moment later.

"What the hell was that about?" Karl asked quietly.

"They want to do their initiation thing for me. Tonight. That's part of what happened this morning while you were with their leader. I was trying to figure out if it was a good idea, which is why I didn't mentioned it when you came in for lunch."

He looked at the crowd. "Then we'd best keep you busy until then. So you don't over-think anything that might happen tonight." He turned to

Rìnmáyọ̀. "So, what other games did you want to see?"

"The Hide and Seek, or a tracking game."

"Chase," said Oluyẹmí. "Following one person through our village. A minute head start. But the area near the priest's home to be off limits."

"Sounds good to start with," Karl said. "You might want to let Dave take over."

They let me have a quick snack in the late afternoon. Then we were back at it until sunset. The moon would rise two hours later, I was told. I spent an hour having a bath. Trying to reconcile the Catholicism I'd learned as a child with what I was about to do. Jesus came up short. What they did here would be more Old Testament. Or even before. Long before.

I remembered about what Marsh had said and seen just before he died. An extremely beautiful woman. The consensus was that she was an old lover, maybe his first wife. What if she wasn't? Dave purred as I pictured her. What did he think about her? A potential mate for me or was she the template of who he wanted for me? No way I could ever ask him about that. I doubted Dave could understand the differences.

Why hadn't anyone in the Coalition ever mentioned the idea of an initiation? Not even Dad. Was there just a party, or some kind of ritual the night before or that night? Maybe Dad hadn't had one either, since he'd grown up outside the Coalition. I'd ask him once we managed to get back. But Sam had grown up in the Coalition. He hadn't mentioned anything, just that he'd been thirteen and a half when his first shift happened. I doubted there was any counterpart in the Coalition or probably the government group to what I was going to experience tonight.

The idea that scientists from the US Army or the CIA of the time had put the ability to shift into men within the past three or four generations did not fit with this village and its allies. How long had there been shifters in the world? A lot longer than anyone in the Coalition leadership wanted to admit. What did the government people believe? Was it the same origin story as I'd been told or did they have a different one? It might be interesting to grab one and just ask him about that. Oh, and ask not very gently if he knew where Justin was. He was at the top of our list of people to find and chastise.

I sat on the porch and waited for them to come for me. Dave was purring in my head. Akínlànà had left a loincloth for me, instead of our usual clothes. After a few aborted tries, I felt it was as secure as I could make it.

The same escort as before. Karl and most of the men trailed along behind us. The front guys held torches. Not flashlights, actual torches. Most of the electric lights were turned off along our route. The dim light of moonrise was starting to creep upward. We passed the priest's house and went into the jungle. Single file now. The sound of a drum came from ahead of us. A slow rhythm. My own heart rate slowed to match it.

This clearing wasn't that large and their lion lay at the middle. The priest sat by his side on a mat. I walked the last few metres alone. Knelt on the mat in front of them. Didn't say anything. Adésọlá held a wooden bowl in his hands, joining us once I was in position.

"A child comes to manhood," Gígalolúwa said. "Is there anyone who would dispute his claim to that state?" He said it twice actually, once in their own language and once in English for me.

No one said anything. I noticed their champion in the circle next to where the old dude had stood. Without a bandage on his arm. Good. We hadn't wanted to permanently cripple him. Another shift, even another partial one, would have healed the minimal damage Dave had caused.

"Is it your wish to leave behind the child and embrace the adult? The hunter and the protector. The father and the warrior."

"I do," I said.

"Who sponsors the child?"

The champion took a step forward and said a word. Then he continued forward and knelt by my side. "He has great honour. I, Abíọlá, will stand as his sponsor."

All this time, the drums kept going, but softer once the priest started speaking. Now the volume went back up. Adésọlá handed the bowl to the priest with a bow.

"The bowl contains the juices and essences of various plants, Ethan. You must drink and the Lion will speak to you." He handed the bowl to Abíọlá, who held it out to me. I'd avoided all sorts of drugs for my entire life, afraid of what Dave might do without me to help him cope with the modern world. But here in the forest, it wasn't the modern world. We'd be safe, no matter what happened next.

I drained the contents of the bowl, not trying to taste it. But it wasn't nearly as horrible as I'd thought it might be. Abíọlá took the bowl back then handed it off to someone else. Then he helped hold me upright. That stuff had a hell of a...

Bright light woke me. Us. We were in fur when I looked at my right hand, or rather paw. I blinked a few times. Dave roused, moved past me and we stretched. The lion lay next to us. We weren't in the village, I guessed by the number and density of the trees. The lion stood and Dave did too. Then we headed off, the lion in the lead. We had no idea where the village was beyond the faint scent in the grass from our trip out here.

It bothered me that I didn't remember anything after drinking whatever was in the bowl. Dave trotted along after the lion, purring. So at least he was happy and maybe he knew more than I did. Not a usual occurrence. After about twenty minutes, we came out into the village's cleared space. The priest's house was a few minutes further around the perimeter, but the lion didn't go into the village proper.

Gígalolúwa came outside after the lion gave a sort of cough. "Welcome back, Ethan and Dave. It is safe to return to human form." The lion went over to him and got stroked. Dave swapped us back. We will now call you by a man's name. Olúgbadé. An honoured name among our, your people."

"Thank you, Gígalolúwa." I bowed my head and Dave purred. "We woke up a little while ago. But I don't remember anything of the trip. Just waking up out in the forest in fur. Is that normal?"

"It has happened that way before. You may remember more in dreams in the days to come." He held out a piece of cloth. I looked down, blushing slightly as I realized I had nothing on. *Right. The loincloth.* "Your escort is no longer needed. You are one of us now. And forever."

"Thank you."

"There is one other thing. They are waiting at the house for you." I must have looked totally confused. "The tattoo, Olúgbadé, showing that you are now a man. It will show up much better on your skin that ours do." He touched his own chest. I could barely make out the darker marks, so hard to see against his normal skin tones.

"I can imagine that's... Wait. Did Karl do your initiation when he was here before?"

"We did not offer it to him at that time. We felt the lions and others from afar were... not ours. Now we know differently." He ducked back into the hut before I could ask anything else. Like, was I actually the first outsider they'd allowed to participate in one of their sacred rituals? Not a lion and white instead of black. I debated going into the house and asking, but didn't. Not now.

We returned to the house without any problems. Akinlabí waited on the porch. He sent a nearby boy off with a few words.

"He will bring the tattoo man. Are you hungry, Olúgbadé?"

"Could have a nibble, but not really. We must have eaten during the night but I don't remember what happened."

"There is food inside when you wish. Karl speaks with our elders."

"I don't think he's thrilled with me for accepting your initiation. But I really don't have a lot of respect for the Coalition in many ways."

A group of young men escorted an older man up to us. He smiled. I saw paw shaped tattoos on all of their upper chests on the left side. Some were harder to see than others, depending on how dark their skin was. I stood and bowed to the old man. Akinlabí removed his shirt as well to show off his. About the size of his hand or his lion's actual paw.

"You may curse us before we are done today," he said. "But we have all gone through this ceremony, and been marked. Are you ready?"

Monster purred, using my vocal cords. "We are." Saying it seemed redundant, but hey, ceremony was ceremony. And I did want to truly belong somewhere. Even with Melissa waiting back at the compound, I needed to experience their ritual in its entirety.

"Sit, and we will hold you while he works." I sat down on the lowest step. Akinlabí sat directly behind me and four of the young me each took an arm or leg. Partial shifts ensured their beasts would reassure Dave as the un-shifted heads and shoulders made me relax. Slightly. The old man knelt between my legs and two other young men came forward with a bowl of ink and a handful of twigs with thorns stuck through them.

I nodded and the old man smiled again and picked up a stick, dipped the thorn into the ink and started to tap on the thorn so it pierced my skin. Dave kept purring, but only inside my head now. I looked up past them and the tapping thorn, seeing a bright sky with no sun and a huge tree in a meadow. It seemed familiar, but it wasn't anywhere I remembered seeing before.

On our way back to the city and airfield two days later, Rìnmáyọ̀ detoured us through a village. "These make objects for the tourists, Olúgbadé. Perhaps you may find sufficient gifts here for those at your home."

I glanced at Karl, who smiled. "I need a few things as well," he said.

Karl handed me a bundle of local money as soon as the jeep stopped. There were a lot of things for sale, and I recognized a few of the people from the feast.

I found a carved lion about the size of a small cat for Victor, along with skirt and blouse sets for Mom and Melissa. Shirts for Sam and Dad. Different colours, and they were as approximate in size as I could remember. *Get actual measurements before the next mission. In case sizes are different from place to place.* Jewellery was much easier.

Some stall keepers wanted to just give the items to me, it seemed.

"What would they charge any American tourists?" I asked Rìnmáyọ̀ the first time, who'd followed me to translate. He looked puzzled. "These folks need money to buy things from the cities. Like more solar panels and batteries. School books. I'm not broke any more, so, pick out what the tourists would pay and double it."

He looked at the wad of bills in my hand. "Fine. You shop and I'll pay the going rates, without the haggling. Many consider that part of the joy of finding gifts or to show how clever they are."

About half of the wad was still in his hand when we returned to the jeep, packages in hand. "Split the rest of it between the girls. Sort of a dowry, or at least money that's theirs. It doesn't change what happened to them, but it's all I can do right now."

Karl handed over what he still held. "Mine too."

Chapter 21

Finding those who hurt the kittens took many lights. But Ethan helped it to understand how they would keep all the female kittens safe and end all the bad males. Good lions would have mates and then kittens.

It was good to be in fur. Many bad males fell under their claws and teeth. They were very close to each other and the kittens were happy once the bad men ended. A good fight. They went back to the lion place and many more were happy. Young Lions sniffed at the females, seeking the ones who smelled best to them. There would be more kittens.

In the blindfold game, Dave stopped. Confused. The one was lion, but not. Ethan did not understand either and removed the cloth. A lion. But not a shifter. Dave did not understand. It was very different.

When the moon gave light, Dave and the not-lion went to a strange place. It was a good forest, with many large trees. But it was dark. Only a few sounds. The not-lion led the way through the darkness. Soon there was a wide meadow full of light that was lower in the middle. A pile of stones like a house was next to a large tree.

"So close, but not yet," Dave heard. He looked around. No one was there but there was a good scent. A hand rubbed his ears and he purred.

"Go back to your world, little lion. Care for your partner. Be as close to him as you can. You will both come to me when it is time to fulfil your true destiny. For now, keep yourselves safe. I see the possibility of much danger to you both in the seasons to come."

Dave blinked. The bright meadow was gone. The not-lion lay next to him in the moonlight. *Hunt together*, said the not-lion as he rose. Dave chirped in agreement. Soon they scented a small antelope. The strange lion allowed him to make the kill and eat first. Then they slept until light came again. When that happened, Ethan woke and they returned to the village. It was good.

Chapter 22

I'd never expected to go to South America. Mexico had been on my list as a place to keep away from various groups hunting me in the past, but I hadn't managed to get there. Yet.

Dave was amazingly calm about the airplane for our return trip. He enjoyed looking out the window when we were low enough to see the ground. I pictured a hawk hovering up in the air to try showing him that what he saw now was what a hawk would see. Wasn't sure if he understood it completely but as long as he was calm during the occasional bouts of turbulence, I didn't mind. Karl was even happier. At least he hadn't mentioned the skydiving course again. I was very sure he hadn't forgotten about it.

First stop was in Columbia. Again, no one checked our bags thanks to the well armed escort that appeared as we picked up our gear bags from the luggage area. They escorted us to a specific customs official who stamped our passports and didn't ask us any questions or open our bags. If there were a lot of international missions, I'd end up needing a new passport in a few years. I did wonder how many missions used small airfields well away from any Customs agents or their stamps. Or if the locals had a stamp set that allowed the teams to bypass the main airfields entirely.

Or maybe that's why Karl wanted us to take up skydiving. I still wasn't sure Dave would understand why we had to get out of a plane while it was still in the air. There had to be movies we could watch that showed teams parachuting into a mission to rescue others. I'd ask Dad when we made it back home. That word still seemed so full of meaning. Dave purred, snuggled close to me.

We rendezvoused with a pair of normals once we were through the official area of the airport. Our security escort nodded at them and headed back into the customs area. Karl seemed to know the normals. I wondered if we'd have to worry about more chickenshit hazing with every new team we met. "Sup," I said. My bag on my right, since I didn't want to risk re-damaging my left side. Melissa might be upset if I did something stupid.

"We have a car waiting," the lead dude said. "It's an hour to our compound. Then you'll be briefed on the mission. We'll head out in the morning. It'll be two days to get there. The roads in the area are poor." The other man rolled his eyes.

We followed them. I found that I could understand most of what was being said from the other travellers. Several ladies commented on my looks. But nicely. I smiled at them as we passed. "Thank you, most beautiful of ladies," I said in Spanish. They blushed like schoolgirls. They'd been the high side of sixty.

"Is he like that all the time?" The other dude said once we were out of the building into the heat and outside air. It stank of jet fuel and Dave didn't like it, but we'd be away from here soon.

"Spreading joy is never a waste of time," I said. "I've already found the one I want to keep, but one should always be polite."

Another man waited behind the wheel of the limo. Our gear went into the trunk and we took the back seats. One man sat facing us, the other joined the driver. By the muffled thump of the door when it closed, I guessed there was armour built into and under the shiny exterior.

"Does Melissa know where we are?" I asked Karl the next morning.

"She does. So do your parents. And Victor. You can call them once we're done with the mission."

I didn't understand why one of the local shifters couldn't have done the jobs the compounds wanted us to do on our four stop South American tour. Dave liked the different scents from the trees, but occasionally detoured to scent mark a tree or piss on something whenever he sniffed another cougar. Or puma, as we were called down here. We also showed the identity game, and talked about how the shifters could connect with their beasts. That might have been the real reason Karl and the Council wanted us to travel. It made reasonable sense and Dave was mostly okay with the planes now. I still didn't want *anything* to do with skydiving. I'd never been a fan of amusement park rides like the roller coaster. Even the Ferris wheel made me nervous when my car was stuck at the top.

Once each mission was complete, the locals handed me a wad of local money and we went to a market area. Dave sniffed at all the new scents, purring in my head. There was enough chatter from shoppers and vendors that the few times he hijacked my vocal cords were lost in the overall ambience.

I filled a second duffel after we finished the fourth mission with all the presents I'd bought. Karl just sighed.

Chapter 23

We'd gone to my most recent range for a week during the early spring. It was odd staying in the campground instead of the cave. Dave enjoyed the change to roam in fur, since there weren't many people around. And we brought back a turkey for supper. But no cattails. They had nutrition but seriously lacked good taste. Victor and I showed everyone where he'd been left alone. I wasn't surprised when he snuck into our tent the first night and wrapped my arms around him and cried. Melissa woke and hugged him too. Thankfully we had a queen sized air mattress and doubled sleeping bags. Victor had started to grow taller but not wider, so he still fit between us.

Melissa took a deep breath when I stopped walking at the top of a rise. "The cave's another five minutes from here. It's pretty flat from now on." The mountain rose another hundred metres or so above us.

"You certainly had a lot of exercise living out here," she puffed. Pulled her water bottle out and sipped as she looked around.

"That's another problem with living underground," I said. "We can't run outside unless it's one of those days and Dave doesn't like the machines. I think it's the hum of the motor. I might ask if we can go out alone some nights, just to give him the fur time."

"Well, I think I'll survive the next bit." She started past me and across the little meadow. I caught up with her in a few steps and we held hands since the trail was mostly wide enough here.

The cave itself was much as I'd left it, including the tarps tucked into the back. Obviously no one had found it, and if any animals had come in here during the winter, they'd left as soon as the weather warmed up.

"How long did you live here?" Melissa asked as she looked around. "It's larger than I imagined a cave would be."

"About a year and a half. As for size, this is good for one shifter. The one I shared on Vancouver Island was maybe three times this size. But it was a lot warmer out there. Rain in winter. I think it snowed once and that vanished the next day so I didn't have to worry about foot prints."

"A lot of things to think about. Survival on your own, even with Dave's help, wasn't easy, was it?" she asked.

I paused to push the memories of wondering if I should just die back into whatever place they infested in my head. Melissa smiled at me and that helped ease the pain.

"No. See that crack? That was my chimney. I used some of the tarps for collecting rainwater and to make a wall across the entrance so no one would see any light from my fire, and to keep the heat in during the winter. Mom sent me a solar light string that made it easier to see in here. Otherwise I used the fire but never bothered staying up very late. The villagers we met in Africa have solar panels on all their roofs so they can have lights well into the evening since daylight only lasts about twelve hours year round."

"Wow." She walked around, touching walls and nearly bumped her head as she walked too close. The dim light made it hard to see clearly.

"That's where I put the bedding," I said. "Lower headroom wasn't a problem that way. If I asked, Dave would give me a fur coat in winter so we stayed warm even without the fire going. Bringing wood in was about the hardest job to survive. I tried to use dead-fall, since it was already dry but sawing a big log into manageable bits took a long time. No power tools and a big saw wouldn't fit in my pack if I had to shift ranges. I didn't want to use an axe since that sound carries a long way."

"That's why the saw chain. How's Dave feeling about being back?"

"He'd really like to go for a run tonight. We shouldn't be seen that way. Since there aren't any real cougars around this area, I don't want to start any rumours about the cougar being back when any bad guys might hear about it. It'll also confuse the locals if there's only one sighting. I'm not sure what they've thought about us vanishing."

"Or you are seen and the bad guys decide to send another group to try to catch you, but you have real help this time and take them prisoner."

"I suggested that..." Melissa stood in front of me and started unbut-toning my shirt. I might not understand much about women, but I understood this message. Dave purred then seemed to vanish.

"Do you want to walk me back down to the campground later, Mister Lion?" She giggled. I did a credible imitation of Dave's purr.

Chapter 24

Karl smiled, about a half metre away from my face. I wasn't really awake yet. Nether was Dave. Looking past Karl's head I figured we were in the Receiving area. Hadn't been taken back to my apartment yet. Good. Back from another drug suppression mission with Bill and his guys. Four days out. At least Victor was calmer about my trips away from him, since I always came back or called if we ran into issues that delayed us.

"Give me five minutes," I said. Monster, Dave growled in my head at being woken. "Hope it's worth waking me up. Dave's cranky."

"We finally have a lead to Victor's people," Karl said. "Get over to my office as soon as you get dressed." Then he vanished.

I managed to sit up. My gurney was near the wall. Bill was gone, as usual. The other three team members were still sleeping. Great. I was usually the last to wake, at least on the trips out. My head felt like it was stuffed with feathers. Dave growled again.

One of the nurses came in and shook her head. "Did he wake you up?"

"Not sure. Said to get my butt to his office. My clothes underneath?"

"They are." She sniffed in disapproval and checked on the others. Paul snored on. At least he was usually quiet.

I slid from the gurney and found my inside clothing. The outside stuff was now being cleaned and my pack was now in that outside storage room. It didn't make sense to me, but we weren't allowed to have our outside stuff in the compound. I kept a few things, namely my wallet and passport, in my apartment anyway. In case of an emergency mission, I told the guys who took away the gear. I dressed and hit the bathroom on the way out. If the situation was so serious that Karl woke me up, he wouldn't schedule any breaks. My stomach growled so I took a long detour past the cafeteria on my way to Karl's office for some portable food.

My dad was also there, which kind of surprised me. Dad didn't go outside much any more except for holidays.

"Hey, Ethan. You ready for some good news?" Dad asked.

I sat down and pulled a sausage stick out of the napkin I'd wrapped everything in. "What's going on?"

Karl smiled. With teeth. "We have the real ID on one of the people you found with young Victor. His DNA finally came up as related to a cousin who just got theirs tested to find their ancestry. That gave us his real last name and the whole thing just snowballed from there." Dave perked up at that news. So did I.

"When do we hit them? Tomorrow?" I asked. "Maybe the day after?"

"As soon as we verify all the intel, so more like a week. They just seem to have one facility where the kids are and we have observers heading there to make sure of numbers and other details before we move in. We need to be covert since we're operating in country, not in some lawless hellhole under orders. The various agencies we work for don't care what sort of mess we make out there. Here, they worry about news coverage of any big operation since they can't control who might be passing by with a cell phone. We need to keep them happy, so we stay very covert."

"So any idea what their deal is? What did they want Victor and any other kids to do once they grew up?"

"Still sketchy on that," Dad replied. "We may need to ask whoever is in charge there. I've been helping coordinate aspects the search and such. Victor's a good kid. Don't want to see this abuse continue. Lucy's been helping too, since Victor doesn't need to be with her whenever he isn't in school as much. He and young Pete get along really well." Both boys regularly came to play with Dave in fur. Pete's older brother didn't. We'd showed him the error of bullying.

"Can we go in full cougar?" I asked. Dave was interested in that idea. "Even the full partial would make Dave happy. If these guys are trying to make shifters, then they should get a taste of what we're really like. Not scared little kids or drugged adults who probably couldn't do more than paws with claws at the best of times."

"You could wear your armour in the partial," Karl said. "In case they're armed and aren't as surprised as we assume that they'll be."

"A late night entry would have the fewest people awake." Dad gave me, then Karl, a Look. "Take out any sentries with trank darts."

I shrugged. "Never give the enemy an even break. Right, Dad?"

Dad smiled. "That's right, Ethan. We need information and that means prisoners, Karl. Really, we should have kept the five men who were with Victor, at least for a couple of days. Quick interrogations, then left them out in the stream with enough sedative to keep them asleep and let the engine fumes finish them off as you did. We'd have eliminated the group months ago. We should also go in with dart guns as our major weapon with taser backups. Send the shifters in partial to rattle the guards on the perimeter if we need one of them to get inside the fence. Then run sleep gas into the HVAC to put all the people to sleep with the aim of no fatalities. Theirs or ours. It's the best way. It will also keep the various agencies off our backs about operating at home without their sanction. That's important if we want to keep operating elsewhere and earning money to support all of our people."

I raised an eyebrow.

Dad smiled. "Used to be Karl's second. I fill in for him if he's out on assignment, like while you were out working in Africa and South America."

"Fine," grumbled Karl. "Spoilsport."

"What happened when Victor's arseholes were found?" No one had said anything so I hadn't known they'd been located. Didn't really care about them but they'd been missed. By their bosses at least.

"The police didn't do any better than we did trying to figure out who they were," Karl said. "It's gone cold on their side. Frozen, in fact."

"It was over five weeks after you left them before they were found," Dad said. "One of the rangers, not Neil, was doing a trail sweep before the snows started. Written off as idiots about the way we thought the incident would be. There were no sign of Victor's prints in the vehicle or even any of yours or Neil's. Mind you, it was pretty messy in there and from the reports they didn't bother looking very hard. I'm pretty sure they were glad to find the whiskey bottles since that's the only reason they had any decent fingerprints to work with."

"Should we tell Victor we know where he came from?"

Karl nodded. "Not yet. Let's have just good news for him. Don't want to raise his hopes too much until we've rescued the other kids."

Bill's eyebrows rose when I headed to the mess hall for a real meal and to fill him in. He was sitting by himself, but his infant son snoozed in a stroller beside him. Dave purred at the baby. "You mean they finally caught a lead?"

"They did. Found a relative to one of the guys, so they managed to ID him, which gave them the rest. No idea on the chain of clues. But Karl thinks there's only one facility. Won't tell me where. Dave's ready to go."

"Still weird you call him Dave." He sipped coffee.

"Are Ralph, Bobby, Simon and Paul up for a covert infiltration?" We'd only been working together for six months and the humans hadn't quite become used to Dave yet. They were okay with our full partial shifts, but my full still spooked them. Karl's plan include swapping me to another team when the next groups changed around. The international pool of teams didn't have many openings. I wondered if they'd just form a new team for us to be in. As far as I'd figured, all the mission leaders, no matter where they were, wanted people who could do a full shift on call. So far, there were two of us so they had to share. The work we'd done after our trip to Africa made all of them want more time with me.

I'd been sure anyone who did a full partial could have done the same jobs I had. But those trips counted against my book reports so I wasn't that upset. Dave was much more relaxed about flying. I still wasn't sure about the parachuting course, which Karl kept mentioning. I kept putting that off but we had watched a half dozen movies about skydiving. Mostly war movies but I'd asked at the compound's library if there were any documentaries or just television shows that showed the fun aspect of it. She'd been dubious about the possibility but promised to look on the internet to download a couple for me.

"They should be. By the way, picked a name for my wolf. Hank. And we scored seven out of ten on the ID test last time. Should have mentioned it while we were out."

"Great. How about the types?" I didn't bother with the testing anymore, except to illustrate for new batches of shifters if we were working with a new group that didn't trust the video that had been sent around. It didn't usually take long for them to come on side. Dave thought the exercise was very boring now, but did like showing off how great he was. Same with the other games, though he liked the chase game best. More like real hunting than anything we did during a mission.

"Averaging better than sixty percent. Getting better." He'd done four out of twenty the first time, with no correct types.

"You've been practising a lot, haven't you?"

"Every chance we get."

We were told that the site was near Fargo, North Dakota. One of the possible areas the lions I'd met long ago might have been heading for. We had a good-sized tour bus with an added trailer for gear, tents and so on. We'd met up with teams from four different compounds at a campground a day away from ours. Apparently we wouldn't be going near any compounds or safe houses to keep any government watchers from learning about our trip. I sat next to different non-shifters from the other teams on Karl's advice after each stop. Letting them get to know me, so they wouldn't panic when Dave made an appearance. Hopefully. Dave would know all of them by scent after the first few days, even if I wasn't sure on their actual names.

A pack of cards appeared after a quick dinner break three rows up from us. Dave pricked his ears. He remembered times he'd helped me catch my opponents' tells and suppressed our own. Another sign that he was far more aware than any other beast in the coalition. My virtual ear rubbing made him purr.

"You want to go play?" Charlie asked me. He had the aisle seat.

"Not this time. I depended on gambling for food money before I came in. I don't play otherwise." Everyone near me looked in my direction.

"That sounds like a challenge." The speaker was a couple of seats behind us. "We're stopping for the night soon." Sunset was at 8ish. Enough time to set up the tents and the kitchen for breakfast.

"Penny poker," I said. A couple of guys laughed at the idea. They wouldn't be for long. I wasn't sure anyone had enough money on them to make it truly interesting for us.

Ten people around two shoved-together picnic tables. The rest of the teams kibitzed from the shadows. All the improvised chips were now in front of me. Pretzels, of all things. The only thing we had in sufficient quantity that would serve as counters. Other than bullets, that is.

"You had *all* the other frigging aces?" Charlie asked in disbelief at my cards. With the two nines and the ace of diamonds on the table and the other two nines and three aces in my hand, I hadn't needed to worry. "I was sure you were bluffing. That's too good a hand to keep hidden."

"Tells are wonderful things," I said. I stood and yawned. Lots of teeth. *We were the best.* Dave agreed. His purr echoed in my head.

We were on the road early the next morning. Another full day of travel. I'd gone for a run once the card game ended. Well, Dave had gone since the campground was deserted as usual in midweek. Bill had the window seat and all the others were full. A weird vibe from the others. Normals and shifters. I wasn't sure why, but I trusted Dave's feelings.

"You get any sleep?" He'd been on watch when I came in. Had my clothes so I could get back to the tents without flashing anyone.

"Enough for now. Planning on a nap soon, maybe another after lunch, but if we need to talk..."

"Nothing too serious. Mostly on using Hank more."

I started my now fairly standard spiel. I thought Bill had heard it before. In fact, I was pretty sure everyone on the bus had heard it at least a few times, but maybe he wanted a refresher.

"That's what you tell the new guys," Bill said when I was almost a quarter of way through. "What else?"

"What I tell people *is* how I started, Bill. Years of work with Dave. Not just the eight months since the identity game started." I tried to find the words to explain what I meant. Wait, there had been a not-completely-terrible book in junior high. Flowers for some guy.

"I'm not sure on the name, but there was a book. Fairly thin. A really dumb guy gets a magic pill that makes him a genius. The catch is that it goes away at the end." I stopped. "No. Bad example. Maybe, more like a kid with abusive parents who keep them in a windowless basement or a closet. No human contact, or damn little. Would you expect that kid, let out into the world at twenty or so, to understand anything about how to make a microwave or a cell phone work without a lot of help?"

Bill stared at me. Our entire section of the bus was silent. A few murmurs from either end showed not everyone had heard me and those that had were filling in the rest. *Shit.* I sighed. Dave was confused. I stood up and held onto the seats for balance. The driver looked at me from the mirror then turned his attention back to the road and idiot drivers.

"No, I am *not* saying that all shifters are abusive arseholes and enjoy keeping their beasts in the dark." *Well, I was, sort of.* "I'm saying that, like most shifters out in the world, you don't really encourage your beasts to *do* anything. I was terrified of a shift when I was fourteen. Didn't look forward to it like the kids here do. Absolute panic and prayed it wouldn't happen again. Then I realized I needed the beast's help to survive on the streets. I actively worked at teaching Dave to warn me when he smelled gun oil. What fear smelled like. What *rage* smelled like."

I turned a little to look at the men behind me. "Years of work, people. Identifying who is a shifter or not is a good starting place. We need to get the teens and even the pre-teens starting to work with their beasts. Ask your beasts for help when you're doing weights, or running. Get outside more. A lot more. Living inside the compounds, especially the underground ones, stifles them. They're hard wired to protect us. The big problem is that they aren't really needed until you're out on the teams. So they stay asleep longer, and it still takes a long time for them to realize that they have a purpose. Even longer to make sure they don't shift anything when you don't want them to."

"Any ideas on that?" Bill asked from behind me.

"Hide and seek, even in the underground compounds. And as shifted as you can get." I sat back down and looked at Bill. "Enough for now?" Bill nodded, maybe communing with his beast.

We stopped for the night. After supper and tent set up, the shifters surrounded me. The normals were behind them. "So, I guess everyone wants to play." *Or they were all going to beat the crap out of us. Or at least try.* Dave was on alert and I was ready to kick off my shoes so I could shift my feet if I needed to.

"A run first," Bill said firmly. "We've been sitting in the dammed bus for too long." He looked at me.

"Okay. We'll start with one lap around the campground for a warm up." We were the only folks here as usual, so we could spread out.

"Second lap, concentrate on linking with your beasts. Let them know they can come watch what you're seeing. It'll be getting dark soon, so think about using their night vision. Shift as far as you can into the partial, even if it's just paws and claws. Do a couple of laps like that. Then slow down. Walk. Thank the beast for their help, no matter what happened. Even it was just a slight shift so you could see in the dark better. Shift back. And picture yourself rubbing their ears. Or bellies. Whatever works to show them you appreciate them and what they did to help you."

"And what about us?" Came from the back of the crowd. The normals.

"If you don't have a beast, just have a good run. Don't try any fancy moves, like shouldering a guy to the side to get him out of your way. If the beast sees something as an attack, it can shift to claws and you'll be headed home. Med bay or the morgue. Don't be stupid about showing off. Tomorrow night we'll do the same, then play some hide and seek."

Halfway around my first lap I swapped to full partial. My shoes were now tied together and hanging around my neck. I held them to keep from getting hit in the chest with each step as I'd forgotten to drop them off in camp. Next time I passed by the tents I'd do that.

A slow lope allowed us to stay on the outside of the group and still keep up. I was beside Bill for a half lap. His partial wasn't as complete as ours. His tail was still missing.

"Tails are good for running fast," I growled. "Rudders for balance and changing direction." Bill growled back at me and I sped up, zigzagging between the other runners. Our tail made it all possible. Dave purred.

The next morning we packed up and stowed the gear and filed back on the bus. All the shifters were quiet. But the vibe of the attitude I couldn't put my finger on was less. The normals didn't seem as whatever either. Were the shifters finally accepting that they needed to change the way they interacted with their beasts? The normals might be accepting that the shifters didn't have much of a clue on using their beasts despite the preference given to them for tasks and possibly pay.

I hoped so. Dave was smug. Happy that we were still the best.

Chapter 25

We surrounded the compound during the early part of the night. No one had spotted us. There hadn't been any movement of guards outside the fence for a sweep since the late afternoon. A couple of them were wandering inside the tall chain link fence, but no one came outside to trip over us. Getting a couple of our people in their uniforms to access the gate had been one of the options for our ingress.

Firsteam Protection read the sign on the front gate. The name meant nothing to me, but word went around quickly through the comms and I was confused at the reaction.

"Who are these guys?" A voice behind me asked. "And why weren't we told they were specforce contractors? The plan is *so* frikin screwed. If there's a whole crew in there we don't have enough muscle or firepower to take them on and do anything besides die stupidly."

Bill sighed and looked over at me. "This isn't their major base. Just where they're keeping the kids and such. Not clear on why no one wanted to announce who they were before we arrived. We have good counts on the staff: thirty guards on three shifts. About fifteen or so caretakers and maintenance staff. We don't know how many shifters, kids and women they have as prisoners. Anyone wants to back off, head to the bus right now. Your choice."

Dave growled in my head. Harm to those who hurt kittens. "These people might be trying to raise their own shifters to compete with us," I said. "But they kept Victor on short rations and really afraid of them. Not sure how they thought he'd be willing to work with them once he was old enough to shift anything, even if he could do anything more than sharper fingernails than normal."

"Let's get the kids out of this hell." That voice came through the radio loud and clear. Lots of agreement came over the feed next.

"Then you know the plan. All groups in position?" More chatter as various teams announced they were ready, which we ignored.

Dave and I were in the lead. In fur. The front gate sentries went down to the darts in seconds and I shifted a hand to type in the access code to the main gate, which the advance team had watched with a really good camera system for the past few days. All of our folk couldn't believe they were so lax at first. The code did not change from day to day. Stupid way to run security, but I was told not to complain about their ineptitude during the final briefing. The biometric part was also easy. The shifter behind me was in full partial and just held the guard up and stuck his eye into the viewer. It was still in his head, by the way: he'd fainted at the sight of the partially shifted wolf appearing in front of him. Fortunately, there wasn't any voice recognition since he was likely to stay out for a few more hours thanks to a trank dart.

After the other outside guards were all down and quiet, sleeping gas was released into the ventilation system. After a short wait, the first group walked in with masks on just in case and started cuffing the enemy and releasing the fifteen kids, the three adult shifters and the three women in various stages of pregnancy, ten women probably waiting for the next round of *in vivo* and one nursing her son.

There was only one cougar boy in the small locked rooms. The rest were wolf. No lions. All the adult shifters were wolf. None of them looked to be in great shape.

"Any idea who this kid and Victor's dad or dads are?" I asked.

"Not yet," Bill said. "Maybe when the med staff wake up, we'll start to get some answers."

We went back to the med bay, where the shifters were. "I wonder why they didn't kill themselves."

"Drugs," said a new guy behind me. I turned, not too quickly or I might scare the guy even though I was in human form. He was from one of the secondary groups that had followed the teams in once the gas had dispersed. "I found the paper copies of their files in the med office. Weren't hidden or anything. All three have been dosed with enough Ketamine to keep them docile. In their food at a guess. Then Ecstasy is used to harvest their sperm every month or so."

"Rate of success?" Bill asked.

"Not that great on first glance. I think most of that data is in the computer files. But having ten women waiting for the next round of in vivo, I'd say it hasn't worked out that well. The oldest kid here is eleven. Found their files too. "

"What about an adult cougar shifter or two? I know they had one."

"Nothing up here. Might be more files in another room. Must have been previous captives who are probably dead. Why?"

"One of the kids here is cougar. His dad had to be a shifter. Plus the kid I found out in the world is cougar. We figured he'd come from here."

"Hmm." He stared at the filing cabinets. "How long ago?"

I had to count months. It had been nearly a year and a half now?

"There's another group headed in with an empty semi or three. We're going to just take everything related to their program with us so we can sort through it all later. We don't want to miss anything."

"Makes sense. I'm sure their bosses are going to be peeved with us at the breach of protocol. I don't understand why they've treated the kids so badly. It doesn't make sense. Telling them they're going to be heroes and rescue people would be the way I'd run it." It was how the Coalition ran their compounds but I didn't say that out loud.

"No idea. Maybe we should ask the head honcho before we leave. There's plenty of interrogation drugs in our coolers. As you said, telling the kids they're going to help save the world is a much better ploy." He blinked, maybe cluing in on the Coalition's reality.

"Good idea," Bill said. "Have your guys look for any way of storing frozen sperm. That cougar might have died a long time ago and they might still be trying to find another. Might have been why they tried that trick with Victor. They must have believed Cindy's story about a friendly cougar and guessed Ethan was a shifter."

"Will do." He waved a hand in the direction of his temple instead of a salute. Not that the Coalition really used salutes. Some normals joined the armed forces to learn new techniques that they relayed to the teams once their hitch was over. Relearning that they didn't have to salute every ten minutes apparently took a while to get used to.

Chapter 26

The three wolf shifters were starting to wake, so I hurried over to the isolation rooms they'd been kept in. There were six cells. So they had built a place to contain more shifters. Maybe they'd been hunting us for a long time. Which one of the now three groups had sent the sniper to the forest near Banff? Maybe he was supposed to shoot me in the arm or leg, so that I wouldn't be as much trouble to get me out of there, probably using a helicopter in a nearby clearing since it would take a couple of days to walk to the highway. But the man's comment that I shouldn't be still bothered me. It didn't fit with this operation or the government guys. Both wanted live shifters to work with or for them, not dead ones.

Bill waited for me in the open area outside the short corridor of cells. So was a wolf I didn't know. "Mark," he said. "I was part of the surveillance team." They were already in the full partial, but still had their boots on, as we did. Bill even had his tail this time. It was nice and bushy, an improvement on the last time I'd seen it. Good. Dave turned us into the same, and watched through my eyes. Being kept in a tiny cell was one of my nightmares. Finding Victor's captors was one of the reasons I'd stayed around. The other, more important one, was still Melissa.

"I just hope they're sane," Mark said. "Otherwise this may be a waste of time."

"May take a day or three for them to finish shaking the drugs out of their system if they've been here for a few years," Bill replied.

A door closed and locked behind us. "We rigged a gas canister into the area's air supply in case any of them are totally bonzo," said someone on the radio. "Gas you all and then we'll pull you guys out. Not sure what we could do with them except keep them unconscious until we get them to a secure location."

The cell doors thunked as they were unlocked from the outer office. All electronic locks, defaulting to locked in power outages. Good if you wanted your prisoners to stay put, bad for any attempt at escape. Dave growled softly in my head.

Rescue them. Take to safe places. Like the kittens. I rubbed his ears. Dave relaxed. "Let's go." I went to the cell assigned to us and pulled the door open. The shifter was in human form, huddled in a corner. A thin pad was rucked up underneath him. No toilet, but a large open drain in the other back corner stank of piss and shit.

"Sam?" I asked softly. That was the name on the file for this room. No last name. He'd been a big guy, I thought. Mostly Anglo looking. Maybe a little Native back a few generations. One arm moved a little. Clearing at least one eye, I guessed. "Just so you know, I'm Ethan. We've come to take you and the other shifters out of here. Please don't attack me or we'll all get gassed. Then the doors close on you. Maybe forever. Okay?"

"What?" Barely a whisper but we had great hearing.

"Ethan. Rescue. Leaving here." Simple was better. Maybe.

His other arm moved and his head rose. Both eyes were wide as he caught sight of me. "Dream. Gotta be."

I went back to human-looking. Dave sniffed, just to be sure. A picture of a wolf appeared over him. Thin with matted fur. Angry. The cameras for the room would show that I'd shifted back.

"Not a dream, Sam. My name's Ethan. Would you like to leave here? Go home? It's been several years since they locked you in here. I don't know how many." *Could they have kept these guys alive for the twelve or so years we guessed the program had been running? Or did they die after a few years from the Ketamine and the stress? After one died they just found others? Was this group one of the hunters of the lone shifters I'd seen over the years? Could be. Maybe we'd find out from their files.*

"Sam. Fellows. Yeah. Leaving here's a good idea." He sat up and leaned against the wall. realized he was nude and put an arm across his crotch in reflex. "What happened to me?"

"Really long story," I said. "Bottom line, you've been drugged with Ketamine and the bad guys here have been trying to breed you and the other two guys to get more boys who can shift."

"Shift?"

"More long stories. Plenty of time to chat later on."

"All's good," came over the speaker system. "Everyone's back to normal. We're getting clothing and food brought down."

"Good. We were worried you guys might be insane."

Sam looked at his hands. "You aren't human. Or..." His wolf was calming, I thought. Dave was purring at it. Or at Sam. Maybe all of us.

"We're totally human, Sam. DNA says so. But we can change parts of ourselves into the animal. I'm a cougar. You're a wolf. So are the other two guys we found. There's a bunch of kids in another part of the basement in this hell-hole. A couple of them might be yours, depending on how long you've been here. We haven't figured that part out yet. We just arrived early this morning. Lots of files to go through. But we're taking everything and everyone with us when we go."

"How'd you find us?" I didn't answer immediately. "More long stories you'll tell me later?"

"Yeah." I squatted so we were at the same eye level. "Really short version is that I was out on holiday in the mountains and nasty dudes with a six year old cougar shifter in tow were trying to find and catch other shifters to bring them here. Namely me, though I doubt they knew my name, just thought there was a shifter in the area. I snuck away with the boy, called my people for help and those guys died. We've been trying to locate this place ever since. We finally had a really good lead about a week ago, and voila, here we are. We'll pull out in a day or so."

"And my choices from here? Another little room?"

"Several. All involve getting out of this cell as the first step. Your next permanent sleeping spot will probably be an apartment bedroom. What's the last year you remember? Or a major event."

He stared for over a minute before he spoke.

"Okay," I said. "That was about five years back, I think. What did you do for a living back then?"

"I was in the army. Near the end of my enlistment. Shit." Eyes wide again. "I'm AWOL!"

"We have contacts in all the branches," I said. "It'll get sorted. Being kidnapped is a great reason for being missing at roll call. There's lots of documentation here for proof. Don't stress on that part of your future."

"Food and clothes are in the main area," Bill called.

I pushed the cell door open. "Need a hand up? Your muscle tone is probably shot after so long in here." I held out a hand. Sam nodded and extended his own. I helped him up and he was a head taller than me. A few wobbles as we walked, but I made sure he didn't go to far off balance.

Out in the lobby of the cell area, there was a long table with six chairs, probably from the cafeteria, a good sized pot of stew, dinner buns and two pitchers of water. Beef stew, though this time we'd just eat it so the guys would know it wasn't drugged any more. Exercise gear and pull on shoes were on three of the chairs.

"Rick and Carl," said Bill as he pointed to the other captives.

"Sam."

The guys dressed, then Mark stirred up the stew and put helpings into all the bowls. Bill and I started eating immediately. Sam tried a bite, then the others did too. I wondered how they were drugged. Food was pretty easy or they could use gas, given the sealed doors on the cells.

"We're setting up in their gym," the speaker dude said. "We want all of you out of those cells. We'll be packing the guards and such in them when we leave here. Seems fitting."

Rick took a deep breath. "So it's over? We're free?"

"Yup," Mark said. "We'll stay with you for a day or three. Get you caught up on the world. Hell, we can carry you if your legs are wobbly."

All three ex-captives looked at me. The shortest guy there. "Doesn't matter how tall or muscled I am, dudes. I could take all three of you, in your best form, even if you were Special Forces, Rangers, or Seals. Okay? Don't try anything now, or I might hurt you. Accidentally."

"He's right," Bill said. "I wouldn't want to fight him for real. Even if we're just sparring, he's deadly." I grinned and Dave purred.

After the meal, a trio of wheelchairs appeared, with more of our guys to push them. All human, since the rescued guys were behaving. Up the elevator to the main floor. There were lines of bodies in the main lobby.

"They aren't dead," Bill said as our three looked at him. "We gassed them, then mostly sorted them out by job description and gave them tranks to be sure they stay quiet until we get them tucked away. The guards will be stuffed into the cells you three were in. Others are going to the kids' cells and there's a couple of the top brass we're going to in- terrogate once they wake up enough to talk. Just to make sure there isn't another base like this one."

"How many of you are like us?" Carl asked.

"About a quarter," Bill said. "Rest are folks we trust and work with all the time." A dude came from a side corridor with a lift truck with a pallet on it. "Good. Easier to move them around."

"Three of them fit on each one," said the dude. "There's another one of these coming from their supply room."

"Let's get you guys to the gym," Mark said.

It wasn't a big space so it looked crowded, set up with pads on the floor. Smaller ones might have been from the kids' cells, others looked like exercise mats. The kids were still sleeping. The women were too. Mostly. Each person had a watcher near them. Some men, but mostly wo- men. They were in civvies, which would confuse the kids, but the shifters relaxed slightly. So would the women, once they woke up. Several tables were set up with food and such on them. Heaters kept the stew warm.

Two hours later, the rescued folk were awake. The kids were sort of huddled together. The women had mostly finished crying, and the three shifters were talking to Bill and Mark. I was redundant there. Fine by me.

Dave sniffed. One of the boys was crying. I went closer. The cougar boy we'd sniffed earlier. Were he and Victor brothers?

"Hi," I said gently as I sat down. All the weapons and armour were out in an adjacent room. In case one of the adults, male or female, weren't as sane as they seemed at the moment. "I'm Ethan. You are?"

He wiped snot onto his sleeve. "I'se Jerry." I felt nothing but relief. Dave purred.

"Hi, Jerry. Why are you crying?"

"He's not here wit us. Dint see him a long time."

"Who? Victor?" A not very wild guess. Jerry's eyes went wide.

"You knows him?"

"I do. When we leave here, we'll go to him. Okay?"

"How?" A couple of the other kids watched and listened.

"A bunch of these bad guys were hunting older shifters. Like those guys." All the kids turned to look at the three, then back at me. "Victor was the bait to catch me. I took Victor to a safe place and I killed the bad guys." Well, that had been the carbon monoxide and the whiskey, but, hey, it was my idea. Besides, short versions were best for now.

"They'se strong," another boy said. Another wolf. Maybe wolves were easier to breed than cougars. Dave still didn't sense any lions.

"None of them are strong enough to win against grown up shifters like us. We know how to work with our beasts. You dudes still hungry? Victor hadn't been fed much, so I guess you all wouldn't mind a snack about now." Slow nods. "Let's get you guys more stew. Okay?"

Soon I had the gaggle of kids around me. I took short steps so they wouldn't trip me. Dave was very happy and I let his purr be audible. I even slept with them, all in one big pile. They'd never heard of blankets before. Heath, a young wolf shifter, had joined me in taking care of the kids. He was taking the wolf boys to a different compound that seemed to be nearby. All the adults would be going there too.

It was a full day later that I left that place. With Jerry. I'd called Mom and Dad to tell them I was bringing Jerry back with me.

Jerry slept on the bed in Victor's room, with Victor watching him once we returned. "I think he and Victor can share clothes for the moment," Mom said after seeing him. "Though I'll have another dresser delivered and I'll take both boys to the stores area later today."

"I'll take them both to the med centre tomorrow," Melissa said. "Ethan, you should come too, since you're the only adult here he knows."

"Sure. He's a good kid. They all..." I didn't know how to say how seeing the kids had affected me. Melissa came over and hugged me. "Sorry."

"Don't be sorry, Ethan," Mom said. Melissa squeezed tighter.

"They'll all need time to recover," Melissa said. "As will the women and the shifters. Victor's doing well in his therapy. Jerry's almost the same age as Victor was, so that should mean he'll progress at about the same rate. Maybe faster since he won't be wondering where his brother is all the time. I'm so glad that the place was found. Pissed that it took so long. Keeping those first men for interrogation would have made everyone's lives much better." I nodded. Her tone of voice was Mama Bear. Or maybe Mama Cougar. Dave approved.

Karl dragged me into his office for an update about two weeks later. Victor and Jerry stayed near each other, though young Peter was mostly with them after school was out. At some point, someone there had decided teaching the kids to read was a good idea, so Jerry could read a simple book, but addition was still a confusing mystery.

"The kids *are* full brothers," he said. "His file was found. Turns out their dad developed an immunity to the Ketamine and attacked when they were taking him out to the med bay to collect another batch of semen. Killed five guards before they shot him. He seemed to have partly shifted, but we haven't found that video footage yet. More than paws and claws, but not full partial. We'll let the shrinks tell them. With your mom to hold their hands, but she'll already know the truth."

"What about their mother? Is she one of the women we found?"

Karl shook his head. "Also dead. Childbirth and neither survived. Happened when Jerry was three and Victor five, more or less. Neither saw her after they were a couple of years old. Five of the kids do have moms that were rescued. They're being asked if they want to keep contact with the boys. Same with the shifters."

"Even if they can't stay together, at least tell me they've found families to adopt those kids. All of them are innocent of whatever was done to conceive them."

"That's in progress. The three shifters we brought out were all army originally. They weren't on active duty and were getting out within the month, so no AWOL issues. Each of them had an interview with that security company. That's the last time they were seen. People they knew assumed they'd been hired on and were dark. Sam was there longest at five years. He has three kids. Older ones are two and four years. The last is in the oven. Two for Carl, one not yet born and two for Rick and the one nursing. They also had stored semen from other shifters they've had in the past, which is where the other kids came from. We're assuming their dads and possibly their moms are dead."

"Accounts for all the kids, then. What was their plan? Keeping the kids starved and afraid of shifting seems really stupid if they ever intended to use them for infiltration and such the way we operate."

"The idiot in charge wasn't really on board with the plan. He lied on all his reports and head office never sent anyone to check up on him. And with the oldest kid at eleven, no one was really expecting any real shifts to happen yet. That would have changed in a year or so. He also authorized using Victor to try to find other shifters. Like you. They were having trouble finding any other shifters leaving the army, so they needed a new source of sperm donors. Since there aren't many shifters out in the world any more, there aren't many who choose to go into the armed forces as a way to make a living. Ron might have become a target in a few years if you hadn't brought him in."

"Makes sense," I replied. "Most shifters born in the compounds go right onto the Coalition teams, never spending time in regular forces where a spy might notice them doing something a normal shouldn't. Not sure how we can track those guys down, but asking who suggested they have a chat with Firsteam might give at least a few leads. Might be a clerk in the personnel department, or, well, anyone on their base."

Dave wanted all those who were involved to suffer. A lot. More ear rubs to calm him down. "Any luck on the finding all of their data? Might have answers in there."

"Techs cloned all their computer storage and we have all of their semen vials. A supply run is due in a day or so. We're still tapped into their communications and we installed tiny cameras in a few spots." He smiled with teeth. So did we. "There's some discussion on contacting them after that to let them know who hit them, but that's way over my head."

"Glad most of the issues are sorted," I said. "Dave's happy too."

"Good. There's another quick mission coming up for Bill's team. A drug gang in Philly. There's a couple of the thugs that we've been asked to terminate by the locals. There's a 'clean up the neighbourhood' activist and her group that they're stalking. We'd rather have her alive so she can start to make a difference there. Pretty good local support for her programs. She's been targeting kids who haven't started using or joined the gangs. Giving them something else to do. Sports and music."

"Sounds good. When do we leave?"

"Two days. Package will be in your hands later tonight. Bill's letting the team know in about an hour."

"Okay. Maps and video of the area ready?"

"Almost. There's just a couple of people at the safe house there. Surveillance and reporting only. They'll give you updates when you all arrive. It'll be a bit crowded in there, but they have enough extra beds for the entire team."

"As long as I'm not sleeping in one of their cells, I'll be fine."

Chapter 27

The apartment was dark when I opened the door and flipped on the living room lights. "Lissa?" I called. No immediate answer, so she might be in the med centre. The people in Shipping would have mentioned if she'd had to leave the compound. It being only seven in the evening meant there might be an emergency. However, I wasn't even sure she knew we were coming back today. We hadn't been sure either.

What with jet lag, and a two week mission to a hotspot in the Middle East, all that I and Dave wanted to do was sleep to adjust to local time. It was also our first real skydiving entry. At least it was during the day. We'd been tethered to Bill, who also had a dart gun in case Dave started to panic. He hadn't, which was a blessing. It also meant we'd be doing more missions like this. Yippee.

I turned the light on in the bedroom as Dave reported Melissa was here. Moments before she sat bolt upright, eyes wide and... puffy. Like she'd been crying.

"Hi," she said, turning slightly away from us. She was still dressed.

I set the package I'd been carrying down on the dresser and went over to her side. Sat beside her and she leaned into a hug. "Just woke up after returning, love. Everything okay?" I was wide awake now.

"Long day yesterday and today. I didn't mean to go to sleep, but I wasn't told you'd be back today. How was the trip?"

"Long and I got sand in crevices I didn't know we had on the infiltration. Dave wasn't pleased." A faint scent. Blood. "Bad cramps, love?" It also meant that she wasn't pregnant. Again. A brief nod.

I knew from past months that she wouldn't talk about it. Talking about other things mostly helped. "There was a decent bazaar on the way to the airfield. Found a nice turquoise necklace. Might be antique. Never knew that that turquoise existed outside of the southwest before this. Apparently it was very popular out there for centuries. That's how it got the name, the dealer said. Turkey's Stone. Real popular over there. Weird, huh?" She perked up slightly.

"I didn't know that either," she said. I kissed her shoulder, as that was what I could easily reach and stood to fetch the package.

"There's also a necklace for Mom in here. The rest is for you." A wan smile. "It's also set in silver. A different style than the southwest pieces you already have."

At least the jewellery distracted her from her pain for a few minutes. Dave purred in my head, happy that Melissa was not crying now.

"Did you want to get supper?" she asked. "I was so tired I just came back here after I finished checking on my patients."

"Could eat. My body thinks it's mid-afternoonish, maybe because we had to take sleeping pills as the plane was about to land so we could be snuck in here on a cargo truck." The clock by the bed read eight pm. "There should be enough for us to snack on left in the buffet tables."

She had me put the necklace on her and I gave her a hug. I wasn't sure what else I could do to help her get pregnant.

Melissa was busy with her patients again the next morning. Snuggling last night was all I could do. Dave picked up on my feeling of sadness and purred at me, and hijacked my vocal cords so Melissa could hear him. Us.

Mom came into the cafeteria when I was having a snack after a light workout. *Wait. Maybe I can ask her for some advice, even if it embarrasses the hell out of us. I think Dad would be even more freaked out than Mom might be.*

"Hey, Mom." I waved and she came over once she'd gotten coffee. "We made it back last night. There's a present for you in the apartment. I can bring it by your place later."

"Melissa and I will need to get larger jewellery boxes if you keep bringing presents like this all the time," she said as she sat down. I shrugged.

"Not sure what else to get you. But. Mom. I need to talk to you. About Melissa. She's..." I couldn't say anything else.

"Missed again?" I nodded. "The downside to being with a shifter, dear. It's nearly two years now."

"More or less. I've seen her watching the little ones in the garden. Or in here. I don't know what else I can do."

"At three years, *in vivo* is a possibility," Mom said, blushing a little. "What have you done? Other than the obvious in timing."

I blushed. It was a good thing that there were only a few people here. "I took a book out of the library two months ago. A really basic biology one and I tried reading it to Dave. Showing him what has to happen for

Melissa to get pregnant."

Mom blinked. "Do you think that Dave could actually help?"

"I have no idea, Mom. Melissa was away that week on her rounds of the safe houses. I think he mostly understood the process. Eventually. He usually doesn't hang around while we're... Um. Last time, he sort of stayed nearby. He wants a kitten too. He enjoys playing with Jerry, Victor and Peter in fur. But he wants us to have a baby. Maybe so he can purr at the baby's beast so it wakes up faster. He purrs at the boys' beasts whenever they're around. I have no idea what he thinks the result's going to be. Might be interesting once they reach puberty to compare them to the kids he hasn't been purring at." *Was Mom trying to distract me?*

"I think you should tell Melissa about the book and Dave's reaction." She smiled. "At a minimum, letting her know that you both want the same thing that she does, should help her cope with her disappointment. It helped me, back in the day." She blushed.

"Okay. I'll see if it's still on the shelves. Let her walk in on us and see it. Hope for a giggle and not a flood of tears. Dave gets upset when she cries and wants to deal with the problem but doesn't know how. This might help motivate him to do something to help. If he can."

I had time that afternoon to find the book. Good. I checked the clock and Melissa should come home in about a half hour. Our general arrangement of eating a little later than usual meant most families with small kids were done and gone by the time we'd get there. One way she was coping with her sadness.

I was about halfway through the book, having gone through the female side of the process which wasn't anything we, really Dave, could change. Dave was paying attention again, which was good. The door opened and Melissa came in and smiled when she saw us sprawled on the couch with the book.

"What are you studying now? Going for a college degree? Or Portuguese?"

"A fair question. Karl does want me to learn other languages. But that's not why I have this one. It's for Dave, actually." I held it so she saw the cover. "Dave's upset that you're upset. I have no idea..."

"You're trying to teach a virtual cougar about human reproduction?" She started to laugh and I relaxed a little.

I put the book down and stood. "I have no idea if he can do anything help the wrigglers, but I figured it couldn't hurt to ask him to try the next time. Or until we hold a baby in our arms. Boy or girl, it doesn't matter to me, though Dave will probably prefer we have a boy."

"So, my not getting pregnant is all Dave's fault?"

"If that makes it easier for you, then yes. I vote we blame Dave for making us wait to bounce a baby."

Melissa managed to find a program in the compound's digital library that showed conception. Dave watched intently at the wrigglers' journey. The people all dressed in white pretending to be sperm confused him slightly but on the whole, he seemed to understand more of the process. We made it to supper about an hour later.

A month later she was less distraught at the advent of her period. That made the whole exercise a win in my books.

Three weeks after that, and a brief mission to rescue a kidnapped family in Mexico, Karl had a better mission for me. Or us. Melissa could come with me this time, but she'd been out of the compound when the team returned.

"There's a lone shifter in a park in northern Georgia," Karl said. "You get another first contact. Melissa gets to keep you company and check out all the shifters in safe houses once you're done with the mission and on your way back."

"Any clue what sort of shifter he is?"

"A big cat in partial so either lion or cougar. It might also be a hoax."

"But you don't think so. Why?"

"He's too near the trails, for one thing. The pictures on Twitter suck for resolution. He's been there maybe two weeks or so. That's when the first sighting happened, at any rate. Four encounters in total. But why he's been seen shifted so often is a worry."

"He must not be very good at detecting the hikers," Melissa said. "But using a full partial makes no real sense. Just hands and feet would give him speed and hunting would be easier."

"He'd certainly be less noticeable with just the paws," I said, then turned to Melissa. "Wanna go for a long drive with me?"

She had dimples, which made both of us happy.

"There's a pull out up ahead," she said a few days later. "Shall we have a picnic, then a short hike to stretch our legs? See if Dave can find any hints? We're well within the shifter's range, based on the sightings."

"Good plan. We're not getting anything just driving with the windows open. Any shifter would tend to stay away from the main roads except for short crossings unless they were trying to get to a new range. At least, that's what I did. If he was spotted in shift near a main road I'd be sure it's a hoax. Or a trap."

"How's Dave doing?"

"He'd like to go for a run pretty soon."

"He didn't get to do much on your last trip?"

"Couldn't do a full shift," I said. "There were too many people around who weren't part of the teams. We had a bunch of local guides and we needed the advantage in that terrain. But he liked rescuing the hostages. There were two kids in with the adults. We carried one out and down the mountain. A little girl. He was purring the whole way."

"It's still odd, how much Dave likes kids."

"I don't really understand it either. Karl also asked us to shift and play with a group of the little boys, then have a session in the gym with all the teens playing with soccer balls. Jerry, Victor, and Pete came too. You weren't back yet."

Melissa, as one of the few trained vets we had in our area, travelled to help deal with injured men in full partial shift in smaller compounds or the safe houses. The medics had found over the years that just shifting back to the human form sometimes made an injury worse, so after missions or training accidents, she'd be brought in to help the regular doctors. If the man's beast could understand that it could shift to the original, undamaged form, the injury generally healed completely. That meant both man and beast had to be free of pain and drugs, which always made the injury worse. They'd started using hypnosis a year or so back to help block the pain and help the person communicate with their beast. She'd found that it helped a lot.

She glanced at me and smiled. "He had a great time, I'd guess."

"Lots of purring. Ten little boys for an hour. Getting his tail pulled rated a quick snarl, but the kids have to learn what's allowable and what isn't. The teens were a lot better now. More of them managed greater changes since the last time we played. And they're trying to use their beasts' senses more. Sam is really motivated. He's really hoping that he'll get to fully shift soon. I don't know if he will, but they're very good with the identity game now. Just over ninety percent. And they're able to identify a lot of people by name, even if they're not shifters."

We pulled into the picnic area and parked close to a table. I got out and stretched. Brought Dave's senses on line. A faint scent near the waste bins. A big cat had been here. So Lion or Cougar. Searching the trash for edibles or useful stuff, I guessed. Not really recent. And no recent people scents. This place wasn't very popular. Maybe it was too far from a town, or not convenient for a lunch stop if you were passing by.

"He was here," I said. "About two weeks or more, Dave thinks. Not many people have been through here since which is why the scent's still sniffable. Might be why he hasn't bothered to come back here. Better use of his time to go where the bins fill up fast. More chance of edibles and semi-okay camp gear to make his life a bit easier."

"Okay. Let's have a quick snack then go for a walk. See if there's any more recent traces away from here. Then head further along the road. Shall we stop at each parking area for a quick check?"

"Sure." I wasn't sure, though. "Checking the trash bins a lot for supplies means he might not be that good at hunting or doesn't have a lot of gear to make a comfortable camp. I did that a lot when I was hiding up in the hills when we first left the city. Since I looked younger than my real age I didn't want to risk being seen by anyone. Didn't want any purchases or get spotted on store security cameras to be traced back to me so that I stayed safer. I was hiding from the police and the hunters so I was very careful about exposing myself. Still, that tactic doesn't do much good now, since there are so many cameras out there that either side can tap into." She opened the trunk and I brought out the cooler.

There weren't any other recent traces of the shifter as we went south. Too many human hikers had been through the trails on the weekends. With no one but us around Dave did have a little fur time but the afternoon sun was soon sliding behind the mountains and Melissa wasn't dressed for spending the night out here, even with both coats and our fur to keep her warm. Dave was now as concerned as I was about the possible shifter. All of us settling down in the car wasn't optimal either.

"Let's find the nearest safe house," I said when we returned to the latest parking area. "I want an update on the sightings." It had taken us three days of travel to get here. With no contact with any of our bases. It seemed odd at first, then I'd started to relax. We didn't go to any casinos, but did have a nice time at the motels. Upscale ones, not the cheap ones as I'd mostly used before. Shifters on the run wouldn't use anywhere expensive and I didn't want to be distracted if we ran into any shifters trying to stay out of sight. Melissa might object if I just gave them the Coalition's 'ohshit' number and let them continue on their way. Then again, having the government guys alerted to where we were would also be a bummer. Better to stay as dark as we could.

"All right." Melissa started to pull out her phone. I still resisted carrying one of the dratted things. Except on missions. Then I wanted all the comm gear the team normally carried. Even in fur, we had a GPS and a radio on a harness or collar so we were never completely out of touch.

"We probably don't have a signal here. We're too low and the mountains will block it. I didn't see any towers up on the ridges."

She sighed at the lack of bars, then pulled out the map and found our location. "There's a major road up ahead. And a motel, from the symbol. They should have a connection, even if it's just a land line."

We had an early supper at their restaurant and Melissa called in. The nearest safe house was only an hour up another decent road, so we just headed there instead of staying at the motel. More security and fewer people to take an interest in us.

"The most recent report was from a sighting by a hiker a few days ago," Johann, the shifter at the safe house said. His wife Kelly was making a snack for us while she listened in. "A partial shift at most. No picture in the report, but from the bits of description I think the guy is lion, not a cougar like you and most of the shifters out in the world."

"That's odd," Kelly said. "There are fewer of them out in the wild because of the pride mentality. Dads tend to stick around and defend their partners and cubs so they have protection."

"Still, it has happened, no matter what kind of beast it is," Johann said. He'd be a big wolf if he managed to shift all the way. "Low fertility is an issue for all types of shifters or maybe the dad was killed, maybe in a gang conflict or well, something truly accidental like a car crash."

"Hard to tell at this point," Melissa said, her hands wrapped around a cup of hot chocolate. I put a hand on hers and got a little smile. We'd keep trying.

"Dave and I have a weird vibe going on," I said slowly. Hot drinks still weren't my thing, so I had a home-made root beer. "No idea why. But I, we, think Melissa should stay with you guys for now. We'll take my pack and a burner phone with no numbers in it and pretend I'm searching for a new range. See if I can find him and talk him into coming in."

"You should say you can't shift all the way so if he is a plant, he won't know it's you." Johann said. I nodded. "Still, it might be better to wait to get a team in to help contain him if he bolts. There's a lot of forest out there, Ethan. It wouldn't take long for them to arrive: a day or three."

"Should be okay. More scents around might spook him. I'll text in each night to let you know our progress. Once we get a recent scent, then you can let Karl know and he can decide if we need backup. The guy doesn't seem to be able to fully shift, which is good. Might not understand tracking either so he'll be easier to hunt if we need to chase him."

There were a few more who could shift all the way now. Sam, to his great delight, was one of them as of four days ago. Three others were wolves and two of the lions, one of them Rìnmáyọ̀ from Africa. Not Karl, even though his beast is a dominant. I wasn't sure how good a relationship and bond they had or if he was trying very hard at making their connection better. Maybe he didn't want the adjustments that came with a better bond. Since he rarely went out on missions, maybe the ability and connection with his lion didn't really matter to him.

None of the science types understood why we could and others couldn't. Neither did any of the shifters. There weren't any physical differences that that anyone could find. The only constant was that we'd

made better contact with our beasts over the years. The beasts were occasionally erratic in their response to orders but on a mission, they could
mostly tell the good guys from the bad ones thanks to the 'identify the
shifter game, which was a great help.

Sam was now off his team while he and his beast George had more
training on the new parameters of their relationship. Turned out that
George also liked playing with soccer balls, since his first full shift
happened as he and the others we usually played with in the gym were
getting ready to play. Sam asked him to shift, expecting the partial, but
got full instead. The tail came in that first time.

"That sounds like a plan," Melissa said.

"What about activating a tracker?" Johann asked. "You should also
take a sat phone for real reports without worrying about getting a cell
signal. That coverage is very spotty out here. The cell companies don't
want to spend the money since there aren't many folk living away from
the towns. The freeways have towers near them but not the older routes.
It'll give me your location when you report in. Daily is better to ensure
we know where you are. That makes it easier to know where you are if
there's a problem and you need help. I can also pop some signal repeat-
ers along the highway either side of your locations so we have an altern-
ate way to be sure where you are between sat calls."

"One of the temp trackers only lasts three maybe four days in the
gut," Kelly said. "What about using your implant? It has a longer range
than a temp one does. We can activate and program it from here. The
program's on our computer."

"They are easier to hide from a physical search," Melissa said. "And it
can be programmed to turn on and off on a regular cycle." They all
looked at me and I felt my stomach cramp.

"What? Did they install one in me already?" I tried to brush it off
but... I'd been unconscious too many times in those first days I'd been in
the Coalition's cells to be sure nothing had been done to me. Dave
growled, but all he understood was that I wasn't happy at the moment. I
didn't want to try explaining anything really complex to him right now,
so I thought about rubbing his ears and that calmed him down. For now,
anyway. I might try explaining more once we were out in the woods.

Melissa sighed. "They did, Ethan. The first base you were taken to.
You might not have been awake from the darts before they put it in."

"Didn't the battery run down already?" She still didn't look happy.
"Weird shit?" My term for the odd bits of gear we were sometimes issued
for an operation. Their power sources were strange and lasted far longer
than anything I'd heard of before. No one was allowed to 'forget' to turn
one in and one new guy had to search back along his path through heavy

undergrowth in a European forest to find the one that fell off his belt. He searched for hours with no luck. Eventually the rest of us were drafted to help. We eventually found it half-way down a steep gully. We had to rig ropes so the guy could reach it safely. Our ride home was delayed by three days. Two of them to find the damned thing and the third to get to the revised rendezvous point for our bus ride to an isolated airfield.

"Weird shit, love. No one mentioned it to you when you returned?"

"No. Neither did my parents. But you knew?"

"And I thought that you already did," she said. "It was in your medical file. I had about an hour to review it before that first weight experiment where we met."

"They thought that keeping me from knowing they could always find me no matter where I went was better?" Dave grumbled inside me. "Trust goes two ways. If they'd admitted it once I came back with Victor that would have been okay. Now... Not so much, love."

"Those transmitters aren't that powerful, Ethan," Johann said. "Three to five kilometres or so, and they absolutely depend on line of sight. If you're behind a hill our systems won't detect the signal. They are programmable. It can be adjusted to shut down for a specific amount of time, then come on line if bad shit goes down. They can't broadcast all the time. Not enough power storage and they're slow to recharge."

"We can get it shut down completely if you want." Melissa's smile was sad. "Or I can remove it for you without telling anyone. It's a fairly simple procedure. Just needs a small dressing to keep it clean."

"When I'm out in the world on an operation, it makes sense to have a tracker like that. I actually worried on that first mission, bogus as it was, about being separated from Tim and the others. They gave me a number and I've given it to several shifters out in the world since then. I had no idea at the time where the compound was or if the number was bogus. If shit went down, well, I'd be on my own again. Having just found my parents and Sam after so long, I didn't want to leave."

"But you did, nearly right after you came back. Why?" Dave noticed that Johann and Kelly had left us alone. I didn't care. I didn't want to fight with Melissa but I had to make her understand why I, we, were upset about this. And other things.

"Because that first trip was nothing but a set up," I said. "To see if I'd try to run away. And then they drugged me and asked a lot more questions about how I survived and what I'd done with Dave before they tracked me down and brought me in. I still don't know what I said." I took a deep breath to calm Dave. Mostly. "Did you see that file too?"

"No. I just know what you've told me about your past, Ethan. The only official file that I've seen is your medical exams and the various metabolic test results. Nothing in there mentioned how your shoulder was originally damaged, just that it was. You told me it happened because of the team forcing you to shift back to human so they could question you, then more damage happened when you were shot. I thought it was amazing that you could shift completely when I first met you. My grandfathers didn't believe that it was possible when word first spread. They're wondering why it hasn't happened before. Or if there is a particular reason that it stopped."

I, we, took another deep breath. "We're sorry, Lissa. Nothing about the tracker is your fault. But I was so afraid of being found by the bad guys ever since my family vanished. As far as I knew back then, the people chasing me that last time and all the other times I'd run from them had killed my parents and Sam when they blew up the house. I didn't know what they'd do to me. Especially if they knew I could fully shift. I only admitted what I did when I was with my family. I didn't mention all the bad stuff to them. Sometimes I... wanted to die. To forget all the pain. I was so lonely for so many years. No friends, no family. Just me and Dave, but he wasn't like he is now. He didn't want to die. I wasn't sure if ending our lives might be better than continuing to be alone. So he... balanced me. Protected me, even from myself."

I saw that she was crying. "I don't have to continue here," I said. "We can just leave or call in a team to try to find this lion once I figure out where he's based. We can go back to the compound. You can check out the shifters on the way. Forget about the tracker. Just be us."

"All three of us," she said with a little smile.

"Soon to be four. Or more." I took her hand. Dave nudged me closer. He seemed intent and focused but I wasn't sure what held his interest. Then Melissa made sure I was only thinking about her and we headed for our bedroom.

Chapter 28

The next afternoon we had a plan, sort of. Karl and the other mission planners weren't really happy about it but finally agreed. Two days after that I was on my own. Almost. I had a small sat phone, along with an altered burner phone deep in my pack. I could provide covert updates with the sat phone. Text messages didn't take long and Johann swore there weren't any government hunters around.

Most of the second day involved getting Lissa's scent off me, my clothes and the stuff in my pack. I didn't want to chance any possibly enemy shifter getting a hint about her. Then I hitched a ride to the southern end of the park and moved up into the hills. Once a day, usually late in the evening just before we camped, I sent off my message. The sat phone gave them my position, so I didn't have to bother figuring it out. I could generally tell where I was by comparing a topographic map to what I saw around me. Calculating my position didn't work as well. I'd added instead of subtracting a few times in training, which could send any rescue party in the wrong direction. That would be unfortunate.

There were now receivers that could pick up my, or any tagged shifter's tracker at every campground, trail head or picnic spot in the area. Plus cameras. That might be how Neil really found me. He'd probably warned by Karl not to mention the tracker. Their ace in the hole to locate me wherever I went. That might have been why he'd been so nervous and afraid when he was alone with us in the four-by. Dave growled softly. Maybe when we went back the next time we went camping there, I'd mention it. If he and Carol were still in residence. Their station might have been shut down now and they'd been reassigned to another spot. Still, we might meet up again.

I struck a recent trail on my fifth day in the hills. Five or six days old, tops. The guy had absolutely no woodcraft because he'd walked straight through a muddy area and left bootprints. And marks where he'd slipped and fallen. He could have gone a few steps to either side of the trail and stayed dry and clean instead of slogging into the mud. Was he really that inept or was he trying to leave these traces to attract a shifter like me?

Or. Was he just a young, clueless city boy trying to survive out here? I knew it could be done, but I'd also had plenty of money to buy supplies and a couple of years to prepare. I'd learned what plants I could eat in the wilds and the types and habits of various critters we could eat or should avoid. If I'd headed out to the forest at fourteen, right after the first time my hand shifted to a paw, would we have survived? Would Dave have been able to shift fully to keep us fed? Hard to know right now. Dave was still mostly a 'what's going on this moment' partner. Searching for details from half a lifetime ago wasn't really possible. I might never be able to discover the truth and I wasn't sure it would matter anyway.

If Melissa and I did have children, they'd know from the start what was possible, so they might be able to do the full shift right away. And maybe we'd go to Gígalolúwa, the shaman we'd met in Africa so they could be initiated, or I could look for an equivalent expert here who had the knowledge needed. More research, but not something we might ever find in the Coalition's library. Maybe Melissa's grandfathers might know of someone since they'd spent years out on missions, plus tours in the military, she'd said.

This guy might be like Ron, a young shifter we'd brought in who'd been trying to survive on rabbits and the park waste bins where he was hiding out. From what his sister said when we took him home for a short stay, he'd lost five or six kilos in three weeks. If he hadn't changed his diet, he might not have survived for very long. I'd gotten a letter from him a month or so back. He was doing well, but in his school work and bonding with his wolf. His sister wanted him to come home for a long visit next summer. His three nieces would be really happy to see him. He might have to put the lock back on the inside of his bedroom door in case there were early morning visitors wanting to play.

I left a message with the news and my thoughts, then stared at the sat phone. I might run into the shifter tomorrow. Or the next day. Or maybe next week, though if I didn't find a fresher trail in three days I'd move from here and go further north. The shifter might have left the area entirely by now, since there hadn't been any more sightings. There weren't many deer sign, which meant only small critters were available. More effort than maybe he wanted or knew how to catch. Or. Still too many possibilities. He might have moved over the ridge and away from the road to look for critters without being seen by hikers.

I decided to keep both phones with me for now. The shifter couldn't be very young, I decided. Early in puberty paws and claws were the maximum anyone knew about. Even me. But *my* hand shifted into a proper cougar's paw, not the partial one that everyone else managed. Most never had much more unless they really worked at it. And by a clear boot print in the mud, the guy had to be taller and heavier than I was. So late teens, maybe early to mid-twenties. What had driven him out here? Was another group hunting him? Well, I might find out. Sooner or later.

If Monster had been able to fully shift when I was fourteen, my foster father would have died no matter what I wanted Monster to do. And probably his arsehole sons as well. I didn't have any real control in those early years when Monster was angry. Nothing would have happened to his wife, I thought. She'd tried to do good by the foster kids but Gordie had beaten most of the fight out of her long before I'd ever known her. I hoped that she was happier without him.

Dave kept sentry most of the night. Nothing happened, which was okay. I'd forgotten how tense life out alone in the world was but the memories were coming back quickly.

The next time I crossed the shifter's trail I stopped and retreated a kilometre or more. This scent was the freshest we'd found: he'd been along here at most a day ago. Took out the sat phone and turned it on. At least this one had a decently sized keyboard.

Very fresh trail. 1 day max. Burying phone this location. Will come back here if we don't make contact today. If we don't report back in two days, the meet-up went badly wrong. Bring the teams in and grab the shifter any way you have to. Love to Lissa. Then I shut the phone down and looked around.

The place I picked was mossy and under trees. It was a sensible place to spend the night, so I pretended that I'd made camp there and unpacked my gear so it would be obvious and spread my scent around if the shifter came back this way before we found him. Then I put the sat phone in a Ziploc plastic bag to protect it from the damp, buried it under a plug of moss and repacked my gear. Then we headed along the shifter's trail.

I'd changed into a clean shirt as I'd packed and saw the tattoo on my chest. The paw, representing my bond with Dave. A suspicion niggled at the back of my mind. Was it wise to show this to anyone I didn't already trust?

A hint of a growl from Dave. That decided that.

"Dave, I want you to hide our tattoo. Just for now. I don't feel right about it being seen." Dave seemed to sulk, then my skin rippled and the tattoo vanished, only to reappear a moment later. It seemed the same. It vanished again. "Thank you." I thought about rubbing his ears. "Once we're heading back to base, bring it back. Okay?" A quick purr.

We found the shifter less than a day later, trying to whack-a-marmot. They are sneaky critters, but good eating. He spotted us waiting at the tree line. He'd been watching a hole and had a stout branch ready to play whack a marmot to stun it. That tactic might work for gophers, but they were too small to waste the time on hunting them unless you had a rifle or there was absolutely nothing else to eat. Trapping small critters like gophers could work with a net over the burrow entrances so that a bunch of them would get tangled up and easier to kill. But then you had to have enough fibre or vines to make a net and know how to do it.

"They don't tend to come out near noon," I said so he could hear me. I took a couple of steps into the sunlight so he could see us better.

"What?" He looked confused by my comment.

"Marmots. Well, around here they're called groundhogs. Regional variations." I looked up and down the slope above a nice meadow. Might be some wild carrots growing in there. "Good place for their summer burrows. Plenty of food around for them. But you won't hit one like that. You have to wait until they come out to feed and they're too far from the burrow to get back in time. Takes patience but they are good eating. Generally do a stew if I have a big enough pot to hand."

"Who -- who are you?" He stood, shifting the stick so it was more like a quarterstaff. I'd learned a lot more about fighting in the past two years. I liked the staff. Gave me lots of options to keep the fight from getting too close. I was still on the short and wiry side, unlike many of the wolves. And the lions. All of them were bigger and heavier than me, so I had to use tactics instead of brawn. Dave wasn't able to make us taller, which was somewhat annoying, but my balance might be messed up if I suddenly got taller, so I'd stopped suggesting that sort of change.

Same thing out on operations. Most guards we were up against were big men, used to hand-to-hand fighting and brawling. However, any guards in my way were generally shocked at my appearance in fur or the partial shift so their size meant nothing. They died quickly and mostly silently. Broken necks to cut down on the cleanup effort but a sliced aorta or carotid if that was necessary.

"Name's Ethan," I said. Silence. A chitter from high in a tree not far away. Chipmunk by the scent. Another critter to small to bother with unless you had a trap and nothing else around that was vaguely edible.

"It's neighbourly to give your name when you've heard someone else's," I said mildly. He still didn't respond. "Well, I'll be on my way then. Seems like you don't want any company. Don't worry about it. I've been in that head space before. A lot. Be well, dude."

When I'd first met Marshall in Banff Park, I'd been about as worried as the shifter seemed to be. My record for bringing in lone shifters without needing a huge team to corral and trank them was the main reason I was here. Even if Karl was nervous each time I went into a situation without a backup team right behind me. I wondered if Johann had asked for a team to come in as soon as I'd left the safe house, just in case.

I made it back into the tree line before the dude called out.

"Sorry, Ethan. I'm Phillip. Phil."

I turned back around and smiled without showing teeth. I didn't want to spook his beast. Which Dave thought was a lion, despite him being nearly as Anglo looking as me. He was also younger than I'd thought. Maybe late teens but not much older. Compared to my nearly thirty, he was still a cub. Dave didn't agree with me. He was old enough to shift into full partial according to the reports and Dave didn't trust him. I thought about rubbing his ears and he calmed a little but he'd keep Phil under close observation. I didn't mind that idea a bit.

"Back to the land living?" I asked as I walked toward him.

He flushed. "No." Then he startled and sniffed. Shocked. "You're..."

"Like you. Different critter, though." I wasn't going to reveal much, not until I knew more about him. I would normally show a paw at this point, but Dave's assessment stopped me. There was a major problem. I was certainly not going to talk about the Coalition until I had a better sense of this guy and his beast. I had a sudden sense of sympathy for Karl and the lack of communication I'd hated. The shoe was on the other paw now. Still, the current plan was a better way to reassure a worried shifter. I'd just pretend to be another wanderer for now.

"I'd never felt anyone like you before." He looked suspicious. "Why are you here? Did anyone send you after me?"

"No. Caught your scent at a rest stop south of here. I was on my way north from Florida. I'd hitched a ride and they were heading down south at the intersection. Stayed in the bush near there that night. There's not many of us out in the wild. The hunters see to that. Just wanted to chat. Run into others every so often out in the hills. Usually we stay together for a day or three. Compare notes on good ranges, where we've seen hunters, that sort of thing. Then we split up. Safer for all concerned."

"Hunters? Who are they? I haven't seen anyone but a few campers around here. Might have been some before. How do you tell it's them?" *The kid was too clueless to have grown up out in the world.* Dave growled.

"Dunno who they are. Never risked trying to grab one and ask. They usually travel in groups of five or six. Came close to me a bunch of times, but... I always spend way more time out in the wild than in towns and such. I swap ranges every couple of years, or whenever I spot guys in suits in the nearby campgrounds. Looking for a new one now, but since you're here I'll head further north. Just wanted a chat, see who was here." *Who or what had chased him out of wherever he'd been living if he had no idea who was hunting us? Another reason not to trust him now.*

"It doesn't end well, having two of us so close unless there's a lot of game in the area and from what I've seen, there isn't much around here. We both need to hunt the same sort of critters and the deer hunters in the fall might run into us. Pretending to be a homeless dude squatting in the forest usually works, but rangers might make you move out if you're in a park. I always have a couple of places set up, so I just move my gear to one of the others once they're out of sight. Move back to the better one a few weeks later."

Phil's grip on the stick loosened slightly. He was still wary, but so was I. Dave was on alert. We still didn't have a good sense of his beast. I doubted he'd done much with it before coming out here. That made a full partial even more unlikely. What had happened to make him do so? I might get him to talk in a day, maybe three. For now, I'd just let him calm down and not mention I wanted him to come with me.

We followed him up slope and into tree cover to a decent sized lean-to, branches tied together with baling twine that had seen better days. We'd passed a number of hay fields before the hills started so he must have brought it up with him. Or he'd gone back to find a bunch when he decided to stay here. He had a fire pit of neatly piled rocks with an improvised cooking grate of angle iron pieces just inside the structure. Enough pine branches were piled on the roof to keep most of the rain off.

A pack more than twice the size of my current one lay beside a pile of pine branches with a sleeping bag on it. A set of nesting pots and a tin plate sat on a stump serving as a table. A hatchet. Decent set up. Way more gear than I thought he might have, given his current ragged appearance. Maybe he'd brought stuff rather than food when he left wherever he'd been living. Assumed that food would be easier to find than camping gear. Mostly true, but not, it seemed, around here.

"Did you find any caves around here?" I asked. "They're nicer in winter than a hut like this. Hard to keep cold drafts out with just branches. I use old tarps for a summer shelter if I'm near a campground. People throw a lot of mostly good stuff away when they head out. I can dump what I've used back into the waste bins when I'm ready to leave the area. Don't want to be humping a lot of gear that's easily replaced. I only look for stuff like tarps and such once I've settled on a new range. A lot of stuff just slows you down or limits who might pick you up for a ride. Works pretty well. Dried food's lighter than canned and pop bottles work for water if you can't find a used cube that's doesn't leak."

"Thanks for the advice. I did find a cave, but it's too high to go hunting down here every couple of days and there's nothing big to hunt up there. Too much bare rock for anything decently sized. I'm taking wood up there to store for winter." He looked around. "I'm down to my last can of stew. That's why I was over there, hunting. Need more cash to go shopping. You have anything?" A hopeful look.

"Couple cans of stew to eat cold if I can't make a fire, but mostly dry pasta mixes, dried beans, and rice since they weigh less and pack better. Best bet for cash with nothing to start with is collecting bottles and humping them to the nearest depot. Harder out here than in the nearest town, but fewer people around is a good idea to keep people seeing you at a minimum. After the weekend you could go scrounging in the picnic areas or nearby campground for the recycling. If there's a big enough town within walking distance, that is."

"That's what I've been doing each weekend. There hasn't been much that's edible. I hadn't thought about the bottles and cans. There's times I see a lot of them if there's been a big holiday."

"They don't have programs in a lot of states, including this one, so that's a hit or miss way to get cash. Some states, like here, just take metal cans for a pittance. Sometimes I panhandle but there's usually homeless guys who have the best places staked out already. I mostly try hitting casinos to raise money for travel. Another thing this state doesn't allow. My best advice for you right now is to try to find a farmer who needs help picking veggies for the next few weeks, frankly. It's hard work but safer than a city. They pay pretty well if you stay away from booze and drugs. Once the season is over, find a friendlier state or a place with a lot more game. You can also just follow the pickers. Keeps you fed and out of sight of the hunters. Your beast shouldn't mind."

He just stared at me. Like I wasn't what he expected. Had he ever met another shifter? The sense of wrongness grew. I'd stay the night and leave first thing tomorrow. Come back with Johann and whoever else Karl could get down here. Grab the sat phone and call in so help would be on the way a lot faster. I faked a smile.

"Still, you're here and so am I. Can help you out a bit on local food sources to give you something to eat on a regular basis. Are there any boggy places around? I saw a few back the way I came, but not many."

"Down nearer the road there's a good sized pond that doesn't drain well. Can't drink it but it's okay to clean off and it's warmish thanks to the sun in the afternoon. Why do you ask?"

"Cattails. There's different kinds but they grow all over. Bit of pain at times to prepare, but they're good eating to balance out your diet when you're living away from grocery stores. Not that great as your only source of food, but they'll keep you going in a pinch." I slipped my pack to the ground just inside the lean-to. "You ever try them?"

Phil shook his head. "I was... in a hurry to leave. We'd gone camping a couple of times, that's the only reason I had this gear handy. The stew and other food was in the cupboard, so I took enough to fill out the pack. Then I... ran."

"Foster system?"

A frightened stare, then he nodded. Hadn't they given him a back story to memorize? If he was a plant, he needed to lull a shifter into stay-ing here until he could signal the others. Or had my guess come close to things he didn't want to remember? Hard to tell right now.

"Me too. My mom vanished one day while I was at school, leaving me behind. Never understood why. I was eight. Hated that last bastard I had to deal with. But I had a year before I left for real." *Would he believe that story? It mostly made sense. Other shifters, mostly the older ones, had been abandoned that way. Easier to start a new life with the minimal documents needed back then.*

"I read up on edible plants and other survival books from the library before I came out to the wilds. You need to get your butt into a town, clean up and hit the library or a used book store. There's lots to eat out here, especially during the summer and fall, but some shit is poison, so you need to know what you're eating. Mushrooms can be the worst, but there's lots of berries that look tasty but will kill you or just make you wish you were dead. We can't go to hospitals like normal folk, even if you have a pile of money to pay for the treatment. Hunters keep watch on places like that, I've heard."

"Thanks," Phil said but he couldn't meet my eyes. Dave growled deep inside me. I had the sense that Phil's beast was frightened. Then Dave couldn't sense him. Phil had to be the bait in an elaborate trap. A more sophisticated one than Victor had been. What reward was he getting for betraying other shifters? How many others like him were out in the woods, waiting for another shifter to come by?

Whoever was behind this couldn't have a lot of shifters this old. So swapping Phil around each summer, or even every month or so, might find others. Like me. But why did *these* guys want us? Would Victor or Jerry have been like Phillip in a few years if we hadn't rescued them? Or was Phil working for a different government agency or black ops group who wanted their own shifters? Too many questions. Sitting Phil down and getting answers was a good plan. Nicely at first. Drugs if he didn't cooperate with the program.

We found a decent patch of cattails not far down slope before we reached the bigger pond. The green tops were a distant memory and the pollen wasn't ready yet, which meant we were after the roots and the lower stalks. I stripped down to my briefs and Phil did as well. He was pasty white, which to me meant he really hadn't been out here for very long. Maybe this was their first stake-out. He should at least have tanned arms and face if he'd been out here more than a few weeks.

Where were the other members of his team? The pack couldn't have held that many cans of stew with the other stuff he had. Dave growled a little. I wondered if the cave was a lie or if the rest of the group was further up or maybe just across the ridge. He hadn't scented anyone else at the camp, but it might have faded after a few weeks. Plus the wood smoke and food smells from his cook fire would have helped overpower any older scents.

"The roots and the lower stem are full of starch," I said with a no-teeth smile. "Great energy source and you can store the dried stalks and roots in your cave for the winter. You'll still have to cook them when you want to eat, but that's life out in the bush and you'll need a fire for heat and drinking water unless you can shift a lot and or have fur all over. One important thing you need to remember about cattails: there's so much fibre in the roots that your gut can't handle it if you just chop them into a stew. Beyond constipated. But if you've got the trots from bad water or meat that's going bad, a bit will help take care of that problem. The lower stem is okay to just cook up and put into whatever you're making."

"So why are we taking the whole plant?"

"Because there is a way to prepare the roots that bypasses the fibre problem." I waded in and used my toes to loosen my chosen root, then pulled the plant up and rinsed off the mud. "Some fibre is good. And the leaves are useful: you can tear or cut them into narrow strips, then braid or twist them together to get cord if you can't find baling twine. Earlier in the spring, while the flower part is still green, you can cook them up in a little water or roast them with some fat if you have it. Small town grocery stores carry lard and shortening in the baking section and they don't need a refrigerator. The upper stalk's still good to chew on now, or chop into a stew. Leave the little roots on, those we can toss in the stew as is. The dead stalks are really good for tinder if your fire goes out. The pollen is good in stews or to make a sort of fry bread if you have some flour to help hold it together, but it'll be another few weeks before it's usable. You can also let the root starch dry out and use it like flour in fry bread or store it up to use for winter stews and such. Pull decent containers out of the waste bins to store the flour in so it doesn't get damp and rot. Plastic, not glass so you don't have to worry about the jar breaking. Had that happen once. Lost about half the starch. Bummer."

"Sounds like an all around good plant." I nodded and pulled up another root. Phil waded in gingerly.

After a couple of tries, Phil figured out the knack of pulling the roots. When we had a dozen or so plants, I got out of the water. It had only been knee deep, but warmish thanks to the summer sun. Another good place to wash out clothing and have a semi decent bath in warm water you didn't have to heat up first. The winter in Florida had been warm enough that we hadn't been very cold, and this wasn't much further north, so anyone living rough here might not need a lot of prep to stay warm and dry without a cave.

We left the cleaned and roughly chopped roots simmering at the lean-to and headed back to the marmots' slope. Two decent sized ones were far enough down-slope that we might be able to nab them. The other five were closer to safety. *Later*, Dave thought. He liked marmot stew.

"We should try to catch both of them," I said softly. "If one gets away, there's still another chance. You take the one further downhill. Okay?" *That would give him a better chance of success.*

Phil nodded. "You don't have a knife, do you?" He held one easily.

I smiled. "I do, but I don't need one right now." I changed the thumb and forefinger on my right hand into claws. At his gasp, I shrugged. "I don't have to worry about dropping a knife if I have the claws. And you don't need much to be considered a monster." *That would give him the idea that I wasn't couldn't shift much. Maybe. What could he actually change? Was the full partial a ruse? Had he been the one to report himself or had his backup done so?* I took a deep breath to calm both of us down. Dave growled softly anyway.

Maybe Phil was just more comfortable with a knife at the moment. Especially since he didn't know us.

Two hours later we dined on cattail and marmot stew. I'd caught mine, Phil had almost caught the other. Enough stew was left over for breakfast and probably another dinner for Phil. I planned to leave and come back with Johann and other muscle as soon as possible. All right, maybe a dart gun. There was something definitely hinky about this guy, even if he wasn't bait in a trap. Dave agreed with the plan.

"I'll head out tomorrow," I said as Phil banked the fire. I'd set out my sleeping bag in the other clear spot in the lean-to. "This range can't support two big predators like us for long. Those marmots aren't going to last long if they're the only decent sized critters around here to eat."

"I've seen a few deer off to the west," Phil said. "They don't come over the ridge very often, maybe because of the road noise. And I've been leery of the antlers. Don't want to get gored."

I yawned as we snuggled into the bag. "Spears work well to slow them down. I can show you how to make one before I head out. Just go for the young bucks. The older ones are smarter. Leave the does unless they're old or injured." I yawned again. Dave was worried. Shit. Phil had drugged the stew somehow. When I'd been setting up my bag? Or was it the water we'd drunk? But why wasn't he....

I sort of heard another voice, then I was lifted up, still lying flat. Dave wasn't with me. I tried to move but couldn't.

"Keep his food and money but burn the rest," the voice growled. Not a beast, just angry. "We'll know if anyone else shows up looking for him. Understand me, sinner?"

Phil's voice was near my feet. Shaky with fear. "Of course. I obey God's will. The Preacher taught me well, sir."

"You didn't shift, sinner?"

"No, sir. He did. Just two claws to hunt with. His right hand. Thumb and forefinger. He did no other shifts that I witnessed. I only used the suit to attract notice to lure such as he is as I was told to do."

Then the world went dark and the wind and a roaring noise surrounded me.

Chapter 29

Dave purred. The kittens barely came higher than Ethan's knees. But playing with them was good. Ethan took off his clothes before the kittens entered and used a towel around his waist to hide his groin.

Dave wasn't sure why clothes or coverings were always necessary. Maybe they were cold without enough fur to cover them. It always gave Ethan fur when he was cold, even if the coverings were on.

"Watch me change, kids," Ethan said. "It'll be fast so don't blink." He was sitting on a low chair the same as the kittens were. Dave moved past him and rolled its shoulders now that it was in fur. The kittens made happy sounds, not afraid of it any more. Good. They all had tiny beasts in them. Ones that slept and grew. When they were grown, their beasts would wake and help them have fur. They would play together soon.

Ethan watched the kittens to be sure Dave understood what they said.

"Petting time," said a female. She did not smell good, but they had their own mate now so he didn't care.

The kittens came over slowly and soon were rubbing its ears and under the chin. It started to purr and that brought joy to them. One picked up its tail and Dave twitched it out of his grasp with a quick yowl of displeasure. That kitten looked sorry, so Dave bunted him a little.

"Look at his paws, boys. Aren't they big?"

The female coughed to get the kittens' attention after a buzzer sounded. Once they were all seated. Ethan suggested that they shift back. Dave sighed. Its time in fur was always short in this big cave.

The towel was near Ethan's knees and he pulled it around their front before sitting up.

"Say thank you to Ethan, boys," the female said.

"And to Dave," Ethan said before the kittens could speak. He didn't like that female either.

A happy chorus of noise echoed in the room. "Dave likes playing with you guys," Ethan said, then turned to the tail-puller. "But don't touch his tail again unless you ask first. Okay?" The kitten nodded.

Their mate returned two sleeps later. Good. Ethan liked to sleep with her. Ethan and their mate were sad and wondered why there was no kitten yet. Dave wasn't sure either. He tried to be present when they mated the next time instead of leaving them alone. Pictured a kitten with a little beast inside. One who could play in fur with it. It wasn't sure the mating worked. It would try again, the next time. To be sure.

An older cub might be in trouble. They would go with their mate to find him. It was good to help the ones like the old one had. Ethan still had sad times when he thought about the old one. But they had their mate now. That made Ethan not sad. Soon there would be a kitten of their own. It was very, very small at first. Dave might not have noticed it, but there was another female around them for a short time after Ethan and the mate went to sleep that dark time. That female smelled very good, but soon that scent was gone. Then they went out of the big cave. That was good. It could play in fur. Ethan was not sad when they could be in fur and keep their mate warm at night.

They finally found the cub. Who was not a cub. A big cat like the dominant was, but the cat did not come forward to sniff and greet him as other protectors it met did. It was lesser, but still should come forward. That was not good. Ethan did not trust the not-cub either. They were tired quickly after the shared food. That was not right.

Dave woke in a bad cave. Darkness surrounded them and a hard floor was under them. There were smells of blood and piss. Fear and anger from those who stood over them. It could not move much. There was hitting and it could not shift safely.

Sharp pain in their right fore-paw. It yowled in anger and attacked with its other paw.

Darkness returned, but there was more blood scent in the air now. The enemies' blood. Not its or Ethan's. Then more pain until it fled. Back to the place it remembered from Before.

A wonderful female scent was in the air of his cave. Then he slept, feeling a hand rubbing his ears. But it was not Ethan. The female sang but he could not understand the words. The female reminded him of the beautiful female that the old one and his protector remembered when they ended. He purred at her a little.

He could not stay awake or open his eyes. But he was not sad. Soon he would be back with Ethan and they would be not sad together.

Chapter 30

My head was fuzzy when I woke. We just lay there, listening and smelling. And hurting. God, did we hurt. Aches all over and sharper pains. I tried a deep breath and it seemed my ribs were intact. Mostly. Dave wanted to rip someone, anyone into tiny pieces. I agreed with him. Then he caught the scents and relayed them to me. Other shifters were here. Our eyes opened to a hellish sight.

A dozen or more cages on knee-high concrete stands. We were in one. It was about two metres wide and maybe three long. One of the other captives was sitting up, so maybe a metre and a half high. The cage was made of bars double the size of my thumb about a hand's width apart. Welded together and buried into the concrete, if I wasn't mistaken. It might be impossible to break free of this cage without help from outside it. More help to escape from the building. Find a phone to call for help.

A spike of pain from my right hand as I tried to sit up made my eyes water. When I was able to see properly, I realized the nails on my thumb and forefinger on my right hand had been pulled off. *Why?*

I finally decided it was because those were the fingers that I had shifted into claws to catch the marmot when hunting with Philip. Did these people believe that would stop the cougar from having claws? And would they try to keep the nail from returning? Shit. *Wait*, I told myself and Dave. He could fix my fingers when we shifted the next time. I'd have to be clear on what to do. For now, I had to be careful in using that hand.

Phil hadn't had any sign of deformed fingers, so maybe I'd be allowed to heal. Then again, he might have been trained as a traitor since he was young. Brainwashed, sort of like Victor and Jerry.

Those idiots had made sure any of the kids they'd bred wouldn't want to use their beasts instead of embracing what they could do.

He was ten now. Jerry was eight. They had regular appointments with therapists in medical to help them cope. I tried to play with them in fur whenever I was home. We all had fun and Dave had fur time.

Enough of the past. I had to deal with the current cluster. I looked around again. None of the captives had any clothing on. Which included me. I looked down at my body. I was covered in a mass of bruises. About half were yellowish and fading, others were still dark purple-red. Minor cuts on my torso but my ankles and wrists were puffy with bruises and swelling. No major bones seemed to be broken but I thought two ribs might be cracked as I took a really deep breath. They hadn't used my face as a punching bag. I wasn't sure why, but there had to be a reason. Maybe they wanted ask questions that they expected me to answer. Expecting that I could talk with a broken jaw wasn't that realistic.

I managed to sit up and found there a band around my neck as soon as I tensed those muscles. A solid metal collar with rings for attaching things and a thicker section at the front of my throat. I hadn't seen them on the others because of their long hair and beards. I couldn't feel a real lock, just a small hole at the left side. With a paperclip, I could probably open it, but I had nothing. Maybe I could convince Dave to make one claw really thin and straight. Maybe.

I'd have to picture exactly what I wanted. And I needed a look at the cage lock. We might be able to do the same thing and escape. Why hadn't the others tried? I hoped that had they tried and nothing worked. But had they given up? They were still alive, so they must still have a hope of escaping. It would be easy to die in here if I gave up hope. Shift one claw and rip open a major artery. No way for our captors to keep us alive.

I tried to speak to the others, but the collar shocked me on the first syllable. I'd heard of collars that shocked dogs to train them not to bark. Must be easy to move that tech into something else. I gritted my teeth so I wouldn't swear out loud. A few moments later, there was a shift in air currents from my right, so I looked that way. A dude in a dark green uniform with no name tag had entered the room. That was the only door, I realized after a quick look around the room's perimeter.

"Animals don't speak," he said. "You will be questioned later to tell us the locations of others like you out in the world. We will cleanse God's world of your kind, abomination."

Like Philip? I didn't say anything else. We needed a clear head to learn more about this place. Escape was not going to be easy. I just hoped Johann and Kelly had managed to figure out how they'd transported me here. I stared at the dude. Roddy, I decided to call him. He looked like he had a long, thick one up his ass.

"If you behave, you will be fed and watered. If you don't, then you will be punished." Roddy pulled a baton out of the holster on his belt. The other captives moved away from him, as far as their cages allowed. I didn't. Another lesson in who had the power. Dave still wanted to rip

him up. *Later,* I told him. He growled. It sounded different now but I
didn't have time right now to play twenty questions with him. Once this
guy left I'd try to find out why that might be.

The baton was a shock stick. There was also a Taser on his belt instead
of a real gun, or even one with darts. So they didn't want us dead, but
why would they want to keep us? Convince us to become bait for other
shifters? Enough torture and we'd agree to help bring others into this
hell? I couldn't believe that anyone with a beast would do such a thing.
But then, Phillip had. Brainwashed? Maybe. We'd find out. The others
had been here possibly for months by the length of their hair, but they
hadn't broken. Yet.

The shock from the stick was enough to stun us, but I didn't pass out.
I should have pretended to since I was hit again right away, which shut
us down.

When I woke again, Roddy was gone. The other captives were eating
from metal pans with their fingers. I couldn't tell what kind of food
might be. A container, which looked like a round cake pan, was in my
cage near the door. I sort of expected it to be empty, given Roddy's comments. I counted. There were seven other shifters in here. By the look of
their hair and beards, they'd been here for several months at least.
Maybe longer. I sat in one of the cage's corners so I could keep an eye on
the door and thought about this place. How did they keep the captives
from shifting and killing themselves?

Hungry, said Dave. *All much hungry.*

His comment was way different from what we'd done before. Those
had been vague images and feelings. *Wait!* He'd never used words before.
How had that changed? *Little food but enough to live,* I thought back, slight
pauses between each word. *No food, can't shift. What senses would be good
now?*

Nose, ears. Reasonable to overheard the guards talking.

Sounds good. If we shift them now, will they stay?

Maybe need more food to keep.

That shocked me. Alicia and the shrinks were going to have a field
day trying to explain what just happened. Maybe I was already going insane from the pain. Or was already insane.

Fool.

That was the last comment from Dave for most of the day. Hunger
cramped my stomach, but I was given water with the rest a few hours
later. This guy wasn't an asshole. He seemed to be concerned about taking care of the captives. Water was put into the pans with a hose not on
full and not sprayed into the cage with no regard for what was in the
way, though that might be what passed for having a bath in here. He also

used a scraper to pull shit out from the cages and into a bucket. The hose also rinsed the piss off the concrete. He finally reached my cage. He had a green outfit on, but more of a set of coveralls rather than a uniform like Roddy wore. A menial worker. But...

"I'm Scott. I'm the night shift here. Behave and you'll be okay. Don't try to use the demon within you to escape. You can't. The cages are escape proof and there are guards outside with both sleep dart and real guns. And you'll be punished for showing the stigma." I looked at him, confused. But I wasn't willing to risk another shock to my throat to attempt to ask him what the hells he was talking about.

"You'll hear the lectures tomorrow with the others. It's too bad that the Devil's agents forced your mother to bear an abomination. But you can be saved. That's why you're here."

Scott left and I slowly drank about half the water, saving the rest for when we woke up. Everyone had thought there were two groups hunting lone shifters. The government one that our ancestors had escaped from and the Coalition, who'd also escaped from someone. Then we'd found the third: the ones who had bred Victor and Jerry, seeking to emulate the Coalition's success in special ops but doing it all wrong. Firsteam: a rival black ops contractor.

Now a fourth one: Religious nutters hoping to save us by torturing us? How had these nutters found out about us? More important: what we could do to escape? Or to die. I took a deep breath. I wasn't giving up right away. Not until I knew that there was no chance that we could escape or be rescued.

I thought about the sniper who had nearly shot me near Banff years ago. He'd managed a few words before he'd died from the fall. That I shouldn't be. Could he be one of these nutters? I still hadn't told anyone about him, but maybe that was one of the incidents that I'd revealed during the drugged interrogation sessions. Karl hadn't said anything about him so I couldn't be sure the Coalition knew about him. When we escaped from here, I'd mention the body. Parts of him might still be there to provide another link to these people. This might be their headquarters, or they might have several facilities. Either way, I wasn't sure there was a way out right now.

The lights lowered and the others curled up to sleep. I lay down to fool the cameras but I wasn't sleepy. I had too many things to ponder and my finger tips hurt each time I flexed my hand.

I did sleep: eventually. I woke when the lights came up and the others sat in the middle of their cages, all facing the same way, unlike when I'd first woken. A screen came down from the ceiling and the image of an elderly man appeared in a Friar Tuck, like the Catholic priests I'd seen whenever Mama Consuela took me to church. I looked around and decided that appearing to be docile might get us breakfast, whatever that was. Dave didn't say anything but I sensed agreement. I sat up, feeling that my body was healing. To keep getting better we needed regular food and water. The others had survived, so I could too. I took the same position as the others did. Kneeling with my hands on my thighs. Two of the other prisoners interfered with my line of sight to the screen but the speakers were set up so that we could easily hear the show.

Ten minutes in I wished for a complete lack of hearing. The speaker must be the Preacher I'd vaguely heard Phil mention before I'd been taken away. His message was not one of the love and light of Jesus. It was about a war between Heaven and Hell. All shifters were the agents of the Devil and had to be cleansed and purified. To keep us from doing heinous things, which he didn't really explain. Killing their version of the righteous maybe. That sounded like a really good idea, if I could get out of the damned cage. Dave growled in agreement. Fortunately, his growl in my head didn't activate the damned collar.

I wasn't willing to pay that much more attention to the drivel right now. Besides, I guessed the program was a regular thing, there would be endless repeats of the basic message if I missed a few minor points.

The diatribe went on for maybe two hours. Maybe longer but I tuned it out, which had the wonderful bonus of blocking my pain enough to relax. None of the others moved the entire time. I tried not to but I had to change position a couple of times as the feeling in my lower legs went away and my knees started to ache from the rough concrete. When the screen finally retracted the others sat against the bars, so I did too. The returning feeling in my legs and feet almost had me swearing at the pain.

Another guy in coveralls came in with a pot on a cart and dished out the meal. I was the last one he fed and was given maybe half what the others were. The other captives must have shared the extra. I looked at the stuff. It wasn't a normal stew, even the bulk canned variety. I picked up a piece of the regular sized chunks of stuff in my left hand and squeezed it. A thin gravy dripped off. Was it-- dog food? *Yuck.* The chunk wasn't hard, so they'd probably added hot water a couple of hours ago so we wouldn't break our teeth on the kibble. Complete nutrition, but for a dog. How well did that work for people?

Roddy had called us an animal, so it sort of fit the mindset these guys had. I looked over at the others. Thin but relatively healthy, it seemed. They weren't beaten constantly since I didn't see any newish bruises. Maybe they'd only been beaten at the beginning of their captivity. *Or if they did something dumb like attempt and fail to escape,* I told myself. And

Dave. We could survive on this shit.

The new guy wasn't as nice as Scott. He sprayed water around rather than filling the pans later that morning. I passed a half hour or so decid-ing on a name for him. Henry, I finally decided. He was a bully from grade two, before my life had been shattered.

The screen came down not long after and another long, spittle-filled tirade from the Preacher filled the rest of the afternoon. I wondered if they were live or recorded. I didn't pay much attention after realising that there wasn't much more content to this one than to the one earlier. The position I chose this time kept my lower legs from falling asleep.

Scott appeared with the evening feeding. My portion was the same amount as the rest. It was the same soft kibble as in the morning. "I was told that you'll be questioned later tomorrow," he said. "Tell the inquis-itors everything you know and it will be better for you. You can control the demon inside you if you try. Pay attention to the lectures. You need to understand why our crusade is necessary for the world's safety."

I shrugged instead of nodding in agreement, so he stared at me for a few moments, then sighed and left the room. The lights went down a mo-ment later. I lay down when the others did. Dave was quiet in my head.

The next morning's tirade came on soon after the lights came up. I sort of did pay attention to it, just to have see if there was anything new. There wasn't. Henry came in before the kibble, pushing a bastardized wheelchair. Four guys in uniforms like Roddy's were with him. The other captives, whom I hadn't decided on names for, cowered in the back of their cages. They knew I was going to have an extremely unpleasant time today. Were probably thankful it wasn't their turn. Again. I almost re-gretted missing breakfast, such as it was. We needed to eat to heal.

A solid metal stick came through the centre of the cage door and the loop on it settled around my neck. It looked like the thing the animal control people use for stray dogs. The man holding it was stocky and didn't have to try twice. I also didn't try to evade or fight it because two other guys holding shock sticks were on either side of my cage. I couldn't escape either of them for long and getting more shocks for nothing wasn't on the current to do list. A fourth guy also had a looped stick but stood near the wheelchair, waiting for whatever the next step was.

Henry unlocked the door and moved to join the first stick guy. They dragged me toward the door. I would have crawled out but they didn't give me any options on cooperation. My neck and face were mashed up against the door bars and I fell out when they moved to the side and the door swung open. I tried to grab the door for balance but my nail-less fingers protested and I couldn't hold on with that hand. Once I was on my feet, the other stick guy put his loop around my neck from the back and pulled while the one in front pushed. Henry vanished but the backs of my knees felt the wheelchair's seat just before I lost my balance and fell back into the seat.

The moment I was sitting down, two other guards grabbed my arms from the sides and put them between curved metal bands on the arms of the chair. Once my forearms touched the bottom, they sprang closed just like a leg trap. *Shit.* A loop of leather came around my chest from behind me. It tightened right on my cracked ribs. I winced. Roddy smiled nastily.

"Feet on the supports, abomination." I glared at the front loop guy, who'd spoken. But I did it. More bindings like those on my arms sprang shut on my lower shins, just above my ankles. I wasn't going anywhere. If I shifted, I might be able to break the bindings or the chair itself. But I wouldn't get far with four shock sticks surrounding me.

The loops were removed from my neck and left just outside the containment room but now all four guards had shock sticks in their hands. Very bad odds for us. Henry, by the scent, pushed the chair.

The trip wasn't far, along three different corridors. Closed doors and we didn't see anyone else. Dave mapped what he could, showing people silhouettes when I looked at closed doors that had sounds coming from them. We ended up in another room about five metres square with reddish brown painted cinder block walls and a grey concrete floor with other stains. A floor drain was more or less in the centre and a long water hose looped on a wall mount near the doorway. The old scent of blood spilled in here was easy for Dave to determine. Shifter blood. And normals. *Had they beaten us in here?*

Dave seemed to agree with my assessment, though he didn't say anything further. *Had we managed to tear up at least a few of the people who'd tortured us? Was that why Henry and Roddy were so pissed at us?* More questions, no answers. Not yet.

The chair's wheels were locked and Henry vanished. The four guards surrounded me. I wasn't facing the door, but a small movement of air and a click let us know when it opened. It was Roddy, who came around to face me. One of the guards brought him a chair. Steel tubing, so it would make a dandy weapon and wouldn't break easily. If I could get loose, which wasn't likely with the now five shock sticks within reach.

"Well, abomination? Do you wish to confess your crimes?"

I gave him my best dubious look, then scrunched my chin down to indicate I remembered what the dammed collar did.

"One who pretends that he's clever," Roddy said. Then he nodded. The guard behind me put his hand against the collar and we heard a short buzz.

Damn. A separate controller, no integral on/off switch.

"Talk."

"So," I said as an experiment. No shock. "You all seem think that I'm the spawn of the Devil? Why, dude?" I tried to sound younger than I was. Any advantage so that we could escape.

"You bear the stigma. We know what you are."

"It's hereditary from what I've figured out, dude." I barely remembered not to call him by my pet name. "I've never done any kind of Satanic rituals. Ever. I went to church when I was younger. I'm Catholic. Still go at times, whenever I'm in a town. Don't burst into flame when I go in or whenever I take Communion." I'd felt nothing but peace in the churches I'd been in.

"But you have killed, haven't you?"

"Self-defence only. Mostly just knock people out so I can get away."

"He's not ready to admit his sins." There was another buzzing near my neck and I felt the shock as I tried to protest. "Take him back to the cages. No food tonight." His shock stick went under my chin. "You'll learn to repent your sins, abomination. You will confess them all to me, soon enough."

I was wheeled back to the cage room by the same route.

Getting me back into the cage was the reverse of the process to get me out. The arm and leg clamps sprang open once both loops were in place, so that control must be on the wheelchair's handles. As the guards were leaving, I gave them the finger. Henry noticed and he 'forgot' to give me any water when he fed the rest. But I felt better for that small act of defiance. It would probably be my last. I needed to keep my strength up which meant I needed each meal that was offered no matter what it was. I just hoped Karl and the others were able to trace me.

Five kilometres was a small distance when I might be anywhere in the world. The other shifters hadn't been able to escape, so the odds that we could do so were stacked impossibly high. But if they weren't part of any group, there was no one who would look for them. Unlike us.

The next time we were questioned was maybe two days later.

"Where have you met other abominations?" Roddy screamed, spittle hitting my face and eyes. "Give them up!"

"I haven't met anyone other than Phillip in the last year," I said. "Not likely the last guy's still gonna be there."

A slap. Dave growled but not using my vocal cords. "Tell me anyway."

"A guy built a little hut in upstate New York. Sanan-something Peak. Older dude who wanted to be near a bunch of little towns so he could hide where he bought food. And where he turned in bottles."

"See, that wasn't hard." The arsehole patted my head and I growled, jerking my head away so he wasn't touching it.

"I'm telling you he likely won't be there." Since the hut was Ron's I was pretty sure no shifter would be in residence. There might be a little scent left, so if Phillip or some other shifter working for them checked, they might be able to report that I'd told the truth.

"Where would he go?"

"How the hells would I know? Somewhere not there!" I wasn't quite shouting but it was close. "We can't send messages to each other. There's no friggin' organised conspiracy of people like me!" I glared and got one back. Roddy broke eye contact first and circled around me. I guessed he couldn't kill me unless he got a lot more information from me on where to find other shifters.

"What about the hunters you told Philip about. Who are they?"

"I have no idea who they are, man. All I know is they mostly wear suits and sunglasses, no matter where they are. They want shifters for something, and I have no idea what they want or where they come from. Whenever I'm in a city for too long, I spot them. Then I run. Don't stop to chat. I've seen a bunch of them with guns. Not ones with darts, though I've seen them sometimes." Silence.

How much had I given away about the two shifter groups? Too much, or would they stay safe? How many troops did this Preacher have trained for his war? Could they take out an entire compound? They'd need shifters to identify any shifters at a safe house, or...

"You and Philip knew each other," Roddy said into my left ear. "How?"

"The beasts. They know who else has one and who doesn't. His sniffed mine then vanished. How'd you brainwash him into working for you?"

"You'll work for us of your own free will, abomination," Roddy said. "Soon enough or we'll fry your brain like we did the others in the cages. Do you want to stay in that room for the rest of your life?"

"I'm not getting staked out to rat out shifters for you, arsehole. Not like Philip. You're not getting anything else from me." *Though pretending to be on side with them might be a way to get out of here. Rip up anyone near me and call in the cavalry.* Dave didn't like the idea, but did want to see Roddy's blood on his paws.

"We will, abomination. We will."

I didn't say anything but growled and Dave growled with me. A shock stick sent us both into the darkness.

We woke back in the cage, with some scrapes on our back. Probably from bring dragged on the concrete floor.

I looked at the other captives. Were they really brain dead? I didn't think so. I hoped that wouldn't be our fate, but I wasn't sure we could pretend to join the nutters.

Dave watched them with me, but he said nothing.

I'd given up, mostly. I counted mornings for a while. Once I reached twenty, I stopped. Stopped eating and drinking. Dave was on side with death. We couldn't save anyone else here, especially not ourselves. He didn't talk much and had mostly reverted back to normal, needing pictures and repetition to communicate. But it wasn't the same. Maybe I'd gone insane from the first round of beatings and just hallucinated it.

At least the pain in my fingers was gone. Dave must have shifted the spots to toughen up the skin where the nail used to be but hadn't replaced the nails themselves. I couldn't tell if the nails were growing back but I wasn't sure how long that process might take. If they started to do so, these arseholes might damage my fingers or hand further, which would be harder to fully heal.

Scott tried to get us to eat but I dumped the tasteless mess onto the floor each time he offered it. He did sweep it up and distribute it to the rest of the captives, which was okay. It gave them a little more energy to survive, if they wanted to. When the tirades came on I didn't bother to pay attention. Just slumped in a corner of the cage.

Roddy was replaced by another arsehole after four sessions in the wheelchair about five or six days apart. Even when the collar was shut off, I didn't bother saying anything as Roddy yelled at me to repent and confess. To tell him where other shifters could be found. At least they hadn't swapped to asking for details about who I thought was hunting us, just where they could find more of us. They didn't realize both groups had more shifters than they could imagine.

Dave pictured him having a heart attack or a stroke from the colour of his face and the veins standing out. If only we were so lucky. That would distract the guards, maybe send one or two out to get help. Then we could shift and try to break free. Kill whoever was in our way. Maybe we'd be killed. I didn't want to leave Melissa, but there might not be any way for us to escape. I doubted that I could fool them into believing that I'd bought into their mindset, unless I'd started the process right away.

The new guy was in black clerical gear, complete with a stole. Dark red, which wasn't any colour I remembered from the times Mama Consuela took me to church.

The collar shut down. I looked at the guy's face and then at his knees. I was losing weight steadily, but Dave's presence gave me more endurance than a normal person had. Sometimes good, it sucked big time now.

"Suicide is a sin, my son," he said almost gently. I didn't buy it. They wanted what I'd never give them voluntarily. "Do you want to burn in hell forever? I can help you." I gave him the finger. With both hands.

The crack of a shock stick against the back of my head took away any other comments I might make. It hadn't been a solid hit so the fuzziness cleared faster than other times. I kept my eyes shut and my head down, pretending to be still be unconscious and listened to their argument.

"You're on report," said the Stole. Angry now. "We need information from him on who else he knows. Philip said that he knows where others are living out in the world. We have a great chance to clear more of Satan's spawn from the ranks of the Damned."

"We should just use the drugs, Pastor Gregory. It's the only way to be sure. He can't lie to us that way. He can repent later on. Or he'll be like the other abominations. I don't understand why we're bothering to keep them alive. They're useless to seek out any others."

"We keep them because the Preacher ordered it. He has a use for them. Confession under drugs doesn't count as contrition and you know it. We cannot grant him absolution unless he is truly repentant. He has many sins, including murder, I'm told."

If they used drugs, I'd doom the Coalition. I knew the exact locations of three major compounds and seven, no eight safe houses. Half of them were manned by older shifters or normals who might not be able to defend themselves against any sort of overt attack. They also had comm equipment and knew of other locations. I couldn't betray my friends. And Melissa. I just hoped she was safe back at our compound. Even the big compounds might not be safe against an attack. I had no idea how many troops these guys could muster or how well trained they might be.

Dave, I thought. *We have to hide. A lot. Can't risk the drugs to make me talk. We can't just shift and hope they won't force me back to human with the shock sticks or the tasers.*

Come down here. There is a place where you will be safe. I will protect you. They cannot force me to tell them anything now. I will try to escape once they let down their guard. Or I will join you in death. Come to me. I was shocked by the return of coherent sentences but hiding the information I, we had, was our top priority. I opened my eyes a crack. No one was around.

How can I get there?

Just jump. I will always catch you, Ethan. I jumped into the darkness. It was so warm. I'd be safe there with Dave.

Chapter 31

Dave stood in cougar form and looked around. It was dark where he was. But warm enough to be comfortable without fur. A blink and there was light from a campfire. His cave. That relaxed him a little. There had been many campfires. The other. Wait. *Ethan* used them to cook and stay warm in the caves he liked to live in while they were in the mountains.

Dave lifted a paw. He was so different now. Ethan was not here. He trotted both ways from the fire. One direction felt different. A hint of fresher air. Ethan wasn't with him in the cave. None of his scent was down here. Where was this place?

The last thing he remembered was pain. Trying to wrap himself around Ethan's mind to protect him. That was Dave's purpose. To protect the other. To make him better than the lesser ones. A female scent registered but it was not that of the mate. Of Melissa. Dave sat abruptly, turning human in the next breath.

"What has changed? How? Why is... I... here?" Before, he'd never been so aware. All of his memories from before waking in here was out of focus in his mind. Simple. Like those of a young child. How had he woken up? The old Dave was like... He didn't know what word to use to describe the old him. Or what had woken him. The pain sticks? Who had the female scent belonged to? He wasn't sure of anything.

"I must find Ethan. He will know what we need to do now." That felt right. Ethan would help him understand. He always understood so much more than old Dave did. He shifted back to his normal form and stood.

As he went down the corridor through the dark rocks away from the fire, he started to glow, which gave him enough light to not run into walls. The flow of air with scents of the outer world led him through the branching tunnels. The passageway was smooth underfoot and taller than Ethan. No cramped passages, no pits in the floor. He almost remembered being in caves like that, when Ethan found places for them to stay in the forests and mountains to stay in during bad weather. Some had been cold and damp. Others were dry and comfortable. Like this one.

Dave realized he was approaching the end of the tunnel. Light that wasn't from him was ahead. It became brighter and brighter until he stood in the entrance and stared around him at the scene.

There was a giant meadow with flowers, butterflies and birds before him, surrounded by thick forest. No scents of others like him. Or of Ethan. He looked up at the sky. No clouds. But where was the sun? Behind the bulk of the mountain? But there were no shadows to show a direction. It was day, or at least bright enough to see well. This place seemed almost familiar but if he had been here before, those memories were locked away in the fuzzy recollections he had of the past.

There was a footpath of sorts through tall grasses and flowers that filled the meadow. It seemed to lead over to the forest. He looked back at the cave entrance. Could Ethan still be in the mountain? Lost in the darkness in a maze of tunnels with no light to see or be able to move safely?

No. He wasn't sure how he could be so certain. Ethan was in their body. That's where he had to go. He had to protect Ethan from the pain.

He trotted across the meadow. It was a vast but shallow bowl. A large stone building was near a very large tree at the bottom of the bowl. The cave mouth was hidden now. He kept checking for Ethan's scent. Or any others like him. Nowhere out here. Maybe later he would come back and explore. If he could leave here and then return whenever he wanted. He wanted to be with Ethan. To protect him. For Ethan to help him understand what had happened and why.

The path led into the forest so he continued along it. There were birds calling softly here, and not far off in the growing darkness a stream burbled along. A few creaking branches from a wind he couldn't feel. But he stayed on the path, even when he could barely see. He did not glow here, which was annoying. He stopped when it was so dark he couldn't distinguish anything of his surroundings.

A sad cry. Loneliness when they had been together for many years. *Ethan, where are you?*

The darkness vanished to artificial light. Men with sticks, striking him. Them. Dave knew Ethan was here with him. He wrapped himself around Ethan's mind as the pain increased. He would protect Ethan. It was his task.

The new pains muted after a long time. No new ones began. A sense of being moved. Scents of blood and anger filled their nose. Words were said but he didn't understand what they meant. Ethan would explain once they were both awake. For now, they slept.

When Ethan woke and was able to remember what had happened to them, Dave was able to pair up his fuzzy memories with what Ethan re-membered. A shifter who had betrayed his people. Phillip. He growled in anger. How could a shifter so betray his partner?

The days passed slowly. Ethan's body gradually healed. Dave pretended that he was the same as before. So limited. He couldn't risk these people finding out what he could do. Ethan did nothing to draw attention to the changes he must have noticed. Since Ethan did not know what this place was, Dave was reluctant to ask him to explain.

The others were like he was. Smart. Just as smart as the human parts of them. He didn't understand how it had happened.

'The body begins to heal,' said one. Dave was startled but Ethan did not hear anything. He dozed through another lecture, leaning against the bars, his injured hand cradled in his lap. Dave had changed the damaged fingers so the pain was less. If they escaped, he would try to repair the nails properly. If he tried to heal them now, Ethan might be beaten again. That would be a bad thing for their survival.

'We do. Where is your partner?'

'In the caves deep in the mountain. As are the others. It was the only way to protect them, and ourselves.' The eldest of the prisoners spoke. 'They might be tempted to betray our people so we hid them as soon as we woke here. You should take yours there. Now. He will be safer there.'

'When he asks,' Dave said. 'Which may be soon. We know things that these will want. Where other shifters can be found. Many of them.'

'Then you must be prepared to take him away quickly,' said another. 'The moment he asks. You can go directly to your cave whenever you will it.'

'What is the mountain?' Dave asked. 'It and the meadow outside the en-trance are somewhat familiar, but my memories of our life together are unclear.'

'As ours are,' another said. 'Our partners are in our caves so these cannot try to force them to make us submit, to become traitors to our people. How were you taken?'

Dave related what he knew of the traitor lion from Ethan's memories. 'I believe these people had him for many years, well before his beast developed beyond a young kitten. It is the only timeline that makes sense to me.'

'It does seem reasonable. If he was young, his beast would not have developed much. Even it it awoke as we have it might be unable to act against his partner.'

Ethan moved, waking again. He blinked, realising the lecture contin-ued, then looked like he was paying attention even though his thoughts were of Melissa. How he was glad she had not come with them to con-front the traitor shifter.

Ethan spoke in his mind. 'Dave, We have to hide. A lot. Can't risk the drugs to *make me talk. We can't just shift and hope they won't force me back to human with the shock sticks or the tasers.'* A different interrogator now.

Dave only knew the only way to keep Ethan safe from the drugs that made him speak without wanting to. In the darkness of the cave, he would be safe. Dave would try to escape with the others. Or he would die and release Ethan as well.

Dave left Ethan in the cave, deep inside the mountain. He was in the way out here. The other beasts had protected their partners. He did not understand how he and the others had suddenly gained so much awareness. To know of the meadow and the sacred mountain. How to get there and back to Ethan's world with no effort. What the others had also known as soon as they woke here. He had not shared his thoughts with Ethan since even Ethan did not understand so many things about this place. This was not the time to truly reveal his awakening. He needed to understand more so that he could explain it to himself first.

When he opened their eyes, they were back in the cage room. But this time, the others knew who was in control.

'Your partner is safe now?' the eldest asked.

'He is within my cave. A fire for light and books to read so he does not realize the passage of time.'

'As ours have,' said another. *'Did you explain our abilities to him?'*

'I have not, since I do not understand how we changed since coming here. Ethan would worry more, I think.' He sensed their assent. Ethan did know that he was different. Perhaps he might go to the cave while the body slept and they could talk. Perhaps. Plan to escape, if they could.

If all the shifters worked together, they might free themselves and send word to their brethren. Karl's beast would understand why all these people had to die. So that they would not harm any other shifters.

He ate and drank now whenever it was offered. But the green men learned nothing from their questioning, even with injections of drugs. Dave had never tried to use Ethan's vocal cords to speak, so it didn't matter how much of the drugs or pain they used. They learned nothing.

'There is a thing that may help us escape,' Dave said once the lights went down over a week later. *'Would you all join me in the meadow?'* He sensed assent and went there himself. Everyone was in their animal form. It was much more comfortable and stable to have four legs than just two.

'I do not recall how Ethan thought of it, but he tried while I was unaware to learn to pass an arm through a restraint as we shifted form. We, well mostly Ethan, could not do so. It is my opinion that since we are now completely aware of our surroundings, we might be able to use his technique to begin our escape from this place.'

'*Through the bars of the cages?*' An older wolf asked. '*I do not think it would work. They are too close together and too thick.*'

'*Through the bands that hold us within the chair, possibly,*' Dave said. '*To take our true form or even a half shift would shock the guards and the one free might be able to push any other guards toward the other cages so that an arm could shift to hold or kill. Then the loose one could use the key the keepers carry to open all the other cages. Then we would leave here or die together.*'

'*It has merit,*' the oldest wolf said. '*How did your human half proceed?*'

Dave nodded. '*A good question. I am not entirely sure. I have only a single image of the time: he began with fingers like so.*' He lay down, changed his front legs to human arms with the elbows resting on the ground. Then he curled the two smallest fingers around each other. '*He asked me to shift one finger and pass it through the other. We were never able to make it work and he gave up after a short time. I believe that he realized that Dave-that-was could not control the speed of the shift and Ethan could not explain the procedure to him well enough to be understood.*'

'*But you contend that we can accomplish the feat? Why?*' Another asked.

'*Since the change is so quick when we were... asleep, it is not surprising he could not succeed. If we are able to will the change to be much slower, it might be possible,*' the eldest said. '*We cannot leave these cages otherwise.*'

'*But how can we practice the technique out in the cages?*' Asked another. '*We have little food and barely survive on it.*'

'*I still have reserves,*' Dave said. '*I will experiment.*' He looked around. '*This place feels good. Is it possible that if we come here for extended periods, the light here might give us all more energy in the outer world?*'

'*Possible,*' said one who hadn't yet spoken. '*But the real power is in the mountain. The place where we hid our human partners. Being in or near that location is, I believe, a more potent energy source. Or at least being within the mountain. There is a grotto that I went to for a time, then stopped. I had decided to die. I... should have mentioned and shown it to all of you when you arrived here. I, well, I was prepared to shift what I could and attack the next time they took me from the cage. I hoped to take at least a few of them with me.*'

'*Can we go there now?*' The eldest asked.

'*Touch one another and I will bring us there. Once you see it, you should be able to go there on your own.*'

The grotto glowed with light with no visible source. Tall columns provided the sense that it was a building, but Dave had never sensed a similar feeling before. It was... '*I do not have words.*'

The others agreed. '*I feel better here,*' said another. '*I agree that if we come here every night and possibly during the lectures, it may give us the energy we need to try the technique our brother's partner tried. Or we can join with our partners within our caves until the body fails and frees us that way.*'

'I would rather attempt escape and bring Ethan back to our body. Then we may both return to his mate.'

'Try the finger exercise when we return to the cages,' the eldest said. *'But be sure the camera does not see anything, or they will punish you, and possibly the rest of us. Late at night might be best.'*

'Agreed,' Dave said. *'For now. Let us relax here.'* They all found places to lie down and curl up. They would take turns remaining awake to give warning of anyone entering the cage room.

Three nights later he succeeded. Slowing the rate of change was nearly impossible. They would be vulnerable until they could complete the change and be free. He reported his success and the method of slowing the change to the rest as they basked in the grotto the next night.

Two hands of days later, they all could do it. Now they started to build up reserves whenever they could access the grotto and not betray their absence. They never saw anyone else there. Were they the only aware beasts in the world? It seemed so but none understood why they had awakened here. For each of them, it had been after the first beatings were mostly over. They had woken in their own caves, as aware as their human partners. None of the partners knew they were smart now. Well, maybe Ethan had suspected, and especially now after he'd used so many sentences when he'd told Ethan to jump into the darkness to reach him.

Ethan would understand why Dave had not told him of what happened in the cave. And the strange female presence. None of the others had mentioned her. Perhaps because Dave-that-was had been more advanced than any other living shifter? If they lived and escaped, he would try harder to understand who she might be. The old one, Marsh, had seen a beautiful woman as they died. Was she the same one? Why hadn't she shown herself when they came here? And what was that stone building or the tree doing here? Was the woman inside the building, waiting for them to come to her? Too many questions and no answers. Again.

The one who had been here the longest spoke while they rested in the grotto during the night. *'If I have tracked the passage of time correctly, there will be an event soon. The Preacher will come in person to show his followers how much success they have had in capturing more of us. We will be paraded before the others who live here and elsewhere, to show their strength. I am not entirely sure when, but within two or three weeks, I believe. I do not know what will happen to us after that. Perhaps we will be killed, or kept for the next show. I was the only one here the last time. Now we are eight. Taken from many parts of the country. That shows there are many who seek to find us.'*

'*Would they take all of us out of the cages for this event?*' The elder asked. '*That way those who free themselves may aid those who partially succeed.*'

'*I believe so. The Preacher always speaks of their efforts to find other shifters in his rants, so he would want to prove to his followers that they were succeed-ing in their mission. Perhaps to gain more money from them.*'

'We shall strike then,' Dave said. '*Store all the energy you can for that change. If nothing else shift hands to paws and teeth to fangs. We will either die or escape together. The robed ones are special targets.*'

'*As are those who torment us,*' said another.

'*But not Scott,*' said a third. '*He has compassion. I do not understand why he joined these people. Perhaps he changed his mind once he learned how we are treated but cannot leave here with any degree of safety lest the robed ones think that he might seek to betray them.*'

'Agreed,' Dave said. '*Are there any others like him?*'

He hadn't encountered anyone else with Scott's attitude. Then again, he and Ethan had been here the shortest time. None of the others knew how or who had targeted them. Two had been found at their jobs, mostly outdoor ones. Others were in a city and were hunted the way the Coali-tion had hunted Ethan. He was the only one Phillip had betrayed. None of the others knew anything of him. If another shifter was captured soon by him, that would tell them that the traitor was still at large. Otherwise, he might have been taken by Ethan's friends when Ethan did not report back quickly. But did the traitor know where this place was? Or any other locations that might reveal information to the Coalition?

Silence. It was hard to wait for an event that only *might* happen.

Four hands of days later, the ceremony began. The first sign was that small groups of male kittens were escorted around the outside edge of the room. Shocked looks from the kittens at the condition of those in the cages. One of the robed ones was with them but nothing was said while they circled the cages in the room.

'*None carry any of our brethren,*' Dave said after another group left. '*Why do they bother to show us to these kittens? Could they all live here? It seems odd that we never saw or scented any of them before.*' The scents on the guards were those of adults. Some women, mostly other men.

'*I doubt they reside here. They may have another place nearby. Their pur-pose could be to frighten these cubs into absolute obedience,*' the eldest said. He was physically the oldest of us. Nearly sixty now. He'd been here half a year, surprised that he still lived. '*To them punishment is the cost of sin.*'

'*Sin is anything the robes do not like,*' said the one who showed them the grotto. '*But their coming means the event is near. I believe that we will be shown to all of their people tonight or tomorrow. It is nearly time for our escape.*'

'Good. We should all go to the grotto as often as we can to fill our reserves. One should remain on guard here to provide a warning when they come for us.'

There were only three wheeled chairs. The rest were strapped down to wheeled tables with weaker cloth bindings, not heavy leather or metal. They might break free more easily and could help the others.

The big room they were taken to had a waist high platform at one end. A theatre? Dave wasn't sure what kind of place this complex had been. There were gasps of fear and amazement when they were brought in through a side door and up a ramp. The bright lights aimed at them made it hard to guess at the number in the audience, but it didn't matter. Death to their tormentors was the main objective tonight. Those who watched from afar were secondary to their escape from this hell. He spotted several large things aimed at the platform. Were they cameras to record whatever happened here? Like the tirades shown twice a day.

Dave was sad that he couldn't say goodby to Ethan or Melissa if the escape failed and they all died. And if those last days together had made a kitten as they'd hoped. Ethan had shown him how kittens were made. He hadn't understood why at the time. Now, he knew a little more. But Dave-that-was had concentrated hard those last nights before they left the compound. The wriggling bits would have enough energy to make a kitten. One with a beast inside would be best, but the other kind would be good too.

He thought that they had succeeded. And Dave-that-was thought a strange female had been nearby those times. Was she the same one he vaguely remembered from his awakening in the cave? He would have liked helping to raise a kitten. He remembered Ethan and Dave-that-was, in cougar form, playing with small human kittens so they would not fear to change. Why were so few beasts able to change completely? He barely remembered that first time he'd shifted into his natural form in the forest. At least now he knew much of what Ethan knew. *How* he had learned those things was another question. Too many of his questions had no answers. But now they had a chance to leave here and live. He and Ethan could talk about many things once they were safe and back with Melissa.

The Preacher started a tirade much like the ones that played twice a day. They didn't pay attention to that noise, but to the smells drifting on the currents of air in the big room. The multitude of lights above them made it warm. A welcome change from the cold concrete of the cages.

'Sleeping darts,' Dave said as he recognized the medical smell. *'Many of these guards have dart guns instead of tasers. They will try to stop us once we are free. Target them first, then the robed ones who have no weapons.'*

'*Many darts will cause death,*' the eldest said. '*Keep moving if you are hit and the guards will keep firing. If we cannot escape one way, we can at least leave this miserable existence behind.*'

Dave felt his chair move forward. '*While they focus on me, prepare to shift and attack.*' He sensed agreement.

"This is one recently captured abomination," the Preacher said. "He was trying to die rather than repent of his sins. But we are trying so hard to convince him of the truth, brothers and sisters. His murders, his rapes and his assaults are all due to the will of his master, Satan, the UnGodliest sinner of all the ages."

Dave started to tune out the meaningless words. But he paused and sniffed since he was so close to the podium. The Preacher held a beast. A wolf, he thought. Is that what had turned him into a madman? For now, it didn't matter. The tirade didn't have any new information. '*Now!*' He shouted to the others. '*Free yourselves and attack!*'

He let the shape of the human body flow as he threw himself to the side. Even the hated collar was left behind. Soon he was standing on four paws and free. A yowl of battle and the Preacher fell before one paw, piss staining the lower front of his robe and blood coursing down the upper. The amount of blood satisfied him and he felt the cowed wolf cub inside the Preacher die with thanks. A hint of another being with him, but he had no time to ponder what that might mean or who it might be. Not with so many enemies surrounding them. He yowled again, hearing the others howl and growl in anger. The people watching began to scream in horror. Good. They should know fear.

Dave sprang toward the guards, standing immobile in shock. Good. That made it easier to reach them. All of his claws were sharp and ready to use. Good. Ethan's fingers would be completely healed if they survived long enough to shift back to his human form.

The screams echoed through the room as the other animals jumped from the higher level and attacked those in uniforms first. Those humans with a little sense tried to run, but that just turned their backs to the danger. Dave snarled and the bodies kept falling around him. There was a sting of a dart landing in his right flank but he refused to give in: Burned the drug out of his system.

'*The gun holders are down. The rest flee. Shall we give chase to kill more of them?*' the other cougar asked.

'*No. There will be other guards nearby, these with real guns. We cannot reach them if we are trapped inside a corridor with nothing to protect us from the bullets. We must reach the outside of this building and run quickly so they cannot find us. Back to the stage. I have an idea.*' Dave turned away from the dead and dying. Walked on bodies with his claws extended into them so he wouldn't slip. And so those left behind would fear shifters.

Ethan had been in a drama class before leaving school and Dave now appreciated the places to hide in the back of such places, hidden from view. There would be doors and corridors without guards. At least a few must lead to the outside of this building. He hoped the majority of any armed men were elsewhere, or else heading to their armoury to exchange their dart guns for ones with bullets.

All but one of the others joined him. '*He is dead,*' said one. '*A dart in his eye and brain. I felt his passing.*'

'*We will mourn him later,*' said the elder. A wolf now. Thin, with patchy fur. Like the rest. Three still wore the collars but that was a problem for later. With the guards dead, they would have time to remove the hated things once they were far from here.

'*This way. I hope.*' Dave led them further backstage.

They soon reached a hallway and a door. Scott stood in front of it. They all stopped. Two started to back up, preparing to flee.

"I'm so sorry," he said. "There aren't any others like you in any of our other places. I hope. This door leads to a corridor with another that does lead to the outside of the building. There's a barbed wire and chain link fence around the perimeter." He held out a strange object. "These are wire clippers so you can get through it quickly. I'll try to bury him properly. Away from here. Wild country. Go quickly. So will I."

Dave took the cutters in his mouth. Scott opened the door and they streamed past him. A few moments later they were at a door that smelled of outside. Still, Dave sniffed it before rearing up and pushing against the opening bar.

They realized it was full night but that was far better than daytime for their escape. Easier for them to hide in darkness than in the paltry shadows of full sun. The others followed him along the side of the building, stopping as they heard a vehicle. The noise grew louder.

They crouched down in the deepest shadow they could find quickly, closing their eyes so no reflection of the lights would betray them. The vehicle passed them without pausing, heading back toward the door they'd come from. Another few minutes and they were at the fence. Dave shifted just his right paw into a hand and started snipping. They slipped through the hole and they headed straight out as fast as they could, then turned toward the rising moon when they entered an open corridor with tall steel towers. Dave heard a small hum over the night noises.

Later, a field they ran through had rabbits. Though not for long. They were plump and probably tasted wonderful, but none of them stopped swallowing the meat as quickly as possible to savour the taste of real food after months of tasteless kibble.

Chapter 32

As the sun started to rise, the eldest led them to a culvert in a dirt road. There were more fields on either side of it, these with tall plants, and hopefully more rabbits, or even mice. Anything to fill their aching bellies. Ethan knew the name of many plants but Dave wasn't sure of the word for these.

'Hunt quickly now,' the eldest said. 'Stay in here during the day so no one sees. Remove collars if we can. Tonight move on. Find more food.'

'And discuss plans while we rest,' said another. 'We have been inside for so long. Must relearn the ways of outside now that we are so different. Bring our partners back to manage the human form so we may hide our nature from any watchers. If those find us again, they will kill us for what we just did. They may also simply kill other shifters to prevent more of their people being killed.'

'It will take time for them to begin their hunt. They must first decide who will take control of their pack,' a wolf said. 'Still, bringing our partners back should be a priority, along with moving as far from here as fast as possible.'

'If we can spare the energy to shift. It may take us time to rebuild our reserves while we spend much energy in travel.' All nodded in agreement. They split up and headed into the plants.

Dave found a nest of mice just on the edge of the field and snapped them all up. And then two unwary rabbits, which filled his stomach for now. A third rabbit was in his way back to the others. He killed it and brought it back in case one of the others hadn't managed to fill his stomach. Or he would eat it later in the day.

'Shall we stay together once we reach a town or find a decent range?' The eldest asked once they had all returned to the culvert. 'Once we can shift back to human form, we can raise money to support ourselves and stay far from these and other groups who hunt us.'

'Ethan did that at places with gambling,' Dave said. 'But I have hints of danger in being there. I do not understand fully. We will also need to find clothing before we can enter places with people.'

'One of us could enter first an area first, then bring back clothing for us all.'

'I think our human partners will be surprised at the change in us,' said one of the younger wolves. 'Mine seldom called on me to aid him in his work. We were out in the forests for long periods. I feel that he would want to return to his previous life. But these hunters found him out in the world. With many of these people still at large, we would be in danger until they can all be put down.'

'All of us face the same issues. Staying together might be best,' the cougar said. 'But living in a city means others may hunt us. In the wild places, we must have a large range to supply us all with food.'

'That may become an issue for all shifters,' the eldest said. 'We must talk to our partners as soon as we can manage it. They will see the advantages of our development, I am sure.'

'There is no way they can shut us out completely,' another wolf said. 'We know of the meadow and beyond. I do not know if our partners could go there or return to our bodies without our aid.'

'We were with the Coalition of Shifters,' Dave said into the silence. 'There are many of our people in their compounds, from all three lines. At first, Ethan did not trust them. But we have a mate there and I will return to her and the kittens we have rescued from other bad places.'

In the end of the discussion, there was little trust for going to Ethan's people for most of the group. Dave understood their feelings and mostly agreed with them. The eldest wanted to go to wild places and stay there.

'Without Melissa, Victor and the rest of Ethan's family, Ethan and I would choose the forest too. If you chose the wild places, remember this number.' He recited the 'ohshit' number. He didn't fully understand why Ethan called it that. He would ask, once Ethan returned to their body.

'The call will bring help. I will contact them once we find a phone, so you may observe how they behave when I return to them. There is no cost to the call, so it can be a phone anywhere in the world. Having allies to fight against these people is good. That will keep any other shifters from enduring what we did.'

The others agreed. While they waited for night to come, one stayed on guard in turns and the rest went to the grotto, to bask in its energy.

The sun setting roused them. One who still wore a collar tried to pull it over his head but quickly gave up.

'I may be able to help. Ethan thought of a possible way to open small locks before he went to the mountain to be safe. Since I knew his thoughts on the method, I know what he envisioned.'

'Anything to get this off. What need I do?'

'Hold still.' Dave managed to shift a tiny hooked claw that could fit into the hole in the collar and the lock opened. The other two came over and he released them as well. The collars were soon buried under a fence line. They all pissed or shit on the spot. They might be smarter now, but they were still animals in their hearts.

Two days later they found a picnic and hiking spot in small hills. They had begun to travel during the day after that second night away from the compound so they could see more of the surrounding countryside and any dangers or opportunities to go into a field to hunt. Real mountains were about two weeks travel away, but they weren't far from a major city by the amount of traffic they heard on the separated highway. There was also a ranger station at the park, currently and thankfully without a ranger. The outside phone was missing the handset and most of the cord, which annoyed him. He hoped there might be a campground nearby so those who didn't want to come to the Coalition might find discarded clothing and other food in the bins without needing to hunt a larger animal that would feed everyone. That would be hard when they were so thin and weak.

'No one has been here for a week or more,' Dave said after testing the scents. 'I will shift fully and go in, then call for Ethan's people. The phone inside should be safe from any vandals, unlike this one.'

'As you will. The rest of us shall go to those mountains to the north for now,' said the elder. 'We can hide in them forever if we stay in fur.'

Two wolves looked at him. 'We will come with you. Our human selves had lives before. We want the option of returning to them. By ourselves, we cannot explain our absence and current condition to our families and co-workers.'

'As you will,' Dave said. He didn't have a lot of spare energy but used it all to become fully human. He nearly fell over, but leaned against the wall in time. He hadn't remembered that Ethan had always been in control of moving in human form. In the cage there was little to do and any obvious exercise was punished. He moved crouched over with his knees bent to help keep his balance without the help of a tail. The door was locked but a shove in the right way opened it. The two missing fingernails were back as they should be. Excellent. Ethan would be glad.

"Toilets for thirst," Dave said. He lifted the seats to make it easier for them. He managed to turn the sink tap on and drank from his hands. Using words was also hard without Ethan's help. He would fetch Ethan back to the body as soon as possible so he could take care of these nagging details. He sensed there was something he'd forgotten in the shift, but dismissed it from his mind for the moment. Making the call was crucial. He hoped there was a safe house or a compound nearby.

The phone sat on a desk and he perched gingerly in the chair. No tail did make that easier. He dialled the number and it rang twice before being picked up.

"How can I help you?"

"This is Ethan Carson," Dave said, concentrating hard on sounding like Ethan. "I'm at a ranger station. Phone number is..."

"We have your location, Ethan. Pickup will be there in... about forty minutes. There isn't anyone nearer that we trust. Do you need medical attention? And is there a safe spot there so you can wait?"

"Hungry, need foods. Clothes. Trees to hide near. Two others come with," Dave said. The sound of a vehicle outside sent the others out the back door. "Others come. I be nearby. Code Melissa."

"Good enough. Stay safe, brother." The line went dead and Dave tottered over to the window to peer out at the parking area from the side so no one would see him. An official car. How could he explain his naked presence without the others becoming involved? Making the man unconscious might serve, but Ethan would not want to cause serious harm to him. A tall man in a uniform got out and stretched, then sighed as his radio squawked. He spoke into it and there was back and forth talking. Then he sighed again, sat back down in the car and left. Dave relaxed.

Dave left the station and pulled the door shut. He nearly walked into the two others brave enough to come with him as they hid in the bushes.

'The others watch from higher ground?'

'Yes. What of the car?'

]A ranger, but called away before he entered the station. He saw nothing of us.' They settled in to wait. Dave thought about shifting back to his natural form but he didn't have enough in his reserves. He remembered the experiment when Ethan and Melissa had met. How Dave-that-was felt after many shifts had depleted the body's energy. The human form would also reassure whoever came that he was not a danger to them or the Coalition. Many had feared Dave-that-was in his natural form at first. Staying in the human form would be best for now.

Perhaps it had been more time than the voice said it would be, but there was still enough good light to see any enemies when a van pulled into the parking area and stopped near the tallest trees. Two men got out, stretched and looked around at the seemingly deserted parking lot.

"Ethan?" One of them called. "We've contacted Melissa and your family. They're relieved and happy you're safe and okay."

The scent of one of them is familiar. Ethan worked with him before. It is safe. But I will go out first to see what they do. Come. The human form was harder to skulk in but they reached the bushes nearest the van quickly.

"Here," said Dave, and stood where they could see him.

"What a relief, Ethan," the man who smelled familiar said. "We picked up the kid two days after your last transmission. Phillip. What a mess. He had no idea where he'd grown up when he was questioned. Kind of like Victor's level of confusion, but with lots of inane prayers that only stop when he's asleep or gagged."

"There's clothing in the back for three," said the other. "Exercise gear so size wouldn't matter. And food."

"Karl wants us to call in as soon as we're at the safe house," the first said. "We'll stay there a day or two, then get you to a bigger place."

Dave nodded. More words were needed. He wanted to be inside a house or compound before he revealed where Ethan was. "Others watch. Not trust yet. Have the number. These, not enough energy to shift back yet. Ran many days to here."

"Okay," the first said. He opened the side door, ready to help them. "We'll let headquarters know once we're under way. All aboard."

Dave entered first. There was no barrier between the front and back of the vehicle. 'Good. Come.'

The van was on a major road shortly after. Dave opened cans of beef stew for the two wolves and the chicken stew for himself. Thumbs were an excellent idea. Water was in sealed bottles. Once the wolves finished their stew, he poured water into the empty cans. Then he looked at the clothing. He managed to get the pants and shirt thing on. But the metal ribbon to close it needed more control with the fingers than he could manage right now. Still, a feeling of incompleteness that didn't make sense to him. Ethan's body was thin, but he couldn't help that. The food available had not really been enough for any of them. Only their access to the grotto had given them the energy to shift and escape.

"We have more high calorie food at the safe house," said the driver. "Help build up your reserves so you can shift whenever you need to."

"Good," Dave said. "Hard to shift back this time to call. Rabbits, mice only. Long time running."

"Have naps if you want," the familiar one said. George, Dave thought his name was. Ethan had liked him. The others lay down on the soft pads but none of them truly slept. But it was good to travel swiftly with no effort on their part. His legs and arms still ached from the strain of running for so long without exercise.

An excellent meal waited for them once they arrived at a long, two story isolated house with several large outbuildings at the edge of a city. Raw beef with fat cut in small cubes for the others, a cooked turkey breast with carrots and potatoes for him. They were given a suite with a dining table and several bedrooms. They had barely finished eating when Karl walked in. The others recognized his dominance at once.

"Ethan, we're relieved you managed to escape. Can you tell us what happened?"

"Not Ethan. Dave." What would Karl do now?

Karl stared for a long time. "You're talking. How?"

"Not know. Much pain." He didn't want to say much until he could talk with Ethan. "Had to do. Drugs to question. Locations like this place keep secret. Ethan hiding to stay safe." Dave finally said.

"Okay. The others did that too? Woke up like you did and hid their human half to protect them?" Dave nodded. "Okay." A long pause. He looked at the two wolves. "I'd guess you haven't come very far from the place you were kept?" All three nodded.

"Went toward moon rise while dark, then toward hills," Dave said. "Land around big buildings flat, no trees. Wire fence. Three nights running. Hide first day so not seen. Found ranger place near here to call."

"I'll relay that. Who were those people? We learned nothing of any value from Phillip. Even with lots of drugs. They obviously didn't want him to give anything up if he was found so they never told him anything about where they were located or who other members are."

"Preacher leads. Said beasts belong Devil, not Gods. Held a beast. Dead now. With others. Many. Others angry so hurt them back. Left there. Seven now. One ended there." Karl's eyes bugged out slightly.

"Shit on a stick. There are bedrooms are just through those doors, Dave. Not cells. Sleep as long as you want. Melissa should be here early tomorrow. She was at another compound helping a shifter after an accident so she's in transit right now. I need to report in to the Council right away. Our people need to know what you told me so they can start to get information on these nutters. We had no idea they existed before now. We need to take them down and warn all the safe houses."

"Tired. Sleep good. To get more food?" The wolves' ears pricked in interest. The meal had been enough to fill their bellies for now, but they would all be hungry again soon. Not spending their energy to chase down mice and rabbits would help them recover faster.

"A guard is right outside the door. Just ask. Sleep well." He rose and left. Dave looked at the others. '*Piss, then sleep? Same room with door blocked.*' They nodded. They were safer together for now.

Melissa had been told who waited for her, Dave realized. "Sorry," he said. "Tried." Then he was being hugged. The others thought it might be an attack at first, but he shook his head. He had pulled on a shirt like those Ethan wore to exercise so he didn't have to bother trying to close the front of the other shirt.

"Dave. Thank you. For trying if nothing else. I know words are hard for you. We're going to stay here for a few more days. More security came with me. We really want to find these people. What they've done is horrible and they have to be stopped."

"Most bad. Only one good." She took a deep breath. "That one left."

"Karl's in the com centre here with a big map. A team with headcams just arrived at the ranger station where they picked you up. They're going to try to retrace your route to find the place. You'll just have to let me know which direction they should go. Okay?"

Dave nodded, relieved. The others joined them on the couch. Easier on joints with little flesh to provide comfort. She smiled at them without showing teeth.

The screen now showed the ranger station. There were three other men, all wearing helmets with small cameras on the side. "They have motorcycles so they can quickly follow your trail cross country," Melissa said. "Cars or a truck might have problems if you all went across fields and through any woods on narrow trails."

Dave took a deep sniff of Melissa's arm. It made him feel better. But she smelled different from before. Was it because he was in charge of the human form instead of merely a passenger within? He pushed the idea aside, but did sense the tiny beast within her. Good. Their kitten grew and was healthy. Ethan would be happy to learn that when he came back. Did Melissa know about the kitten yet? She had not mentioned him so perhaps she was not yet aware of her condition.

Maybe Ethan would realize that they were with her and return to his body without Dave needing to go and fetch him. It would be a difficult journey while he was still so tired from starvation and the run. He should have gone to the grotto last night while their bodies slept. He would suggest it to the others later if they had time to nap later today. She stroked his hand. That made him want to purr in contentment.

"I'm going to pan the parking lot," said the leader. "Tell me when I get to your line of travel." He moved slowly. When Dave saw the trail they'd come down, he nodded and Melissa said to stop. "That trail?" one of the others yipped in agreement. "Good enough." Those motorcycles were much quieter than he recalled. Ethan had known similar machines that deafened him in the city when they were young. These were much better for sneaking up on an enemy. He thought Ethan had ridden others like it on the missions. So much of their life together was hard for Dave to make sense of. When Ethan returned, they would talk. And Ethan would explain what Dave did not understand. Together they would try to make sense of why Dave was so smart now.

The riders made it to the culvert where they'd spent the first day in only a few hours. Dave heard his stomach rumble.

"We're making good time. If this is your first stop the compound has to be very close by. Any report from the drones?"

They didn't hear any response. Melissa shrugged. "Are you guys hungry again?" She must have heard his stomach as well. All three stared at her. The two in animal form licked their lips. Dave nodded. "I thought so. I'll order the same as last time? Two for beef, one poultry?"

"Yes," Dave said. "They wait there? Why stop now? We ran far to reach that place. Came there early light. Hunted for food in plants before resting and stay hidden."

"It's just for a little while. The drones are flying ahead of them. They can go high like birds and take pictures of the area the team is approaching. We don't want our guys to ride into an ambush or run into the people who held you. If we know where they are, we can arrange our own ambush and capture prisoners to question about who they are. Was it full dark when you left the compound?" Dave nodded.

"You spent the first day in that culvert?" Another nod. "Smart. It would hide you from their drones, if they had them and were searching for you. They might have been too busy cleaning up any mess and dealing with their injured to chase you. I think it's likely they're still there. Why would they think any of you *could* call for help, after all. Is there anything you can tell us about which way you'd come from?"

"Collars to stop voice. Buried near fence there. Big corridor of tall steel things ran down to get away quick near the prison."

"Really tall steel structures? Was there a kind of a hum in that area?"

"Yes," Dave said. "Faster to run through grass than trees at night."

"There's a transmission corridor showing west of there. I'll get a drone moving down it." Karl's voice held satisfaction.

The team headed for the fence line and quickly found the collars, possibly from the scent of their piss. One man put them into a clear bag and sealed it to keep the stink away from them. "We'll take them with us. Anything else here that we need to find?"

All three shook their heads and Melissa relayed that.

"Good enough. On our way."

Melissa went to the door, opened it and asked for the food. Then she came back and sat beside him and took his hand. She and Ethan often did that, he remembered.

Karl came in before the food did. "One of our drones is on approach to a likely place. Good thing you remembered the transmission towers. Really cut down on the search area. There's a lot of woods around there." He touched his ear and the picture changed.

It looked almost right to Dave. "Angle high. Night when cut fence. Not see other things."

"He's going lower well outside the fence," Karl said.

The compound seemed to be the right one, but it was now empty from what the drone revealed. The riders approached with caution and the main gate was unlocked. They didn't go far in case of traps. Other drones started investigating the rest of the buildings. Two big vans, one filled with many men stopped at the gate. The drone controllers were in the other and only opened their side door for fresh air.

"We'll have a full team go in to search it top to bottom and we'll also trace the ownership documents. You guys did well. Can you change back to human soon? Or bring your other selves here?" The wolves looked at each other, then shook their heads.

"Hard," Dave said for them. "Different shape hard to balance, use. Words few. Small cages so no moving there. Others much time there."

"The human half of the partnership needs to come back to their bodies before they shift to human," Melissa said. "I'd suggest that Dave might want to switch back to cougar if he can. He'll be more comfortable that way since he isn't used to having only two legs. I'd like to have all of them in the med room for quick physicals now and more extensive ones once we're at a major compound. I can tell they've been malnourished and I want to find out what any other physical problems these forms have before they shift back. Any minor injuries may have been healed during this shift but I'd rather know what else might be wrong now so we can prepare to help them."

That sounded good to the others. And to Dave. Food came and smelled good. This was more like the stews from the cans Ethan liked. "You need the elements from foods other than just meat," Melissa said. "This stew has extra vitamins and minerals to help you all recover. There's nothing to hurt you or make you sleep. Though, you may find you are sleeping more for the next few weeks. Try to dream about your human selves. Let them know it's safe to come back." Dave picked up the bowl of chicken stew but left the spoon where it sat. He didn't trust his hand's fine motor control yet. Ethan always made such things seem so easy.

Maybe Ethan would come back soon. He sighed. It was easier to go and fetch Ethan than to wait. He could rest later in the grotto and Melissa would not be alone. He would tell Ethan about the kitten when he went there. Child. Their son. They would all be happy.

The others could also fetch their partners back and stay in their caves to rest. He still thought there was something that he'd forgotten to do. Ethan would tell him what it was when they were all back at the compound.

Chapter 33

I thought I was sleeping a lot, but wasn't sure anymore. There was no real way to track the passage of time in the cave. There was no windows or cracks to see outside and the fire never needed more wood. It just kept burning, providing light and warmth. The cave was similar to the one I'd had when I rescued Victor, but it was larger. Wider passageways but I didn't explore much since the fire's light didn't didn't show much once I was a few paces away from it. And Dave, the beast, wasn't in my head anymore. I wasn't sure how long I'd been here, but Dave had told me to stay put. So the nutters couldn't question me about how to locate the Coalition's compounds and safe houses. They might have a lot of people so could try tactics other than a major frontal assault.

The safe houses would actually be easiest to take out, since they were mostly standard construction with maybe a panic room in the basement and scattered surveillance equipment to track who came to visit the nearby campgrounds. Two or three people who might not have much training to stop them like Neil and Carol. Torture or drug them into revealing other locations. The cascade of losses could cripple the Coalition.

A lot of the teams were always out of country or at least outside the compounds on assignments so even the bigger ones might not have enough guards and team members to truly protect them if a lot of the nutters had any training or equipment. The school was another weak spot, though I wasn't sure where that was. The letters I received and sent went by internal mail, not any official postal service. But I was sure someone I knew could betray that location.

"Dave?" I called into the darkness at the end of the cave. There was an old fissure just ahead almost like the one I'd used as a latrine at the real world cave but I never seemed to need to use it now. I went back to the fire pit and turned on another of the solar lights so I could read a favourite novel. I wasn't sure how Dave had made them appear. That they were from my memories was the only thing that made sense to me.

Dave came into the firelight without a sound. I'd finished at least six thick books. I stared. He was so much thinner, and his fur was dull and dry looking. What had happened? How long had I been down here?

"Dave, are you okay?" I dropped the book and it vanished before hitting the floor.

'Tired. Many things happen. Must come back now.'

"Come back where? The compound?"

'Melissa waits. Kitten.'

I stared again. "She's pregnant? Finally?"

'Kitten grows. Come. Hold tail if need. Long journey. Tell more later. Tired.'

"Okay." I let Dave lead but we didn't go toward what I'd thought of as the outer entrance, but instead went to the other end of the cave. "Doesn't this go further into the mountain?"

'Go down to leave.'

It freaked me some, but Dave started to glow once we left the fire's light. The path was narrow but always flat. It went up and down but I never had to crouch down, climb up or down anything vertical, or crawl through a pinch point. "This isn't a normal cave, is it?"

'No. Silence. Respect.'

I kept quiet and followed along as other passageways joined with ours. The path eventually opened up from the side of a hill into a bright meadow, but I'd never seen or smelled flowers like these before. Or seen such a bright day without a visible sun in the blue sky. It was almost familiar but I couldn't place where I might ever have seen anything like it.

I looked around. Over to one side was a large medieval-looking stone tower. At least six windows spaced up the side meant it was both taller and further away than I guessed at first. Or it might have been built for dwarves. Hard to tell from the angle but we stayed well away from the bottom of the bowl. I didn't recognize the tree's type off hand.

Dave ignored both of them so I didn't ask. Yet. We must have been rescued if he knew Melissa was pregnant, so we'd have plenty of time to talk about what had happened and to explain how and why Dave was so advanced now.

We walked through the long grass and flowers. Brightly coloured butterflies and birds flitted around us. On the other side of the meadow we went into a forest with about half firs and pines and half regular oak and maple trees, which became darker and darker. Dave didn't glow here. We stopped in the blackest of places. There was a hint of birdsong and a small stream but I couldn't see anything. All I was aware of was my grip on Dave's tail. I'd started to hold it during our travel though the forest once it was dark enough that I couldn't make out the path.

'*Now to wake,*' Dave said. Then he yowled.

My eyes flew open and I sat up. I was in a bedroom. A small light on a desk showed a completely normal bedroom, not the cave.

'*Good,*' said Dave. '*Go piss.*' He sounded exhausted.

"Okay," I replied. I pushed the covers off the rest of the way and realized that my arms were really skinny. Much like Dave had been. What the... I made it to the bathroom by using one hand on a wall for balance. Once inside and the door closed, I looked at myself in the mirror. My hair was scraggly but my beard had been roughly trimmed. I finished the necessary and flushed. Wondered about a shower but I wanted to find Melissa first. If she was here. And if I could stand and walk reliably.

I stared at my chest in the mirror again, then touched the spot in disbelief. The tattoo over my heart marking my initiation by the Lion was gone. As if it had never been. *Wait. During that tattooing, I'd looked up. The African sky was bright blue with no clouds that day, but I couldn't see the sun from where I sat.* Had we been in that meadow before? But why was the tattoo gone? Had Dave hidden it for some reason? Bad things had happened to us, I guessed. Very bad considering how we looked at the moment. Maybe. I'd ask Dave later. The present was more important.

Without Dave's help, I couldn't tell if Melissa'd been with me, but the second pillow on the bed didn't look like anyone had slept on it. There was a sound of a door opening and closing in the main room. I wrapped a towel around my waist just in case it wasn't her, came out, and Melissa stood there. "Hi, Dave. How are you feeling today?" Relief that she was all right filled me.

"Not Dave," I said. "Ethan. I'm back." A smile lit up her face and she hugged me. My arms went around her and I felt tears running down my cheeks. And hers.

Two wolves came out of another bedroom. I recognized them, but didn't know them. They waved their tails once as a greeting, then went past us toward the bathroom. Melissa saw the confusion on my face.

"They escaped with you, Ethan. There were several others who didn't want to come in with Dave. I should tell Karl you've recovered. We've all been so worried. He'll let your parents and Sam know that you're back."

"I don't remember any of what happened, Lissa. But Dave said you, we, are having a kitten now. Finally. A baby." I glanced down at her tummy, then back to her face.

Her smile warmed my soul. "Three months. At first I wasn't sure, since I was so stressed by your capture. Then the morning sickness started. Your mom dragged me down to the med bay. That confirmed it."

"I... I didn't want to think that you'd died. But if you never came back, at least I had..." She took me by the arm. "Get dressed. Food should be in the kitchen and we'll talk later. About everything."

I was on the other side of the bedroom door a moment later. From the sounds, Melissa was crying, then the outer door opened and closed. *She'd thought I might be dead? But she'd have our baby so... What had happened to me? The last thing that I remembered right now was getting back from a hostage rescue and playing in fur with the little kids and teens.* I turned to the dresser and closet for clothes. The usual exercise gear was easiest for now. A shower after a meal would be a good idea. And shaving, or at least trimming back the growth.

High calorie, high protein was the theme of the meal. Which wasn't breakfast, more like lunch. Stew, bread, cheese and bananas. The two wolves came out of the bathroom, sniffed me before settling on the couch. I noticed there were bowls of stew in the oven, being kept warm. They ate on the couch and I refilled their water dish. After they finished the stew, I peeled their bananas and broke them into chunks. They ate them happily. I'd never imagined that any sort of canine would like bananas. Both headed back into the bathroom. I heard a flush, but did not want to know how they'd dealt with the toilet. At least Dave had been in human form.

Karl showed up just as we finished eating, Melissa with him. Her eyes were a little puffy from crying but she'd thankfully stopped. I wondered if everyone knew I was okay. I wasn't good at dealing with crying partners. Dave usually wanted to rip apart anything that made her unhappy. If it was me, I wasn't sure how he'd react. He was different now. Probably as smart as I was. How would that change our relationship with him and Melissa? A full threesome, not a two-and-a-halfsome.

"The living room for now," he said. Melissa sat next to me on the couch and the wolves joined us. "What's the last thing you do remember, Ethan?" he asked.

"Getting back from a hostage rescue and playing with a classroom of little boys and then the teens. I'm guessing the next mission went really wrong. Who are the wolves? They seem familiar, but I don't recognize them as the ones we know who can do the full shift."

"You and Melissa went out together to find a shifter up in the hills three days south of our compound: Chattahoochee National Forest, just into Georgia. You found him, and it seems that he was a plant by a group of religious nut jobs. They took you to a compound in northern Alabama by helicopter and then tried to drive the Devil out of you. These wolves, and several others, were also there. Their beasts are ascendant at the moment. So was Dave until this morning. They all hid their human halves to protect them. Possibly from brainwashing so they'd go out looking for other shifters to catch. Dave hid you to protect the safe houses and compounds you know actual locations for. The safe houses would be easy to overwhelm. We've sent out warnings to all our people, just in case. Moved team members to the more isolated safe houses and adding more cameras and other warning systems. Twice daily check-ins so we know if anyone's been attacked. We're as protected as we can be."

I stared. Nothing like that was in my memory. I just shook my head.

"We aren't sure how, but Dave helped these two and the others escape. He called in for pickup at a nearby ranger station. We also don't know how it happened, but Dave is a lot smarter than any other beast, maybe barring the ones he escaped with."

"When he brought me back he spoke and acted like a normal person. I've no idea where I was. A big cave system but I don't think it was real. Not sure where I am on the insanity scale." Melissa squeezed my hand and that helped me stay calm.

"Dave wasn't very comfortable with human speech so we don't have a lot of the details. However, we were able to find the physical location of the nutters' base with their help and there are teams searching it for clues to who these people are. It used to be a boarding school but not recently. Last sale was six years ago. A religious group took it over but we've never heard of them before and we don't think that was their main base. They didn't leave much behind but took their wounded and all the bodies with them. Their leader as well, we've assumed. Dave said he had a beast, which might be how he knew about shifters. It must have driven him insane and he started a religious cult to foil Satan's plans."

"Weird," I said. "So how long a memory gap do I have?"

"It's been nearly three months since you vanished," Melissa said, squeezing my hand. "We did pick up Philip, who was the lion who betrayed you a day or two after you went missing. He's been full of *God's will* and *the Preacher said* with little relevant information on the group or your location. He had a costume hidden in his shelter to wear to fool the hikers who saw and reported him. He is adamant that he couldn't ever shift or the Devil would take his soul. Maybe seeing you and hearing how you were treated will jolt him out of his convictions, but he really might not know anything useful if they risked letting him out into the world by himself. There were microphones hidden in his shelter, which is how they knew to come fetch you, probably by helicopter since there were no vehicles on the roads that didn't check out."

"So what happens to us now?"

"We keep feeding you up and hope Dave lets you know what happened once he recovers. As for these two, same idea. Once they have enough energy and their human halves come back, they'll be offered the same options. Stay with us or go back to their lives. One of them may want to report back to the ones who didn't come in with you, just to let them know what happened and that they're all right."

"What all the leaders want to know is how Dave and the others became more aware," Karl said. "Sentient. Thinking beings instead of just beasts. The shrinks are going nuts trying to figure out what happened. Word is spreading very quickly. You have any ideas, Ethan?"

"Not a clue. When Dave brought me out of the cave, he was different. Really tired, but that could be because of how much weight we've lost. I don't know how long I was in the cave. Had a stack of books and the solar lights that Mom sent me from the last range. It didn't seem like nearly three months, though. I don't remember anything of being captured or being in their hands. Maybe he was able to block those memories so I wouldn't remember. Or it's just the shock of getting caught."

"Lots of reasons, but the same result," Karl said. "Any contact with him at the moment?"

"None. I know he's inside me, probably back in the cave I woke up in. Having a nap or just resting. He looked terrible. Really thin." I looked over at the wolves. "Like them, actually."

"I'm not surprised," Melissa said. "You lost nearly twenty kilos. The others must have lost the same or more. And none of you have much muscle tone left from being confined for so long."

"This is so bizarre," I said. "So for now, I get to eat, sleep and snuggle." Melissa chuckled and squeezed my hand again.

"Get back into shape, too. Near as we can determine, you had no exercise during the time they had you. Then you and the others ran over fifty or sixty miles on just a couple of rabbits or so each. So being nice to your body is a good idea."

"Good plan." I turned to Melissa. "Maybe we could have a short nap after I have a shower and shave?" She like to feel skin, not fur. Although, she liked Dave's fur. I didn't quite understand the difference. Maybe his wasn't as scratchy as a beard was.

She blushed but Karl couldn't restrain a snicker. From their expressions, I thought the wolves were laughing as well.

Two weeks later, Dave was quiet inside my head, but at least he was back. The two wolves managed to shift and their human parts were in charge but neither knew what had happened in the hell compound. Their beasts were still recovering, Melissa guessed. We'd all seen a few pictures of the place we were kept. If they hadn't hidden us, PTSD time for sure.

Greg and Steve were the wolves. Both were four or five years older than me and they'd managed to stay away from all the factions until six or seven months ago.

"Dave's back, but he's still tired," I said at breakfast. It was still high in calories and protein but I was gaining weight and muscle. "Not sure if he'll be ready to tell me anything in the next day or so."

"Still, that's excellent news," Melissa said then looked at the others. "Yours shouldn't be far behind."

Steve nodded. "Still trying to decide if we can head back out to our lives or if we need to stay hidden. Though, knowing we can call in for help in an emergency is a relief. I have no idea how the nutters managed to target me in the first place. They might come after me again once I'm back home and that wouldn't be a good idea, especially if we killed at lot of their people during our escape. If my beast is as smart as Dave is, I think discussing the future with him would be a good plan before any decision is made. We've got to cooperate now. I can't just make decisions on my own. About most everything, it seems. Kinda like being married, though it's not quite like that."

"Your memory might return in a month or two or your beasts may let you know what happened. If you can't go back to your old lives, we have teams that go on covert operations to help fund the compounds, here and in other countries," Melissa said. "That's an option, especially if you continue to be able to do the full shift. We don't understand why *all* of you were able to do so. There's only... ten or so, that we know of outside of your group. Ethan was the first one the Coalition encountered. Many of our shifters can do a full partial. That generally panics the guards they need to eliminate on their way to rescue people or take out drug lords. We have a low injury and fatality rate because of what our shifters are able to do and learn."

"Still no idea how they became so aware," I said. "And the place Dave put me was really strange. It was a big mountain cave, but there was only one exit to the outside. Took a while to get out. All the paths were smooth and level. No drops, tight squeezes or other weird shit like I've run into in other cave systems. That's why I don't think it was real."

The others didn't recall anything about being in a cave. Just one minute they were living their lives, next they were here. Maybe their beasts had kept them asleep in the caves as soon as they became sentient. Which would make sense. I wondered why Dave hadn't done the same for me. Maybe he'd wanted to come visit, but hadn't been able to do so. It might have taken more energy for him to come to the mountain than he really had available. Or he hadn't known what to say that wouldn't totally freak me out.

"I think the shock sticks you found near the cages we were kept in might be responsible," Greg said. "I never had much contact with my beast before this. Could barely change my hands to paws so I didn't have much trouble staying human as I grew up. It was even easier once I was working in a state park as a ranger. Still, that was about as far as I ever shifted. At times I needed its strength but I never did that where anyone could see me. I think the nutters used the shock sticks on us a lot, especially at the beginning. Occasionally after that if they thought we were trying to escape. Maybe the shocks have an effect on the beasts' development. But I certainly wouldn't want to put anyone through that as an experiment." Steve and I nodded in agreement.

"I also had an outdoor job, oil surveying," Steve continued. "So I was out in the wild places a big chunk of the year. He liked it out there. Didn't like me drinking or using drugs while I was off shift like many do in that sort of job, which meant I'd saved up quite a bit. One of the guys told me yesterday that they've recovered my ID and such from the compound. I want to check my accounts later today. Still wondering about going back to my life. But I never found anyone to be with. Kind of what Ethan said. None of them smelled right, though I didn't use that term at the time. I'd like to meet some women from your group. See if anyone clicks with me. I'm not sure on the covert ops idea but I'm more than willing to help take down the Preacher's people once you find their main base."

"You could do the surveying in summer and help run a safe house come winter or when you're off shift," Melissa said. "I'll pass on the request. There's a major compound near here. A day or maybe two and we'll go there. You can meet the women and see how it goes."

"And we would be unconscious during that drive so we don't know how to get there. In case," I said. Then I thought of another issue. "Have they been tagged yet?"

"Tagged?" Greg asked with a frown.

"Implanted tracking devices. And no." Melissa looked at me. "Ethan had one put in without his knowledge or consent when he was first brought in. He was justifiably angry about the deception when he found out. We're trying to be more... transparent about such things now. But we still have to worry about infiltration by those working for the other program we know of. And now these religious nutters."

They nodded. Melissa turned back to me with an odd look. "Ethan, do you remember *when* you found out about your tracker?"

"I'm not sure. Not too long ago, I think. But you were there. I'm sure of that. You thought I already knew, but were sad when you found out I didn't. When was it?"

"It happened while you were preparing to go look for the lion shifter just before the nutters took you. We were trying to be sure that you could be found if things went wrong. Your memory of that time may be returning." Her smile was strained. There might be something else she wanted to say but didn't want anyone else to hear.

"Not really looking forward to that," I said. "But it might help sort out who these guys are. Easier to take them all down."

We left the safe house in a commercial type van late at night. The driver handed us pills as we boarded. I just took them. Greg and Steve sighed and took them as well. They had air mattresses for us to lay on, which was a lot more comfortable than the bare metal or just a blanket. Melissa and I snuggled up before we went to sleep.

I woke in a bedroom. The other pillow was dented and the covers disarranged so she'd been here with me. Not waking in the Coalition's version of Shipping was a good thing. I really hated those gurneys. Sometimes Dave woke first and we thrashed around, especially if they'd put any straps on us. We'd dumped the damn thing over a few times now, so our compound people mostly knew to just wheel me back to the apartment and put me to bed. Melissa must have warned these folk before we left wherever we'd been.

I went out and found the bathroom. There were two other bedroom doors. Dave sniffed for me, but didn't say anything. Greg and Steve were behind the doors, still asleep. They'd been in hell, as we'd started to refer to it, longer than I had, so it was taking them and their beasts longer to recover.

I showered and shaved. It was good to keep the fur off my face but I needed a barber to deal with my hair properly. When I lived in the forests, I just tied it back or did a back braid so it didn't get into my eyes while I was hunting. Took a knife to it if the length started to bother me. There was probably a barbershop here if we were in a larger compound. For now, breakfast, or any meal was in order.

There was a guard outside the main door. I knocked on it to warn him I was opening it.

"Morning, or whatever," I said with a no-teeth smile, since he was a shifter. Wolf. He smiled back the same way. "Any chance of some food?"

"Of course. Are the others still asleep?"

"At the moment, but they should wake up soon or I can wake them when the chow gets here."

"I'll have the kitchen send food up, and let Dr. Kalan know you're awake. About ten or fifteen minutes til the food gets here. Okay?"

"Thanks." I was confused for a moment, then remembered that Kalan was Melissa's last name.

I shut the door and went to the couch. The TV remote was on the coffee table and I hit power. The screen came on and I channel surfed until the food arrived. It was breakfast, which was okay by me. Sausage, bacon, hash browns, eggs over easy and toast for three. A big glass of apple juice for me and sealed, insulated coffee mugs for the others.

The guys woke at the smell of food and decided on eating first, then cleaning up.

I left the TV on an all-news station while we ate. Getting caught up on the world would also help them, and me, adjust. We'd nearly finished the meal when Melissa came back in.

"Hi, love," I said. "You were up early. Everything okay?" She smiled.

"Excellent. It was time for my regular check up. The baby's fine. My blood pressure's back to normal. Stress, your mom thought. Now that you're back, I'm relaxing."

I stood up and hugged her. "I'm so glad that one of the little wrigglers finally learned to swim fast enough to win the race."

"Pardon?" Steve asked as he set down his coffee mug.

"Shifters have lower fertility rates than normals," Melissa said. "Ethan and I have been trying for nearly two years to have a child. His parents only had two boys, nearly six years apart."

She paused. I was confused for a moment. She was giving them the option to talk about their past. Greg looked at Steve and shrugged.

"My parents had three girls plus me," Greg said. "Fifteen years between us all. Dad died in a car accident when I was six and I was the only boy. Not sure on how my grandfather died or much else about him but I never knew him. Mom never really talked about him so I'm not sure if she knew him either. I lived at home until I started my job as a ranger. Hid the beast as much as I could, but maybe my mom knew why I was hiding out in my room more once puberty hit. But we never talked about it. I'm wondering if I should talk to her about Dad's ability now. It could be important to find out if I might have a few cousins who need help to deal with what we are. I should also ask her just how my dad really died. She might have told us kids what she did to have an explanation that didn't reveal anything about him being a shifter. She couldn't trust that someone else might be after the family or just me, even if he was dead. Erring on the side of caution and keeping quiet was a good plan."

We all took a breath. A car accident might have been helped along by one of the groups but leaving Greg with his mom indicated it might have been just one of those things. But the watchers hadn't taken me away after I thought my family died, so maybe his dad had been killed by an idiot group, or it was just a tragic accident. Damn. More questions. Not a lot of answers. As usual.

"I just have one sister," Steve said after a few moments. "My dad married really late and died of pneumonia when I was twenty-three. He was given up for adoption by his mother, so I have no clue about my grandfather or any other relatives. Dad taught me to hide the beast when it first started showing, so I did. Maybe his father didn't realize his mom was pregnant. If it has taken you guys two years of trying, he might not have known. Our daughters don't change, do they? Dad wasn't sure, but my sister never showed any of the signs. I have a couple of young nephews now- should I worry about them?"

"No," Melissa answered. "The ability travels only in the direct male line. That is, any sons *you* have will be shifters, and the same animal as you have. Our current theory is that whatever allows the shift is on the Y chromosome. We think that's why so many shifters out in the world don't know their fathers or grandfathers. My grandfathers are cougar shifters and have been in the Coalition since their escape from the government. They were young children at the time and didn't understand why they had to move suddenly. Their parents never explained anything. Most of the daughters of known shifters join the effort as support staff and marry other shifters. I went to vet school to help deal with the problems the animal forms have. My sister is into computers and works on the information gathering side. My brother is based in South America right now and just found a woman he wants to be with."

"They encourage keeping the types together," I said. "So be sure any women you consider are from the wolf lines. Your beasts should be able to tell, especially now, but ask just in case. Mind you, I'm sure a lot of the unattached women will be introducing themselves to you once we start eating in the cafeteria. They'll know you're wolves, so women from other lines won't approach you. Maybe."

That practice had really annoyed me and especially Dave-that-was. None of them smelled right to him. And the perfume on one in particular made me sneeze. Being allergic to that perfume had also frightened the people there. They mostly thought we were dangerous and liable to attack anyone at anytime, courtesy of a government spy named Justin. He was still in the wind. Or maybe the nutters had grabbed and killed him.

"As I said, we're pretty sure the necessary genes are on the Y chromosome, but we don't want to risk the crossover. No one is sure what might happen if there is gene leakage into the females over the years and they have a son who is from another lineage. There are enough stories in the tabloids of partial shifters. Just imagine a wolf-lion cross." Melissa blushed a little.

"Makes sense," Greg said. He finished his coffee. "Gonna grab a quick shower, then maybe we can bump the gym here?"

"Not hit?" Melissa asked with a smile.

"Hell, no," Steve said. "Gentle exercise. My legs and arms are still feeling the strain of that run."

I asked my escort to detour to their barber shop for a decent haircut before I went to exercise. He had a dart gun. So did Greg and Steve's escorts. It made sense, given the nutters' insanity. I'd be worried we might try attacking someone to get a message out on our location if I was in charge of this compound.

Karl found me on my way to the gym. "Any word from Dave?" My escort dropped behind so we could walk together.

"Not quite, but my memory seems to be coming back. It'll probably take longer for Greg and Steve's beasts to come back since their human halves were away so long. I'm surprised they managed to get them back and shift to human so fast."

"Think they'll stay?"

"Allied, for sure. Maybe hiding out with us until we find the nutters. But they're considering joining. Thanks for the change in procedure, Karl. Not tagging them or drugging them for information is helping build the trust they need."

"We're still worried about infiltration," Karl said. "We've learned nothing from Philip, even with drugs. It's been decided that he simply doesn't know anything about their facilities or he was kept inside at a minor location before they took him to the area were you found him. The computers at the nutters' compound were all trashed. Melissa's sister Deborah is on her way there to give a hand. She'll probably come through here with her report since this is the closest large compound. Just a warning, Ethan."

"I wonder if she'll smell good to Dave," I said. "Or if she'll be neutral."

"Don't complicate my life any more this week, okay?" He pointed at a sign. "Gym's that way. Go. Get fit. We need you for missions in the next couple of months. As soon as the docs clear you. No first contacts for the next while, just info gathering around well placed targets so we can take them down quicker and easier."

"Full shift and they ignore me and the camera." Karl smiled. I'd done them before, but convincing Dave that he had to follow a particular path had been hard at times. With him aware and a full partner, it should be a lot easier. "See you later." We went in and there were a bunch of teens playing basketball at one end. Greg and Steve were by the weight machines. With light hand weights. I went to join them.

Not much time passed until we were done. Another shower was on my list. Greg and Steve weren't doing any better.

"Shit," Greg said. "I'm still a marshmallow." One of the escorts nodded in sympathy.

"According to our searches and the time you were last seen, you were in there for five months, sir. So it could be a couple more weeks before you're fit enough to leave no matter where you decide to go."

"Any idea what's happened with my stuff? I had an apartment. No roommate. I'm not sure if my family or whoever reported me missing might have packed it up."

"We found out that it was packed up after two months by your family. Furniture, clothing and such went into a storage facility. Calling your family or friends should be possible, sir. We have excellent spoofing that will hide our location. Once you and the techs decide on a story, that is."

"Right," Greg said. "I have no idea how to explain where I've been."

"Are your fingerprints anywhere in the system?" I asked.

"Doubt it," Greg said. "Never in any trouble that way, but the cops might have checked my place for fingerprints or for DNA once I was listed as missing in case a corpse turned up. Why? You have any idea on how we can explain what happened to me and Steve?"

"Thought of a plan that might work. You went on a quick holiday out of country, maybe down to Mexico or to one of the Caribbean islands, were mugged and bopped on the head. Coma or complete amnesia. No ID, nothing in the system and voila, no way to contact anyone. You wake up and called a friend to let them know what happened. Then we get you back to your family, even if we have to smuggle you across the border to wherever so you can officially fly back home. Maybe insert your names into the flight databases so everything looks legit, but those might have been searched already."

"Same story could work for both of you," the escort said. "I'll have the techs double check what's in the federal databases on you. They can cross reference any local news or police reports about your disappearance."

"Good idea," Steve said. Both men seemed relieved by the thought of going home safely. Reassuring their families that they hadn't died.

Dave was more present in the next few days, but still seemed tired. *'Dave, is there anything we really need to know about the nutters to help find the rest of them?'*

'I have nothing else that could identify them. Do not ask again.'

'Okay. Glad you're back. Can I ask about the mountain?'

'Later. After the kitten comes.'

'I have one more question. What happened to our tattoo? Did you hide it?'

'Ah. That was what I missed. It returns.' I looked down at my chest and it was back, but Dave had gone back to wherever he was hanging out. Prob-

ably back in the cave to have a nap and recharge.

Karl wasn't thrilled when I told him what Dave didn't want to discuss, but they were actually getting lots of information from the detritus left behind. The cleanup had been fast but the people doing it hadn't realized that they should have just burned the place to the ground. Fingerprints, for example, were on *every* surface. Enough of them were in the various systems the Coalition could access that we could get names. Quite a few of them had even been in the military at some point, which would explain how they grabbed people from their homes. But how many trained men had our partners killed that night? A lot, by the amount of blood on the floors of the auditorium. I occasionally wondered why and how they'd found Philip and where he was from.

The church that owned the place was a weird one based on the rantings of the Preacher and his talking about the end of days. No one had seen him for three weeks, the hackers found out. The week before we escaped. He'd probably been on site, and was now in an unmarked grave in the woods Or under a martyr's cenotaph at their main compound, wherever that was.

"The last couple of his weekly broadcasts were repeats, not new ones as usual, it seems. They have a secure website but the outer security on it isn't that great. They may want people to find it. It's one way to get new recruits and more money coming in," Karl said. He and the leaders of this compound sat around a big table with me, Greg and Steve. And Melissa, of course.

"Dave said he was dead so there's probably a lot of jostling to see who gets to be the new Preacher. He might have been the only shifter in any position of authority," I said. "I'm not sure how he convinced people to go along with his ranting, but I think the group's been around longer than we might think. With at least two compounds and maybe more, that's a lot of money to account for. We know where we were kidnapped from, and our partners might know where the others had been when they were grabbed. But these guys are spread all over the US. At least."

"Mine didn't sense any beasts in any of the other people there. Is there any sign of anyone coming back to that compound?" Steve asked.

"None. And it wasn't officially owned by the church, but by one of the members. We found a picture of him in the Alabama DMV and his blood in the theatre area. A lot of it, so we're guessing he's dead."

Karl opened a folder and showed us a man. Stuck up expression.

"Roddy," I said after a moment. "He was there. Wanted me to confess my sins as a spawn of Satan. Didn't believe that I used to go to church and didn't burst into flames when I went in."

"His name isn't Roddy," the wolf leader said evenly. "Why do you use that name for him, Ethan?"

"I know it isn't his real name. I use nicknames for people if I don't know their real ones. Wolfie." I was glared at in response. I shrugged.

"We targeted the ones who tortured us," Steve said. Everyone now looked at him. "Flashes from my beast. He's decided he likes the idea of a name, separate from mine. James is my middle name so he'll use that for now. Anyway. There was a big event they were filming, and we were taken from the cages for display. We broke loose, shifted, and well, it was a slaughter. Then we bugged out before reinforcements could find us with big guns with bullets instead of just sleep darts and Tasers."

"That's probably why they don't want us to remember the details," I said. "PTSD, here we are."

"The auditorium had a number of places with blood on the floors or chairs. Lots of drops and splatters were in the hallways leading out into the other areas. The teams assumed each site in the auditorium was at least one injured or dead nutter. We might get around to collecting the hallway samples but they'll be a jumble of sources. We have our labs running the DNA samples against various databases. Same with the finger-prints in the living areas and offices. We haven't bother gathering fin-gerprints in the public areas, at least for now." The lion leader. Almost as dark as Karl was. Fairly dominant but less than Dave. The wolf-type was almost as dominant as Karl. It really didn't seem to matter to them. Maybe because most of the beasts were so unaware of what was going on around them despite their dominance level. If the average beast became more aware, it might shuffle priorities for their human partners.

"We've set up cover stories for both of you," Lion said. He pushed a folder at each of them. "Have a look at them and let us know if they will work and your decision. We believe that the nutters will be in consolida-tion mode for the next few months, so we don't think they be trying to kidnap anyone else or trying to track you down. You'll get a phone num-ber for a safe house near you, but you won't know exactly where it is. We are taking a risk, allowing you to return to the world. Please don't make us regret it."

While Melissa was busy checking with the other shifters who lived here, Dave and I had time to chat. About a lot of things.

We found the best place for visible privacy was on top of the bleach-ers in the gym. No one bothered us as we climbed up the open end. I took the precaution of taking along a pillow, since I knew how hard those seats were.

'I woke in the cave,' Dave said. 'Possibly after the first of the beatings. Everything I knew of our life together was... out of focus. Many things made no *sense to me. I had no idea where you were.'*

"No context on the memories, I guess," I replied. "Like starting a book in the middle, but you'd seen a few pages here and there with no idea what order they were supposed to be in."

'Can you tell me of our life together? I think that if you remember details, then I may also access them.'

"Well, you started waking up when I was eleven or so. No shifting, but when we were in Africa, I realized…"

'Africa? When was that?'

"Um. Not that long ago, actually. That's where I got the tattoo. We were initiated by their shaman. Their priest. I don't remember anything of what happened after I drank the extremely psychoactive concoction they gave me. But during the tattooing, I looked up and the sky was a lot like the one outside your mountain. Beautiful blue, but no sun visible. Any hints on what happened during that trip?"

'Not really. Our minds are linked, so as you remember events and people, I can access that learning. Now, that is.' He paused. I just leaned back and watched some kids playing soccer. Thought about Africa and everything that happened to us there.

'I think.' Almost a sigh. *'I think there was someone there. And when I woke in my cave after the awakening. A woman, but I never saw her. Just that her presence was there. A scent.'*

"Her scent? Um. You know that there's only a few women Dave-that-was would allow me to consider dating? The rest, they weren't right by some criteria I never really understood. That started as soon as you started to shift my hands. But. Could you, he, have been looking for someone that reminded him of the woman Marsh saw when he died?"

Dave vanished. I sighed and climbed back down after a few minutes. Helped the kids with their footwork until it was time for supper.

I'd nearly fallen asleep when Dave reappeared. *'I wish to try something, Ethan. While you dream tonight, I will help you remember some things. I think it might be faster and easier to let me experience your life with me than for us to find time to talk as we did today.'*

"Okay. See how that goes."

Waking up, I was exhausted. Like I hadn't slept at all. Dave wasn't nearby. Maybe he was as tired as I was. When he reappeared, I'd just finished a shower.

'I do not think that is a good technique to use,' he said.

"I agree. Don't feel like I slept at all, but I don't remember anything that I might have dreamt. Did you learn anything about the woman?"

'Hints. No facts, but I believe we have encountered her several times, other

than when Marsh and his partner died. I am even less clear on what criteria Dave-that-was used to determine if a woman was suitable. Your thought on the woman in red is possible, but that would mean neither of us remember any encounter that early in our partnership. It must have been profound for it to have affected my view of who might be a suitable female for you.'

I finished towelling my hair and got out my shaving kit. "What about the explosion? That's the biggest trauma we went through before you woke up. Losing the family. Thinking we'd be alone. I was eight, so Dave-that-was wouldn't have been very awake. But Dad said no one was sure I was a shifter when I was young. At least, that's the excuse they gave for not bringing me in. What if the woman had done something to us back then?" I forced myself to lather up to shave. "One of the reasons you developed a lot more than most beasts ever do because we were linked together more than most shifters ever do."

'Which means she is something we may never understand.'

"I wonder if we can get a letter to Gígalolúwa. He's the priest of the tribe in Africa. He might have some ideas. We might even be able to go there, if we can convince Karl to let us go. He has a list of missions he wants us to do, he's said. It's probably very long and getting longer by the minute. I don't know what sort of computers they have in their village, but a video chat might work okay to ask some basic questions."

'Might there be books we can read to learn more to start?'

"I never looked in that section of the library. We can drop there by after breakfast."

'Good.' He vanished again, maybe to continue a nap if he'd been awake all night. I sighed and started shaving. Having him aware was going to be weird to get used to. But if he wanted to track down the woman in red, it would give him something to do. Dividing up our awake time might be difficult, but we'd adapt. We had to.

Greg and Steve went back to their lives two weeks later. But they'd keep in touch. Both had found women from wolf lines who were acceptable to their partners. Since the majority of shifters were wolves, it kind of made sense that there would be mostly wolf line women in all the compounds. I did wonder if that was one of the criteria Dave had used, or if it was easier to find a suitable partner with an aware beast. Maybe they just weren't as picky now as Dave had been back then.

The couples would officially meet each other once the fuss of the men's returns died down. Otherwise, too many questions might be asked and make it into the news coverage of their return. The guys didn't live anywhere near each other, which would also limit the chances of anyone thinking they'd been in the same place. On the other hand, it meant the nutters were all over the country, not just a local problem in the south-east. They also had a lot of money available, since they must have used a helicopter to remove me from Philip's camp. There hadn't been any significant traffic on the roads for the cameras to pick up. That meant a few powerful supporters, or a shitload of ordinary folk. I wasn't sure what might be better. No one else could decide that either.

The main teams withdrew from hell about the same time. Melissa's sister was coming back with us to visit. We were due to head back to our home compound next week with her, Karl told me.

"Hi, Ethan. How do I smell to Dave?" That was the first thing Deb said to me after we shook hands.

"Um. We weren't trying to sniff. Just so you know." I did not want Melissa mad at me. Looking at another woman the wrong way could make your current girlfriend very upset. And if she was pregnant, you strayed at your own risk. More wisdom from various gang members I'd known. A pissed off girlfriend could hand you over to the cops if she made a call. That, I didn't have to worry about. But still, keeping Melissa happy was high on my priority list. And on Dave's, it seemed. He'd found a couple of books on anthropology in the compound library and he could get our body up at night and read while I slept with no adverse effects on either of us. Plus he could take cougar naps during the day in case he wanted to shift to get some exercise. We hadn't arranged a time to play with soccer balls with whichever shifters wanted to come.

"But I want you to." A hand came toward my face.

I wanted to take a step back but Melissa was holding my other hand. I looked over at her. She smiled and nodded. I sighed. Leaned over Deb's extended hand. Dave sniffed.

"Nice, but we prefer your sister." But I got the impression that Dave-that-was would have considered Deb if we hadn't already met Melissa. Not that I would mention that detail. Not until I was comfortable with her and the reverse. Her attitude confused me. And Dave, listening in. Human customs still baffled him but now he could ask for explanations. Her insistence made me as confused as he was. Maybe more so.

"But you'll know the difference between us, even in an emergency?"

"Yes. Why are you so concerned about me being able to tell you apart? You don't really look alike." Melissa was slightly shorter than her sister and her hair colour was a lighter brown.

"Just in case." Deb looked at Melissa. "You can keep him. I guess Mom was right."

"Thanks, Sis." Melissa smiled at me. "Ethan, were you going to the gym this afternoon?"

"Yes." I said it slowly. "Unless you have other plans for me. Us." A more recent bit of advice, this time from Karl.

"Not at the moment. Deb and I need some girl time to chat and catch up. I'll see you for supper, okay?"

"Sure. See you then." I didn't run from them. I walked. With purpose. That would be my story if anyone asked.

Mom and Dad wanted to have supper with us the night we arrived home, so we all sat together. Victor and Jerry decided to sit with Peter and their friends from school since they couldn't monopolize the conversation as usual. Melissa was a little quieter than usual but Deb filled the silences with stories of other places she'd lived in and visited for computer cracking. And I was still confused. Why was it so important for her that I never mistake Deb for her sister?

Sam was late for supper but we'd saved him a seat anyway. "Sorry, but I needed to finish a report once I woke up," he said as he set his tray down. He smiled at Deb. "Just back from a mission. Glad to meet you, Deb." He sniffed at her hand after they shook and Deb snarled. "Sorry, but you do smell good." A hopeful smile met with her frown.

"And I am *not* available." A growl, deep in her throat. Almost a cougar's growl.

Sam did the sensible thing and started to eat. I thought about when we'd first sniffed Deb. There hadn't been anything but faint male scents around her. Co-workers, not good friends or a partner. But she'd been at the hell compound for a couple of weeks. Enough time for any scents to fade and laundry to have taken them from her clothing. I added one and one which meant... I decided to chance sticking my foot down my throat.

"Is your partner going to join us here?" I asked. "You've been away from her for nearly a month, I guess."

Everyone around the table stared at me. I shrugged. "I've met a few other women like you over the years, Deb. No big deal. You could have just told me, instead of trying to hide it. Dave and I were going nuts trying to figure out why you were acting so weird about us being able to tell the difference between you and Melissa. Knowing your preference right off would have made it much easier to understand."

"It's not common in these circles," Deb said with a glare in my direction. Mom looked confused for a moment, then clued in. Sam and Dad took longer, being males without a lot of exposure to the modern world.

"But it is elsewhere," Melissa said. "She's always been... sensitive to talking about it outside the family."

I drank apple juice and shrugged. "I don't care. I've found someone to care about. I am more interested in what you found in the hell compound's computers but that's not a subject for the dinner table."

"That's quite true, dear," said Mom with a quick smile at me. "Deb, your brother is based in South America, Melissa said. Have you ever been down there to visit? Dan and I were thinking of a place to get away later this winter. We haven't had a real vacation in years, just the odd week of camping or a quick stopover while we were on assignment."

"I haven't, but Roger's letters say there's a lot of wonderful places to visit. I could write him and ask for specifics if you want." Deb was a lot calmer now. Relaxed. Good.

"That would be wonderful, dear," Mom said.

"And what about Victor and Jerry?" Melissa asked. "Do you want to take them with you?" Mom and Dad looked at each other.

"Perhaps they could stay with you and Ethan," Dad said with a smile that showed some teeth. "Give you both some practice before the big arrival." I translated that as *we need a holiday from everything. And everyone.*

"Victor and Jerry are happy about becoming big brothers," I said to Deb. "I missed out on that with Sam, but they both like the notion. They've been talking to their classmates with siblings."

"Any idea if it's a boy or girl?" Deb asked Melissa.

"Still too early to tell," she replied. "Though I hope it doesn't take as long for us to have a second." We hadn't told anyone that it was a boy. I'd tried to remember if anyone knew about Dave's ability to detect shifters before they were born and couldn't be sure.

"Have the current one first," Dad said with a smile. "And be prepared to kiss sleep goodbye for the first year. At least."

"Dave's actually looking forward to having a kitten of our own," I said. "Even before he got smart, he wanted a kitten to help raise to be strong. So nothing bad would happen to them."

"He knew that I was pregnant as soon as they returned," Melissa said. "My scent changed, Ethan relayed from him. I was so worried about what was happening to Ethan that I wasn't really paying attention to how I was feeling until the morning sickness hit."

I hadn't heard about the search for me yet. But again, not a topic for the table. Maybe I'd catch up with Karl in a day or so.

"Where's the bait dude-- Philip?" I asked instead.

"He's in a very secure location," Dad said in a tone of voice that said he wasn't having an easy time. Good. But he had information or something that Dave wanted. I wasn't entirely sure how I knew that. He hadn't mentioned it out loud. Or in my head. We definitely had more than one channel of communication going on now. Why it was happening, that was another question with no answer in sight.

Author's commentary

Greetings!

You may have noticed that Monster's pov chapters have changed from volume one. Showing Monster's evolution to Dave and beyond was difficult to include. I did want to show him in the earlier parts of the series to provide a counterpoint to Ethan's point of view of the same incidents, so this is a two person first person work. Go figure.

Titles are one of my weak points, which is one reason the chapters don't have individual titles. However, you may have noticed that the titles of the first and the current volume are almost familiar. <u>Lonely Together</u> was suggested by the song <u>Happy Together</u>, by the Turtles. Since Ethan and Monster share a body, but Ethan can't live in a city or around many other folk without various groups trying to capture him because he has Monster inside him, he is lonely, but with Monster trying to make him not sad, it seemed a fitting title.

This volume, <u>Always my Love</u>, is more properly <u>Never my Love</u>, by The Association. Ethan has finally found someone whom he can love without Monster/Dave becoming irate. He has very exacting standards and the pair had only encountered three women that he would accept.

The third and fourth volumes still haven't let me know their titles. I need to go through the Billboard listings again to find songs that resonates with the difficulties and joys that Ethan and Dave have to face before they finally track down the Preacher's people and learn more about the origin of all the shifters. And maybe having a quiet chat with Justin. Which group did he actually defect to? The government one, Firsteam Protection or the Preacher's people. Or another group entirely?

Lee F. Patrick Calgary, Alberta
December, 2020

www.ingramcontent.com/pod-product-compliance
Lightning Source LLC
Chambersburg PA
CBHW020119030726
47498CB00006B/2176